PRAISE FOR THE COLLECTOR

"I loved this book from the first page! Dante isn't just your run-of-the-mill YA bad boy...he's a villain. A real villain, who you often won't like in the beginning. But at the same time, you can't take your eyes off him because he's hot, witty, and just fascinating. And all the while you'll be thinking, I can't wait to see this boy's world get rocked."
— Wendy Higgins, author of SWEET EVIL

"Victoria Scott's smokin' hot paranormal debut, THE COLLECTOR, *left me breathless at every turn with its sizzling anti-hero, unlikely heroine, and the epic romance that unfolds between them."*
— Mindee Arnett, author of THE NIGHTMARE AFFAIR

"Sexy boys, high stakes and heart-pounding romance combine in a book that's full of humor and heart. I loved spending time with Dante Walker. Next book please!"
— Talia Vance, author of SILVER

"Dante Walker is dangerously smooth, lethally seductive, and cocky enough for ten alpha males combined. This is a book that lives up to its hype and will garner fiercely devoted Dante fans."
— All Things Urban Fantasy

"It comes down to perfect pacing, a killer voice and a motley crew with flair and personality."
— Girls in the Stacks

"Author Victoria Scott has created a deliciously appealing main character, a story that feels very much an original, with pacing that moves lightning fast. And with a few surprises that will keep readers enrapt, THE COLLECTOR *is an exhilarating and absolutely riveting must read."*
— Fiktshun

THE COLLECTOR

A DANTE WALKER NOVEL

THE COLLECTOR

A DANTE WALKER NOVEL

VICTORIA SCOTT

This book is a work of fiction. Names, characters, places, and incidents are the product of the author's imagination or are used fictitiously. Any resemblance to actual events, locales, or persons, living or dead, is coincidental.

Entangled Publishing, LLC
2614 South Timberline Road
Suite 109
Fort Collins, CO 80525
Visit our website at www.entangledpublishing.com.

Edited by Liz Pelletier

Print ISBN 978-1-62061-242-2

Manufactured in the United States of America

First Edition April 2013

The author acknowledges the copyrighted or trademarked status and trademark owners of the following wordmarks mentioned in this work of fiction: Chuck Taylor, Dumbo, Rainbow Brite, Armani, GQ, Smurfs, Nobel Prize, Lady Gaga, Martha Stewart, Skittles, Godzilla, Styrofoam, Playboy, Bergdorf Goodman, Neiman Marcus, Nordstrom, Versace, Target, LASIK, Lincoln, Escalade, Cheetos, Bose, Match.com, The Three Stooges, Nirvana, Beyoncé, American Express, Biggie Smalls, Hugo Boss, Kenneth Cole, Safari, Midol, Care Bears, Nissan, System of a Down, Marlboro Reds, Doritos, Anderson Cooper, Eminem, Dom Perignon, Louis Vuitton, Pandora, Korn, Christian Louboutin, Gucci, BMW, Jay-Z, Prada, Botox, Dolce and Gabbana, Jimmy Choo, Starbucks, Oscars, Sherwin-Williams, Glock, Justin Bieber, The Jonas Brothers, Popsicle, Disneyland, Dumpster.

For Ryan,
who insisted he loved me over French fries.
You are my person. I love you, I love you.

"All my life, my heart has yearned for a thing I cannot name."

—Andre Breton

What's up, people. Name's Dante.

Last summer, I met this chick in Chicago. Homegirl said she dug my red Chuck Taylors, and I dug her fashion sense. We got to talking, and somehow, as the sun set and night crawled over us, I told her…everything. I don't know why it came out. But it did, all the same. The chick, a writer it seemed, asked to share my story with the world, and for whatever reason, I agreed. It is what it is. Sometimes I like to gamble. That's how I roll.

So this is it—my life, told by her hand. I guess this story was bound to leak one way or another. At least from me, you know you're getting it straight.

That is, if you trust a demon.

—Dante Walker

CHALLENGES

"Pride is the master sin of the devil, and the devil is the father of lies."

—Edwin Hubbel Chapin

1

THE ENVELOPE

I'm in a slump, off my game, throwing up bricks, swinging and missing.

I'm having an off year.

My boss isn't pleased, and he's not the type of guy you want to piss off either. He's the ultimate a-hole who doesn't buy excuses, even the champion ones I'm slingin'. But hey, it's a job. And generally speaking, I'm damn good at it.

I am The Collector.

It's not as bad as it sounds. I'm kinda like Santa Claus. We're both jolly guys with a passion for frosted cookies, the color red… and sorting souls. My job is simple: weed through humanity and label those round rears with a big red *good* or *bad* stamp. Old Saint Nick gets the good guys, and I get the fun ones.

Two years ago, I was just your average seventeen-year-old guy. That's a lie. I've never been average. I look like a movie star and move like an athlete. That didn't change when I kicked the bucket. It's okay to be jealous, to covet me. It's a delicious sin—tastes like chicken. But don't envy my success as a collector. I earned it. Like

Michael Jordan, I shot until I never missed. If there's a bad soul anywhere on planet Earth, I can smell him out and turn him in. Bag and tag.

Boss Man runs the Underworld, and I'm his number one guy up top. I'm so good, in fact, that I train the other five collectors on how to be more awesome. It doesn't take a genius to understand the game: collect souls that are sealed.

Seals are our friends. I say it slowly, because patronizing people is fun.

It's an easy gig. So easy, I've been bored lately. Maybe that's why my numbers have slipped. But don't fret. I got this. I've never met a hurdle I didn't like.

In fact, stumbling toward me is a herd of business suit–clad men way too old to be this wasted. What are they even doing on New Orleans's Bourbon Street? Being creepers, that's what. A guy with Dumbo-sized ears breaks away from the pack and heads toward a girl half his age. His arms swing in great big circles until yellow liquid splashes from his plastic yardstick drink.

Way to bring your A game.

The girl turns toward her friend in an obvious attempt to avoid eye contact with Drunk Ogre Man. But no matter. He whirls her around, shows her his colorful beads, and attempts to pull up her shirt. That's the deal, right? Beads for boobs? Not this time. Homegirl slaps him and storms off, her heels *click-clack*ing down the paved road.

Ogre stares after her, and his friends howl with laughter. His red-rimmed eyes go big for a second, and then he starts laughing, too. He got off pretty easy, all things considered. But we're not done yet. Or better yet, *I'm* not done yet.

I gaze at the guy in a way only I can. A warm yellow light crawls over his skin and flickers. It almost appears as if his body is on fire. This light is his soul, and I can see the thumbnail-sized rectangles called seals that partially obscure it. Seals come from being bad, or as I like to say, *exciting*. If I could come back from the dead, the things I would do. I'd go out with a bang. But I can't. And unfortunately, collecting leaves little time for recreational activities, if you know what I mean. So I just keep punching the clock and doing what I do best.

Amidst the dude's mini black seals, there are other seals. *Our* seals. Collectors' seals are bigger than the ones you get automatically when you sin and therefore do a lot more damage. In order for Boss Man to know who's done what, our seals are different colors, and already this guy looks like Rainbow Brite. Now he'll have one more to add to the others. I flick a finger, and a sizzling red seal—the length of a human palm—attaches to his light. He didn't feel a thing, but he certainly deserved it. His soul light dims just a little more than before. Once his light is completely covered, it's over. Finis! We'll collect his soul and bring it downstairs. I form my hand into a gun. "Pow!"

Another one bites the dust.

Today I'm playing my part on Team Hell like a heavyweight. The game works like a gas gauge. On one side is hell, on the other is heaven. That little orange bar tips back and forth between the two, depending on who has the most souls. Collectors are Boss Man's insurance policy that Big Guy (A.K.A., lord of the heavens) doesn't win, but he should chillax. No one ever gets the upper hand. If they did, it'd mean the gates of heaven—or hell—would spill open onto earth.

Or some fairy-tale crap like that.

After Boob Man is gone, I stand in the doorway of the Cat's Meow bar, watching people do the same things that led me to where I am now. This city is one of our standard posts. Since there are billions of people and only six collectors, we have to concentrate on specific areas, or we'll never get anywhere. Most people go to Judgment Day, which may or may not mean eternity in hell, so Boss Man likes to bring them in before that happens if he can. And New Orleans, well, it's one of the easiest places to make quota.

Seals fly from my fingertips with ease. I don't have to think too hard about it, and for that, I'm thankful. I like this part of my job, the nameless faces. Collecting souls is nothing personal. I'm an equal-opportunity sealer. I'm not sure I could do it any other way.

But I guess I'm going to have to learn. I shove my hand into my pocket and rub the sleeping white envelope. I can almost feel it pressing against my thigh, as if it's alive. As if it has tongue and teeth.

I spin around and see Max running toward me in a gray Armani shirt. "Dante. Oh, Dante. Seal me! Seal me so hard!" He grabs my hips and pumps his toward mine. "Oh, Dante! You're so hot when you seal souls."

I shove my idiot-of-a-best-friend off me and laugh. Max dances around in a circle with one leg pulled up, and people move away as if he's mentally unstable. He and I are the only collectors that like to remain visible to the living. The other four roll incognito. Max finishes his dance and brushes his shoulders off.

"What the hell was that?" I ask.

"My new move," he says matter-of-factly.

My fellow collector is six years older than me but acts like he's thirteen. We met a couple of years ago after he kicked the bucket and came onboard. He talks so fast, I have trouble understanding him sometimes. I like to think he was the World's Best Car Salesman before he croaked.

Max spreads his arms out and gestures to his suit. “Hey, what do you think of my new threads?” The only thing Max likes better than money is the stuff money can buy.

“Not too bad.”

“Not too bad?” He covers his heart in mock offense. “Shit. This work of art is on the cover of *GQ*. Know what else? George Clooney wore this very suit to a party last weekend.”

“No, he didn’t.”

Max runs a hand over his clean-shaven jaw. “No. No, I guess he didn’t. Think anyone else would buy that? I might try it on the honeys tonight. Oh, check this crap out.” He reaches down and tugs his pant leg up. The gold cuff wrapped around his ankle is decorated with Smurf stickers. “One of the other collectors did this after I crashed last night. Can you believe that mess? I can’t get the damn things off.”

I roll my foot around, feeling my own cuff pinching my ankle. The heavy restraint enables collectors to walk the earth. It allows us to eat, breathe, and carry on a normal existence among the living. It also allows Boss Man and the other collectors to know where we are if they’re close by. A little Big Brother if you ask me, but then again, we’re given the option to remove it, if you call breaking off your cuff and dying a final death an *option*.

Max elbows me. “Who’re you fantasizing about?”

“No one. I’m thinking about these damn cuffs. I wish there was a way to stay here without them.” Max doesn’t realize I know exactly where these cuffs came from. And I can’t tell him. The only reason I know is because Boss Man explained it while training me for my pending promotion. Maybe I shouldn’t be proud that the devil tells me his secrets. But I am.

“Well, there ain’t. So you can just get over that one, pretty boy.” Max rubs behind his neck and squints against the sun. “At least we're able to get out of hell from time to time. Besides, why are you even tripping about it? Everyone knows you're getting promoted to Soul Director. Then it's permanent placement on earth, *hombre*. It's like you hit the Underworld jackpot. Speaking of jackpots, I feel like gambling. I've got the itch."

"I bet you've got the itch," I say.

"You're nasty, you know that? Just foul." Max walks backward away from me, bumping into people as he moves down the street. "You nasty, you nasty. You mama said you nasty!" And then he's gone. Vanished into thin air.

I shake my head at his dramatic exit. I feel bad for not mentioning the envelope. But he'll just make it into a big deal. I pull it out and stare at it. Inside is the name of my target: Charlie Cooper. Boss Man wants her soul, says he'll forget my recent downslide if I deliver. This is unusual. He typically doesn't pinpoint specific people, and I *hate* that it's going to make things personal. But I'm not here to question, only to do my thang.

It's not like I have much of a choice.

I'm on it, I told Boss Man when he handed me the envelope. *Like white on rice.*

I didn't say the last part. He wouldn't appreciate the humor.

2

HITTIN' THE HOOCH

I'm standing outside a two-story colonial house in a neighborhood so sweet I feel like gagging. *Cooper* is spelled out on the brick mailbox. I'm in the right place. As if I wouldn't be.

The front door is painted a rich, bright red. The corners of my mouth curl into a smile. Have I mentioned my love affair with red? It's a beautiful, trusting relationship. Nothing coated in such a wondrous color could ever be bad. I stride up the walkway, run my hand over the red wood, and sigh. Then I see something that ruptures this magnificent moment.

At the end of the walkway is a cat. It struts with arrogance. You'd think it just won the Nobel Prize. But it didn't. Know why? Because it's a freakin' cat. In case you missed the memo, I. Hate. Cats. I loathe them. They're built with creepy little teeth and finger blades. I don't know about you, but I'll pass on *that* freak show.

The cat sees me and rolls its eyes. It does. I swear it. In my head, I imagine punting it across the street. I throw my arms up like a human goal post and scream, "It's good!"

Behind me, I hear a *click*. I spin around and see an old woman who clearly thinks she's a young woman glide through the red door… She's wearing a silk kimono that shows way too much old-person leg. Her processed blond hair is sprayed out around her face, and she's wearing more makeup than Lady Gaga. Without noticing me, the woman bends at the waist and reaches for the morning paper.

Thanks for the invitation. As a matter of fact, I will *come in.*

I breeze past her into the house. I'm sure she felt something, but her eyes persuade her otherwise. That'd be my shadow kicking in, the thing that allows me to become invisible whenever needed. It's the only kickass ability collectors have, thanks to our cuffs.

Inside the house, I catch the scent of old people. You'd think the young girl would cancel out the smell of dinosaur, but it doesn't. Not even close. I wonder where the chick's parents are and why they aren't around.

Every inch of the house is covered in flowers and lace and screams tacky. It's like Martha Stewart vomited, and this is the crap that came out. I shake my head. These people need an interior designer. Stat. Mother would never have let this happen. She had refined tastes, and Dad was boys with Benjamin Franklin. Thinking about my father makes me remember That Night, and my stomach lurches.

A muffled voice creeps down the stairs. I'm too far away to hear what's being said, but I know it's her. Heading up, I imagine what kind of chick I'm dealing with. If Boss Man wants her soul, she's got to be pretty bad, and I always did dig the bad chicks. In fact, most things I dug when I was alive were bad. Guess that's how I ended up here. Most people got this thing in their head saying they'll be with Big Guy when it's all over. But let me tell ya, spend every day living only for yourself, every day indulging in little sins that *aren't that big of a deal*, and one day I may be showing you the ropes in hell. Amen.

At the top of the stairs, I shake off my shadow, making myself visible again, and run through the rules in my head. I can do pretty much anything to bring this girl in, but I can't physically hurt her. All collectors know hurting a human could trigger war on earth between Boss Man and Big Guy. Everything else, though, is fair play. And I'm not above pulling some dirties to get what I want. I swim a hand through my hair. It's showtime. I push her door open…and my chin drops.

Her bedroom is painted a blinding shade of pink, and glittering posters drape her walls. A queen-sized bed stands in the middle of the room, shrouded in a sheer pink canopy. So many pillows litter her duvet that I'm sure she must sleep on the floor. There isn't a surface or shelf that isn't covered with glass figurines. It's a room built for a seventeen-year-old who still believes she's a princess.

My target has her back to me and is blabbering away on a retro corded phone. It is, of course, decorated in pink and white rhinestones.

"I know. I know. This final is going to be way hard. Like, ridiculous hard."

Her voice has the slightest Southern ring which might have been endearing, had I not been pressed for time. Boss Man made it crystal clear I have ten days to complete this job, and I always come in under deadline. There's too much riding on this to screw up. If I deliver this one measly soul, I'll be promoted to Soul Director. Like Max said, that means permanent placement on earth. And let me tell you, never having to visit the Underworld again? Serious motivation.

I knock once on the open door and sigh.

"I don't think I'm sleeping from now until finals are over. If

I don't get an A in this class, my grandma will skin me alive and make it look like an accident."

Come on, get a clue. I knock again and clear my throat. The girl spins around. My eyes widen at the sight of her. *This* is the girl Boss Man is after? She looks like a porcelain doll…beat three times with an ugly stick.

I take it all in: glasses, frizzy blond hair, a spray of pimples, and a stick figure so not attractive on a seventeen-year-old girl.

"Oh. Em. Gee. I have to let you go. There's a guy standing in my doorway," she says into the phone. Then, quieter, "Yes, very. I've got to go. Tell ya later." The girl hangs up, and an enormous grin stretches across her face. She grabs a lock of blond hair and curls it around her finger. "Hi."

"Hey," I say. "Your grams let me in."

"Oh, yeah? You here from the pharmacy?" She continues smiling like a lovesick moron. I can't help but smile back.

"No, I'm here to see you," I say, which apparently pushes her over the edge. The girl's eyes widen, and she does this whole nervous laugh thing. I shake my head, but it doesn't affect her. "Are you Charlie?" She nods, and her expression changes. Only slightly, but I pick up on it. She's surprised I know her name. "I just moved here. My mom knows your grams. She said I should come by and introduce myself. Said we might get along. Name's Dante."

Charlie's blue eyes study me from behind her thick glasses. "Where you from…*Dante*?"

"Phoenix." Lying has always come easily to me. Don't judge.

"Why did you guys move to Peachville?"

"Mom got a new job here. Said she always wanted to move to Alabama. Something about the trees in the fall." Here's a free tip: adding details to lies makes them more believable.

She nods her head as though I said something profound, then turns and walks to her window. For the first time, I notice she's wearing purple jeans. My God, it's like she stepped straight out of an '80s movie. Her wavy hair falls to mid-waist, and I think how she looks better this way. From the back.

"You don't want to stay for breakfast, do you?" Her words are slow to leave her mouth, as though she anticipates rejection. On the contrary. I can't believe how easy this will be. She couldn't be more desperate. Still, I take a second to respond. Girls fall faster for guys who are indifferent.

"Yeah," I say as casually as possible. "Why not." When she spins around, I notice her cheeks are bright red. "You all right?"

"Oh, yeah. It's just when I get—" Charlie covers her cheeks with her hands. "You'll love my grandma's cooking, that's all."

All the way down the stairs and into the kitchen, Charlie yaps away. I nod and smile and smile and nod, and when she turns away, I form a gun with my hand, place it to my temple, and pull the trigger. This girl is starved for attention. It's amazing to me when people are totally unaware of how bad they are at socializing.

Something else I notice is her limp. She has a subtle walking issue, and I'm wondering whether it's from a birth defect or an accident and why no one's done anything about it. It's the twenty-first century. White coats can fix anything.

We spill into a small kitchen with a black-and-white tiled floor, small circular table, and cabinets the color of cat vomit. Though the kitchen's decor stinks, the smell of something wonderful pulls me away from Charlie's chattering. Bacon. Right there cooking on the stove. Yeah, I know. I'm dead. But I can still eat like a sumo wrestler. And if that deliciousness isn't on a plate in front of me within two minutes, I'm eating it straight from the pan.

As if on cue, Grams breezes into the room with a plate in hand. She stops in place.

"Mmm…I've always dreamed of having dessert for breakfast." Grams ogles me, a playful grin on her Botox-filled face. She's thinner than I like my grandmas to be, but the ring of naughty in her blue-gray eyes captures my affection.

"Grandma!" Charlie moans in embarrassment.

"Child," she says, without turning away from me, "why didn't you tell Grandma we were expecting a handsome guest?"

Charlie shakes her head and smiles at me like we're in this together. "This is Dante. He just moved here from Phoenix. I think you know his mom. Didn't you let him in?"

Grams's dyed-to-match eyebrows furrow. No worries. I got this. "My mom's name is Lisa Walker. You guys met at church, I think?" She glances away and bites the corner of her lip. Now I just have to bring it home. "She said you'd remember her."

"Oh, yes," she says slowly. She stares into my eyes as if the answer is there. "I do. Just took me awhile to place her. I love Lisa. Wonderful woman."

"She said you might say something like that."

The deep lines on her face smooth with relief, and she laughs lightly. "'Course I remember Lisa." She motions to a chair at the kitchen table. "Sit. Sit. We need to get the two of you fed. There's enough for you and Charlie to share. You'll be going to Centennial High, I reckon?"

She's talking to me, of course. I cock my head toward Charlie. "I'm going where she's going."

Charlie's mouth falls open. It takes her a moment to stutter a response. "I—I go to Centennial."

"Yep," I say. "That's where I'm going." Grams gives an approving nod and sets down a plate covered with eggs and toast. And bacon. She sits across from us and takes a pull on a water bottle.

"Grandma," Charlie asks, "aren't you going to eat?"

Her grandma lifts her water bottle. "I'm all set."

Charlie turns to me. "Grandma loves water. I mean *loves* it. She says our bodies are made of the stuff, and if we don't drink enough of it—"

"We'll shrivel into beef jerky," her grandma finishes.

"Well," I say, thinking Grams is off her rocker, "to each their own."

"Exactly!" Grams yells, sloshing water around in her bottle.

I lean over Charlie's plate and take a bite of crisp bacon. I imagine it melting on my tongue.

Grams puts her chin in her hand and gets all daydream-y. "I haven't seen muscles like these since I met my Rudy, God rest his soul." She seems to be talking to herself, but I can obviously hear every word. "Dark hair, blue eyes, and skin so tan it's like the sun bent down to kiss ya."

I glance at Charlie, who's covering her face. "Grandma, *please*," she begs.

I don't know what she's complaining about. I'm really starting to like Grams, though I doubt if she knew what I was she'd be tossing the compliments around so freely. In fact, I bet if the woman so much as spotted my tattoos—the dragon covering my back or the tree tatted from my elbow to shoulder—she'd flip her shit.

Charlie stands up, walks over to her grandma, and kisses her forehead. She lingers there, like she doesn't want to leave her grandmother's side. "I'll see you after school," she says finally.

At the front door, she pulls a lime-green backpack over both shoulders. I cringe. Everyone knows you're not supposed to wear it on both shoulders. It seems too eager.

Charlie glances at me and presses her lips together like she's deciding something. Then she says, "You, um. You want to walk to school together? It's okay if you don't. You probably need to go home and get some stuff first. Or maybe you're not starting school until next semester."

Every sentence sounds like a question. I quirk one side of my mouth. "I'm right behind you." Charlie grins like a lunatic, and my own smile leaves my face as I watch her cheeks turn bright red with excitement. So *that's* how it happens.

I stand and walk over to Grams. I rub her back and thank her for breakfast. Old people love physical contact—I'm guessing her more than most.

She bats her eyes at me. "You're so very welcome."

The smell of rum hits me like a hurricane. So Grams is hittin' the hooch, is she? Maybe the tats wouldn't blow her mind, after all. I eye her closely, and her face drops when she realizes I know. I wink and squeeze her shoulder. *Your secret is safe with me*, I say without speaking.

Charlie heads out the door, all smiles and sunshine at watching the moment between her grandmother and me. She's too naïve to realize her grandma's a drunk, and I'm not going to tell her. Not yet, anyway.

As Charlie is leaving the house, she somehow trips on the threshold and nearly face-plants onto the ground. I roll my eyes. How is it possible out of all the people in this world, *this* is the soul I've come to collect?

3

THE SOUND OF LAUGHTER

Apparently Charlie doesn't have a car. "But don't worry," she tells me, "we can *walk* to school from here."

Thrilling.

It'll only take a few lifetimes, what with her limp and all.

Charlie carries a brown lunch bag in one hand, and every few minutes she digs Skittles out of her pocket and pops them into her mouth. I have no idea how she survives high school. She's a disaster. It's kind of tragic. Why is this girl still alive while I'm a walking corpse?

I can't stop staring at her mouth. It's the only part of her that's passable. Of course, it never stops moving.

"Don't you think?" she asks.

I meet her eyes. "What?"

She nudges me with her shoulder like we're long-lost pals. "Someone's been daydreaming. Want some sugar?" Her open palm is a stained Skittles mess.

"I'll pass," I answer. I'm not sure how this chick stays so tiny. She eats like a hippopotamus. Deep in my pocket, I rub my thumb in circles over my lucky penny. I'm trying to figure out how to corrupt this girl, and she keeps asking me silly questions.

Focus, Dante.

I narrow my eyes and do what I'm trained. At first, her body is exactly the same: short and skinny, like a weed that needs plucking. But then it changes. The familiar warm yellow light crawls over her skin and flickers.

Ah, soul light. If I could drink it, I would. The color of a human soul is the same for everyone. It's the seals that make the difference. I count how many she has, then clench my hands into fists. There are twelve seals on her soul. Only twelve.

Great, I've come to collect Mother Teresa.

Inspecting her soul closer, I notice some of Charlie's seals are from collectors. I know because I see bursts of color: purple and green and orange and whatnot. Every collector can place seals, and you can tell who sealed a soul by the color. Most of hers are green. That'd be Patrick's work. Naturally, I was the one to train him.

The fact that Charlie has any collectors' seals means Boss Man has probably had her watched for some time, or at least the Peachville area. Staring at her, his reasons are lost to me. But it doesn't matter. I've got to collect her either way. If I don't, and she dies, she'll go to Judgment Day, and Boss Man obviously doesn't want to take chances.

Her soul is clear of any of my red seals, but that won't last for long, 'cause Papa's come to play. "How much farther?" I ask.

"Just on the other side of this hill," she chirps. "Like I was saying, I'm not sure if you'll be able to enroll this late in the semester, but at least you can see the school and stuff."

"I wouldn't worry about it."

Charlie glances at me, and her eyes crinkle at the corners. "I think you're nice, Dante."

"That's 'cause I *am* nice."

She gazes ahead and walks in silence for almost a full minute. It suddenly feels strange to be near her and not hear her speak. The massive trees hang in a canopy over the road, stretching to greet one another, their leaves dead.

Toothy jack-o'-lanterns sit on porches and watch us pass. One looks like it's mocking me, so I flip it off. Charlie sees me. She throws her head back and laughs long and hard. The sound startles me.

I wonder what it would feel like to laugh like that, with complete abandon.

•••

Charlie tugs me into the front office and announces me as a new student. The woman behind the desk eyes Charlie, then me. I know what she's thinking, that I'll ditch her by lunch. That we're in two separate categories: the loser, and the guy who *calls* people loser.

I turn to Charlie and place my hand on her head like I would a dog. "Be a good girl and wait in the hall for me?" Her smile falls as if she expected this, but she nods and turns to go. I watch her walk out of the glass doors, where kids pass her by like she's not even there. Like a ghost. I glance back at the woman behind the desk. She's no older than thirty-five, but she eyes me with the bitterness of someone much older.

"How's it going?" I ask. She raises an eyebrow. "I need to enroll." She laughs without smiling. "Look, I *need* to enroll. And I need the same schedule as Charlie."

"Well, none of that's going to happen. It's Friday. We only enroll students on Mondays. And we're halfway through the semester. You'll have to wait until January." Now she does smile, because bursting my bubble is the highlight of her day.

I eyeball her tattered clothing and bad hair, and I smile right back. Because everyone has a price, and it just so happens hers is cash. I pull a wad of bills from my pocket and flip a few hundred dollars onto the table. "Think you can make a miracle happen?"

She stares at me like she might slap me, and for a second, I think she might. But then she chews the inside of her cheek and glances over her shoulder. "There's a security guard, like, ten feet away. I could have you kicked out of here."

"For what? Being awesome?"

She crinkles her nose like she smells something bad. That stank is called desperation. That's what I'd like to tell her, anyway. Instead, I wait while she shoves the cash into her purse and hands me a blue slip of paper. "Show this to your teachers if they ask why you're there. Good luck on your midterms," she jeers. "Go ahead and follow Charlie's schedule. I'm sure you guys will be great friends."

I point a finger at her. "Thanks, babe."

"I am not your *babe.*"

"Whatev."

Outside the office, Charlie's leaning against the wall. A pile of books are stacked in her arms, and she rests her chin on top.

"You really need all those books?" I ask.

"You can never be too prepared, right?" she says. A guy shoulders his way past her, and Charlie's books clatter to the floor. She dives to the ground to scoop them up.

"Watch yourself," I tell him, because he almost hit me, too.

The dude turns and flips me off.

Right as the guy's about to turn the corner, I flick my wrist in his direction. The yellow of his soul flips on, and seconds later, a small red seal attaches to the light. That prick needs to learn some manners. I form my hands into guns and fire them off in his direction. "Pow! Pow!"

"What are you doing?" Charlie asks from the floor.

"Nothing you should worry about." I roll my shoulders. Man, it feels good to seal souls. Like eating a little slice of bacon. I think about turning around and sealing the soul of the lady who accepted my bribe, but I'm too distracted by Charlie's bumbling. "Why don't you put some of those books in your backpack, Charlie?"

"Oh, no," she says, her eyes widening behind her glasses. "That causes back problems." She swings her long hair over her shoulder. "So did they let you in? Can you go to classes?"

"Yeah, I can go." The realization that I'm back here, in high school, pours over me. Isn't the one upside of death a free ticket out of this crap hole? At least the high school I went to was nicer than this. We had the kind of school portrayed in movies. This place, on the other hand, is the Walmart of high schools: scuffed linoleum floors, ratty double-decker lockers, and plastic everything.

"So you're in. Nice!" Charlie beams.

I meet her eyes and say slowly, "Cool."

"Cool what?" she asks, her face pulling together in confusion.

"It's *cool* that I got in, not *nice*." She glances away, and I can tell I hurt her feelings. Crap. In order to have a bad influence on this girl, she's got to like me. "Then again, what do I know?" It's a lame attempt at making her feel better, but still she perks up.

"No, you're right." She swims her hand in front of her face. "It's coooool."

I grab her hand and pull it to her side. "Let's just go to class, all right?"

• • •

Three excruciating hours later, I'm walking Charlie to lunch. I used to think teachers were idiots, and two years later, I'm sure I'm right.

Kids are pouring out of the four hallways that spill into the cafeteria. The overhead lighting is so bright, I have to shade my eyes. Something squeals loudly, and I ready myself to kill some sort of rodent. But it's Charlie. Apparently, whoever's walking toward us warrants this kind of hysterical reaction.

"There's my Char-Char!" a girl sings as she nears us. She's every bit as tall as I am and twice as thick. Charlie hugs Amazon Girl and then turns to me. "Dante, this is Annabelle."

No. No way. That name is reserved for females with grace and elegance, not this girl. This girl is…beastly. "Annabelle," I say. "It suits you."

Annabelle laughs deeply and tosses an arm around Charlie, who I can only imagine is being crushed by the weight. "Yeah? 'Cause I always thought Godzilla was more fitting."

I laugh so hard I snort. Charlie narrows her eyes at me like I did something awful, but I've decided I like this chick. She's got spunk. And something tells me her soul has been sealed a few times.

"Nice kicks, by the way," Annabelle says. She stares down at my bright red Chuck Taylors, the ones I almost never take off.

I spin them to the side so she can get a better look. They're a flippin' work of beauty. I nod in her direction. "Thanks."

"Did you just move here?" she asks. Annabelle's chin-length black hair is like a helmet, and heavy bangs make a hard line across her forehead. Nothing moves as she speaks.

"Yeah, his mom is friends with my grandma," Charlie says

before I can open my mouth. "He had breakfast with us this morning."

"That right?" Annabelle glares at me with accusation in her green eyes. She doesn't think I'll be sticking around and doesn't want Charlie to get hurt. How endearing. "And now you're going to sit with us at lunch?"

"Yep," I say. "Now what's a guy gotta do to get grub around here?"

A few minutes later, I'm sitting with Charlie and Annabelle and staring at cardboard food on a Styrofoam tray. I'd like a one-way ticket back to Grams's kitchen, please. I'm about to suggest this when a guy moves toward Charlie and drops down beside her.

"Hey," he says in a small voice.

"Blue!" Charlie squeezes his upper arm. I'm surprised by all these friends popping up. Charlie doesn't strike me as the kind of girl who has *any* friends, much less more than one.

The guy collapses against her. What is it with all these people using her as a crutch?

"I'm going to flunk chem," he says like a deflated balloon. The guy's built like a pasty-skinned streetlamp. I want to pull him aside and tell him about tanning beds. Or sunless tanning lotion. Something.

"No way," Charlie says. "I'll help you study."

Blue—er, whatever—looks right at Charlie with big blue eyes and grins like a moron. I've seen that look before. It happens right before sex and broken hearts.

"Really? Yeah, that'd be great," he says. "I don't know why I'm doing so terrible. Guess I'm not smart enough. That, or my teacher hates my face."

Charlie rubs his back, and he hunches into her touch. The guy's slow, drawn-out words and defeatist attitude reminds me of Eeyore from *Winnie the Pooh*. Man, my dad loved *Winnie the Pooh*. When I was twelve, I accidentally broke the handle off Dad's Pooh coffee mug, and the next day he glued on two new ones. He called it his insurance policy. My dad was always doing funny crap like that.

Blue rolls his head of blond curls around like he's relaxing his neck, but really he just appears drunk. I bet when this guy gets wasted, he crawls into his bathtub and cries. Annabelle pulls a jumbo package of powdered sugar–covered doughnuts out of her bag and tosses them to Blue. They hit him in the chest.

"Nice catch." Annabelle snorts.

Blue picks them up and eats them one after another, and somewhere between the sixth and seventh doughnut, he notices me. "Hey," he says, as if I haven't been sitting here the whole time.

I nod. "'Sup."

Blue gazes at me and then Charlie like he can't understand why the hell I'm sitting next to her. You and me both, brother. "Charlie, you, uh, going to introduce him?" he mumbles.

"Mmm." Charlie stops drinking her neon-orange soda. "Oh, yeah! God! Sorry! This is Dante. He just moved here." She shoots me a big smile. I try to return it without seeming turned off. Without thinking, *Braces. Heard of 'em?*

"He had breakfast with Charlie this morning," Annabelle adds slowly when she catches Blue's eye.

Blue's head whips toward Charlie. So he *can* move quickly. Even quicker is the hurt that floods his face.

Relax, I want to say, *that ain't* ever *going to happen.*

4

DAYDREAM CHARLIE

I'm staring at what's left of my food—which is most of it—when Charlie gets up from the table. She picks up her tray, and I think she's about to put this garbage where it belongs. But she dumps the leftovers into napkins and stuffs them into her backpack. I can't even stomach eating this junk, and she's going to repurpose it as a midday snack.

Annabelle stops discussing last night's Knicks game with Blue and glances up at Charlie. "You going where I think you're going?" Charlie bites her plump bottom lip. Annabelle nods. "That's what I thought."

I bump Charlie's hip with my shoulder, and she glances down at me, startled. "Where you going?" Charlie pulls in a breath but doesn't say anything. "Come on. Spit it out."

Blue shoots me a look of warning, and I'm wondering what he and his hundred-pound-self are going to do about my attitude. This may be my assignment, but it doesn't mean I have to be all excited about it. In fact, it's probably better I'm not.

"I was going to stop by the journalism room." Charlie says it so quietly I cock my head to hear her. I hate mumblers. I've had enough with Blue and his ever-present mumbling already. We don't need two spineless people at this table.

"Speak up, Charlie," I say. "If you have something to say, then say it out loud." Blue huffs from between gritted teeth. I meet his eyes and raise my eyebrows. He holds my glare for a moment longer than I expected he would, then glances down. That's what I thought.

Charlie sticks her chin out and says louder, "I'm going to the journalism room to watch the broadcast." She nods. "Yeah."

I smile at her and stand from the table. "Well, let's get crackin'."

"You want to come?" she asks, her eyes round and vulnerable.

"Sure, why not? What else do I have to do?" *Besides seal your soul and drag you to hell.*

"Great!" Charlie gives her friends an *OMG! He's coming with me!* look and glances back in my direction "It's on the other side of the building near the gym. We can just…walk from here."

As opposed to taking a train?

People watch as Charlie and I weave our way through the long, bench-like tables. Heads move together, and whispers are exchanged. A group of girls giggle, and one waves at me with gusto. I'll be back for them later. I've got to collect Charlie's soul, but that doesn't mean I get a free ticket out of my normal duties. If I could finish this job *and* seal a ton of souls while I'm at it, that promotion will be mine fo' shizzle.

Right as we're about to leave the cafeteria, I see a guy waving an orange envelope around like a winning lottery ticket. Three guys near him peer over his shoulder as he reads whatever's inside. I glance around and notice more orange envelopes in giddy, greedy hands.

I suddenly want one of those orange envelopes so bad it makes me sick.

When I was alive, I was never left out of anything. In fact, I would've been the one passing out those damn envelopes. It feels weird to be on the outside. I throw my shoulders back. But who cares, right? If I wanted to, I could own this school in a matter of days.

The echo of squeaking tennis shoes and thumping basketballs lets me know we're near the gym. I wonder if Annabelle and Blue ever break from talking basketball long enough to actually play. Hearing the repetitive sound of balls clanking off the rim makes me want to ditch Charlie and join the game. Unlike those jokers, I hit nothin' but net.

Charlie stops in front of what I guess is the journalism room. She stands outside the doorway, not going any farther in. Whatever she wants to do, she wants to do it from here. On the left side of the room, there's a long gray table with three stools tucked beneath it. On the other is an enormous black camera and a stand holding cue cards.

I notice a girl strut toward the center stool. She holds a stack of papers and silently mouths the words she's reading. When she's done, she drops them onto the table and glances around the room. My back stiffens when her gaze meets mine.

The girl's got enormous brown eyes, smooth brown skin, and long dark hair. She's like a bucket of caramel, and I'd like to taste every part of her. And string me up and flog me if she isn't built like a *Playboy* centerfold.

"That's Taylor," Charlie says like I just ran over her dog. "She's head of the journalism club. And pretty much everything else." She watches my face closely and continues, "I could introduce you."

"Uh-huh," is all I manage because I can't stop watching Taylor nibble her lip and smile at me. Two guys wearing red football jerseys file past Charlie and me and sit on either side of Dream Girl. A second later, two more students walk into the room and set up near the camera. A guy as tall as a soda can climbs up onto a short platform and plays with the camera. He nods at a freckle-faced girl standing close by, who counts down from five, and the room falls silent.

"Hi! I'm Taylor Fitch, and this is your Weekend Play Plan. With me, I've got Brad Setterfield and Clint Moers from our very own Centennial football team." Taylor does an adorable *woot-woot* with her arm, and I fall in lust all over again.

I glance at Charlie to make sure she's still there and then look right back at Taylor.

But then I stop.

My eyes slowly return to Charlie. Her face is…alive. Eyes. Ears. Mouth. They're completely open and alert. Even her head has a daydream-y tilt. Maybe she's crushing on one of the jocks? But no, her eyes are glued to the same thing mine were—Taylor.

"What are you staring at?" I whisper.

Charlie's eyes never leave their subject. "This," she whispers back. "Her."

"You got a thing for chicks?" I ask.

Charlie rolls her eyes and smiles. "No. It's…the whole being in front of a camera and being so *good* at it. Sometimes they even do these things live, and she still does everything perfectly."

"She's just reading the cue cards." I point to the cue card stand as if it isn't obvious.

"You say it like it's no big deal." Charlie's face drops, and I remind myself what I'm here for.

I nudge her. "So why don't you join the club? Maybe you can go on camera sometime." Charlie shakes her head but doesn't say anything. "Why not?"

"It's not that I have a problem talking to people." Yeah, I gathered that much. "But I can't go on camera in front of the whole school and be like her." Charlie points to Taylor's shiny hair and shinier smile. "She's so...captivating."

"Please. She's just flirting with the camera. You know how to flirt, don't you?" Of course she doesn't.

"Well, yeah," she says. "Everyone knows how to flirt."

I doubt she has any clue how to reel a guy in. Even if she did, she'd have no idea what to do with him. I suddenly have an image of Charlie trying to hold onto a fish as it flops around between her hands.

The freckle-faced girl announces that they're done filming, and the beauty behind the table gets up and saunters toward me. I have to stop myself from shoving Charlie out of the way.

"Hey," the girl purrs. "I'm Taylor."

I try to appear uninterested. "Dante."

"New here?" she asks.

"Yep." I say, barely looking at her. Uninterested. It always works.

"Then you'll want this." She hands me a glorious orange envelope. Pow! "It's an invite to my party Saturday night. Give you a chance to meet people."

"We'll see," I say. Taylor gives a smile that says she knows I'll show. And she's right. Because this party will serve two purposes: it'll give me the chance to corrupt Charlie and ravage Taylor. Caramel Mama is already walking away when I speak up. "Hey, 'Taylor,' you said it was?" She nods. "Well, this is Charlie. She wants to be in your little club." I flip my hand toward the journalism room behind us.

Taylor glances at Charlie, then back at me. "I don't think so."

Charlie hits my arm. "Dante, I don't have to be in the club.

They probably already have enough members. It's fine."

"See," Taylor says. "It's fine."

My blood boils. If there's one thing that pisses me off, it's singling people out. Taylor starts to walk away, but I grab her wrist. "Except it's not, actually. Charlie wants to be in the club, so let's just get her in there, all right?" Taylor narrows her eyes. "Besides, if *she's* here all the time, *I'll* be here all the time."

She thinks about this for a second and decides she still has a shot at us hooking up. She's probably thinking how great I'd look on her arm. It'd be the other way around, but whatever. "Fine." Taylor studies Charlie's face. "But you can't be on camera. No way."

"That's great! Thank you." Charlie cheeks redden. Even though she thanked Taylor, it seems there's some deeper emotion swirling beneath the surface of her eyes.

Taylor touches a pink fingernail to my chest. "See you at my party."

I don't like the way Taylor treats Charlie, like she's a Porta Potty, but I need to hold onto my invite. "See ya."

As soon as Taylor is out of earshot, Charlie lights up. "Oh, my God. You're amazing. That was so amazing! You basically just told Taylor to shove it."

Charlie's eyes are so big and excited, I can't help but laugh.

"It's no big deal," I say. This could turn out to be really good. Charlie needs someone to take up for her at this school, and her friends certainly aren't in a social position to do it. If she thinks I have her best interests at heart, she'll trust me. And that trust will be the perfect stepping stone on the path to corruption. As if to prove this theory to myself, I tell Charlie, "Hey, let's do something fun."

Charlie beams. "Yeah? Like what?"

"Let's get outta here."

She takes a small step back like I'm explosive. "We've got to go to class, though. The bell's going to ring any second."

"Come on, Charlie. We'll go somewhere fun. Haven't you ever wanted to be a little rebellious?" I can tell the answer is *no*. I need to get her to bail on classes. I need this small victory over Ms. Pious, or else I might as well call this assignment hopeless now. "Look, this is my first week in Peachville, and my first day at Centennial. It's kind of overwhelming. Is it so bad that I want to just spend some time alone with you?"

In my entire life, I've never seen anyone smile the way Charlie is smiling at me right now. And for a second, I actually feel guilty. But then she opens her mouth and says, "Okay, let's do it."

And just like that, the guilt is gone.

5

MALL HELL

"This? This is where you wanted to go?"

Peachville's only mall is crowded for the middle of the day. Don't these people have jobs? Or lives? The mall has a tile floor that turns high heels into a headache, and the fountain centerpiece attracts only fake greenery and screaming children. "I told you I'd take you anywhere you wanted to go, and you choose here?"

Charlie bites into a sugar cookie. She's still nervous I borrowed her grandma's car without asking, but she's starting to relax. "I love the mall. Don't you?"

"Yeah. I mean, it has its uses." A woman with a stroller races past me and nearly takes off my right arm. No "excuse me" equals one tiny seal for you. I take a moment to seal her up right, then turn my attention back on Charlie. "It's Friday, though. Don't you want to try and dig up a party for tonight instead of hanging out here?"

She brushes crumbs over her blouse. "I don't really like parties."

"Charlie, have you ever been to a party?"

"Yeah. I mean, sort of." That means *no*. "I go to birthday parties and stuff."

"I'm talking about a real party. Like the kind Taylor's throwing. Do you ever go to parties like that?" Charlie shrugs and shakes her head like it isn't a big deal. "Hey, why don't we go to Taylor's party together tomorrow night?"

She stops walking and stares at me, her head bent to one side. "Why? Why do you want to take me? And why are you being so nice?"

So she does understand this is abnormal, someone like me hanging out with someone like her. I calculate my answer. "A lot of people at my last school were really shallow. And I was part of that crowd." Okay, so that much is true. "I decided this time would be different. I want to find friends who are…real."

Charlie's face pinches into a smile, and I almost feel like cupping her chin. I take another gander at her mouth and decide if it wasn't for those crooked teeth, she might actually have one solid asset.

"So how 'bout that party?" I nudge her.

And…the smile's gone. "I don't think that's a good idea. I don't really fit in with those people."

I decide to drop the subject for now, but one thing's for sure—we're going to that damn party. "Hey, can we swing by Bergdorf? If we're going to be at the mall on a Friday, we might as well have some fun."

Charlie gawks at me like I've gone bat shit. "What's a Bergdorf?"

"You're kidding me, right? This place doesn't have a Bergdorf?" She shakes her head. "What about Nordstrom, or maybe a Versace?" More head shaking ensues. I take a deep breath and spin in a circle. I spot a Neiman Marcus. It'll have to do. "Let's go in there."

"Nice," she says as we head over to the store. "I usually just get my stuff at Target. They have cute clothes."

"Oh, Charlie." This time I can't help myself. I rub her back and laugh. She smiles up at me with a look of awe. For some twisted reason, I think of my mother. This is the way I always wanted *her* to look at me.

The moment I enter the store, I come alive. I flag down an associate and tell him I need his help. The guy has dark, slicked-back hair and a black leather jacket over a starched shirt. He reminds me of a preppy James Dean. As I pile clothes into his waiting arms, his pupils dilate and take on a wild shade of cash. Commission makes people crazy. I bet psych wards have a whole wing dedicated to rehabilitating commission-paid peeps.

I'm about to ring up when I see Charlie eyeing a bright red dress. She may be an uggo, but that dress would turn anyone into a rock star. "Grab the dress," I yell across the store. "My treat." Charlie takes the dress off the rack and holds it against her. Over my shoulder, the associate holding my clothes snorts. "What?" I ask him.

"No, nothing," he says with a laugh.

I laugh, too, but in a different way. "No, really. What's funny?"

The guy thinks we're sharing the same joke, so he opens his fat mouth and says, "That dress was made for a lot of people…"

"And?"

"And you know, she's not really one of them." The guy realizes I'm not laughing anymore. "I don't mean to say—"

"I know what you mean to say. You just said it." I take the clothes out of his arms and throw them. "Changed my mind. I don't need this off-brand crap." His jaw drops open, and I have an urge to shut it with my fist. I'm the only one here who's allowed to judge. He's lucky his mouth didn't earn him a seal.

I head toward Charlie, and right as we're about to leave, the guy decides he's not going to let me embarrass him. "Not my fault your girlfriend's a train wreck." My head snaps around. Already her eyes have that glassy, watery appearance.

Oh, no, you didn't. Oh, yes, he did. *One seal for you, coming right up.* His soul light flips on, and—ah, snap!—look how many seals this guy has. He's pulling some serious recreational badness after hours. Spotting a few of my fellow collectors' colorful seals amidst the small black ones is more proof that Boss Man's had Peachville scouted for some time, searching for something big. I briefly wonder why I never knew about it before.

Leaning back, I smile wide. Sealing this soul is going to be jolly good fun. I toss a seal his way and relish in the crackling sound it makes when it adheres to his light. He's maybe one or two seals away from being collected. I do hope I get the pleasure of bringing this one in. He'll go on living after he's collected, of course, but as soon as he dies, he'll meet up with his soul in a happy little place called hell.

"Come on, Charlie. Let's go." She follows me out but doesn't say anything. I sit down on a bench near the fountain and motion for her to sit beside me. The dude was out of line, and also a bit off-base. I mean, Charlie's definitely not a looker, but who's to say she won't be when she grows out of her bad skin? Or finds the right hair stylist. Or hires an orthodontist and gets LASIK and puts on some weight and gains a morsel of confidence. I've seen it happen. High school dork morphs into cute college prep. "You know that guy's just being a prick, right?"

"Yeah. It's not a big deal." Charlie acts like she's watching the kids play, and she even manages a half smile. I'm surprised how well she's handling the whole thing. A lot of girls would break down over something like this.

"You know what we should do?" My body rushes with energy. "Something crazy. I have an idea." I take her hand, and we move to the exit closest to where we parked. "See that kiosk right there?" Charlie nods. "Let's take something?"

Her eyebrows pull together. "Like, steal it?"

"*Steal* is an ugly word, Charlie. What we're doing is letting loose. Something you should do more often." I take her head in my hands and turn it back toward the kiosk. "You see, when you live life—I mean, really live it—you don't care what anyone says about you because you're suddenly, exhilaratingly *alive*." She gazes at me, transfixed. "Do it, Charlie. Just try it out. If you hate it, we can return whatever you took. No one will know the difference."

She gives a wicked smile, and I bite my upper lip to stifle a laugh. I could get used to having a sidekick gone rogue. I'm all set to give her advice on how to approach the kiosk, but she slips away before I can. She moves toward the cart of knickknacks, stealth as a leopard despite her slight limp.

As she approaches her destination, I slide my hand into my pocket and absently squeeze and release my lucky penny.

Like a pro, Charlie scouts the guy who mans the cart, determines his coordinates, estimates how much time she has.

Then it's done.

With a subtle sweep of her small hand, she stuffs something into her pocket and makes her way toward me. Charlie presses her lips together, and her eyes become enormous. She's trying to stop herself from laughing, and so am I.

As we head toward the exit, I turn around and see the guy staring at us. He takes a step forward and stops. *Crap, he knows*. He didn't catch her in the act, so he's not sure what to do. If he accuses her and he's wrong, it'll cost him his job. He waits too long, and now it's too late.

Charlie and I burst through the double glass doors, and she erupts with laughter.

"Holy crap," she says. "That was crazy!" She pulls her stolen hairpin out of her pocket and shows it to me. I raise my open hand over my head, and Charlie tries to jump to give me a high five. She's too short, and it makes me double over and laugh, too. The sight is so ridiculous.

"What now?" I say.

Some of the excitement in Charlie's face falls away. "I should really get home. My grandma will wonder where I am. And oh, man. Her car. We've got to go."

"Come on, we're on a roll," I plead. "Let's do something else."

Charlie wraps her arms around herself. "No, I really need to go. I've never skipped school before, and I've certainly never stolen anything. Especially not my grandma's car."

"Like I said, we didn't steal her car. We borrowed it."

"Yeah, Dante. Hanging out with you has been, like, so fun." She puts her hands on her hips, a sign that I shouldn't push my luck. "But I need to go home now."

"All right, let's get you home. Keys." Charlie tosses me the keys, and I somehow catch her disastrous throw.

I let her walk in front of me while I think about what I'm about to do. I'm not sure why I'm hesitating. There's no time to hesitate. Ten days. That's all I have. And there's no gray line for theft.

I stare at Charlie until a shining light engulfs her small frame. It's so bright, so devastatingly bright. I point my finger and release a seal. It attaches to her soul and stays there.

And damn it if she doesn't turn around at this very moment… and smile.

6

WATCHFUL EYES

I pull up in front of Charlie's house and kill the engine of her grandma's '90s Lincoln. Right now, I'd like to find a hotel and call it a day. But this job isn't your typical nine to five. So I turn to Charlie, who's busy destroying her nails, and say, "Want me to come inside for a while?"

She takes her fingers out of her mouth. "My grandma still isn't home, or she'd be outside with a butcher knife already."

Good. "That's too bad. Where is she?"

"Her friend Ilene usually picks her up on Friday afternoons so they can gossip," she says. "That's why she wasn't here when we came by earlier."

"Does your grandma work?" I ask.

"No. She used to be a cosmetologist. She even did makeup for movie stars when she was younger, but she doesn't work anymore."

I inspect the big white house in front of us with its black shutters and red door. It's nowhere near the size of my parents' crib, but it still must have cost some cash. I'm guessing money's tighter now that Grams is retired.

"Want to see what my grandma has stashed in the fridge?" she asks.

"Definitely."

We climb out the car, but instead of heading inside, Charlie walks across the street to the densely treed area facing her house.

"What are you doing?" I ask.

She pulls napkins out of her backpack and unwraps the leftovers she stashed from lunch. "These raccoons used to get into our trash, but my grandma bought these heavy-duty lids to keep them out. It worked, but I feel kinda bad for them, you know?" Charlie tosses the food toward the trees and heads toward the house. "If my grandma found out I was feeding them, she'd freak."

"Your secret is my secret." *Even if you are a hippie nut job.*

Charlie unlocks the front door and goes in, but I stop in the doorway. I turn around. Then I turn around again.

I feel something. No, I *sense* something. And it sure as hell isn't raccoons.

Across the street, it's so thick with brush, I can't tell if something's there. I take a few steps forward and listen. I don't hear anything, but I know it's him.

A collector.

The sensation never lets me know how many collectors are near, but reason tells me there's only one. Feeling like an idiot, I say, "Max?" But there's no response. There are only six of us, yet this guy's sportin' shadow. Why won't this dude reveal himself? I know the only thing that can kill a collector is to remove his cuff, but right about now I'd like to give other alternatives a shot. I run through the collectors in my head. In addition to me and Max, there're Patrick, Anthony, Kincaid, and Zack. And I can't imagine why any of them would follow me. In fact, I'd think they'd be afraid to. Not only do I have Boss Man's ear, but I'm the one who performs their continued training. And there's no secret why that is: I'm the best.

I walk back toward the house, glancing over my shoulder the entire way. When I get to the door, Charlie is there. "It's nothing," I say before she asks. "Let's raid the kitchen."

Charlie and I dig out three bags of chips, one can of artichoke dip, and two cans of orange soda. We chow down, and I try to shake the odd feeling that a collector was outside her house. But I can't. I don't understand who it would've been, or why they came here.

As I watch her tip back her drink, all I can think is, *Why Charlie?*

I've got to get this assignment moving quicker, and I know how to do it. The thought makes me gag, but I know it'll work, and I don't have much choice. If another collector is watching on the sly, then it's time to bring out the big guns. I'd like to show him how smoothly I operate.

"Hey, Charlie," I say, taking the orange soda out of her hand and setting it down. "Let's hang out in your room." Her blue eyes widen, but she doesn't protest as I take her hand. "Come on."

"You want me to bring up the chips and stuff?" she asks. "I'm addicted to the Cheetos, but I wish my grandma would buy the puff kind, you know? I always ask her to, but…" Charlie rambles at Mach speed. She's nervous. And she should be. I doubt this girl has ever visited first base…or even been to a game.

I lead the way up the stairs and push her bedroom door open. The pink overload blinds me as I enter the room. Though I've seen it before, I'm still not prepared for how *loud* it is.

I sit on her bed and shove some of the pillows onto the floor. She doesn't seem to mind, which surprises me. Charlie takes her stolen hairpin out of her pocket and grips it in her hand. She stares at it as though it might suddenly sprout teeth.

"Why so glum?" I ask in my seduction voice.

She rolls her tongue over the inside of her cheek and says quietly, "I want to return it."

"No, you don't."

"I do," she insists.

I bite down, not at all happy she's killing my vibes. Ready to drop the subject, I hold my palm out. "Give it to me," I say. "I'll return it."

She hands it over like she's happy to be rid of it. I stuff it in my pocket, where it'll stay. That seal of hers ain't going nowhere. It's not like you can rob a bank one day, then return it the next and expect a full pardon. Please.

Charlie smiles, thinking her sin is absolved, and plucks a porcelain figurine off her window ledge. She tosses it back and forth between her hands. The way she does it seems…careless.

"That one your favorite?" I ask, trying once again to pull game.

"What?" Charlie peers at me, then down at her hands. "Oh, yeah. It's beautiful."

No, it's ridiculous.

"Actually, it's pretty dumb, isn't it? All this pink and lace and little girl propaganda." She sets the ornament down gently as if she feels bad for what she said. "My grandma decorated this room before I got here. I didn't want to hurt her by changing it, but this place really is over-the-top girly."

My shoulders tense. I hate that I don't know as much about her as I thought I did. It makes me feel unsettled. It's been a long day; I shouldn't have to do background work at this point. But it is what it is.

"How would *you* decorate it?" I lean back on the bed and cross my arms beneath my head.

Her eyebrows inch upward. "Well, first I'd get rid of the damn figurines. I want a room that says I'm seventeen, not seven. Then I'd pull these pink drapes off my bed." Charlie grabs the drapes, tugs them off, and wraps them around her shoulders. "And oh, the paint. The pink has to go. Instead, I want one bright red accent wall."

"Really, red?" So the girl does have some taste.

"Heck, yeah. It's my favorite color of all time."

"Seriously?"

"Yeah. It's so bold, so powerful, so…everything I'm not." She jumps onto the bed and stretches her arms to touch the ceiling. Her shirt rises just a bit, and I catch a glimpse of firm white belly. It's almost as blinding as the room. "And here! Here I've always wanted storm clouds. I know it's cheesy, but I still want them." Charlie starts jumping up and down, and my body bounces with her movements. "And a softer bed! One I can get better height with." She jumps higher and higher, her words stilted by her movements. "I believe. Jumping. On beds. Is good. For. The soul."

Watching her makes me laugh, even though I'm frustrated that she's killing my panty-dropping moves. She reaches her hand down and says, "Come on."

"Come on what?" I ask.

"Jump with me."

"False. Not happening."

Charlie grabs my arm and pulls until I'm sure it's going to rip out of its socket. For a tiny thing, she's pretty strong. "Fine. Whatever." I stand up on her bed. "This is stupid."

"Oh, really?" Charlie jumps up and down real slow at first, then faster and higher. "*Is* it stupid?"

"Very." I try jumping a little. My mother would never have let me jump on my handmade-in-Tuscany bed. As I start to get some height, I find the experience to be pure awesomeness. Will I ever admit it? Nope. But Charlie probably doesn't need an admission since I'm grinning like an idiot.

She grabs my hands, and we jump around in a circle, laughing like hyenas. I'm about to fall off the edge when Charlie's grandma walks into the room. "What in heaven's name are you two doing?" Her words are stern, but her smile says she's happy I'm here and that Charlie has a new friend. "I see some wild animals got into the kitchen and didn't clean up."

Charlie drops down onto the bed, then bounces off the side. "Sorry, Grandma. I'll take care of it."

"No, no." Grams waves her long red nails toward us. "I wouldn't want to disturb your circus act. You guys hang out. I'll make dinner. Just…door open okay, Charlie?"

Charlie's face flushes, but she nods.

After her grandma leaves, I say to Charlie. "I should probably go." There's no way I can pull a Don Juan now, and I'd rather not be roped into staying for dinner. I've had enough Charlie for one day, even if it wasn't the *worst* day I've ever had.

She says she'll walk me to the door, but I tell her I can see my way out. As I'm halfway down the stairs, she sticks her head out of her room. "Hey," she says. "What are you doing tomorrow morning?"

I press my lips together and shake my head.

"If you want to come by around eight, I'll show you something awesome." I nod, but my brain is screaming, *8:00 A.M.! What?!*

I'm at the bottom of the stairs when Charlie adds, "Wear tennis shoes."

I pull my mouth up to one side and point down at my red sneakers as if to say, *Would I ever take these puppies off?*

She laughs. "You okay walking home? I could drive you."

Charlie knows how to drive? "Nah. I live close by, remember?"

She waves like a pageant queen and sidesteps into her bedroom.

I laugh to myself before moving to open the front door, then remember to mind my manners. I back up a few feet and stick my head into the kitchen. Grams is standing at the sink tossing back her plastic water bottle of rum. My eyes fall to the countertop near her right hand. A dozen brown prescription bottles lay open. Goose bumps rise on my arms, neck, legs—and everywhere else on my body.

Sick. People. Freak. Me. Out.

I'm dead. This shouldn't bother me, but my mind is already supplying terrible diseases she's carrying. Things like the Ebola virus. Also, I'm no doctor, but I'm fairly certain you're not supposed to party with booze and pills in the same sitting. I think back to when I first met Charlie. She asked if I was from the pharmacy. Does she know Grams is hopped up on enough meds to bring down a rhinoceros?

I try to make it out unheard, but Grams spins around and spots me. Her lips curl into a wide smile. Then her eyes snap to the pill bottles. The smile falls from her face, crashes to the floor.

"High blood pressure," she says.

I don't believe her for a second.

Grams steps toward me, and I try to take what I hope is a subtle step backward. *Get away. Get your sickness away from me!*

She notices me backing up and stops. Hurt fills her blue-gray eyes. Before I can think of something to say, I turn and walk out the door.

I need to get away from this house. Away from Charlie and her big, trusting eyes. Away from Grams and the look she just gave me. What am I supposed to feel? Guilt? Shame?

No.

I won't.

I am The Collector.

I walk to the closest pay phone and call the only cab in Peachville. When the driver picks me up fifteen minutes later, he asks, "Where to?"

"A car dealership," I say. "The best you got."

7

PULLING WEEDS

At 7:45 A.M., I leave Wink Hotel and head for Charlie's house. After a night of sleep and frivolous spending, I feel like myself again. Like Dante freakin' Walker, the best damn collector on planet Earth.

I'm going to collect Charlie's soul. I'm not going to feel bad doing it. It's my job. It's nothing personal.

This morning, I'm relishing the perks of working for the Underworld. I press my foot down on the accelerator, and the deep rumble of my candy apple–red Escalade growls. My new baby girl has black leather, Bose surround sound, and twenty-two-inch rims. Match.com couldn't have created a happier couple.

Outside Charlie's house, I honk once and wait. I want to see her face when she walks out the door. She's going to like this ride as much as I do. Only lovers of red can truly appreciate this beauty.

As I'm watching her door, I feel something outside my window. I glance to my left, but there's nothing there. At least that's what my eyes say. But I can feel the collector watching me through his shadow. Watching and waiting for me to botch this assignment.

A tapping sound to my right sends a chill up my spine. Charlie is smiling through the passenger window. Her backpack is slung over both shoulders, and she's dressed in dark jeans and a tie-dyed T-shirt. Tie-dye? Really?

She opens the door, and her wide gaze darts around, taking it all in. "You've got to be kidding me."

"I'm telling you, I'm not."

"It's so awesome!" she says through the hand over her mouth. "Where'd you get it?"

"It's mine. Mom said she'd buy it for me if I moved to Alabama peacefully." I wave my hand around the interior. "I chose peace."

"I'd choose peace, too." Charlie climbs into the passenger seat, then tosses her bag into the back. "Let's name it."

"Name my car? No."

"Yes! Ooh, let me do it. How about Elizabeth Taylor? She was flashy and looked good in red."

"You want to name my car Elizabeth Taylor?"

"Not want to. Did. It's done."

I pull in a long breath. "Can you just tell me where Liz needs to go?"

Charlie claps her hands together and tells me where we're headed. I punch the address into the nav system, and twenty-five minutes later, we're parked in front of Peachville's ghetto. I was sure a city with the name *Peachville* couldn't have a rough part of town, but I stand corrected.

Decrepit houses line the streets, barely a foot between them. Chain-link fences enclose weed-infested yards, and iron bars protect the windows. I watch Charlie from the corner of my eye.

"You got a death wish?"

"Trust me, okay?" she chirps, even though it's way too early for chirping. Charlie slides out of the car and waves at a yellow school bus parked near a crumbling curb. People start pouring out of the bus and heading toward her. They're carrying paint buckets, flower pots, sod, and lots of tools murderers use.

"Charlie, can you please clue me in?" I ask, getting out and stretching my legs.

She opens the back door, grabs her backpack, and pulls out two long-sleeved T-shirts. I grab one as it flies toward me and read the bright, obnoxious logo: *Hands Helping Hands*.

"What does this mean?" I ask. Then it clicks. "Oh, no. Uh, huh. I don't do manual labor. And I certainly don't do it at 8:00 A.M. without coffee."

"Hands Helping Hands is a charity," she says. "I do this every Saturday morning. It's so much fun. You'll see."

It will not be fun. And I will not see.

I notice Blue and Annabelle walking toward us carrying shovels. Blue's eyes narrow when he sees me. Annabelle squeezes his arm as if to calm him and says, "She got you, too, huh?"

"Apparently." I take the shovel from Annabelle and turn to Charlie. "So what are we doing, and how long are we doing it for?"

She pulls the long-sleeved Hands Helping Hands shirt over her tie-dyed embarrassment. "Some people on this street want to improve the appearance of their homes. And we're here to help do that."

She points to a minuscule house with peeling blue paint. "For that one, we've agreed to strip the paint off the front patio and repaint it." She nods toward a home right next to us. "This one will get yard work: weeds pulled, flowers planted. That kind of stuff. There are five houses in all, and we'll work in teams to help get everything done. You'll be with me, Annabelle, and Blue. We're going to be doing this house."

Charlie limps toward the house with the defunct yard. I run my hands through my hair and have the urge to rip out a fistful. I yank on the long-sleeved shirt that announces I'm a chump and head after her, dragging my shovel behind me on the pavement.

As the Three Stooges act a-fool, I work in silence. I'm not sure how this is fun to them, and I'm not sure how I let this happen. Charlie and I should be doing terrible, soul-sealing activities. Instead, she somehow swindled me into *volunteering*. The word has a bad aftertaste, and I'd kill for a beer to wash it down with. Still, as much as I despise this, there's a part of me that admires Charlie's sudden take-charge attitude. If she could only learn to use that same confidence at school, she might not be such an outcast.

Then again, this *confidence* of hers has me doing crap I don't want to do.

I jam the shovel into the dirt and wipe the sweat from my brow. "Why do you guys do this?" Charlie, Blue, and Annabelle stop what they're doing and watch me, but no one says anything. "Any answer will do."

Charlie takes a few steps toward me. She knows I'm not happy. And why should I be? She tricked me into wasting my Saturday morning helping people too lazy to help themselves.

"Dante..." She glances over her shoulder at Blue and Annabelle. The pair pretend to inspect a fire-ant mound, but I know they're eavesdropping. "I like doing this. These people need our help. And it makes me feel good. Doesn't it make *you* feel good?"

"No, it doesn't," I answer honestly. I jab my thumb toward the house. "Why doesn't the person in this house get off their ass and do this themself?"

Charlie's eyebrows pull together. "Because the person in that house is eighty-eight years old and restrained to a wheelchair."

Great. Now *I'm* the ass. I've got to be more careful if I'm going to get this girl to come to the party tonight. I'll give her the day, but tonight…tonight it's my turn.

I relax the muscles in my face and chest. "I guess that's good. Helping people who can't do things themselves."

"But they do things themselves. They do!" Charlie's mouth tugs into a smile. "See, we call it Hands Helping Hands because the people we help agree to help others. Like, for example, this lady we're helping today, she's agreed to work as a suicide hotline volunteer from her home. It turns into this great system of people helping each other."

Something flutters in my stomach. "Charlie, who started this organization?"

She shuffles her feet and brushes dirt off her hands. "Uh, we all did."

"Whatever, Charlie, you started it," Annabelle yells, then resumes her pretend fire ant inspection.

"That true?" I ask. This isn't good. Somewhere in the back of my mind, I'm wondering if this is the reason Boss Man wants her. But it's a tiny operation. This wouldn't make a dent in his numbers.

"I guess." Charlie pushes her glasses up her nose, then pulls her wavy blond hair into a ponytail. She's fidgeting, and I'm not sure why. "We started this—er, *I* started this—because there were so many people out there being helped who wanted to repay the favor."

She and I have very different worldviews. I think most people receiving help have no desire whatsoever to do crap for anyone else.

Charlie twists her hands together, and I know there's something else she's not saying. "How'd it start?" I ask.

Her eyes find mine, and I know this was the question she didn't want to answer. "It started with a group home, a place for kids under state guardianship." Charlie glances at Blue and Annabelle, then back at me. "I was, uh…I was one of those kids. My parents died in a fire when I was twelve." She pauses, but I stay quiet and let her finish. "I was the only one who got out of the house. Because I didn't have any living relatives, I went to live at the home." She points to her hip and tries to smile. "The way I walk is a souvenir from that night."

"So your grandma…?" I ask gently.

"Isn't my grandma. She adopted me three years ago. One time I told her she was like the grandma I never knew. She loved it so much that I just kinda started calling her that. I think it helps avoid questions from people we meet."

"So this organization you started, it helps you?"

"Yeah, I think it does. When I was at the home, there were so many wonderful people who helped me recover. Most of them were volunteers. It made me feel grateful, but it also made me feel indebted. I asked around, and a bunch of other kids felt the same way, so we decided to do something for other people.

"We started doing things during our free hours for people within walking distance. The only thing we required was that the people being helped agreed to help someone else." Charlie waves toward today's volunteers. "And now, three years later, over two thousand people have received help or helped someone else."

Two thousand? Two *thousand*? What if she keeps doing this? She'll never accumulate enough seals to be collected. What's more, every second these people spend helping someone, they're neglecting the important business of collecting new seals for themselves.

Still, I'm relieved. For a moment, I thought this might be the reason Boss Man wants Charlie. And while two thousand is a lot of shiny, happy people, it's not enough to do serious damage. Which brings me back to my original question: *Why her?*

Charlie picks up a plastic sleeve of yellow tulips and sticks her tongue in her cheek. "You good with all this self-revealing?"

"I'm glad you told me." I squeeze her hand, then pick up my shovel and follow her back to the garden we've created.

For the next two hours, I don't complain when the temperature drops. Or when Blue mumbles. Or when Annabelle talks about old black-and-white movies ad nauseam. All I can do is pull weeds. They are never-ending, and for that, I'm thankful. Because it keeps my mind off the image of Charlie being pulled out of her burning home while her parents are on the inside—dying.

I wonder if she cried when it happened. I wonder if she screamed so loud, she sounded like someone else entirely. I wrap my hand around a weed and tear it from the ground. Then I do it again. And again. This I can control. But these thoughts that tick away in my head, I can't.

Because they hit way too close to home.

8

WHAT THE EFF?

Charlie is unusually quiet as I drive back to her house. For the first time since I met her, I hate the silence. I need her to talk, to say something. Anything.

Then I wonder if she needs the same from me.

I glance over at her. She's staring out the passenger window, watching houses blur past us. The sky is overcast, making her sucks-to-be-a-teenager pimples less visible. I open my mouth, then close it. Then I open it again. "Want to listen to music?"

Charlie glances over at me like she forgot I was driving this tank. I turn on the stereo and flip through radio channels until I find a Nirvana song. It seems right. Dark, haunting, tortured… something we can lose ourselves in.

"You like?" I ask, turning it up.

She nods at first. Then she decides to be honest, scrunching her nose up and shaking her head with a barely there smile. I flip to a Beyoncé song and pause.

Another small head shake.

"What's your favorite station?" I ask. "Maybe there's something that'll get us in the mood for tonight."

Charlie laughs and lets her head fall back. "You're not going to let it go, are you?"

"Nope. So you might as well pick out a party dress." I nod toward the radio. "And a party song."

Charlie studies me for a moment, then reaches for the radio and flips it off.

"This is my favorite."

"Off?" I ask.

Charlie rolls down the window. She lays her head on the open window frame. "I like the sound the world makes."

I shrug, roll my window down, and listen when we come to a red light. I hear a mockingbird singing and a man raking leaves. I hear a dog barking and a plane flying overhead. There's even a low rumble of a lawn mower in the distance, and I somehow hear that, too. Personally, I'd take Nirvana. But as I watch Charlie listen to her favorite station, I realize she has something most never will—peace.

I pull up in front of her house, and Charlie opens the car door. I grab her arm before she can get out. "Pick you up at nine?"

She puts a hand on top of her head like she's thinking. Then she says, "My grandma will want me home by midnight."

Score! "Cool. See you tonight."

"I can hardly wait." Charlie rolls her eyes, grabs her backpack, and heads for the front door.

I've got to get this chick more excited about tonight. She needs to be in the right frame of mind to do things she never would before. I drum my fingers on the steering wheel and watch Charlie let herself in her house.

And then I have it.

I back out of the driveway and head to Peachville Mall, where one sexy red dress awaits my credit card.

• • •

James Dean meets me at the entrance of Neiman Marcus. He's about to give me a big excited welcome when he realizes it's me. He does the thing where he acts like our confrontation never happened, and I'm totally down with that. Whatever gets us to not have a conversation.

I grab the red dress in size anorexia and head to the counter. The cashier behind the register asks if anyone helped me out today. I shoot a glance at James Dean, who is busy avoiding eye contact, and say, "Nope."

She nods and tells me it'll be $140.89, and I hand over my limitless Amex Black. The cashier raises an eyebrow and takes the card from me like it's made of explosives. She turns it around in her hands, and I have an urge to throw my arms up and scream, "Pow!" Some people say the Amex Black card is a myth. Those people are also referred to as *poor*. Even thinking the word makes me itch.

Cashier Lady puts the dress in a garment bag and hands it over with the receipt. "I don't need a receipt," I say. "It doesn't matter." I like the look on people's face when I say this. It's a mixture of envy and detestation and makes me feel like a gangsta, like Biggie Smalls.

I'm heading out the door when curiosity stops me. I swivel around the garment bag slung over my shoulder, and flip on James Dean's soul light. I'd like to see if it's time to bring him in.

But wait one effin' minute. I inspect his soul light…and I see glittery pink seals atop the other ones. *What the hell?* No one, and I mean no one, would seal souls with sparkly pink seals.

I take a step closer, but of course they're still there. What's more, I can see soul light filtering through the pink seals. It's like these new seals are breaking down the old ones.

My eyes fall to my feet as if they'll help kick-start my brain. I can't think of a single thing that can destroy our seals. We sure don't have the ability to do it ourselves. So where did this come from? What changed?

James Dean is crossing and uncrossing his arms. I'm no doubt making him nervous. I steal one last glance at those pink seals and leave the store. Then I locate the bench Charlie and I sat on only yesterday.

I'll be damned if I'm going to let someone destroy *my* work. Why did that chump even get those pink seals? For being *good*? If that's the case—and this isn't an isolated incident—this could be the reason my numbers have slipped. It's not like I sealed any fewer souls before my assignment.

My assignment.

Charlie.

I raise my head and pull in a quick breath. *It's her.* This is the reason Boss Man wants her, the reason he's had Peachville on his radar. He's been searching for her. I'm positive. Charlie was here with me yesterday. She must have done something to that guy. Did she do it on purpose? Has she been playing *me* this entire time?

Oh, crap, does she know who I am? Or what I'm here for?

No way.

The dress bag lies across my lap. It doesn't feel good in my hands anymore. I want to toss it in the closest garbage can, but I need to continue as if nothing has changed. Because it hasn't. Charlie's soul must still be collected. Once that's done, I'll get promoted, and my numbers will go back to normal.

Now that I've got the big, dramatic mystery that is Charlie figured out, I'm feeling good. I've got the upper hand again, and I'm sure from here on out, everything will be hunky-freakin'-dory.

9

CONSEQUENCES

Max is going through my overnight bag when I get back to Wink Hotel. My favorite part about this is that he doesn't stop when I walk in the room.

"Hey," he says. He pulls out my black Hugo Boss dress shirt, then holds it up to his nose and sniffs loudly.

"Dude. Stop." I pull the shirt from his hands and toss it on the bed.

"I just love your scent," he says in his chick voice.

"You and everyone else, my friend." I drop down onto one of the queen-sized beds, sticking my hands beneath my head and crossing my ankles. "What are you doing here?"

"Came to pay my favorite collector a visit. That allowed?"

Max pulls out my shoes and holds them up to his own to see if my feet are bigger. I crumple up the Boss shirt and throw it at his face. "Stop being creepy, Max."

"What? I'm looking for something to network in. I got to get laid, man. I mean, by someone other than your mama."

I jump from the bed and fly across the room, my hands balled into fists.

"I'm screwing with you, dude." Max raises his hands in defeat. "Sorry, bad joke."

"Max, I swear I'll break your cuff off if you ever mention my mother again."

"You wouldn't. You love me too much." He gives me his car-salesman grin, and I cross the room and drop back on the bed. "Besides, who needs this damn cuff, am I right?"

For a fleeting second, I consider telling him what I know—the story of where our cuffs came from. But I won't shatter the trust between Boss Man and me.

"So, how you doing with the girl?" he asks.

I glance at him from the corner of my eye. "How'd you know?"

"Are you kidding? Everyone knows. You're the talk of the town, pretty boy."

The fact that everyone knows about my assignment drives me crazy. Now it feels like there's this huge spotlight on my back, and everyone's allowed to watch.

I fill Max in on almost everything, including the part about the pink seals. But I decide not to spill about the collector outside Charlie's house—mostly because I don't want to sound paranoid. When I'm done talking, Max's face goes slack. He pushes my overnight bag onto the floor and sits on the opposite bed. "I didn't know that's why Boss Man sent you to collect her. You really think she has the ability to cancel out our seals?"

I nod.

"What are you going to do?"

I place a hand on my forehead. The truth is I don't really know what I'm going to do. I've proven to myself that I can push Charlie to sin. And I've already sealed her soul once. But how am

I going to do it enough times to collect her in less than ten days? The weight of this assignment suddenly feels like it's sitting on my chest, like a fat walrus just hanging out.

"Honestly? I'm not really sure," I say. "But I've been thinking. Out of us six collectors, I've always been the top performer. I've brought Boss Man more souls in two years than others have in ten." I look at Max. "No offense to the other collectors."

He shrugs. "Ain't no thing but a chicken wing."

I laugh. Leave it to Max to make anything into a joke. "Anyway, I'm thinking Boss Man will spot me a few extra days if that's what I need."

The goofy grin on Max's face falls. He runs a hand through his hair and turns toward me. "You're not seriously thinking about asking for an extension."

I shrug and pull my lips together as if to say. *Why not?*

"Dante, Boss Man will have a conniption fit if you don't bring this girl in. He doesn't want to chance a Judgment Day. It's why he's stuck you on her. So you gotta figure something out."

"Like what?" I need him to have the answer, because right now, I feel clueless. Max is right; if Charlie died before being collected for hell, she'd go to Judgment Day, and she'd be a shoo-in for heaven.

Max rubs his chin and then the sides of his face, which aren't as perfectly shaven as usual. "The Assistant gave me something."

My heart stops beating for the second time in my life. Nothing good comes from Boss Man's assistant. Whenever he's too worked up to deal with something himself, he passes it off on her. And she does whatever's necessary to get the job done.

Max stands up and reaches into his navy-blue sports coat. I feel my skin prick with sweat in anticipation. When he pulls his hand back out, he's holding rolled-up pieces of paper. My muscles relax, and I release a breath I hadn't realized I was holding.

It's only paper. How bad can it be?

Max hands me the parchment. A red ribbon is tied around it. For a moment, I enjoy this simple pleasure, my fingers touching the silky red ribbon. *Such a great shade of red.*

I unroll the document and glance at Max. His face is contorted in an *I share your pain* kind of way. I glance down and read the first words that catch my eye. I realize I'm not breathing again. I'm not doing anything besides staring at the jumble of letters that open their nasty mouths and scream

SOUL CONTRACT.

I drop the contract in my lap. It's useless. Someone like Charlie would never agree to an exchange. "Did you read this?" I ask him.

He pulls his mouth up on one side. That's a *yes*.

"I didn't know we used these anymore," I say.

"Apparently we do," he says gently.

"Have you ever—"

"No." Max shakes his head. "Never."

I stand up, and the contract drops to the floor. "What am I supposed to do? I can't show her this. I'd have to expose myself. I'd have to expose all of us." As I say this aloud, I wonder if it matters...if she already knows who we are. "She'll freak out. She'll think I'm lying. It'll push her away." I cross the room and stop in front of the hotel room window. "There are a thousand reasons why this is a bad idea."

"I'm right there with you," Max agrees. "But what can you do about it?"

"I'll bring her in on time. The right way. There's no way I'm risking our asses for this girl." I turn from the window. "Besides, even if I needed to use it, it'd never work. This girl is so damn *happy*. She wouldn't sell her soul for anything I could give her."

"Well, if you didn't like that, this is going to feel like a swift kick to the nuts." Max fidgets with his jacket collar. "When the Assistant gave me the contract, she told me there'd be—how'd she put it—Donkey Dick–Sized Consequences if the girl wasn't brought in on time."

"Well, isn't that just freaking wonderful. Consequences. There will be consequences." Every time I say *consequences*, Max winces and nods. "Glad to hear the Assistant still has her sense of humor."

So now my promotion—and who knows what else—is riding on this assignment. This is turning out to be a grand ole time. It's not that I mind the added pressure. I thrive under pressure. No. I thrive under normal conditions. Under pressure, I blow people's minds. Besides, what's the worst they'd do? Deny my promotion?

I let that sink in—the realization that I could lose my only chance to escape the worst place anyone could imagine. Max is biting his fingernails. "Max?"

"Yeah," he says way too loud.

"I'm going to bring this girl in. I don't need the contract."

Max smiles with his entire face. "There's the guy who trained me, you sexy son-of-a-bitch. I knew you could do this. I told the Assistant, I said, 'Do you even *know* who you're dealing with here? Pffft. Pffft.'"

"You definitely didn't say that."

"Nope. I sure as hell didn't. That woman would've cut my junk off. And I need my junk. Especially tonight. What with all the Peachville honeys I'm trottin' with." He pops his collar and struts toward the door, trying to make his usual dramatic exit.

"Max Turner, born a lady-killer, died a lady-killer…and damn it if he isn't *still* lining 'em up and knocking 'em down."

Max freezes at the door, his hand on the silver knob. He

throws me a small smile over his shoulder. "I wasn't always like this, Dante. People change when shit happens."

He walks out the door, and I wonder what he meant by that. The only Max I've ever known is the guy he is now, so I don't buy what he's selling.

I reach inside my pocket and fumble for a second, fingering lint. Then I feel it—my penny. I pull it out and roll it between my thumb and pointer. The date and the word *Liberty* are misaligned. It's called doubled die, and it happened over half a century ago in 1955, when workers at the Philadelphia Mint screwed up. Their error made this penny worth several hundred dollars. But for me, it's not about the value.

It's a lifeline to my past.

Shoving the penny back into my pocket, I pick the soul contract up off the floor. I don't need to read the fine print. Like every other collector, I've heard the stories. And I'm sure I'm right about Charlie. That she'd never agree to it.

Which means exactly one thing: I've got to play this night like a P-I-M-P.

10

RED DRESS

I pull up in Elizabeth Taylor at exactly 9:00 P.M. Fighting the urge to honk, I kill the engine and walk to the door, the garment bag folded over my arm.

After Max left my hotel room, I decided on classing it up for the party. I'm sporting my black Boss dress shirt—sleeves rolled up, of course—dark jeans, and my red Chucks. Even sprayed on my favorite scent, Safari. Because it's a little dirty, like me. If Charlie doesn't dig my get up, I'll expose her for what she is: asexual.

Grams opens the door after I've knocked only once. I guess she was expecting me. Her eyes drink me in, and a smile finds her mouth. "If I didn't know better," she says, "I'd think the devil just showed up on my doorstep."

Normally I'd laugh my ass off at the irony of this statement, but I'm strung out, so I feel like shoving a bright light in her face and screaming, "What do you know?!"

Instead, I smile as Grams puts an arm around my shoulder and leads me inside. I'm wondering if there'll be a moment when

Charlie glides down the stairs like she's a completely different person. But nothing like that happens. Charlie is sitting at the kitchen table to my right when I walk through the entryway. She's eating a bowl of cereal, looking like she always does—unkempt.

I walk into the kitchen with Grams hovering way too close. Charlie pushes her bowl away and stands up. There's an awkward moment where we half-hug, half-fumble. Then Charlie spots the garment bag over my arm.

"What's that?" Her eyes widen.

"It's for you," I answer, holding it out to her. "Open it."

Charlie takes the garment bag and unzips the front. When she pulls out the red dress, Grams groans this long, "Ohhhh, myyyyyy Gaaaaawd."

"You got this for me?" Charlie asks. I nod, and she twirls around with it held against her like she did in the store. "Should I wear it tonight?"

"That's the idea," I say, sitting down at the kitchen table.

"Grandma?" she squeaks.

"I'm right behind you, baby."

Charlie and Grams head up the stairs toward her bedroom. Why it takes two people to put one dress on one body is beyond me.

Charlie's bedroom door clicks shut, and a few seconds later, the doorbell rings. Grams sticks her head out and yells down the stairs, "Man Child! Can you get the door?"

I head toward the entryway and listen as Charlie tells her grandmother not to call me Man Child. When I open the door, Blue and Annabelle are standing on the other side. Blue is holding two movies and a pizza box. His pinched expression looks like he just smelled his own asshole.

I take a few steps away and say over my shoulder, "By all means, come on in."

Annabelle swivels around my side and stands in front of me. Her mouth is pulled into a smile, but her voice holds a note of accusation. "You watching movies with us tonight?"

"Not exactly."

"Then what are you doing here?" Blue mumbles.

I ignore Blue's question because it isn't worth answering. Annabelle is still standing in front of me, so I step around her and plop back down at the kitchen table. She must take this as an invitation to chat because she sits across from me. Blue lingers near the door, leaning against the stairwell railing.

"So if you're not watching movies with us, what are you doing tonight?" Annabelle asks.

"I'm going to Taylor's party."

"Mm-hmm, mm-hmm." She nods like this is a reasonable answer. "And who would you be going with?"

"I'd be going with Charlie."

Blue doesn't move, but I hear the *click* of his teeth slamming together. Annabelle must, too, because she glances at him and says, "Oh, come on. Is that really a surprise, Blue?"

She jumps from the table and heads across the entryway to a small den. Once there, she opens a closet door and searches for something.

"The mother lode!" she cries.

Annabelle holds a trunk the size of a microwave against her chest and wobbles back toward the kitchen table. I flinch when she drops the trunk on the table and beams at me. "In this trunk," she says with a serious face, "is God's gift to women."

"Chocolate?"

"No."

"Midol?"

"What? No."

"Tampons."

"Stop guessing," she says. "In this box is Charlie's grandma's makeup stash. I've waited three years to bust into this thing. The time is now." Annabelle unlatches the makeup box and lifts the lid ever so slowly. I half expect pixie dust to float out of the box in a twinkling, magical cloud.

Annabelle gasps when she finally peers inside. "It's better than I ever could have imagined." She pulls out mini racks of colorful pastes and powders. Grams may be a makeup guru, but she can't apply it to her own face. Actually, it's a case of applying too much. She doesn't understand restraint.

"So you going to do Charlie's makeup or something?" I ask. I'm hoping I'm right. The better Charlie feels tonight, the more trouble I can get her in.

"Charlie? No. This is *my* time. First I'm going to hook up with Bobbie Brown, woman of great mystical makeup powers..." She pulls out blue eyeliner and gives it a lustful look. "Then I'm going to hook up with Bobbie Davids, boy of great basketball skills."

"What?" I say.

"What?" Blue echoes.

Annabelle stares at us like she can't understand why we're confused. "I'm going to make myself into a hottie, then make out with Bobbie Davids at Taylor's party." She brings the blue eyeliner to her eyes and leans toward a prop-up mirror. "I knew tonight was going to be awesome. I just had this gut feeling, you know?"

"Annabelle, you can't go to Taylor's party," Blue says.

I'm glad Blue spoke up, because the last thing I need is Charlie's crew ensuring she stays her same ole prude self.

"Who says I can't go to the party?"

"Your lack of invitation says you can't go," he answers.

"Whatever. It's not like there were formal invites or anything."

I pull the orange envelope out of my pocket and lay it on the table.

Annabelle stops mid-stroke and stares at the invite, then at me. "You've got to be kidding me. She handed these things out? What is this, the sixteenth century?" She rips the invitation out of the envelope. "It says it's for you plus a guest. I guess *a* guest means *one*, huh?"

Blue and I nod in unison. I'm glad we agree on one thing.

"What is she going to do, kick us out?"

We nod again.

"Bobbie Davids would see me kicked out on my ass." Annabelle takes a second to think about this. "Well, what if I want to go, anyway?"

"Anna, don't ditch me, all right?" Blue pleads. It's a little pathetic, actually. But I try not to judge, since he's doing me a solid.

"No, you'll come, too!" Annabelle gets up from the table and grabs his hands. "I'll do your makeup, sweet cheeks."

"Funny." Blue yanks his hands away. "I'm not going to that party. We're not invited, or we'd have an invitation."

Annabelle's smile crumbles. She walks over to the table without saying another word and starts loading the makeup back into the trunk. I know the stand-up thing to do would be to invite them along. It's not like I couldn't sweet-talk Taylor into letting them stay. But I have an assignment with a big, blubbery D-day, and I'm not letting these two get in the way.

Annabelle is sliding the makeup trunk back into the den closet when I hear Charlie's bedroom door open. It's about freakin' time.

Grams glides down the stairs, and a second later, Charlie limps out. She's as happy as a Care Bear, and I'd love to say she looks like a beauty queen, but she doesn't. What she does look like is *passable*, which I'll take. And for the first time I'm reminded Charlie is seventeen. Her blond hair is piled on top of her head, and she's wearing a tasteful silver necklace. The red dress is killer—strapless, tight through the middle, and ruffles that end mid-thigh—but her lack of curves does nothing for it. Then I notice Charlie has a rack. Color me shocked.

I quickly glance away when I realize Grams thinks I'm staring at Charlie's boobs with more than friendly interest.

Blue smiles like she just gave birth to his firstborn son. I roll my eyes at how obvious he is.

You can have her body when I'm done with her soul, I want to tell him.

When Charlie reaches the bottom of the stairs, she takes the hand Blue is offering. "Do I look okay?" she asks, her cheeks reddening with excitement. "The dress is so great."

Blue opens his mouth to say something, but he's way too slow and way too inexperienced to handle this.

"Charlie," I say, pausing for added effect. "That dress is nice." I lean in close and whisper in her ear, "But you make it… *hypnotic*."

Charlie's face lights up like a Christmas tree. She grabs the bottom of her dress in her hands and squeezes. Then she turns to Annabelle and Blue. "I'm so sorry, guys. I tried to call your cells to tell you about tonight."

It's no biggie." Annabelle shrugs a shoulder and smiles. "Next week."

When I notice Grams is staring at me like she's about to offer a one-way ticket to her bedroom, I decide it's time to roll. "If you'll excuse us," I say, "I'm going to take Charlie with me now."

Grams and Annabelle shuffle so we can reach the door, and Blue shoots me an I'd-like-to-cut-your-Achilles-tendons look.

I place my hand on the small of Charlie's back and lead her

from the house. As I'm opening her car door, Grams steps outside and yells, "Home by midnight, or I'll whip you both."

Charlie cringes, waves at her grandma, then slides into the passenger's seat. I close her door and jog to the other side and get in. As I back out into the street, I notice a blue Nissan parked in front of her house. It has about the same appeal as a ninety-year-old with a heroin problem.

"Whose car is that?" I ask.

Charlie points a finger at the POS. "That's Blue's blue. We call him Scrappy."

I decide that's why Blue and Annabelle rode the bus to volunteer this morning. That thing makes a unicycle seem like reliable transportation.

Charlie is staring at me.

"What?" I ask without turning toward at her.

"Nothing," she says. "You just look really nice. And I'm really happy you're taking me to this party."

"You are? I figured you might be having second thoughts."

She shakes her head and tugs the top of her dress up, which is suddenly having an issue trying to cover up her chest.

"Well, that's good." I start Liz and pull out into the street. "I want you to let loose tonight. Try some things you wouldn't normally try."

"Like what?" she asks.

"Nothing crazy," I answer. "It's just…look, you don't like when people judge you and your friends, do you?"

She shakes her head.

"Then just try to be open-minded and not judge the people at this party. You never know, you might even have fun." I reach over to turn on the stereo, then stop. *She doesn't like the radio*, I remind myself.

"Okay, I'll be open-minded," she says.

"Yeah?"

"Yeah."

With Charlie here beside me, I realize it was crazy to think she knows what she's capable of. Not a chance. She has no idea she has a stash of glittery pink seals inside her body, and I'm definitely not telling her. The less she knows, the better.

I squeeze her knee and concentrate on finding Taylor's house. We drive the rest of the way in silence, and strangely enough, it feels perfectly normal. Eventually, Elizabeth Taylor pulls off onto a dirt road, and we take it for a quarter mile. At the end of the makeshift road is an enormous two-story farmhouse with a wraparound porch on the top and bottom levels.

Music is blasting from the house, and a smile finds its way to my face. I park the car and open Charlie's door. She bites her lip, and I tell her everything's going to fine. But that's not entirely the truth, is it? Because this party isn't going to be *fine*.

It's going to be the beginning of her end.

11

THE PARTY

I knock once, then let myself in.

Charlie doesn't move from outside the doorway. "Shouldn't we wait out here?"

"No, Charlie. If you're invited to a party, you just go in." I'm going to have to be careful tonight. She's not used to parties, and I need her to mesh so she doesn't get all holier-than-thou.

Charlie trails in after me like she's expecting an alarm to sound.

Inside Taylor's fridge, I grab myself a beer. "What do you want to drink?" I ask as I pop the top and take a pull. The beer rushes down my throat, and I shiver from how damn good it feels.

"Oh, I'm not drinking." Charlie bites her nails and glances around. The kitchen is empty. In fact, the whole house is empty. Party must be in the back.

"Come on, Charlie. We talked about this on the way over. People drink at parties. You're at a party." I step toward her and run my hand down her arm. "Trying new things, remember?"

She wraps her arms around her waist, then smiles and nods.

"Thatta girl." I grab a strawberry-kiwi wine cooler from the top shelf. A shot of tequila is what I'd like to feed her, but I figure I better ease her into this.

I slide the wine cooler across the kitchen counter, and she grabs it. More beer finds its way down my gullet as Charlie twists the cap off her drink. She takes a small sip.

"Not bad," she says. She takes another sip.

Thank goodness for small miracles. "Ready to get crunk?"

"Get what?"

"Join the party."

"Oh, yeah," she says. "Where is everyone?"

"Probably in the back." Following the thumping sound of bass, I lead the way through Taylor's house and find a sliding glass door in the living room that leads outside. When I pull it open, the music washes over me.

Two speakers are built over an enormous deck that extends into the backyard. A dozen people sit on benches built along the inside of the deck, and from the sound of it, there are even more people farther out in the yard.

I nod *what's up* to a few people and keep moving. Charlie stays near me as we head down a flight of wooden stairs descending from the deck. At the bottom of the stairs, she stops and makes this surprised sound.

In front of us is a clearing half the size of a football field. Beyond that are giant trees with white paper lanterns hanging from the branches. I'm a bit impressed myself. The parties I used to throw were limited to kegs and a bonfire. Guys don't really do decorations.

Though this party is all *fancy*, the kegs are still in attendance, which is pretty delightful since I've already killed my beer. I crush the can and do a long-distance toss to the trash.

"Ready for another?" I turn around and face Charlie, who still has ninety-nine hundredths of her drink left. "Charlie, you're nursing that thing. You need to drink it."

She breaks her gaze from the lanterns and turns her drink up. I put my hand on the bottom and keep the bottle upturned for much longer than I'm sure she intended.

"There you go," I say when she forces it back down. It's going to take more than a wine cooler to earn Charlie seals, but I know where one wine cooler can lead, and that's where we're headed. Drunk people lose their inhibitions. People without inhibitions sin. Therefore, Operation Get Charlie Wasted has been launched. "One more good pull like that and we'll be ready to hit the keg."

"I knew you'd come."

I turn around and see Taylor heading toward us. Over her shoulder, I spot a guy's legs flailing in the air. Keg stand. Jealous.

"How long you been here?" Taylor wraps her arms around my waist and pulls me into a hug. Her boobs press against me, and I briefly wonder if they'll make a full appearance tonight. The bright orange shirt she's wearing is pushing those puppies up and over, and it wouldn't take much to make it happen.

"Not long," I say. "Good party."

"'Course. I only throw the best. Come on, let me take you around and introduce you." She loops her arm through mine and starts to pull me away.

"Hang on." I pull my arm away. "Charlie, you want to walk around with us?"

Taylor notices Charlie, and her face puffs up like a blowfish. "I didn't know you brought a date."

I shrug because there's no best way to handle this. Tearing into Taylor will be tonight's dessert, but I can't have Charlie upset.

"It's okay," Charlie says. "Think I might just hang out on the deck."

Taylor grabs my arm again, and again I pull it away. "I'm not ditching her, Taylor."

"Okay. Fine." She smiles likes it's no biggie. "I'll be around if you decide to be social."

I face Charlie as Taylor sashays toward a small group of girls. "Yes. Before you even say anything, yes. I want to hang out with you. No, it's not fine that I ditch you. We came together, we're partying together."

Charlie grins. "I wasn't going to say anything. But thanks." She turns her wine cooler up and drains it dry. "Did you still want to go to the keg?"

"Damn, girl. You *do* know how to party." I lead her toward the keg and fill up a red plastic cup. "Here you go, sweetheart." I grab one for myself, and we sit down on the deck steps. "You having a good time?" What I mean to say is, *Are you feeling your booze yet?*

"We've only been here, like, ten minutes," she says in a completely sober voice. "But, yeah. I'm having fun."

"Cool. How 'bout we make it even more fun?" I stand up and yell out across the clearing. "What's up, people! Who's up for a drinking game?"

Several drunkards give a slurred yell of excitement and raise their plastic cups.

"On the deck. Five minutes."

I nudge Charlie, and she heads up the stairs, whispering to me over her shoulder. "I've never played a drinking game, Dante."

"Don't worry about it," I tell her. "It doesn't take much athleticism."

People crowd around us in a circle and await the drink-a-thon. I break past the crowd and climb up on a bench. My heart is pumping, and my mouth is smiling, and I feel like I belong.

"Everyone ready?"

Zombie-esque slurring.

"Okay. The game's called I've Never. For the two of you who don't know how to play, I'll explain the rules. I'm going to yell something out, and if you've done it, you have to drink. Here we go." I raise my glass up in the air. Charlie is watching me with big eyes and red cheeks.

"Hmmm. Let's see. Okay, I've never gone to Centennial High School." People grumble and take a drink of their beer. I do, too. And more importantly, so does Charlie.

"Next. Uh, let me think." I glance at Charlie and act like I just thought of something, like she happened to give me the idea. "I've never volunteered before." Taylor makes a big show of drinking, and so do several other people. I bet they've never volunteered a day in their life. But the girl in the red dress has, which is why she places the red cup to her mouth.

Charlie smiles and shakes her head like I'm flirting. Taylor's eyebrows furrow, and she whispers to the girl standing near her.

I decide to let up for a couple, or Charlie will know I'm purposely targeting her.

"I've never been in a fistfight." I take a big swallow of my beer and watch as several other guys, and a few chicks, join me.

One more freebie and it's back to Operation Get Charlie Wasted. "I've never had a one-nighter." People laugh and drink up, and my eyes nearly explode out of my skull when I see Miss Charlie Cooper sneak a drink.

"Game over. Thanks for playing." I jump down from the bench and lean in close to Charlie. "You've had a one-nighter?"

Her whole face changes colors. *Damn right, I just busted you.*

"It was last summer. It wasn't a big deal."

"Who was it?" Not that I care.

She shrugs. "Just some guy I met. He was staying at the same hotel as me and Grams."

I stand up straight and run my tongue over my teeth. Charlie getting it on with some random guy on the beach? Who woulda thunk. "You make it a habit of mugging down with strangers?"

"We didn't mug down. We just kissed and stuff. Not that it's any of your business." Charlie turns and heads down the deck stairs toward the clearing.

I run after her, wondering if she realizes that *kissing and stuff* doesn't really classify as a one-nighter. "None of my business?"

She shakes her head.

That's it. She's officially feeling her alcohol. And holy crap, she's heading to the keg again. "You want another one?"

"Yeah. Beer's gross, but it's good for my brain. I like the way it fizzles in there."

Good for my brain? The collector part of me snatches up her cup and pumps more frothy yellow liquid. But the other part of me, the human part, feels a twinge deep in my gut. She's getting drunk because of me. This fact is 95 percent pleasing, and 5 percent…something else. I can't think about the something-else part. Especially since Charlie is half walking, half staggering toward a guy who's sure to blow her off.

"Hey there, football man," I overhear her saying.

Sweet Jesus.

I jog after her and grab her shoulders. "There you are, Charlie. Why don't we go back up on the deck and hang out?"

"Dante, stop." She pulls away from me and grins up at the disheveled guy three times her size. "I want to talk to Vince Haggard."

Vince's face lights up, and he glances at his buddies. Together, they laugh like they're one person, which they sort of are. Charlie doesn't realize they're laughing at her. She only laughs with them and makes sweet love to her cup of beer. I've got to get her to slow down before she becomes *that* girl.

"Hey, why don't I get you something mixed? I bet there's good stuff in the house." What I mean by this is, *I bet there's Coke in the house, and you'll have no idea it's virgin.*

"I've changed my mind," she says. "Beer tastes like gold nuggets and baby kittens. Which is exactly why I'd prefer another one." Charlie upends her cup. I'd like to say beer spills out onto the ground. But it doesn't. Because Charlie has already polished it off. In, like, two seconds.

This is getting ridiculous. If she keeps going like this, she'll be passed out within an hour, and passed-out peeps tend to refrain from sinning. I need a distraction, something to get her mind off drinking.

Taylor is a few feet away, and I have an idea.

"Hey, Taylor," I yell. "Good times." I raise my glass, and she smiles with one side of her mouth. "How about another game? Maybe a sober one so the lightweights can play."

She glances at her friends, and her half smile grows wider.

"Yeah, I got a game we can play," she says. "But only since you asked."

12

HIDE AND GO SEEK

Everyone gathers around as Taylor explains the game.

"This game is like Hide and Go Seek, but with a dirty little twist." She sweeps her dark hair off her shoulders and continues, "Guys, you stand near the deck stairs. And girls, when the guys start counting, we'll run out into the woods and hide."

A guy who's way too small to be categorized as male asks, "What do we get if we find you?"

"Exactly," she says. "That's the twist. If you find a girl, you get to bring her back to the deck and kiss her."

The guys cheer their approval, and I look at Charlie. This isn't exactly what I had in mind, but maybe it'll be good. Maybe she and some guy will hook up. From the looks of it, there aren't a ton of *good influence* dudes here. The right boy toy might push her to sin and make my job easier.

Taylor raises her hand to get the guys to shut up. "The game is over after ten minutes. If there are more girls on the deck than in the woods, the guys win. More girls left in the woods, we win."

The girls and guys begin to separate. The girls inch toward the woods, ready to run, and the guys linger near the stairs.

"Okay, losers," Taylor jeers. "Turn around and count to fifty so we can beat your asses."

Right before I turn around, I steal one last glance at Charlie. She's set to run like this is the freaking Boston Marathon. The smile on her face sweeps from ear to ear. For some stupid reason, it makes me excited to play Taylor's dumb game. I'm about to go into counting mode when I catch Taylor eyeing me. She winks and mouths the words, *Find me.*

Maybe. Not the worst idea I've ever heard.

I turn around and listen while some douchebag counts and the girls run into the woods like a pack of wild dogs. When Homie finally gets to fifty, I turn around and watch as thirty guys run crotch-first toward the woods.

Me? I'm taking it easy. There's nothing out there I care about.

A minute later, I hear the first chick squeal echo through the trees. Footsteps fall close by, and I see a guy dragging a girl toward the deck. When he gets to the clearing, he flips her over his shoulder and races up the stairs. Then he presses his lips to her. Or eats her face. I can't tell from here.

The whole thing has a barbaric, caveman ring to it, but I'll admit it's pretty entertaining to watch.

I lean against a tree as more and more girls are pulled out of the woods. Taylor's waiting for me, no doubt, so there's no need to rush. Somewhere near the deck, the caveman leader yells, "Five minutes."

Leaves crunch under my red sneakers as I set out to claim my prize. I wonder if Taylor will let me drag her back by the hair. It's an enticing thought.

I don't get ten steps before I see Taylor being pulled toward the clearing by Vince. She spots me and delivers a few friendly death rays.

Right back at ya, babe.

Oh, well. Game's over for me, but I'm curious how Charlie made out. Or who she made out *with*.

When I get to the clearing, I scan the deck. I don't see Charlie anywhere. Maybe she's still hiding. She's a clever girl. I wouldn't put it past her to be one of the reigning champs.

Then I freeze. Something horrible occurs to me.

"Taylor," I ask. "How much time is left?"

She laughs, but it doesn't reach her eyes. "Oh, I don't know. Three minutes or so."

I glance around and notice none of the guys are coming out of the forest. Or going back in.

Oh, fuck.

"There are still girls left out there." I can hear the pleading in my voice, and it makes me want to kill something. Anything.

"None worth finding," someone yells.

Everyone laughs at Shithead's comment, but instead of breaking his jaw, I run.

I'm about to crash into the woods when Taylor yells, "Two minutes, sweetheart."

Branches whip across my face and snag my Boss shirt, but I don't care. Charlie can't be the only girl left.

"Charlie!" I yell. "Where are you?" If I can't find her in time, I want her to at least know someone was looking. "I'm going to find you!" I try to sound like we're having fun, but I know it's not working.

I search behind trees and dig through shrubs, but I can't find her anywhere. Then I hear a sound that makes my breath catch.

Behind me, I see Charlie curled into a ball. She's leaning against a massive tree, and her arms are wrapped around her knees. *I can deal with this*, I think. But then she raises her head… and her face is my undoing.

Behind her glasses, her eyes are swollen and red and so filled with hurt that I fear I may actually murder someone. That I will end someone's life.

Her lips part, and she says only, "They all saw me. But they just kept walking."

She starts crying again, and I don't think, I just move. I sweep Charlie into my arms, and I carry her toward the clearing. She lays her head against my chest, and I know I will rip someone's throat out if they say a single word.

A hush falls over the crowd as I appear with her in my arms. I start to climb the stairs, still carrying her, when I hear Charlie mumble something.

"No," she says quietly. I try to hold onto her, but she pushes away from me. "No," she says, louder. "Put me down. Put me down!" Surprised, I place her on her feet. She tugs her dress up and ascends the rest of the stairs, chin held high. I climb behind her, wondering what's happening. Charlie straightens her back and approaches Taylor. "You knew that would happen."

Taylor grins.

"Did you tell them to leave me out there?" Charlie continues..

Taylor acts offended. "I would never do that," she says, shaking her head. "They did that on their own. Such jerks, am I right?"

Charlie flinches. Maybe Taylor *didn't* ask the guys to ditch her, but I also know that only makes it worse. I slide the glass door open to Taylor's house. We're going home. I'm taking Charlie home.

We're almost inside when I hear Taylor snicker. I turn around. I'm too ready for a fight to ignore the sound. "You have something to say?"

Charlie touches my arm to try and calm me, but it doesn't work.

"No, nothing," Taylor says through a laugh. "Just noticing that even you didn't want to kiss her."

I cross the deck in three strides and get two inches from her face. "I'd watch what comes out of that fat mouth of yours."

Taylor leans in even closer and lowers her voice. "I'll say and do whatever I want, asshole. And another thing, you better watch your step at Centennial, because I could destroy you and your mutt-faced girlfriend."

I throw my head back and laugh long and hard. Then I lean in and whisper in her ear, "You don't know who you're fucking with, princess. Ain't *no one* do bad like I do."

13

INNOCENCE

Charlie is silent most of the way home. I try once to get her to talk about what happened, but she just half-smiles and says she's fine. So I do what most guys do—I shut up and hope things get better on their own.

The thought of Charlie getting left in the woods makes me grip the steering wheel tighter. I have this sudden, crazy urge to smash my windshield out. I'm not sure what good it would do, but I imagine it all the same. If Charlie does have the ability to release *good* seals, no one at that damn party should ever receive one, even if for the rest of their lives they live like saints.

There is nothing I can do to protect her from the pain she feels. What's more, it's not my job to protect her. In fact, it's quite the opposite, and crap like tonight doesn't make it any easier.

Inside my glove compartment, the soul contract reminds me I have another option. But it's not that simple. Yes, the contract would speed things along. But a girl like Charlie would never agree to the terms.

Beside me, Charlie's chin rolls back and forth along her

chest. She's halfway between sleep and consciousness. Every few seconds, she releases these tiny snort-snores. How can someone be cruel to this chick? It's like picking a fight with a chipmunk.

Her cheeks no longer hold their scarlet shade, and in the dark, her face almost seems pretty. It's unfair that people like Taylor are born with good looks, while the Charlies of the world spend their lives being bottom-feeders.

For a second, I allow myself to imagine Taylor's face if Charlie were to become beautiful. The thought is delicious.

Charlie is good and intelligent and should know what it's like to have true and utter confidence. Not just the kind she has inside her charity, or even the bit she displayed tonight, though that was promising, but the kind that makes people notice when you walk by. Boss Man has targeted her, and nothing will ever stop that agenda. But once I've collected her soul, her body and mind will stay on earth for the remainder of her life.

Doesn't she deserve the best while she's alive?

It feels like I'm talking myself into using the soul contract. But I can't decide whether it's to make this easier for me or better for her. I don't know.

Charlie does another snort-snore, and I glance over. Her bottom lip hangs open, and she's breathing long and deep. I'm certain she's moved from quasi-sleeping to passed the hell out.

When I glance back at the road, I sense someone standing in the middle of the street. *Shit!* My muscles clench, and I jerk the wheel to avoid leaving roadkill in my wake.

Charlie bolts upright, and her hands splay out. I do the thing where I throw my arm over her chest like my mother used to do. Elizabeth Taylor screams to a stop.

"What!" Charlie yells. "What's going on?"

I whip my head around and search for the person in the

street, but they're nowhere to be seen. My heart pumps so fast, it's painful. I'm guessing for Charlie, too, because she's breathing hard.

"Did you see something?" she asks when I don't say anything.

I run my hands through my hair and breathe out through tight lips. "No. I thought I saw a deer, but it was nothing. I'm just tired."

Charlie studies me for a long time, then turns back to the road. "I'll stay awake with you."

"Cool," I say. "Thanks."

She reaches for the stereo. "Music?" I nod, and she flips through the channels until she finds a System of a Down song. "You like this kinda stuff, right?"

"Yeah. That'll work."

Charlie and I don't talk for the remainder of the drive, which is fine with me. I'm too busy having conversations in my own head. I know what I sensed in the street. I just don't know *who* I sensed. The collector watching me is getting too far up my ass. There was no reason for him to pop out in front of my car like that other than to mess with me. Does he realize what could've happened? What if I'd lost control of the car? I may be immortal, but I can still feel physical pain. And what about Charlie? Does he realize hurting her could mean war on earth?

The part that bothers me most is not which of the other five collectors is watching, but what he's searching for. He must know about the assignment. And maybe he knows about the soul contract, too, and is waiting to see if I'll use it. But why screw with me in the meantime?

When I pull up in front of Charlie's house, she's asleep again. So much for staying awake. I nudge her a few times, and she opens her eyes and wipes drool from her mouth.

Nice.

"Are you going to be okay?" I ask.

"Of course. Why wouldn't I be?"

Of course.

I smile, and she slides out of her seat, a bit unsteady on her feet. She's about to close the door but stops. "Hey, Dante?"

"What's up?"

"Thanks for taking me to the party."

"Seriously?"

"Yeah. It's just…no one's ever asked me to go before. And the first half was sorta fun." She sticks her thumb and pinkie out and mimics drinking. I manage a half laugh before she continues, "I know things didn't go great, but it's nice to be a part of the fun. It makes me feel like I'm living. Does that make sense?"

My whole body seems to pull into itself. I can't believe after everyone kicking the crap out of her tonight, she's *grateful* for the experience. At first, Charlie struck me as being so young. Maybe it's her naïveté, or the fact that she's brimming with dorkiness. But as I watch her hand trace light circles over her hip—a small curve in her body I never noticed before—I realize Charlie could be attractive to the right person. It's in the way she sees the world. Like she's lived a hundred lives before this, and now she's got it all figured out. When in fact, she's just a seventeen-year-old girl.

Charlie Cooper had something terrible happen to her. She watched as her parents burned alive. Anyone would say she has a right to be angry. To be reckless. To weave a string of sins, each one worse than the last. And yet, she somehow manages to have this… this innocence.

She has every reason to be exactly like me.

But she's not.

For one small moment, I envy her life. I can't help wondering how things would be different for me if I'd lived the way she does. It's a thought I typically never allow myself to linger over. But with her, I can't help it.

I can't think of the right words to tell her how lucky she is. Or how, now that I think of it, that dress doesn't look so terrible on her. So I just say, "Good night, Charlie."

She smiles, and it takes over her entire face. "Night."

14

DECISIONS

I lay awake in my hotel room. For the past three hours, I've been tossing and turning like a druggie in rehab. The soul contract is driving me crazy.

To use, or not to use: that is the question.

I have to forget about the way I saw Charlie tonight, with her innocence all up in my face. And I can't think about how doing this to her either way makes me feel…off. Boss Man gave me a job to do, and if I don't do it, someone else will. And that someone else will get my promotion, because sure as shit, Boss Man's owning her soul in a week. So I have to make a decision. I need to be the collector I was sent here to be, and use the tools at my disposal.

I am Dante Walker.

I am not merciful.

In order for me to use the soul contract, I'd have to be sure she'd trust me completely. Even more, I'd have to be sure I could follow through to the very end, because once a soul contract is signed, it'd be the only thing the Underworld talks about.

My other choice is to collect Charlie's soul the tried-and-true way. But that has proven to be more than a little difficult.

Either way, something has to happen. I can't let her walk around destroying our work with her pink seals.

After another half hour of wrestling this issue, I shoot up in bed with my decision made. I will collect Charlie's soul without the contract. If the collector watching me is waiting to see what I can do, I'm going to give him one hell of a show.

I had the right idea a few days ago, and now is the time to put it into action—when she is at her most vulnerable. I swing my legs over the side of the bed and throw on my clothes. The clock reads 2:30 A.M. when I shut the hotel door behind me and jog toward my Escalade.

As I drive to her house, I run over the scene in my head. I'll seduce Charlie tonight. I'll take every part of her body for my own, and tomorrow she'll be a doll in my arms. Putty I can twist and mangle.

When I finally arrive, my heart is racing, and I know there's no turning back. I scale up the lattice to her window and knock quietly. The last thing I need is Grams killing our moment.

After the fourth knock, Charlie slides her window open, and I crawl inside.

"Dante?" she asks, her voice thick with sleep. "What are you doing here? It's, like..." She glances at her nightstand. "It's almost three in the morning. Is something wrong?"

I move toward her to do what I came here for. Her lips fall open when I pull her in close to me. My hands wrap around the sides of her face. I stare down at her. The moment hangs between us. She needs to think this is love. There's no other way she'll submit.

Her eyes open wide, and I see in them something that makes

me sick: trust. She'll do anything I ask, and I know why. She cares about me. In two days, she's opened her heart the way I never could. She believes I am her friend. Me.

Dante.

A fraud.

I drop my hands from her face and step back. Charlie releases a quick breath. I wonder if she knew what was about to happen. She has to. I glance at her, barely able to raise my head. She's dressed in a red silk above-the-knee slip. Something I can't believe she owns. And even though she's wearing this thing that says *I'm Down to Mess Around*, she still exudes this *purity*.

I don't want to hurt her. I really don't. But I won't miss my chance to leave hell.

Her hair, her skin…the way she walks. Her appearance prevents people from realizing how amazing she is.

But not anymore.

I step in close and take her hands in mine.

"Charlie," I say, "I'm going to make you beautiful."

15

SURPRISE!

I pull Charlie down on the bed and sit beside her.

"What are you talking about, Dante?" Charlie stares down at her feet. I know I've hurt her by implying she's not beautiful, but we have to face facts to move forward.

"There are some things you don't know about me," I answer.

The realization that I'm going to expose myself crashes down on my shoulders. They hunch over from the weight. This could go wrong so many different ways. I haven't really thought about how I would say this, because I never thought I would.

"I'm sure there are a lot of things I don't know about you. We've only known each other two days."

Stalling, I point to the clock. "Technically three."

She seems confused, then turns to glance at the clock. I expect her to laugh, but she doesn't. "Okay, three."

I stand up from the bed and put my hands on my head, lacing my fingers together. Then I shake my arms out and sit back down.

"What is it?" Her voice brims with concern, and it only makes me feel worse about the lies I've told her. This is exactly why I hate making things personal.

"What I mean to say is I haven't been honest about who I am," I tell her.

She leans back. It's hardly noticeable, but I notice it all the same. "Well, this seems easy enough. Just tell me the truth. Who are you?"

I'm a collector sent from hell to manipulate you into sinning until I can collect your soul.

This doesn't seem like the best way to start. So instead, I say, "I didn't come to Peachville because of my mom's new job. I came for you."

Charlie swallows. "What do you mean you came for me?"

To seem like I care, I cover her hand with mine. "My mom doesn't live down the road. *I* don't live down the road. I'm staying at Wink Hotel near the plaza." I squeeze her fingers. "Charlie, my job was to find you."

She wiggles her fingers free. "Why?"

I don't know what to say next, so I decide to just leap. "I work as a collector."

"Like a debt collector?"

"No, Charlie." I crack my knuckles. Here goes. "I work as a *soul* collector."

Charlie starts laughing and stands up from the bed, leaning on her good hip. "My gosh, Dante. It's three o'clock in the freaking morning. If you wanted to mess with my head, why didn't you do it at the party?"

"I'm telling you the truth."

"No, you're being a jerk. And I want you to leave."

"Charlie, listen." I cross the room and grab her elbows. "I'm a collector. My job is to place seals on people's souls."

"Why are you talking to me like I'm an idiot?"

"I don't think you're an idiot," I say. "I swear I'm—"

"Okay, fine. Let's say you're a soul collector," she says mockingly. "How'd you get the job?"

"I was deemed the best for the position."

"By whom?"

"By God."

I don't know why I say this. Maybe because there's no way I can tell her who actually employs me. But now that I've said it aloud, I realize the idea is brilliant. If I can convince her I work for Big Guy, she might agree to the contract. It's not like there's anything in the fine print specifying *where* her soul goes.

"By God?" Charlie's eyes narrow. "And why does God want my soul?"

"Because it's pure." Though I'm lying, somehow this part feels true.

"You got some sort of proof you work for God?"

"No, I don't, but—" I stop. Wait a second. Heck, yeah, I got proof. "Okay, I'm going to do something, and you have to promise not to scream or do any other loud chick thing. 'Kay?"

She seems unsure, but nods anyway.

I press my lips together and pull on my shadow, leaving her seemingly alone in the room.

Charlie stumbles back and bumps into her dresser. A dozen crystal figurines teeter. "Dante?" she says, her voice quivering. "Where'd you go?"

I remove my shadow and reappear.

Her hand flies to her mouth. "You just disappeared," she says through her fingers.

"Word," I say. "It's called shadow. All collectors can do it with one of these bad boys." I reach down, pull up my jeans, and point to my gold cuff—my Achilles heel. "The reason I never wear shorts."

"What. Is. That?" She runs her hands over the smooth metal.

"It's my cuff. It allows me to collect souls, and use shadow, and walk the earth after death."

Charlie's eyes become enormous. "After *death*? You're trying to tell me you're dead?"

"Yeah. And the cuff keeps me alive. Honestly, Charlie. Do I look like the kind of guy that'd wear this for fun?"

"No. But you don't look dead, either." She bites her lip, thinking. "If you're so dead…how'd you die?"

Every muscle in my body seems to ache at once. Though this is a reasonable question, I'm not prepared for it. My throat seems unbearably dry, and I'm not sure I can answer. It's been so long since I've allowed myself to think about that night.

Charlie must see the pain in my face because she says, "Oh, my gosh. You're being completely serious. You're, like, dead."

My stare falls to the floor. I can't meet her gaze. I don't want her knowing this about me. But for some reason, the words tumble out. "Yeah. It was a car accident."

Charlie wraps her arms around my waist and hugs me. I bury my face in her hair and squeeze my eyes shut. "My dad wanted to go to the store to get brownie mix, of all things. He begged me to go, said he needed backup." I let my head fall back. "This damn deer was just standing in the street."

It's like I can't stop. *Stop!*

"He died first. I watched him. I watched my dad die. After that, I just kind of let go."

Charlie leans back and raises my chin, and in that moment, I see something in her eyes I hadn't noticed before. It's compassion, yes, but there's something else. Though we met almost three days ago, it seems like she's seeing me for the first time. "Hey," she says gently. "It was an accident."

I nod.

Her arms around me suddenly feel less like a friendly hug, and more like something else entirely. Against my chest, Charlie's words hum near my skin. The sensation sends a shiver down my back, though I can't imagine why. "He didn't know that would happen."

I nod again.

"You and I aren't so different," she says, rubbing a small hand up my arm. "Except that I somehow survived."

Survival is the exact reason I'm here. To get a second shot at life on earth. I reach inside my pocket and touch my penny, the one Dad gave me on my seventeenth birthday. The one I told him was *not my thing*.

Rubbing my face, I push him to the back of my mind. This whole conversation has gotten way too emotional, and I have to put a stop to it. We both died that night, but he went one way, and I went another. And now here I am.

"Listen, you know how I told you I'd make you beautiful? I have something for you." I pull the contract out of my back pocket and hold it out to Charlie.

"What is it?" She takes the contract and watches me expectantly.

"Well, like I said, I'm a collector. I came to collect your soul."

She cringes, and all the things I'd just seen on her face, things that said she saw something in me—they vanish. I try to soften my approach.

"I know that sounds bad, but isn't that where you want to go when you die?"

"Heaven?" she asks.

"Sure."

"Yeah. Yes. But I'm not ready to die now." Her eyes widen with fear. "There are things I still want to do. And what about my grandma? She'd have no one."

I see my opening to close the deal, and I take it. "That's the best part. You'll go on living even after your soul is collected. And in the meantime, we'll give you anything you want in return."

"Like a selling your soul kinda thing?" she asks.

I smile and shake my head. "Yeah, exactly. It's a win-win."

"I don't know. This feels weird."

"There's nothing to feel weird about. Think of it as a gift. You want us to have your soul anyway, and we're willing to pay for it."

"I know, but it's strange to think I'll be walking around soulless."

I squeeze the bridge of my nose. I'm so close to ending this, I can taste it. This needs to be over for my sanity's sake. "Charlie, a million people would kill for this opportunity."

She crosses the room and plops down on her bed. "This is a lot to process at three in the morning."

"People are more open to grand ideas at three in the morning," I say. "Charlie, let's just do this. You can be beautiful, and I can finish this job."

I hear a strange noise escape her mouth. If I didn't know better, I'd think it was a sound of pain. "What if I don't want to change?" she says in a small voice.

"Everyone wants to change." I take the papers from her and unroll them on her nightstand. I'm not sure if I'm supposed to use a magical pen or something, so I just pull out the one I brought from Wink Hotel and hope it works. "Here. I got you a fancy pen and everything."

Charlie's face contorts into an unreadable expression. "You brought a pen?"

"Well, yeah."

She takes it from me and rolls it between her fingers. "You were sure I was going to sign this, weren't you?"

"No," I say. "I just figured—"

"That I'd agree to anything you asked?"

Red Alert! Red Alert! Backpedal!

"Charlie, I'm doing this for your own good."

"For my own good? Like, because I'm so pathetic?" Though she speaks in a soft voice, her words cut through me.

"That's not what I meant. But…"

"But?"

I fumble with my belt buckle. "But you could look so different."

"I want you to leave."

"Charlie—"

"Leave!"

I stumble backward. Never could I have imagined Charlie yelling. It shakes me to my core. I reach toward her, but she steps back and squares her shoulders.

I tuck the contract back into my pocket and pause beside her window.

"I'm sorry, Charlie," I whisper. I'm not sure she hears me, and I'm definitely not sure I mean it, but it feels like the right thing to say.

I climb down the trellis, slide into my car, and stare up at her room. For a moment there, I really thought it was going to happen. But I should've known it wouldn't be that easy.

As I drive back to the hotel, I realize just how bad I botched this. She knows who I am. She's not going to sin if she thinks I work for Big Guy. And the contract is a no-go.

I may not be able to complete this job.

And now all I can think about are those damn *consequences*.

16

ANGRY CHARLIE

On Monday morning, I search everywhere for Charlie. I went by her house yesterday, but her grandmother said she was out.

My ass.

I catch up with her in first period biology. She sees me staring, I know she does, but she doesn't acknowledge me.

"Hey, Charlie, you going to ignore me forever?" I ask from the desk next to hers.

She glares ahead at the whiteboard like I don't even exist. This is something I never thought I'd experience, getting dissed by a girl like Charlie.

"I know you hear me. Will you just let me talk to you?"

Nothing.

"Look…" I glance around to see if anyone's listening and lower my voice. "You know I didn't mean anything by it. I think you're great." I can't bring myself to say she's beautiful as is. She's not. "Come on, let's ditch this class. I'll take you—"

"Dante, you have something you'd like to share with the class?"

I scowl at Mr. Gordon. He has one eyebrow raised like this affects me. I shake my head and roll my wrist, motioning for him to go ahead.

"Glad I have your permission." Mr. Gordon raises his arm to the whiteboard, and for the next sixty minutes, I alternate between watching Charlie ignore me and admiring Mr. Gordon's yellow pit stains.

When the bell rings, I try to play it cool, like I've lost all interest in her. I know the drill, when girls get pissed, you gotta let 'em come to you. That's why people compare chicks to felines.

Except my strategy fails. Charlie grabs her lime-green backpack and storms from the room before I get a chance to show her how much I don't care. Instead, I find myself jogging to keep up with her.

"Charlie, wait."

She keeps walking, pumping her short little legs to outpace mine. Seriously? I've got, like, a foot on this girl.

I grab her arm and pull her toward me. "Will you just stop? You're acting like one of those girls."

"You mean a girl like that?"

She points to a girl with long, shiny hair and even longer, shinier legs. *Hot damn!*

"A *beautiful* girl?" Charlie pushes. She steps toward me. I know she's going for intimidating, but she's too small to pull it off. Silly rabbit.

"Yes, exactly," I say. "You're acting like one of those shallow chicks."

"Why? Because I care about how I look? You know, I realize I'm not pretty. But that doesn't mean I want you pointing it out to me." Charlie glances away, gritting her teeth. "Guess I hoped that maybe you thought…I don't know…"

She trails off, so I open my mouth to jump in. I need to convince her to sign the damn contract. But I also need her to stop looking at me like that—like I hurt her in this deep way. Before I can say anything, the bell screams overhead.

"I've got to go to class," she says, sighing.

I let go of her arm. "I'm going where you're going, remember?"

She doesn't rush off, which is a small miracle I'll take. We walk side by side to Alabama History, and she doesn't complain when I sit next to her. The class feels even longer than the first, and I vow never to enter high school again when my ten days are up. When the bell finally rings, I get up to walk Charlie to lunch. She catches my eye, then heads out before I can stop her.

Dumb. I thought we were past this.

In the cafeteria, Charlie sits down at her usual lunch table. Blue and Annabelle are already there, and Blue's jaw tightens as I close in.

"Charlie, can we please talk?" I say.

Annabelle stops pulling grapes out of her brown paper bag, and her eyes widen. "What's going on?" she asks.

"Nothing," I answer.

Annabelle and Blue turn toward Charlie.

"It's nothing," she confirms.

I run a hand through my hair and decide I need a peace offering. But the only thing this POS cafeteria has is faux food.

But there *is* a vending machine, and I know one thing Miss Charlie loves.

I grab my wallet out of my back pocket and head toward it. Standing in front of the huge glass box, I pull out enough money to buy every last bag of Skittles. Then I do the fun thing where I put in a bill, and the machine spits it back out. Dollar goes back in. Dollar comes back out. *Damn it! Do you want the freaking money or not?!*

After fifteen and a half years, I drain the machine of Skittles and walk back to the cafeteria table with my loot. I'm feeling pretty proud of myself until I notice Charlie's not there.

"Where'd she go?" I ask, my pockets and hands full of glossy red bags.

"Where'd who go?" Blue mumbles.

"She went with Taylor," Annabelle says. She points toward one of the hallways, and I start to go in that direction. But Annabelle stops me. "Wait. Dante."

I turn around, and one of the bags plops onto the tile floor.

"Don't go after her. She's obviously pissed about something." Annabelle pauses, hoping I'll fill her in on what happened. When I don't say anything, she asks, "Did something happen at the party?"

"You haven't talked to her since Saturday night?" I ask back.

She pops a grape into her mouth and shakes her head.

"Yeah," I say, "something happened."

Still loaded down with candy, I drop down into a chair. Annabelle tosses powdered sugar-covered doughnuts at Blue, and this time he manages to catch them.

"Lunch of champions, eh?" I say, trying to make conversation with Blue. It certainly beats the staring contest we're having.

He wipes sugar from the corner of his mouth and takes his sweet-ass time answering. "Something like that."

"You know," Annabelle starts, "Charlie really likes you."

"Yeah?" I say. These are her friends. I have to pretend what they say matters.

"Mm-hmm. Then again, she cares for just about everyone. Even people who don't deserve it."

I study her closely, but it doesn't seem like she means me.

"But you," she continues, "you've really gotten under her

skin. And you've only been here, like, three days." Annabelle turns her milk box up but keeps her eyes on me. Then she crushes the empty box in her hand. "Where'd you say you were from again?"

Wait? Is she trying to intimidate me? Because if she is…it just might work. Bitch be scary.

"I didn't," I answer.

"Phoenix, right?"

"Sure."

Blue takes the lead from Annabelle and locks eyes on me as he slowly chews a doughnut.

"Why'd Charlie go with Taylor?" I ask her, ignoring Blue's stank eye.

The muscles in Annabelle's face relax. "I don't know. Taylor said she wanted to apologize. That's why I was asking about the party."

I can't believe Taylor would apologize. Unless it benefits her in some way.

Blue brings up the Knicks, and he and Annabelle discuss the fundamentals of run-and-gun basketball.

"Do you guys ever actually play?" I interrupt, relieved by the change in subject.

"Play?" Annabelle asks, her dark eyebrows rising.

"Yeah. Play. As in, do you play basketball?"

"Hell, yeah, we play!" Annabelle says at the exact moment that Blue shakes his head.

"Well, which is it?" I ask. "Do you play or not?"

Annabelle balls up her lunch bag and throws it at Blue. "Yes, we play. He just doesn't want you there."

"Where do you play?" My legs twitch just thinking about getting on the court. Or field. Or track. Anything I can compete in.

"At the Rec. It's on the north side of Peachville." Annabelle steals a glance at Blue, who stays mute. He's not a man of many words. But if he were, I could imagine what he'd say right about now.

I bite the inside of my cheek. I have no freaking idea why, but my stomach flips. "I'll play with you guys." There. It's out. No big deal.

"No," Blue says. *Now* he opens his mouth? Apparently moving in on Charlie is bad, but stealing the court is intolerable.

"No, huh?" I say.

"No."

Blue gets up to leave, but I hold up a hand. "Don't bother. I'll go." I don't want to sit here any longer. I have the confidence of a killer whale, but being shot down by these losers stings.

Intimidation Annabelle calls after me. "Ah, come on, Dante. You can play." But the damage is done. So I stalk off all butt-hurt and head outside. Elizabeth Taylor gives a wide chrome grin. I slap her hood and hop inside. "Let's get some smokes, girl."

I rev her engine and drive to the closest gas station. I've got a few minutes left of lunch and know just how I'd like to spend them.

The guy behind the counter hands me a pack of Marlboro Reds and a black plastic lighter. The second I walk outside, I flick the grind and light my cigarette. I pull in and push out two long drags, and it feels great.

I quit smoking after I died, which is pretty ironic. It's not like I care about keeping my dead body healthy, but it felt like a good time to stop. Mostly it's the smell that kills me. But right now, there's no better scent on earth.

Beside me, I get that nagging feeling like I'm being watched. And it's getting hella old. "Want one?" I ask the invisible air to my right. Holding the pack of cigarettes out, I wonder if the collector will finally show himself. I count three beats, then drop my arm and stub out my cigarette. "Chickenshit."

Turning to go, I feel something hit my back. I stumble a couple of steps and spin around. *Did someone just push me?*

My eyes flick around, searching the area. I don't spot anyone, but it doesn't matter. I know who it was. The collector either accidentally bumped into me or just took a cheap shot. Blood pounds against my temples, and I fantasize about breaking his jaw, but I can't do anything if he won't show himself. Today's Monday. Within six days, I'll finish this assignment.

Then Boss Man and I are going to clean house.

• • •

When I get back to school, I have to jog to get to class on time. I don't feel like dealing with angry, sweaty teachers this afternoon, so I make the effort. The second I enter the classroom, I realize Charlie's not there. Which can't be right. That girl wouldn't miss a class if someone threatened her life.

I stand at the entrance of the classroom without moving and realize the entire class is watching me do nothing. Someone clears their throat, and I take the hint to stop being a creeper. At least now I can sit in the back like a socially capable person. Charlie's a front-row kinda girl.

My math teacher's a chick, so I check out her rack for a while, then lie down on my desk for a nap. Maybe when I wake up, class will be over, and I can hunt my assignment down. But right as I'm drifting off to the teacher talking about an algorithmic something or other, I hear Charlie's voice.

I snap upright and see that it's coming from a television. Wait, what? Why is Charlie on that ridiculously outdated TV? My jaw goes slack as Teacher Lady kills the lights, and I realize that

Charlie is broadcasting in the journalism room.

No. No. This can't be good. Taylor would never relinquish her spotlight unless…

Oh, crap.

17

PISSED-OFF DEMON

Every muscle in my body tightens, and I shoot up from my desk.

"Mr. Walker?" the teacher asks.

I glance at her, then back at the TV. My gut tells me to go to the journalism room. *Now.*

"Mr. Walker," the teacher says more forcefully. "Is something wrong?"

I watch as Charlie shuffles some papers in front of her. She's smiling, but the corners of her mouth twitch wildly.

"Dude, you're blocking my view." I turn around and see a guy with greasy hair munching Doritos. His eyes are glassy, and he's obviously been hittin' some medicinal marijuana. He laughs, and his bloodshot eyes narrow. "Dude, what's *wrong* with you?" He laughs again.

I grab the open book on my desk and make a move to leave. But Charlie's voice stops me.

"Hello, and good afternoon. I'm reporting live from Centennial's prestigious journalism headquarters." She accentuates the word *prestigious,* and people in the class laugh. I saw the room she's in with my very own eyes. It was four walls and a busted-ass table.

She made a funny. Charlie Cooper actually made a funny.

"Dude!" Stoner Guy says.

I glance at him again, then sink down into my seat.

Charlie grins into the camera, and her voice pitches higher. "We've got lots going on this week, so grab your notebooks, poise your pens, and get ready to blow a solid ten minutes of class time."

Someone whoops next to me, and I have to raise a fist to my mouth to cover the huge smile I'm wearing. *Get it, girl!*

For the next few minutes, Charlie lists off upcoming football games, student council meetings, and something about bus schedules—all with a dose of wit and charm.

I keep glancing around to see if everyone sees what I do. This isn't the same girl I've known the last four days. She's confident. She's eloquent. She's…not Charlie. I narrow my eyes and lean forward. I notice she's staring slightly to her left.

Ah, cue cards. That explains it.

Charlie lays the last sheet of paper off to her right, signaling that she's done with the broadcast. "I'll close with the most exciting part of today's broadcast, the Halloween dance!"

More whoops around the classroom.

"As you know, it'll be held in the gymnasium. We'll be selling tickets during lunch all week. So don't forget to buy yours, or you'll be left dateless like me."

Charlie stops. Her smile falters, but she quickly recovers. "I would know…only ugly losers…" She stops reading the cue cards. Then she gazes right into the camera and freezes.

People in the classroom laugh nervously.

Taylor. She messed with the cue cards. I should have known. *I should've known!*

I bolt from my desk and run for the door.

Behind me, I hear the teacher yelling my name, but there's no way I'm stopping this time. My sneakers thump against the floor as I run down the hallway, into the cafeteria, and down another, longer corridor. I'm heading to the journalism room, but I stop suddenly when I hear the sound of quick footsteps coming from the closest bathroom. Somehow I know it's her.

The bathroom doesn't have a door, just an entrance that turns sharply so you can't see inside. I don't even check to see if anyone's watching. I just go halfway in, knock on the wall, and say, "Charlie? You in here?"

The footsteps stop briefly.

Yep. It's gotta be her.

I go the rest of the way inside and find her pacing in front of the restroom stalls. Her back is to me as she says, "You can go, Dante. I'm fine." But when she turns to pace in the opposite direction, I see the truth. Her face is pink and blotchy, and her eyes hold so much pain, it rips something apart inside of my chest.

My hands curl and uncurl, and my breathing comes harder and faster. Who do these people think they're messing with? This girl has been assigned to *me*. Boss Man wants her soul, which means anyone messing with her is messing with me. And they're about to find out exactly what that's like.

I turn abruptly from Charlie and storm toward the hall.

"Dante," she says. Her voice becomes urgent. "Dante, don't."

I head down the hallway, gaining speed, unstoppable.

As I round the corner, I see Taylor and one of her boy toys laughing. They're having a grand ole time mocking *my* girl. The guy sees me, and his mouth turns up on one side. "Oh, here comes the boyfriend. Did you catch our show, *boyfriend*?"

I don't stop. I keep moving. One second, Dickhead is standing upright, and the next my fist slams into his jaw. He hits the floor with a hard *thud*. I jump on his chest and throw my fist over and over into his face. I'm a big guy, there's no denying that, but what's more, I'm a motherfucking *demon*. And now the guy below me knows what it's like to piss one off. When his eyes roll back in his head, I stand up and wipe blood from my knuckles.

Then I look at Taylor.

Fear sparks in her eyes. I approach her slowly. She backs up until her shoulder blades hit the lockers behind her. "Dante, I—"

I cover her mouth with my hand. "Shut up."

I step so close, I can practically feel her heart beating. The hand not covering her mouth flicks, and her soul light flips on. Just as I expected, she's coated in sin seals. What I don't expect are the two sparkly pink seals. *What the hell? Did Charlie do this?*

Right now, I don't care. All I care about is delivering what this girl deserves. Usually, the size seal I can assign is based on the sin. But this time—just this once—I'm going to take a little liberty.

I close my eyes and pull as much as I can out of my core, then I let go. A seal the size of Canada attaches to her soul light. And oh, sweet mercy, I can tell Taylor feels it. Actually *feels* that I just took something sacred from her.

My mouth curls into a smile.

"Pow, bitch."

18

CALM AFTER THE STORM

When I turn around, Charlie is there. She stands in the middle of the hall, her arms rigid at her sides.

I close the distance between us and put my arms around her. I have no idea why I do this, but it seems right. She lays her head against my chest for a moment, and then I take her hand.

"Come on," I say. "Let me take you home."

I lift her chin, and when she gives a firm nod, I put my hand on the small of her back and lead her to the parking lot. She slides into the passenger seat, and I start the engine. I can't stop thinking about the pink seals on Taylor's soul, about how they got there and why Charlie gave them to her. It doesn't add up. I know she doesn't know about her ability, but maybe it'd be better if she did. It's something I need to think about.

I glance at Charlie. Her face is drained of emotion. "Want to talk about it?"

She shakes her head and stares out the window. But after a few seconds, she turns and glances at me. "I'll be fine, you know. I was fine."

I throw her a *give me a break* look and turn back to the road.

"It wasn't as bad as it could have been," she continues.

"Did they mess with the cue cards?" I'm sure I'm right, but I want her to confirm what I already know.

Charlie sighs. "Yeah. They were pretty bad. I'm lucky my brain shut off when it did." She laughs to herself, though I know she doesn't think it's funny. "It was a creative way to make an idiot out of me. I'll give her that."

"Taylor will get what's coming to her."

Charlie fidgets in her seat. She wraps her arms around herself, then glances at me. "What did you do to her?"

I know exactly what she's talking about, but I opt for playing dumb. "What are you talking about?"

"I mean, I saw the way she looked when you got close to her. Did you...do something?"

I roll my shoulders back. This is dangerous territory. The less Charlie knows, the better. Lies are slippery little beasts. "I just made sure she wouldn't mess with you anymore."

"How?" she presses.

"Why'd you want to do that broadcast, anyway?" I ask, dodging her question. "What is it with you and being on camera?"

Charlie chews her fingertips, and I pull her hand from her mouth. It's beginning to be a game we play.

"I like reporters," is all she says.

"Really? Why?"

She starts to put her fingers back in her mouth, then stops herself. "I don't know."

"Sure you do. So what is it? You got a thing for Anderson Cooper?"

She smiles. "No. It's just...I don't know. The night of the fire, everything was so chaotic. My neighbors were crying, and the firemen were asking me to describe the layout of the house, and everything was so *loud*. And amidst it all, I remember this lady. Her hair was pulled up into one of those twists." Charlie motions to her hair. "And she just…sat there and held me for what felt like forever.

"Finally, this guy with a camera comes over to her and asks if she's ready. She asked if I would be okay alone for a bit, then nodded to the cameraman. But before she got up, she took off this yellow suit jacket and put it on me. Like, she put my arms through the sleeves and everything. Then the guy counts down, and this woman, she just…came alive. As I watched on, she stood there, calm as a bird, and told the world what happened. And I remember thinking…yeah, people should know. They should know about my parents. It's important." Charlie glances at me. "You know? It *was* important, right?"

I nod, and for once, I squeeze her hand without an agenda. "Yeah, it was."

"So, anyhoo." She shakes her head back and forth as if to erase the tragedy. "I decided when I got older, I wanted to be like that woman. Telling people when important things happen. Someone has to do that. Otherwise, people just get forgotten."

When we pull up to Charlie's house, I go to kill the engine, but she stops me. "Dante, I want to be alone for a while. Okay?"

I have six days left to seal the deal, and I can't afford to give Charlie alone time. But I can't bring myself to push her, either. So I just say, "Want me to swing by tonight? Do dinner or something?"

"I'm supposed to hang out with Annabelle tonight," she answers.

She'd rather hang out with Annabelle than me? What the H?

"That's cool," I say. "Maybe we can grab an early breakfast

tomorrow before school."

"How about I call you?" she says.

"If you haven't noticed, I'm not packing."

She scrunches her nose up. "You don't have a cell phone?"

"Neither do you."

"Yeah, but you're, like, loaded or something."

"I hate cell phones," I say. "I feel like…if I want to talk to you, I'll find you."

"Well, if I want to have breakfast tomorrow, then I'll be here. If not…" She shrugs, then laughs, and I'm happy to hear it's authentic.

"I'll be here at 7:30 tomorrow," I say. "Maybe I'll get lucky." That did *not* come out right. But no worries. It sails straight over her head.

I'm thinking we're good here. That Charlie is back in happy-go-lucky spirits. But as I watch her head up the walkway, I can see the way her shoulders sag. Annabelle's not coming over tonight. Which means Charlie's going to sit alone in that blasted pink room of hers and dwell.

I glance at my glove compartment where the soul contract rests, knowing this is a perfect time to go for the gold. She's weak right now, susceptible. I should go inside and make her see that things could be different for her. Instead, I back out of the driveway and head toward Wink Hotel. Alone.

• • •

Lying in bed, I toss and turn. I realize I've done this a lot the last three nights, especially since I'm no further along on this assignment than I was four days ago. Unless you count that one measly seal Charlie received for minor theft.

I secretly hope Max will appear at this very moment and tell me what to do. Even though I trained him, right now I need a second opinion. How do you get a girl to sign a soul contract when she's perfectly content with her life?

The muted television suspended in the corner casts a blue-green glow over the room. I glance at the clock—1:23 A.M. Somehow I find enjoyment in this, the fact that the numbers are consecutive. I drift off thinking about other times I like—3:33 because there are three threes and 11:11 because it's the only time with four of the same number. As miniature clocks swirl behind my eyes, the one next to me keeps ticking, and eventually, sleep takes me.

• • •

"Dante," I hear someone say. "Dante, wake *up*. My gosh, you sleep like a grizzly bear."

Hands shake me, and I bolt upright. Charlie stands beside my bed, washed in the TV's light. She's working her bottom lip between her teeth, and her cheeks are bright red.

"Charlie Cooper," I say, rubbing my face, "what are you doing in here? You scared the crap out of me."

"Dante the Collector scared? Of me?" She's teasing, but her face is crinkled with worry.

"How did you get in here?" I throw the covers back, cross the room, and dig through my overnight bag for jeans and a T-shirt. Even though I'm half asleep, I wonder if she's checking me out in my boxer briefs. Then again, who *wouldn't* check this out?

I make sure to give her a good view of my tats as I drag on my jeans: the dragon covering my back and the tree stemming from my elbow, growing up my bicep, and branching over my shoulder. The tree is barren and completely wicked. I know, because I specifically told the tat guy that I wanted it to look *wicked*.

"Mr. Stanley gave me a key at the front desk," Charlie answers. "He's friends with my grandma."

"So he just gave you a key?" I pull a gray Armani T-shirt over my head. "I don't think they're even allowed to say what room I'm in."

She rolls her eyes. "This is Peachville, Dante. Not Phoenix. Or wherever you lived." Charlie sits down on my bed, sinking into a heap of tangled sheets. It's strange seeing her there. In my bed. Where I just was.

I sit on the opposite bed, and my knee jerks up and down. "So what's up?"

She runs her hands over her thighs and stares up at me. Her eyes are wide and alive, and I suddenly realize what she's here for.

"I'm ready," she says. "I want you to make me beautiful."

CHANGES

"Beauty's sister is vanity, and its daughter lust."

—Unknown

19

THE DOTTED LINE

For a moment, I just stare at her. I'm, like, speechless. Never did I think I'd hear those words, *I'm ready*. But Charlie had taken a beating the past couple of days, and what was it Max said last night?

People change when shit happens.

"Dante?" she asks. "Do you still have that contract thing?"

I nod.

"Can you explain how it works again? This time I'll listen."

My eyebrows rise, and I nod again.

"Is it here somewhere?" Now she's the one staring at me. I can tell I'm freaking her out by not responding. I've got to snap the heck out of it before she backtracks.

"Yeah," I say finally. "Yeah, it's in the car. I'll grab it."

She lies back on the bed while I slide on my red Chucks. I try not to notice the way her thighs press against the mattress.

"Be right back," I tell her, but she doesn't say anything.

I jog out to the car. In my gut, I have this strange feeling. Like some completely wasted chick just told me to get condoms. And I agreed.

I pull the contract out of Elizabeth Taylor's glove compartment, then head back inside. Because I forgot the key, I have to knock and wait outside my own room until Charlie opens the door. Her eyes fall on the contract as I move inside and sit down on the bed.

"So what's the deal?" she asks. "I just sign…and you make me pretty?"

I unroll the contract and try not to seem clueless—even though that's exactly what I am. I haven't done this any more than she has.

The contract has a place for both our names and pretty much spells out that for each request she makes, she forfeits a piece of her soul. Okay, seems easy enough.

"It looks like you just sign, then ask for whatever you want." I shrug. "And then I guess we give it to you."

"As in, you're not sure?" she says.

I raise my voice and straighten, hoping she'll buy my forced confidence. "I'm sure. It's very simple. We do it all the time."

"Really?"

"Totally."

She reaches for the contract, and I give it to her. Her eyes roll over the words. "It doesn't say a whole lot, does it? You'd think for something like this, there'd be lots of legal stuff."

"We like to make things easy." I'm hoping my use of *we* makes it sound like I know what I'm doing.

"So all I do is sign, then make my requests? And when I've used up all my wishes or whatever, you'll take my soul?"

"Exactly." I taste acid in the back of my throat.

She lays the contract on the nightstand between us and pulls in a big breath. I really look at her in that moment: her frizzy blond hair, skinny, curveless body, and bad skin. These things make her appear average at best. But there are other things I hadn't noticed before. Things I can't stop studying now that she's considering this. Things like her sweeping cheekbones, ones models would murder for. And her neck, long and graceful like she was meant to wear ballet slippers. And of course, her mouth. Which I've always thought was beautiful.

I mean, passable.

That was weird.

My shoulders tense when I think about this whole contract thing. Charlie's the only girl I've ever met who loved her life. Like, *really* loved it. And now she's going to change it. All because Boss Man wants her soul.

And because I want a promotion.

I want to ask her why she's changed her mind. I'm sure she's been picked on her whole life, so what's different now? But I'm scared to press. Scared if we talk about it, she'll change her mind. Scared she might say *me*.

She opens the nightstand drawer and pulls out a pen. I'm about to tell her where to sign, but she finds the line on her own and puts the pen to it. She hesitates and glances up at me. There's something strange in the way she's holding my eyes, like she just remembered why she's doing this. I wonder if she can tell I'm holding my breath.

"Thank you for this, Dante," she says. "I'm sorry I got mad before."

Her kindness is suddenly too much. I reach to jerk the pen out of her hand, but before I can, she signs her name on the dotted line: *Charlie Cooper.*

She hands the contract and pen up to me, a grin sweeping from ear to ear. "Your turn."

I take it from her, cross the room, and lay it down on the

dresser. She can't see the look on my face, the one I want to tear off with my fingernails. There's no reason I should feel this...*guilt*. I'm a collector. This is what I do. I don't know any other way.

For a second, I wonder if I can stop this. Maybe if I don't sign my own name, it'll pause this whole ordeal.

"Dante?" Charlie says from the bed. Her voice is thick with concern.

I turn and face her, and she must notice the struggle in my features, because her mouth opens, and her eyes widen.

"What is it?" she asks. "Did I do something wrong?"

I can't stand the sound of her voice. I can't stand the way she's looking at me. And I can't *stand* the crap she makes me feel.

I slam the pen down and sign my name before I can think.

It's over.

It's done.

My lips pull up into a halfhearted smile, and I glance back at Charlie. She's waiting for me to tell her it's okay. So I do.

"You did the right thing."

She nods her head and smiles, but her eyes find the floor. Then it's like something occurs to her. She hops up from the bed and runs to the bathroom, limping and bumping into me on the way.

"Where you going?" I yell.

I scour the room thinking I missed something, then go after Charlie. Inspecting herself in the mirror, she turns her face from side to side. She seems excited at first, but then her mouth slopes downward.

She glances at my reflection. "It didn't work."

I lick my lips. "I think you have to actually ask for it to happen."

"I did, though."

"When?"

"When I was out there," she says. "Right after you signed."

I rub the back of my head. "I didn't hear you say anything. Maybe you have to say it louder." *Or maybe you have to fax it in? Or mail it via sea turtle. Who effin' knows.*

"You think I have to say what I want out loud?" she says. "That's kind of embarrassing."

"You didn't say it aloud?"

"No, I just…prayed for it. To God, you know."

Oh, no.

"I think," I start. *Careful, Dante.* "I think you have to say it aloud so there's, like, a witness. It's probably why we both had to sign."

Yeah, that sounded good.

She *hmphs*, then walks past me into the room. "Okay, so I'll just say it aloud."

"Okay." I sit across from her, and though I still feel a twinge of guilt, I can't help being excited to witness this. She's going to be beautiful. Charlie Cooper…is going to be beautiful.

She folds her hands in her lap, closes her eyes, and opens her mouth.

20

I WANT

"I want—"

I lean forward, nearly falling off the bed. I can't wait to hear her say the words: *I want to be beautiful.*

"I want," she repeats.

Come on! Come on!

"I want to have beautiful hair."

"You want what?"

"Beautiful hair," she repeats. "I want to have beautiful hair." She lifts a lock of frizzy-fried blond hair and grimaces.

I'll admit better hair could do wonders for the girl, but what about the rest of her? Why not get rid of the bad skin or crooked teeth? Or her limp, for that matter? "Don't you just want to do everything at once?" I ask.

She shakes her head. "No way. I don't want to go too fast. I need time to think about what I want."

Great. The last thing I need is her dragging ass on this. "Maybe you should just ask to be beautiful, and the things that need changing will change."

She doesn't answer me. Instead, she stares at her hair. "Why isn't anything happening? It still looks the same."

I glance at her hair. It *does* look the same. "Maybe you have to say it louder. Try again. And while you're at it, go ahead and ask for a few other things."

She presses her lips together, then takes a breath and nearly screams, "I want beautiful hair."

Nothing happens.

I sigh and fall back on the bed. Why can't anything on this assignment ever go right? "Why do you even want better hair?" I ask. "Why not bigger boobs or something?"

"Dante!" Charlie throws a pillow at me. I grab it in midair and throw it back. She laughs and falls back on the other bed. "I guess I always wanted to be one of those girls that can do the hair toss."

"The hair toss?"

"Yeah," she says. "That thing where the girl smiles all flirty-like, then tosses her perfect, shiny hair over her shoulder? I want that."

I glance over at her. My breath catches in my throat. Her hair is...*glowing*. As calmly as I can, I ask, "Why else do you want to change your hair?"

"I don't know," she says. "Ooh, yeah, I do! I want to do all those cool styles."

Charlie sits up, and her hair glows brighter. She doesn't even notice. She's on a roll now, and her cheeks burn red.

"I want to do those messy buns and low side ponies and maybe have cute, sideswept bangs."

Brighter and brighter. And now...now it's changing. Growing longer and fuller.

"I've always wanted to do all those things, but with hair like mine, it's a lost cause." She pulls her hair from behind her head and gazes at it. "My hair's always just...it just..."

I start laughing.

Her eyes go big, and then she runs into the bathroom.

"Ahhhhhh!" she squeals. "My hair! Oh, my gosh, my hair!"

She races back into the room and swirls around. Her hair sprays out in a thick, shiny blanket. The color is a perfect shade of blond, like she walked right into Bergdorf and asked for their very best.

Charlie rolls her arms beneath her hair and lets it fall in a wave down her back. "It's gorgeous," she breathes. "Don't you think?"

For a moment, I forget all about the contract and just relish the grin on her face. Though her smile is less than perfect, it does something to me, makes my chest tighten in a good way. It also makes me feel as if I did the right thing. Then her soul light flips on, and like I don't even have a choice, a seal floats from my chest and attaches to her light. It's smaller than the one I gave her at the mall, and I realize then that it'll take a lot of beauty wishes to completely collect her.

But judging by the happy dance she's doing around the room, that won't be a problem.

21

SHINY, PERFECT HAIR

The next morning, I pick Charlie up, and we go to our early morning breakfast. She's left her hair down, and it is…stunning. I never thought good hair could do so much for one person. I suggest she audition for a shampoo commercial.

She laughs.

I don't.

"Where we headed?" I ask.

"You didn't make reservations for our date?"

I'd have spit out my coffee if I'd had any. A *date*? Damn, Princess Cooper got some overnight confidence. When I glance at her, I see she's smiling. My shoulders relax.

"Thought you'd know best," I respond. "I'm basically a tourist."

"Metro Diner it is," she says.

"*Metro?* They're really taking liberty with that word."

Charlie giggles and tosses her hair over her shoulder.

Oh, sweet Joseph. She just tried out the Hair Toss.

Inside Metro Diner, we grab a table near the back. A waitress who clearly ate a water buffalo for breakfast waddles to our table.

"Order?" she says.

I open my mouth to answer, but Charlie beats me to the punch. "Two Greek omelets with extra feta, salsa on the side. And two large OJs."

Big Bertha scribbles the order down and turns to go.

I grab her arm. "Hold on there, sweetheart. I'm sure the omelets and orange juice are to *die* for. But I'm also going to need black coffee and two sides of bacon."

She stares at me like I'm the least interesting thing she's seen next to exercise.

"You do have bacon, right?" I ask her blank stare and heavy breathing.

She nods and waddles-slash-thunders away.

"Food's pretty healthy here, huh?" I ask Charlie.

"Like you'd care." She snorts. "Exactly how much bacon do you eat?"

"Enough to put your Skittles addiction to shame."

The bacon comes out burnt, and the coffee tastes like a donkey's ass, but the Greek omelet is actually pretty awesome. We eat our breakfast, and Charlie flips her hair at the end of every sentence. Which is saying a lot.

At one point she stops and stares at me.

"What?" I ask.

"It's just…so you can eat and stuff?"

"Yeah, so?"

She glances around and leans toward me, boobs pressed against the table. "But you're dead."

"Damn straight."

"Then how do you eat?"

I wipe my mouth with the paper napkin. "My body was scavenged before I could start to…umm…"

"Decay?" she says, her nose scrunched up.

"Yeah, exactly. Then they placed this cuff on my ankle, and I was back in business."

She peers out the window, thinking. "So you're like a living person? Blood flowing? Heart pumping?"

I nod. "Yep. I was just out of commission for a few days during the funeral and burial. Then the next thing I knew, I was gasping for air."

"You were alive again," she says, filling in the pieces.

"I wouldn't say *alive*, exactly."

She tongues the inside of her cheek. "But you *are* alive."

"No, Charlie. I'm not. I'm dead. All this—" I beat my chest. "—it's artificial."

She takes a small bite of her omelet and tries to change the subject. I'm glad she asked her questions and that I answered without screwing up—without exposing who I really work for. I watch her wash down the omelet with radioactive orange juice and realize she still doesn't know about her ability. That she can undo my seals with her blasted pink ones. I have questions of my own, questions I want answers to, but they aren't going to come from her. And for that I'm thankful.

After breakfast, I drive Charlie to school and suffer through three hours of mind-numbing classes before lunch. When the bell rings, I follow her out of economics and into the cafeteria. We didn't see Annabelle and Blue when we got to school this morning, and even I'm a little excited to see their reaction—to see if they'll even notice.

Blue's face changes the moment he sees her. His eyes narrow, then widen, and his lips parts.

Guess he notices.

Charlie does the Toss, and his mouth stretches into a smile.

"Hey, Charlie," he mumbles. "Did you…do something?"

She slowly lowers herself down into the chair across from him, tucking one leg beneath her. It's hilarious watching Charlie attempt grace, but I give her mad props for bringing the confidence. If she only knew how much that same confidence could improve her overall appearance…

"What are you talking about?" Charlie asks coyly. "*I* didn't do anything."

Annabelle glances up from a magazine, and her jaw drops. "Holy mother of God, what did you do to your hair?"

Charlie laughs, but it has a ring of nervousness to it. I can tell she doesn't know how to respond.

"My friend flew in from L.A. to visit family," I say. "She's a stylist."

Charlie chimes in. "Yeah, and she did my hair."

Annabelle gets up from the table and walks to our side. She runs her fingers through Charlie's hair, and her eyes get all crazy, like she might be packin' a chainsaw. "What did she put in it? No. No, I don't care. Just…how do I get it?" Annabelle eyes me. "You will tell me."

"Don't know. She's super weird about her trade secrets."

"That's okay," she says. "I don't need to know. Just tell me I'm next."

"Sorry," I say, my palms turned up. "She's flying back this afternoon."

Annabelle acts like I just ran over her cat, which I would if I saw it. She lifts Charlie's hair to her nose and breathes in.

"Okay, that's enough." I pull Charlie's hair away from Annabelle and point her to her seat.

Annabelle stomps back to her chair like she's seriously considering kidney-punching someone, or burning the school down. Something.

"Anna, your hair is beautiful the way it is," Charlie says.

Annabelle points her plastic fork at Charlie. "You will not talk to me."

Charlie leans forward, her face pulled together. "Are you being serious?"

Annabelle rolls her eyes. "No. But you better call me next time Jesus comes to Peachville."

Charlie laughs, but at the same time, she gives me a look from the corner of her eye—like we're sharing the secret that Jesus really *did* come to this country bumpkin town.

"What are you reading?" I ask to change the subject.

Annabelle holds up *First Shot Magazine*. "They did an entire issue on black-and-white movies. I thought I'd see what they put in here."

"You dig those old movies, huh?"

"It's my favorite thing next to basketball. Speaking of, we're playing after school today. You in?" Annabelle grins, then she yelps and glares at Blue. "Seriously? That hurt."

"Nah," I say. "I got stuff to do."

"Shame," Blue says under his breath.

I crack my knuckles and zone in on his mumbling mouth. I'm so over this crap. "You know what, I changed my mind. I wouldn't mind kicking some ass today."

"Yeah." Annabelle nods. "That's what I'm talking about. Charlie, you want to come? He's going to need directions to his final resting place."

Charlie shoots a glance at me, no doubt startled by the *final resting place*. "Sounds good," she says. "What time?"

"Seven o'clock."

Blue stares at Charlie. "You're going to come?"

She shrugs. "Sure, 'bout time I check you guys out."

I'm surprised Charlie hasn't gone before. Then again, I guess it's not fun if you don't have a prayer of playing. With her limp, I doubt anyone's let her near a court.

As lunch period wraps up, I spot a beauty queen strutting toward our table. When she does the hair toss, I realize Charlie's still an amateur.

"Hey," Hot Girl says to Charlie.

Charlie gazes up at her. "Hi."

Hot Girl shifts for a second, like standing there is physically painful. "My friends and I were just wondering if you got your hair done or something."

Charlie's eyes shine. "Yeah, I did. Thanks for noticing."

"Uh-huh," Hot Girl says. "Where did you go?"

Charlie points to me. "His friend from out of town did it."

The girl shakes her head. "Tragic. I can't find a hair stylist to save my life in this crap hole." She sighs. "Thanks, anyway."

As the girl walks back to her table, Charlie turns to face us. Her eyes are the size of watermelons.

Hells, yeah, I think. *That was perfect.*

22

B-BALL OR BUST

When Charlie and I arrive at the Rec, Blue and Annabelle are already on the court. I'm surprised to see there's no one else waiting to play. I guess the citizens of Peachville aren't big into physical fitness. Which makes me wonder what they *are* into—I'd guess cattle herding. Or pig farming. Something real intellectual like that.

Annabelle is trying to spin the basketball on the tip of her finger and doing a fairly impressive job. It rotates several times before tipping over and thumping against the floor. She chases after it and notices us walking toward her.

"Hey, hey!" she says. "Look who showed. Ready to get your ass handed to you?"

She's talking crap, and I'm loving it. In my book, it's all part of the experience. Playing clean isn't my style.

She tosses me the ball, and I catch it with one hand. Basketball is one of many sports where having gigantor hands helps. I take the ball, dribble it behind my back, then drive it to the rim for a reverse layup.

Annabelle laughs. "Oh, so you think you're hot, do you?"

"Girl, I got swag for days."

Charlie claps like she's enjoying this and settles on the floor near the wall. Then she proceeds to twist and untwist her shiny new hair like she couldn't be happier.

"How do you guys play?" I ask. "One on one?"

"Yeah," Annabelle answers. "Blue and I'll play first, then you'll play the winner. We play to fifteen. Cool?"

"Works for me." I walk over to where Charlie's sitting and lean against the wall.

Annabelle takes the ball to the three-point line, and Blue stands a few feet away, ready to guard her. She smiles at her opponent, fakes to the left, and makes a beeline toward the basket. The ball thumps against the ground as she dribbles. Then she lifts it smoothly into the air, and it swishes through the net. She throws her arms up and whoops. Then she holds out a finger and says to Blue, "That's one, busta."

Annabelle tosses the ball to Blue, and he takes it to the top of the key. I cringe, thinking how brutal his game will be, but before I can imagine his flailing fundamentals, he pulls the ball above his head and shoots it calmly into the air.

And it hits nothing but net.

From almost twenty feet away.

Damn!

Annabelle sneers. "Never saw *that* coming."

For the next few minutes, I watch the game unfold. It doesn't take long to identify their strengths. Annabelle's a master of the inside game, and Blue's got pinpoint accuracy from behind the arc. It's clear Blue better understands the fundamentals, but he's losing ground because he lacks aggression.

Though he's afraid to throw his weight around, he manages

to win the game by a couple of points. Annabelle accuses him of cheating and slumps down beside Charlie.

She eyes me and waves a sweaty hand toward the court. "You're up, big boy. Sorry I couldn't be the one to shut you down."

I hop up, eager to show what I'm packin'. It's been too long since I've given my red sneakers a workout.

Blue won't meet my eyes. He tosses the ball to me as if to say, *Take it out.*

I grab the ball, flip Blue like a turnstile, and lay it up with no resistance. It's like he's not even trying to stop me. When he gets the ball, he immediately shoots, and again he swishes it.

Kid's got a nice touch.

Déjà vu—I take the ball out, drive it to the hole, and lay it up like it's nothing. Blue takes the ball, but this time I get right up on him, hand in his face. I'm daring him to take it to the basket. Instead he tries to launch another jump shot. I leap straight up and swat it away.

"Get that crap outta here," I yell as I retrieve the ball.

Over my shoulder, I see Blue's jaw tighten. Good, maybe that block got his ass fired up.

I take the ball to the basket for another uncontested layup, then turn on Blue. "What the hell are you doing? Why aren't you playing?"

"I am playing," he mumbles.

"No. No, you're not." I step toward him. "Why aren't you guarding me? What are you afraid of?"

Blue chews the corner of his lip, and his face reddens. He's pissed off.

"You've obviously got mad shooting skills, so why won't you play a little defense?" I shove the ball into his chest. "Stop being such a pussy."

Blue lines up for another shot from the top of the key, so I lunge for it, thinking I can't believe how predictable he is. But then he pivots, spins to the left, and takes the ball right to the freakin' basket.

"*Damn*, son," I say.

I laugh, and surprisingly, so does he. Blue and I have a strange relationship, if you can even call it that. On the surface, I hate that he gets in the way of my assignment, and *he* can't stand the amount of time I spend with Charlie. But if Charlie were taken out of the equation, it almost feels like we could maybe—and I do mean *maybe*—be friends. But as it stands, it'll never happen.

For the rest of the game, Blue unlocks his inner aggression, and his game improves dramatically. Every once in a while, I steal the ball or block his shot. And a few times, he does the same to me. In the end, I win. But not by much. And I can only imagine what a few more weeks of this could do for his game.

Charlie grins from the wall as we approach her. Her face is glowing, like this is the most fun she's had in years. I wonder how long it's been since she's played basketball, or anything for that matter. Probably not since before the fire…since she was a little girl. My heart throbs. "You know what, Charlie? It's your turn. Get on out here, girl."

"What? No." She laughs. "I'll pass, but thank you."

She's turning me down because she's afraid. Because she's so used to saying no, she can't imagine saying yes.

So I don't give her a choice.

I toss the minuscule girl over my shoulder and listen to her scream as I carry her to the free-throw line. I grab the basketball and place it in her hands. "Shoot once, and I'll let you go."

She looks over at Annabelle and Blue, then back at me. "I can't."

"Bullshit."

She tries to limp past me, but I move to stand in her way. "Just shoot, Charlie. It's not a big deal."

She drops the ball. "I don't want to."

Blue makes a move to come out on the court, but Annabelle stops him.

I pick up the ball and put it back in her hands. "Sure you do. Everyone wants to play. They're just afraid of looking stupid." I brush the rich blond hair from her eyes. "But you know what's stupid? Not trying. So just…try."

She rolls her eyes. "You'll leave me alone if I throw it one time?"

"If you *shoot* it. I'll leave you alone if you *shoot* it one time."

Her mouth cracks into a smile.

There it is.

Charlie bounces the basketball a couple of times, and it's the most pathetic thing I've ever seen. It barely makes it back up to her waist.

"Just shoot it, huh?" she asks, eyeing me.

I nod and step back.

She glances at the rim, takes a deep breath, pulls the ball up—and shoots.

It's the world's worst shot. The worst. But it makes me so damn proud I could freakin' scream.

"Did you feel like an idiot?" I ask.

"Yeah," she says through a laugh.

"It's not so bad, though, huh?"

She shakes her head, and I gesture toward her friends like she's free to go.

"Give me the damn ball," she says, pushing her glasses further up her nose.

I raise an eyebrow, and the grin on my face is so huge it actually hurts.

I hand her the ball. She shoots again, and this time she gets closer. At the last second, she stumbles toward her bad hip, and I grab her until she's steady on her feet. I'm definitely not noticing how much I like her soft chest pressed against mine.

"You got it?" I ask.

"Ball," she demands.

"Hell, yeah," I say too loud. I jog after the ball and hand it to her.

Charlie takes six more shots, improving each time. She starts leaning to the right before she shoots, compensating for her injured hip.

She bounces the ball three times and fixes her eyes on the basket.

Come on, girl.

I can practically hear Annabelle and Blue holding their breath, and my heart is pounding so hard, I can feel it in my hands. It's ridiculous how my body's reacting.

Charlie licks her lips, raises the ball…and shoots.

Swish!

We all stay quiet as she turns around.

"Piece of cake," she says.

Blue runs onto the court and pulls her into a hug. Guess his on-court confidence is sticking with him off court, too. My mouth forms a tight line, though I have no idea why.

"If that doesn't mandate pizza," Annabelle says, "I don't know what does."

"Pizza!" Charlie yells.

"You didn't eat before I picked you up?" I ask. "I would have taken you somewhere."

Blue's eyes narrow. Guess our bonding time is over.

"Yeah, I did," she answers. She doesn't say anything else, like she's not sure what that has to do with anything. Truth be told, I could eat again, too.

"Y'all want to go to my house?" Charlie glances at the three of us, and I get this strange floating sensation from being included so easily. Like the four of us are a group now.

Annabelle raises her arm. "In."

Blue nods.

They all look at me.

"Yeah, cool," I say.

I try to hide my smile.

23

SYMPATHY

I pound the silver bell to get Pizza Guy's attention. There's a carved jack-o'-lantern near the bell, and I'm positive it could move faster than the kid behind the counter. After taking a quick shower at my hotel, I realized I couldn't just eat—I was *starving*. And as soon as The World's Slowest Person moved his rear, I'd get our pizza and tear into it like a wildebeest.

Ten centuries later, I slide two greasy brown boxes onto the seat next to me and drive to Charlie's house.

After I knock, Annabelle opens the door and grabs the pizza from me. Her black hair is wet, and I can still see the comb lines. "Did you eat any?" She eyes me suspiciously and lifts the box lid.

"I ate it all." I walk into the living room and flop down on the couch beside Charlie.

"I expected as much." Annabelle carries the pizza into the kitchen and comes back out with paper plates and napkins stacked on top. She sits down next to me, making me the Oreo filling between her and Charlie.

"Where's Blue?" I ask.

Charlie pulls a slice of cheese pizza out of the box. "Upstairs with Grandma. He wanted to check on her, since she's not feeling well."

My stomach tightens. I know Charlie doesn't realize how many meds her grandma is taking and what that implies. "What's wrong with her?" I venture.

"She's just got a cold or something, but I still feel bad," Charlie says. "I offered to bring her some pizza when it came, but she didn't want any."

I glance down at my hands, then up at Charlie. "A cold in October? It's a little early."

Her eyebrows furrow likes she's thinking about this. "Yeah," she says, frowning. "Guess so."

I don't push the subject. I'm not sure I want Charlie distracted by her grandmother's condition. Whatever it is.

"What's this profanity?" Annabelle says, interrupting the uncomfortable silence. She's staring down at one of the pizzas. Particularly at the half I reserved for myself. The one with Canadian bacon. "Who put pig on the pizza?"

Charlie leans forward, sees the bacon, and laughs. She points to me. "That'd be the newbie."

"Sick," Annabelle says. "You're nasty."

"Not as nasty as your game," I say, leaning back.

"If you want to talk smack, you came to the right place."

We lock eyes, trying not laugh, and take a bite of our pizza at the exact same time.

"You guys are idiots," Charlie says. Then her eyes land on the stairwell. "Blue, you okay?"

Annabelle and I turn to Blue. He's trying to smile, trying to assure Charlie everything's okay. But the smile doesn't reach his eyes.

"Yeah," he answers her. "I'm just tired from all the *defense* I played tonight."

Good one, I think. *Make a joke so she doesn't know how sick her grandma really is.*

I'm thinking how strange it is that he seems to know something's up when Charlie doesn't, but then I turn and catch Charlie's eye—and I see the truth. *She does know*, I realize. *She just doesn't want them to worry.*

I'll never understand the friendships Charlie has. Friendships where it doesn't take cash, or hookups, or saying the right things to stay in the circle. No, Charlie's friendships are different. She tries to protect her people, and they in turn protect her. They accept one another's imperfections and support one another. My friends weren't like her friends, which makes me wonder if I ever had any at all.

I watch Charlie laugh with Annabelle as Blue descends the stairs. I can't stop thinking that her friends must see what I do in her, what my boss sees. Her innocence, her purity.

This clean lifestyle seems to make her happy.

And I wonder if being more like her could have made me happy.

Annabelle hands me a plate with four pieces of pizza and nods to pass it down. It changes hands and ends up in Blue's lap. He picks up the first piece and destroys half of it in a single bite.

"Movie?" Charlie asks.

Annabelle jumps up, runs into the kitchen, and comes back holding two movie boxes. She raises them. "*Breakfast at Tiffany's* or *It's a Wonderful Life*?"

Everyone groans.

She throws them on the coffee table and sinks down on the couch. "You guys are tasteless."

"You carry those things around with you?" Blue asks.

"They're not *things*," she says. "They're classics. And I got them when you took me by my house to change."

Charlie raises the remote. "TV?"

"Yes," Blue and I say together.

"Sorry, sweetie," Charlie tells Annabelle. "I'll watch them with you this weekend if you want."

"Meh," Annabelle murmurs.

Charlie turns on the TV, and we end up watching a rerun of the *MTV Movie Awards*. A few minutes into the show, my curiosity strikes. I glance at Annabelle, then at Blue.

I wonder.

I've never really cared before, and I don't make it a habit to peek unless I'm assigning seals, but I just can't help myself.

At once, their soul lights flip on. From the looks of it, Blue and Annabelle are living boring, hygienic lives, though the latter's isn't *quite* as clean as the former's. I yawn. What a waste.

An hour later, Annabelle and Blue get up to leave. I stay behind, and Blue's none too happy about it.

"You're not coming?" he asks me.

"Nah, I'm going to stick around for a while."

He glances at Charlie, then at me. His arms fall limp at his sides, and I can tell he's hurt. I guess he thought that after the party, she and I weren't hanging out alone anymore. But he's wrong. We're just getting started.

The two pull away in Blue's car, Scrappy, and I turn to face Charlie. "Want to chill in your room for a while?"

She smiles and nods, and I follow her upstairs.

Playing basketball was fun, but now it's time to work. I've got to convince Charlie to move faster on her requests and finally fulfill the contract. More doing, less thinking—that should be my mantra.

We move into her room, and she softly shuts the door behind us. I sit down on her bed. "Charlie, have you thought at all— "

"I'm ready to do more," she interrupts.

"What?" I ask. "I mean, you are?"

She shrugs and nods.

I rub my hands together. "Yeah, that's what I'm talking about. So what are you going to do?"

She picks up a crystal figurine and leans against her dresser. "Drumroll."

I mimic drumming and grin.

"I want to lose the glasses." She takes them off and holds them out. "Exhibit A."

"All right, yeah," I say. Though I'm wondering why this takes a soul contract. Can't she just get LASIK? Or contacts? But I guess if Grams can't afford to buy Charlie a car, she probably can't buy her those things, either. Still, looking at Charlie, I'm not sure why she needs to lose the glasses. They're not so bad. They're kind of fitting, actually. She just needs to make them more fly, maybe get some Versace frames up in there. Then she could be Charlie with style. Instead of Charlie being someone she's not.

But my job isn't to question this.

It's to push her.

More doing, less thinking.

Charlie sets her figurine and glasses down on the dresser. "How should I do it?"

I cross my arms. "I guess the same way you did last night."

"What did I do?"

"Well," I say, thinking, "first you said it aloud. Then you started listing reasons why you wanted it to happen. So maybe just try that again."

She laughs a little. "I can barely see you."

"I look really hot right now."

She laughs harder and pulls her hair up into a ponytail, like this is going to help the magic or whatever. Her lips part, and my heart pounds so hard, I can't stand it. "I want to have beautiful, perfect eyes," she says.

I want to stop her and suggest she'd better specify 20/20 vision, but she plunges onward.

"I've always wanted to wear blackest-black mascara and buy one of those kits with the trillion shades of eye shadow. But what's the point with these?" She nudges the glasses on the dresser. "It's like, no matter what I wear, I still feel dressed down. Oh! And I want to do that thing where I bat my eyes when a boy flirts with me."

When? When *a boy flirts with me?*

"I want people to notice the color of my eyes for once." She stares at me and says quietly, "I bet you don't know what color they are, do you?"

I'm glad she can't see my face, or she'd know the answer. I inspect her blond hair and fair skin. "Blue," I venture.

She pulls on her earlobe and smiles. "You just guessed. But that's okay." She puts her hands on her hips and says again, "I want beautiful, perfect eyes."

She closes her eyes and breathes evenly. Her hands fall to her sides, and she squeezes them into fists, like she's willing this to happen. She takes one last, long breath and opens her eyes.

Then she races to the bed and leaps up. She jumps up and down on the mattress. Up and down. Up and down. "I can see! I can totally see!" she says in a scream whisper so her grandma doesn't wake up. "Oh, my gosh." She stops jumping. "It really worked."

I walk to the dresser and grab her glasses. Then I open the window and pretend to throw them out. She jumps down from the bed, races across the room, snatches them away, and tosses them out the window.

"Charlie!" I say, laughing. "You actually threw them out the window."

"Oh, you *saw* that?" She holds up two fingers and points to her eyes. "Crazy, so did I!"

She's standing so close, and it's like I can taste the excitement rolling off her. Charlie looks outside, then up at me. Her eyes *are* blue. Not the kind that's muddled with gray, but a sharper shade of blue. The kind of blue you find in a Crayola box.

They're open wide, and I can't help but...but...

I slowly reach out and run my thumbs over her eyes. They close beneath my touch. She doesn't open them when I pull away. She just stands there, her chest rising and falling.

In an instant, her soul light flips on. I'd almost forgotten about the seal, but apparently the contract overlooks nothing. From deep in my chest, a red seal appears and floats toward her. It attaches to her light, clinging there. Seeing what I've done, I clench my hands.

"Good night, Charlie," I say gently.

She smiles, her eyes still closed, and nods.

I leave and tug the door closed behind me. Outside her room, I dig my hand into my pocket until my fingers find the cool copper. I try and focus on the blurred *Liberty* pressed into the coin's side. Then I glance down to where I know my cuff is, and for a tiny moment, I'm disgusted with where it came from—with how Boss Man made these things. I wonder what Charlie would think if she knew the secret I know. The one I can never tell.

I squeeze my eyes shut.

This is an assignment. She's *an assignment.*

I hear her on the other side of the door, moving around the room. She's probably crawling into bed. I suddenly imagine what she's wearing—whether it's that same red silk thingy—and if she's already beneath the covers. I bet she's even more angelic while dreaming. Blood burns in my veins. And in the pit of my stomach, a mixture of anger and guilt makes me nauseated.

Because it doesn't matter. In the end, no matter what I think about the girl sleeping in that bed, I won't forfeit my promotion. I won't return to hell.

I won't choose her life over mine.

The top stair creaks when I hit it, but something stops me. Grams's door is cracked open, and I can hear her coughing up a lung. A shiver shoots up my spine, and all I can think is, *Freaking disgusting.*

I head down two more stairs, then hear coughing again. Grams coughs so hard and so long that I'm sure it's the last sound she'll ever make. Then she stops and gasps for air. I squeeze my eyes shut, pull in a breath, and head toward her door. It sways open beneath my hand, and I spot Grams lying in a full-sized bed. There's a window near her, and the moon casts shadows over her purple silk comforter.

I take a few quiet steps into the room and stop when she turns around. She doesn't seem surprised to see me. Like she knew I'd be here at this very moment.

Grams opens her mouth and coughs again, and I fight the urge to bolt. On her nightstand, just out of her reach, is a glass of water. I cross the room, put one finger on the glass, and slide it toward her.

Then I do bolt.

I shake my whole body out and roll my head quick like a

boxer, trying to get rid of the heebie-jeebies.

"Dante," Grams croaks.

I freeze.

"Thank you," she finishes.

The tiniest of smiles touches my lips, and I descend the stairs and leave.

24

IDEAS ARE A-BREWIN'

Wednesday morning I wake up with a start. I realize I'm halfway through my ten days, and I don't have much to show for it. I need to speed things along. The problem is, I can tell I'm dragging my feet.

Though I won't admit why.

When I get to Charlie's house, Grams opens the door. She's dressed in her silk kimono, acting like nothing happened last night. Like she didn't almost croak.

"Hey," she says. "Charlie rode with Blue to school."

I fold my arms in front of my chest. "Oh, yeah?"

She nods.

"So," I say.

Mr. Awkward rolls up between us, lights a cigarette, makes himself comfortable. It's the same bastard who shows up after you've bumped uglies with a stranger.

Grams breaks the tension by smiling. She slaps me on the shoulder. "Don't worry, kid. I won't tell anyone you've got a heart."

I try to match her smile, but my mouth won't cooperate.

Instead I say, "What's wrong with you?"

She takes a sharp breath and gazes over my shoulder into the woods. "Food poisoning."

"Uh-huh." I run a hand through my hair. "When you going to tell Charlie about that food poisoning? So it doesn't, like, blindside her."

Her blue-gray eyes snap to my face. "That girl's been through enough."

I hold her stare. Charlie *has* been through enough. Still, she knows something's going down with Grams. But not everything. And she deserves to. But I decide it's not my place.

Grams is still glaring at me, so I nod. "Guess you're right. See you around."

Her face warms. "See ya, good-lookin'."

• • •

Classes drag by, and I can't find a spare second to talk to Charlie. The time between classes seems shorter somehow, and for the hundredth time, I curse having to be in school at all.

When lunch—and sweet freedom—finally arrives, I find Charlie and her clan at their usual table. Charlie's lashes are long with black mascara, and above them, a shiny brownish-gold color is spread over her eyelids. It's the first time I've seen a touch of makeup on her.

It looks good.

She looks good.

But I'm still not sure it was necessary.

The cafeteria is alive with commotion, and the sounds of excited voices pierce my eardrums. It's the damn Halloween dance. It's been like this all week, horny boys and clueless girls scrambling to find dates and buy tickets during their precious social hour.

Gag me.

"That is a terrible face." Annabelle draws a circle in the air to reference my face. "What's the problem? You look like you're about to crap your diaper."

I drop down next to Charlie and say, "It's that." I point to the black-and-orange-clad ticket table.

"You don't do dances?" Annabelle asks. "Is it because you can't dance?"

I lean forward. "Trust me, I can— "

"It's okay." She nods toward Blue. "Blue can't dance to save his life."

I eye Blue, but he just shrugs and works his PB&J.

"Annabelle, I got moves that'll bring you to your knees," I say. "I just hate school functions."

I nudge Charlie for backup. She digs her hand into her pocket, then pops Skittles into her mouth. She stays quiet.

"Charlie? You like that kind of stuff? Dances? School crap created because it's a *safe alternative for the children*?" I end with air quotes.

"She's a chick, ain't she?" Annabelle asks. "We girls are prewired to like things that make you suffer."

This is not good. I am not—I repeat, *not*—going to that damn dance. Then again, I'm not sure what I'm worried about. The dance is three days away. By then, I'll have Charlie's soul all wrapped up with a fat red bow. I just have to give her a reason to ask for more beauty changes.

"If you guys want to go party, why don't we go tonight? Why do we have to wait until Saturday?"

Annabelle glances at Blue, then at me. "What'd you have in mind?"

Crap. What did *I have in mind?*

"Something great," I say, stalling. "How 'bout I pick you guys up out front after school?"

Charlie grins, and Blue nods, but Annabelle's not convinced—which surprises me.

"Why should we go anywhere with you?" she says.

"Wow. Okay. Did I do something?"

"It's what you didn't do." She nods at Charlie.

I study Charlie, but I have no idea what Annabelle's talking about.

"Her glasses," Blue says. "She's not wearing glasses anymore."

Oooh. That's right. I'm not supposed to know. I should be surprised. I should be all, *Charlie, where are your glasses? You look great!*

I glance at Charlie and feign surprise. "Oh, wow. Where are your glasses? You look great!"

She gives me a knowing smile and says, "I got contacts this morning as an early Halloween present from Grams."

"Halloween present?" I say. "Is that a thing?"

"Totally," Charlie says.

"Not at all," Annabelle and Blue say.

I focus on Annabelle. "We solid? You in now?"

She cocks her head to the side like she's contemplating. Then she grins and says, "In like a mofo."

When lunch is over, Charlie turns to me, expecting me to walk her to class like I usually do. I put my hand on her waist, surprised at the bit of curve I feel. "I'm going to take care of some stuff. I'll see you outside after school. 'Kay?"

"You're going to skip?" she asks.

"Is that so surprising?"

She laughs and shakes her head. "Guess if you're dead, you're not afraid of flunking out."

"No, sweets, I'm not." I let go of her and head outside. I've got four hours to dream up something that'll make Charlie beg to cash in that contract. And I've got a damn good idea brewing.

25

LET'S ROLL

When the final bell rings, I'm waiting in the parking lot. I see the three goofs sauntering toward the car, bundled against the cold. Charlie points toward Elizabeth Taylor, and a few seconds later, the three climb into my car. Annabelle and Blue crawl into the back two captain's chairs, and Charlie sits shotgun.

No one says anything for a minute. Then Annabelle breaks the silence. "Sooooo...where're we going?"

I open the console, pull out four tickets, and spread them in a fan. "Vegas, baby."

No one says anything, which is great in my book. I'm all about the shock value.

"Everyone, listen closely." I pause to make sure I have their attention. "First, pull out your cell phones."

Blue opens his mouth. "This is not going to—"

"I said, pull out your phones." I roll my hand in the air. "Let's go, let's go. Move your asses."

Annabelle smiles and pulls out her cell. Blue follows suit. Charlie doesn't have a cell, but no biggie. She can borrow her girl's. In fact, it'll work out better that way.

I point to Annabelle. "Call your mom and tell her you're staying the night with Charlie." Then I point to Charlie. "Call Grams from Annabelle's phone, and tell her you're sleeping over at Annabelle's." Blue's turn. "Blue, call your mommy. You're staying the night with Dante Walker. I'm the new kid in town, and you feel sorry for me."

They consider what I just said, and slowly, three smiles surround me.

I nod at Annabelle. "You first."

Everyone makes their calls, and a few minutes later, Blue clicks his cell shut.

"So she said okay?" Annabelle asks him.

"Yeah," he says, grinning. "I can't freaking believe it. She never lets me stay out overnight during the week. But she got all sympathetic and stuff."

"Wait," Charlie says. "Are we going to make it back in time for school tomorrow?"

"Nope." I hand them three notes from their *parents* explaining to the school that their kids are sick. "Your perfect attendance will finally pay off. No one in that school will think their golden children played hooky."

The three take the notes from me and study them.

"They appear legit," Annabelle announces. "Props."

Charlie glances at me. "Well then," she says. "What are we waiting for?"

• • •

The excitement is palpable as we drive to the Birmingham airport. I've got Eminem's old stuff blasting through the speakers. Annabelle is throwing her head around, and her short black hair is flying through the air. Blue keeps pushing her away when she gets too close, but even he's laughing. And for the first time, Charlie seems to be basking in the music's beat, her body rocking back and forth in the seat.

This is my best idea to date.

We get to the airport, park, head inside, and wait to board the plane. Every few minutes monotone announcements come over the speakers. I keep hoping it's *our* monotone announcement, saying it's time.

"You still excited?" I ask Charlie, whose leg is spastically pumping up and down.

She stops moving her leg and shrugs a slender shoulder. "Eh, nothing I don't do every day."

"That right?"

Her eyes find mine, and I'm startled by how blue they are. They say everything she doesn't. She's thrilled. She's alive.

She's wondering what the hell she's gotten herself into.

I start to slide my arm around her shoulders, but the attendant announces that it's time to board. We grab our backpacks and walk down the long Jetway to the plane. When we get to the entrance, my crew goes too far. I reach out and grab Blue's shoulder.

"We stop here," I say.

He shakes my hand off. "This is first class."

"Yeah," I answer. "I don't do coach." Blue can't hide the excitement on his face, though I know he'd love to.

"How are you this loaded?" Annabelle asks when she figures out where we'll be sitting. "Is your dad like in the mafia?"

I cringe. "Something like that."

She must notice the look on my face because she drops the subject.

Charlie and I sit together, and Annabelle and Blue sit across the aisle from us. The captain comes on and welcomes us and says how long it'll be until we hit Sin City. Fifteen minutes later, the plane rolls gently down the runway.

Then it races.

Charlie's face is pressed to the window, and right as the plane's wheels leave the ground, she fumbles for my hand and squeezes. I glance down at her palm in mine, and my breath catches. I squeeze back. Holding hands is such an intimate gesture. One I've never really thought about before now. I stretch my fingers out and wrap them tighter around her cool skin. Her eyes never leave the window.

That's what makes it okay.

Blue and Annabelle order food and drinks and just about everything the attendant offers them, and Charlie continues to stare at the clouds.

I lean toward her ear. "It's beautiful, huh?"

Her head whips around, and for a second our faces are way too close. I quickly pull back.

"I've never flown before," she says.

My head falls to one side. "Really? You guys never went on vacation?"

"Yeah, we did. We just always drove."

"You like it?" I ask.

"Like what?"

"Flying."

She turns and gazes out the window again. "I do."

26

SIN CITY

When we land in Las Vegas, Charlie is asleep. Her head rests against the window, her hair spilling over her face. I reach up and push it away. She doesn't feel anything. No harm done.

The pilot comes on over the speaker again and startles her awake.

"Holy cow," she murmurs. "I fell asleep. Are we here?"

I nod, and she leans forward to wave at Blue. Annabelle is also asleep, but unlike Charlie, her sleeping is less...blissful. She's snoring and smacking, and Blue's been putting bits of paper in her mouth.

Blue roughly shakes her awake.

Annabelle immediately swallows, and down the paper goes.

"That was so mean," Charlie says in her sleepy voice.

Annabelle coughs and glares at Blue. "What did you do? Did I just swallow something?"

Blue pulls her into a hug. "You're my best friend in the whole world."

"Get off me, leech," she says, smiling.

We get off the plane and head outside, where I hail a cab. In the distance, I can see the distinct pyramid shape and the light that shoots from its top. It's a skyline I've seen many times before. Growing up with a father who's always away and a liberal, free-spirited mother, it was easy to do as I pleased. And with more money at my disposal than any kid should have, my options were endless. Thinking back on my life, it's a wonder I died the way I did. It was so…anticlimactic.

"I can't believe we're here," Charlie says. She's staring out the window at the skyline as we pull away from the curb. "It's amazing."

"It's even better up close," I say.

"I can't believe we're actually in Vegas," Annabelle breathes. "I mean, seriously."

"I know," Blue says. He looks at Charlie, though I know he's talking to me. "I'm glad we got to come."

I smile. "Just wait until we get to the hotel."

Twenty minutes later, the cabbie pulls up to V Hotel, Vegas's newest gem. I pay the driver, and we grab our backpacks and head inside. The *clang-clang*ing of slot machines rushes out to greet us, and as soon as we step foot in the lobby, Charlie starts pointing.

She gawks at the walls that change colors every few seconds and the chandelier made of clocks. She rubs her hands over the small, strategically placed beds that suggest all kinds of nasty things. And finally, she beams at the man behind the counter, who's dressed in head-to-toe leather and handing me our room keys. I'd like to think his attire is due to Halloween this coming Sunday, but somehow I doubt it.

I give each person their own key, and Annabelle jumps up and down.

"Our own rooms?" she says. "Get. Out."

"I won't."

We head down the hall, and Charlie shakes her hips to the pumping, pulsing music. The walls are lined in red velvet, and the floor is decked in black-and-white tile. Overhead, vintage records dangle in a chaotic pattern. The entire place is built for partying, which is exactly why I chose it.

Blue and I walk side by side. Every time a chick passes, his eyes nearly pop out of his head.

I lean toward him and whisper, "They make 'em kinda different here, don't they?"

He straightens, and his face reddens, but he acts like he doesn't know what I'm talking about.

Inside a glass elevator, I push the button for the thirtieth floor, and we shoot up. Every time we pass a new floor, the roof of the elevator changes colors. Annabelle and Charlie start announcing the colors as if we can't see them for ourselves.

When we get to our floor, the girls rush out to see their rooms. I point Blue in the right direction, and he gives me a look like he resents the guidance. I'm not sure what it'll take to win him over.

Nor do I care.

Annabelle and Charlie disappear into their rooms for about sixty seconds, then burst out and run into the other person's room to see if anything's different. It is. Each room has unique décor, though the entire floor's theme is *vanity*.

Not sure how we ended up on this particular floor.

Oh, wait, yeah, I am.

I peek into Charlie's room, and she is, of course, jumping on her bed. The wall behind the headboard is made entirely of glass, and behind it, the city is brilliant. Every time she jumps in the air, the city seems to hold her there. Like she's one of the buildings. Like a sparkling new attraction.

Annabelle comes rushing in, but I stop her at the door.

"Hey," I say. "You mind if I talk to Charlie for a sec?"

Some of the excitement drains from her face, but she nods. "Hey, Charlie," she calls over my shoulder. "Come knock on my door when you're done talking to Dante."

"Anna, will you make sure everyone is in my room in two hours?" I ask her.

"Two hours? It's, like, nine o'clock now. We're not doing anything until eleven?"

"Correct. The cool kids show up late. That's the way it works." I wink and close the door.

Charlie drops down on the bed. She seems confused until I close the door behind Annabelle and sit across from her in a sky-blue loveseat. The enormous, posh room is decked out with mirrors. They smother the three non-glass walls, and even the chandelier is made of tiny circular mirrored plates. Scattered among the wall mirrors are photographs of famous people gazing at their reflections. Covering the black tile floor is a huge white shag rug, and outside there's a balcony with a see-through floor.

If this place doesn't make her want to be beautiful, I don't know what will.

Charlie curls her legs to one side and looks at me expectantly. It's like she knows what this is all about.

"You like it?" I ask. I pick up a miniature pumpkin near the loveseat, no doubt added to the decor during October.

Her eyes take in the room. "It's so, like, over the top."

"It is, isn't it?"

Silence hangs between us. I want her to ask for more beauty. If I can help it, I'd prefer not to push. That way, I can finish this assignment with a clean conscience.

So I wait.

Her bright blue eyes grab my attention. "Dante," she asks hesitantly, "why'd you bring us here?"

I push my tongue against the back of my teeth and think of how to respond. I decide on the truth. "Peachville was suffocating me. I needed to get away for a while. And why not come with friends, right?"

Okay, the partial truth.

She brushes invisible crumbs from her shirt. "It wasn't because…you thought I'd ask for more if you brought me here?"

I pretend ignorance. "More what?"

She pulls her mouth up to one side and narrows her eyes. She's not buying it.

"Oh, more contract stuff," I say. "No, I didn't. I just wanted to have a good time."

Nothing else. Don't say anything *else.*

Charlie chews her lip, then smiles and nods. "Okay."

And just like that, she believes me. It boggles my freaking mind how trusting she is. I decide to take a chance. "Why? Were you thinking about asking for more?"

She crosses the room and opens the door to the balcony. Sounds from the street flood in: cars honking, people yelling, music thumping. Her back is to me when she asks, "I don't know. What do you think?"

I put my elbows on my knees and lean forward, trying to act casual. "I mean, I guess if you were going to ask for more, why not do it here, right?"

From here, it seems like her shoulders tense. But I decide I'm imagining things.

She turns around wearing a grin. "Maybe I will. Why not?"

"Great! Good." I stand and walk toward her. I put my hands on her shoulders. "You only live once, Charlie. You and I know that better than anyone."

A flash of hurt sweeps through her eyes, and my chest tightens. I shake her gently by the shoulders. "Hey, you know I didn't mean anything by that."

"Yeah, I know." She nods her head, though her gaze falls to the floor. "You only live once."

"Exactly. How 'bout this? You get dressed, and I'll take you and your friends out on the town tonight. Show you what it means to party."

"I don't have anything to wear."

I eye her crumpled T-shirt and jeans, and her busted-ass sneakers. She's got a point.

I lift her chin until she meets my eyes. "Don't worry about that," I say. "I got you, girl."

27

CALL IN THE TROOPS

When I get back to my room, I call down to the front desk. Some dude picks up on the first ring.

"Concierge. How may I help you this evening, Mr. Walker?"

"Yeah, I need to have some things delivered to my guests' rooms."

"Certainly, Mr. Walker."

I rub my forehead, thinking. "I need someone who does makeup and someone else for hair. Oh, and maybe one of those people who makes your nails look all good."

"Yes, sir, a nail technician." I can hear him smiling through the phone. "We have one on staff."

"Yeah, that. Also, I need a stylist. I need them to call my guests to get sizes and then bring them clothes to hit the club in."

"Is there anything else?"

I glance around my room. "Yeah, I need two bottles of Dom and the biggest, fattest bacon cheeseburger you got."

"Would you like to charge this to your room, sir?"

"Yeah, put it on my Amex."

"Thank you. We'll have the stylist call your guests right away. Would you like for the stylist to visit your room as well?"

I glance down at my red vest, navy button-down, dark jeans, and Louis V belt. Meh.

"Sure," I answer. "Send her my way."

"We'll have them up shortly."

I hang up and walk to my bed. It's big enough for me and six chicks. Pow! After eyeing a Pandora radio mounted onto the wall, I flip through the channels until I land on Korn. The music blasts from the speakers, and minutes later, someone knocks on my door. It's the booze. Not a moment too soon.

The guy who brings it in waits awkwardly in the doorway until I sign the check and put a twenty in his hand. Then I pour my old friend, Dom, into a crystal flute and toss it back. Champagne's made for sipping. But I'm made to party, so whatev.

The stylist calls and later brings up a gray sports coat and red V-neck shirt. I consider her choices.

"You done good," I say.

She gives me a tight smile, then rushes off to take care of the other three.

I glance in the mirror. Surprise, surprise—I look finger-lickin' delicious. And that's important, because I'm about to visit Charlie. If I can't get her to ask for more requests, the least I can do is ensure she picks up a few more seals tonight. That'll be a hell of a lot easier if I strut my business. Ugly people are a lot of things, but influential is not one of them. I grab a glass of champagne, muss my hair, and bust out the bedroom eyes.

The clock reads 10:45. Good. That's all the time I need to get Charlie in the right frame of mind. I open the door to my hotel room, cross the hall, and knock once on her door.

A guy in his early thirties opens the door. "What do you

want? I'm busy."

"Who the hell are you?" I ask.

He cocks a hand on his hip. "Who the hell are *you*?"

"I'm the guy paying for this room."

His hand falls to his side. "Oh. Well, I was hired to get this girl ready to go out tonight."

"Yeah, I know. I'm the one who hired you."

"Mm-hmm. Mm-hmm." He shakes his head as if to say, *And?* Then he glances over his shoulder. "Look, we've still got a lot left to do. I can't stop mid-session. Can you come back later?"

"Dude, get the hell out of my way."

I push the door open. The room is in complete disarray. There are curling irons and makeup kits and racks upon racks of short dresses and shiny blouses. Near the closed bathroom door are discarded white robes and pink push-up bras, and strewn across the bed are more beauty products than I've ever seen in my life.

I turn on the guy. "What happened in here?"

"Magic," he says. "And don't think magic means miracles because it doesn't. So manage your expectations."

I have a sudden urge to beat this guy's face in. Instead, I sweep my arm across the bed and sit down as random crap clatters to the floor. The guy turns away and heads toward the bathroom. He knocks—or rather, *bangs*—on the door.

"Enough, already," he yells. "I've got to do her hair."

"Screw off," some chick who isn't Charlie yells back.

The guy shoots me a look like he can't believe she just said that, like we're sharing the frustration. He turns back to the door and puts his mouth near the crack.

"Listen here, you busted-ass bitch. You better open this damn door before—"

Busted-Ass Bitch swings the door open and immediately

palms his face and shoves. "Get. Back."

He bucks up like he's going to hit her, but she just sashays by him and into the room. "Come on, Charlie." She pulls a plush white chair near a mirror. "Sit here."

I peer over the dude's shoulder, curious what they've done to her—if she'll even look human. The smell of perfume and powder wafts out, making my nose itch like crazy.

And then she appears.

Something in me catches.

She's not beautiful, exactly. But she looks...she looks...*nice*. Maybe it's that I'm accustomed to her face, the way her cheeks glow when she's excited, or the curve of her mouth when she smiles. It's her face—*Charlie's* face—and in a strange way, I like it the way it is now. Without any changes.

My legs are restless, and I have to stand from the bed. I move toward Charlie without thinking. The stylist chick keeps rattling on, so I point at her and say, "Shut. Up."

Her face scrunches in disgust, and she flashes an irritated glance at the dude, who only flips her off.

Charlie freezes in place. Her mouth quivers like she wants to smile, but she's not quite sure how to react.

No one speaks as I move to within a few inches of her. She's wearing a sheer, long-sleeved blouse. Beneath it, I can just spot her black bra. The blouse hangs loosely over skintight leather pants that clutch her tiny ankles. I also notice she's swaying, teetering on black Louboutins with red underbellies. Her hair falls over her shoulders, untouched for now.

None of this is what surprises me.

It's her skin.

It's...flawless.

The red patches have vanished. Pimples—gone. Left in their

wake is smooth, porcelain skin that begs to be touched. And why shouldn't I?

I reach up and run the back of my hand over her skin. Her eyes close, and she breathes in. I'd like to say she's being stupid. Holding her breath like that. But my breath is gone, too—lost to this moment and the girl with doll-like cheeks.

Right as I'm wondering about the seal associated with this request, her soul light flips on. Before I can comprehend what's happening, a seal appears from my chest and rushes forward to attach to her light. There's still plenty of light left, but for the first time, I can see that headway is being made, that it's much dimmer than when I met her five days ago. My stomach clenches at the sight.

Homeboy kills the moment by grabbing Charlie's arm. "Sorry, love, but I need her now."

I stand, transfixed, and watch as the guy parts her long blond hair down the middle. He then curls a few pieces with a flat iron and shakes her hair out between his fingers. "The trick is not to overdo it," he says to no one in particular.

The stylist swoops in and puts the final touches on Charlie's makeup. "Voilà!"

The twosome guide Charlie to a mirror, and she takes herself in. She runs her hands over the silk blouse, her soft hair….the gold necklace around her neck. But her eyes never leave her face. I wonder if she did it as soon as I left her room. She must have, or the makeover duo would know something's up.

Even the skin on her neck is clearer, and it gives her whole face a kind of radiance only preggos get.

"You happy?" I ask her. I'm still standing near the bathroom. I haven't regained function of my legs yet.

"Damn straight she's happy," Hair Guy says. "We just turned

her into Cinda-freakin-rella."

I've had about enough input from the staff, so I stick cash in their sweaty palms and wave them toward the door. When I turn back to Charlie, she's beaming.

"It's good, huh?" she says.

I laugh. "It's good. So you asked for…?"

"Better skin," she finishes. "I thought, what the hey. How many times am I going to be in Las Vegas with my best friends?"

"I concur," I say, though I'm not sure I do. It's my job to ensure she executes the contract, but did she really need this done? She would've outgrown her flawed skin, and it wasn't even that bad. Not when she smiled, anyway. Because when Charlie smiled, you didn't notice anything else.

Walking around her in a tight circle, I inspect the change. Seeing her up close, I know she's nearer to becoming traditionally beautiful, but a part of me aches for the way she used to look. Will I ever see her strawberry blush of excitement in these new, smoother cheeks?

I'm about to reach out for another sample when someone knocks on the door. Charlie takes a quick backward step, and something in her eyes says she's disappointed we're interrupted. Two seconds later, someone knocks again. My skin flushes with annoyance.

"You guys in there?" I hear Annabelle yell.

I smile and put a finger to my lips. Charlie covers her mouth, but her laugh breaks the barrier.

"Yeah, I can hear you laughing," Annabelle says. "Freaking let us in. I thought we were meeting in Dante's room. We've been standing out there knocking for, like, ten years."

I cross the room and swing the door open. "Ten years, you say?"

"Give or take." She strides past me wearing a tight black dress and scarlet high heels. Her dark hair is bobbed *Pulp Fiction* style, and she's got long gold earrings that brush her shoulders.

"Annabelle, you look great." I can't believe I'm saying this, but it's the truth. She's a big girl, but in that body-hugging dress, it's obvious she's super-sized in all the right places. I never noticed before, but with a little elbow grease, she could be a real hottie.

Annabelle squeals for two seconds when she sees her friend all glammed up, then races into Charlie's bathroom to dig through the makeup the stylists left behind.

Over my shoulder, I spot Blue standing in the hallway, waiting to be invited in. He's fumbling with his cuffs to avoid eye contact. The stylist hooked him up with a black button-down, dark jeans, and brown cowboy boots. Very urban cowboy. It suits him.

I slap his hands down and pull his head up. "Head up, *hombre*. You're *GQ* tonight; act like it."

He bites the inside of his cheek to keep from smiling.

And then he sees Charlie.

28

PRE-PARTY

Blue's entire face opens like a lion's mouth. He takes her in—the tight pants, the loose blond waves. And of course, her skin.

Charlie sees him and immediately smiles. There's no reservation about it; around him she's comfortable. "Hey!" She swirls in a circle for Blue. "What do you think?"

He doesn't say anything, but he does cross the room to stand in front of her. "You look different," he says softly, as if this remark is for her ears only.

Her face pulls together, and she fiddles with the gold necklace lying on her chest.

"Not in a bad way," he quickly adds. "But definitely different. In a big way."

"The makeup people did an amazing job." Charlie turns away from Blue, but he spins after her, orbiting her body with his own.

"It's not just that." He reaches up and takes her face in his hands. His thumbs pull up to trace the line of her jaw. "Your skin," he says. "It's perfect." Blue's eyes flash in my direction. It doesn't last long, but it's long enough to make me uncomfortable. Why is he looking at me? He couldn't possibly know something's up.

What I'm really thinking, though, is that he needs to back off. Blue's a good guy, and he's spoken his mind, which is admirable, but Charlie's *my* assignment, and if he isn't careful, I'll let him know that in no uncertain terms.

Annabelle appears from the bathroom, her arms filled with miniature bottles and tubes of makeup. "What's going on out here? Why's everyone all quiet?" She moves to stand beside the two of them. This time, she really studies Charlie's face. "Okay, what are you doing behind my back? Why do you look hotter every time I see you? And what is up with your skin? It's baby's-ass smooth."

"I did a treatment the stylists recommended," she answers. Annabelle's mouth opens like she's going to demand the same treatment, but Charlie cuts her off. "It hurt so bad, though."

"It did?" Annabelle asks.

Blue takes a small step backward, as if her fabricated pain somehow hurt him, too.

Charlie nods. "It was the worst. They said to expect pain, but I had no idea it would be so intense."

"Does it still hurt?" Annabelle asks.

Charlie cringes like it stings just thinking about it.

I stifle a laugh. My assignment is getting better at this whole lying thing. Still, I better break this up before more questions get asked.

"Why don't we go to my room and pre-party for a while?" I grab Annabelle's waist and guide her toward the door. She stares over her shoulder at Charlie the entire way.

"Maybe I could handle it," Annabelle mutters.

"No, you couldn't," I fire back.

Blue and Charlie follow us into my room, where the radio is still blasting *let's effin' party* music. Annabelle forgets all about

Charlie's new, flawless skin the second she sees the champagne. She races to the cart and pulls the bottle up.

"How did you get this?" Her eyes land on me, a mixture of excitement and fear swirling behind her dark irises.

I take the bottle from her and pour a glass. "I called down and ordered it."

"And they didn't card you? Or did they? Do you have a fake or something?"

"I don't have a fake ID," I say. "I have a credit card." I hold the glass of champagne out to her. She stares at the shiny crystal like it's battery acid, then quickly changes her mind and sweeps it out of my hand.

"Annabelle, you're going to drink?" Charlie asks.

Annabelle shrugs and brings the glass to her lips. "When in Rome, eh?"

Blue cocks his head to the side, then approaches the booze tray. He pours a trying-to-impress-Charlie-sized glass of Dom and toasts Annabelle's flute.

Thank goodness for friends. They're making my job a lot easier tonight.

I pour another two servings and hand one to Charlie. She takes it without complaint, and the four of us raise our glasses. "To tonight," I say.

"Hear, hear," Annabelle says as the flutes clink together. Then she pumps her hips against Blue's ass, and he shoves her off, laughing. "And thanks to Dante for hooking us up: first-class tickets to Vegas, our own rooms, stylists, champagne. A girl could get used to this."

"No problem," I say. "Glad you guys could come." What's crazy is that what I'm saying is true. I haven't been to Vegas in what feels like an eternity. And Annabelle, Blue, and Charlie—they're all so thankful for the trip. They're nothing like my old friends.

We go out on the balcony and watch the cars slink by beneath us. The lights of the city are overwhelming from this height. It's like the city is everywhere and everything. And we're all a part of it now.

I watch Charlie's face as she leans over the railing and peers down, and then up at the sky. She's not smiling like I expect—she's more curious. She catches me staring and raises the champagne to her lips. When she pulls it away, she giggles. It doesn't take long with champagne.

The music inside changes to a lame slow song, and Annabelle and Blue groan.

"I think that's our cue," I say.

"Where are we going?" Blue asks.

"Somewhere that'll blow your feeble mind." I collect their glasses and put them on the dresser. Then I walk toward the door and hold it open. "Let's roll."

Annabelle and Charlie link arms and race ahead of us. They stop and make faces in the mirrors hung along the hallway. Charlie pauses for longer than Annabelle, no doubt inspecting her skin. Her friend has to keep tugging her away.

Downstairs in the lobby, Blue nods toward the casino. "Any way you can get us in there?"

"Probably. But where we're going is much better."

Blue's eyes linger on the flashing lights and chiming bells of the casino as we head outside the sliding glass doors and into the night. Charlie tugs a lightweight Versace coat around her middle as I hail a cab.

The cabbie pulls up and asks through the open window, "Where to?"

I lean down, putting my hands on the sill, and tell him, "Holy Hell."

29

HOLY HELL

Annabelle and Charlie are singing when we pull up to Holy Hell, making a bad song sound worse.

"Here ya go." The cabbie turns around and eyes me expectantly, like he somehow knows I'm the chump paying. He swipes the cash from my hand and turns to face the busy street.

Charlie and Annabelle have already climbed out of the cab, and Blue is trying to get out on the opposite side. He's dangerously close to getting run over.

I briefly wonder if I care.

Guess it would suck. A little.

The club, Holy Hell, is five stories of delightfulness. There's a line wrapped around the building, but there's no way I'm waiting in that thing. In fact, I doubt it ever moves. That's just where they stick people they don't want inside. The Vegas has-beens and never-beens.

When Blue finally lurks up beside us, I ask him, "You know how to slip someone cash?"

He looks at me, trying to comprehend what I'm asking.

"Here, watch." I pull a hundred out of my wallet and fold it until it's hardly visible. Then I tuck one corner between my ring and middle fingers, folding the rest in my palm. "What's going on, man?" I say to Blue and hold my hand out.

He glances down at my hand, then shakes it with his own.

I spread my ring and middle fingers slightly, and the bill drops into his palm. When he pulls his hand away, he sees he has the bill.

"You got it?" I ask him.

He nods.

"Okay, your turn. You try it on me now. Don't let the bill drop. If it does, we're shit outta luck." He nods again, but just in case he doesn't understand why I'm showing him this, I say, "You have to learn how to do this. I don't want problems when people question your prepubescent-looking ass. Cool?"

His nostrils flare, and he tucks the bill between his fingers, holding his palm out to me. "What's up, dude?" he says through his teeth.

I shake his hand.

His technique is perfect.

"That was terrible," I say. "But it'll have to do."

I pull out another bill and wrap my arm around Charlie. Glancing back, I notice Blue is doing the same with Annabelle, but his eyes never leave the arm I have around Charlie's waist. I smile inwardly, then lead the way to the bouncer and shake his hand.

The bouncer does a quick lift of his chin and pulls back the red velvet rope. People in line shout profanities. Blue makes the pass, and the bouncer closes the rope behind the four of us.

"You done good, Blue," I say.

"Like I give a shit what you think," he replies.

I throw my head back and laugh. "Kid, you hang out with me

any longer, and you'll be picking fights with black belts."

He jams his hands in his pockets, but his dimple fights to make an appearance. Ah, our touching love-hate relationship strikes again. Tear.

Inside the club, we stop at a small booth, and I pay the guy stamping hands. Blue pulls out his wallet, but I wave it away and toss a little respect his way for offering.

The holding room we're in is tiny, maybe ten feet by ten feet. On the right is the guy I just paid, and on the left is an elevator. In a stroke of luck, we're the only ones waiting outside of it. Charlie shoots me a nervous glance, and I give her a soldier's salute.

After a few seconds of waiting, the bell for the elevator *dings*. The four of us pile inside, and Charlie glances at me. "Which floor?"

I shrug. I want her to pick. I'm curious.

She leans toward the buttons. There are four floors above us and a basement, six floors in all. Near the buttons is a gold sign with dark, blocky writing that reads, PICK YOUR POISON.

Annabelle nudges her. "Pick a floor, girl. I'm ready to get my dance on."

Charlie twiddles her fingers in front of the buttons, then pushes five.

I groan.

"What?" she asks. "Did I choose wrong?"

"No. You chose exactly as I expected you would." And I'll get to spend the next hour somewhere I don't belong. Irony—it's a bitch.

The elevator races upward, and when the doors slide open, Charlie gasps.

We walk out into Holy Hell's top floor. Brilliant white cotton drips from the ceiling like puffy clouds, and small crystals dangle beneath them. The white tile is pristine and coated in feathers, and the walls are covered in a soft shade of blue. In front of us, a long bar twinkles with tiny lights, and every chair, couch, and stool is wrapped in bright white leather.

The effect is heaven on earth.

Punch me.

The girls squeal and run toward the middle of the room, where people are dancing to oldies and sipping frothy white drinks. The room's only redeeming quality is the sporadic platforms where chicks clad in skimpy angel outfits dance seductively.

I fist-bump Blue's shoulder. "Want a drink?"

He nods without hesitating.

Damn straight.

Instead of heading to the main bar, I lead Blue toward a massive ice block. Above it, an angel girl stands waiting. I hand cash up to her, and she mixes two white drinks and pours them through the top of the ice block. The liquid rushes through tiny groves like a mountain stream, then spills into two frosted glasses.

Blue's eyes widen. "Bad."

"Indeed." I hand him his drink, and we go to find the girls, who we realize are already dancing like drunken idiots. They grind their hips toward each other, and I wonder why the slightest bit of booze turns chicks into lesbos.

"Having fun?" I yell over the music to Charlie. She's doing a pretty decent job of dancing despite her limp.

"Ooh." She takes the glass from me. "This looks yum."

I didn't actually intend for the drink to be hers, but I guess it does more good down her throat than mine. Still, I best keep an eye on her. I remember how loopy she got after two beers at Taylor's party. If she gets wasted, she'll end up passing out instead of enjoying delicious sins o' the evening. Not good.

Blue moves in to dance with Charlie, but I step between them before he can. I wrap my arms around her waist and lift her own around my neck. She pushes her head into my chest, avoiding my gaze. This causes a small smile to lift my mouth.

I wonder if she's ever been kissed before. I don't mean kinda kissed, like the crap she mentioned at Taylor's party. I mean *really* kissed.

No freaking way.

Which means if I kissed her, it'd be sort of like her first time. Oh, man. Which means she has a lot of other *first times* to experience. Thinking about Charlie doing the dirty, I laugh, but when she looks up at me, I stop. A warm sensation spreads between my shoulder blades when I really think about her in bed with some dude. It's actually not funny. Not at all.

"What's wrong?" she asks.

I lay her head back on my chest. "Nothing," I say. "Let's just dance."

Behind me, Blue shoots me death stares as he dances with Annabelle.

I know, dude. One second you think I ain't half bad, the next you want to castrate me. Touché.

We dance for half an hour before I can't stand the happy, bouncy music any longer. I grab Charlie's hand and tap Annabelle on the shoulder. She spins around, taking Blue with her. Blue's eyes fall on Charlie's hand in mine. He grimaces.

"Let's see some of the other rooms," I say.

"Yeah!" Annabelle screams too loudly. Her eyes are round and glassy. I don't have to guess why. She visited the ice bar more times than I cared to count. "What's on the other floors?"

"I'll show you."

Charlie digs her heels in. "Aw, I don't want to go. I love this room."

Over the last five days, I haven't heard her ask for much. The fact that she does now makes it difficult to deny her. But I feel uncomfortable here, out of place. My skin itches, and a chill runs down my spine from being surrounded by these fake angels, despite how cheese ball they appear.

"Yeah, it's pretty cool," I admit. "But the other rooms are more fun."

Her lips pull up to one side as she considers this. I tug on her hand, and when her eyes meet mine, I give a well-practiced wink.

She melts.

"Okay." Charlie pouts, and I have to stop myself from staring at her lips. "Let's go."

We pile into the elevator, and Annabelle reaches across me and pushes the buttons for every floor besides the one we're on.

"Seriously?" I glance at her, and she's clapping her hands. Charlie claps with her.

"We want to see what's on all the different floors," Annabelle says.

"Fine, but our final destination is the basement." I shake my head but smile once I turn to face the elevator doors. I'd want to see this whole place if it was my first time, too.

The elevator opens on the fourth floor, and Charlie and her two friends push me to the back so they can see out. They don't get off, just crane their ostrich necks to get closer looks. The fourth floor is like the fifth, but not quite as over-the-top heaven. Three has a 'seventies dance show vibe with flashing lights and trippy music. People move in a slow haze, and the bartenders are dressed as ghosts.

Charlie shoots a glance in my direction.

"Purgatory," I say.

Her mouth splits into a smile, but then her face contorts. Understanding reaches her eyes. She knows what's coming.

Floor two is noticeably darker. Shades of violet splash across the room, and the music has an ominous ring to it. Annabelle wraps her arms around herself. "Oh, man," she says. "This is going to get creepier, isn't it?"

The elevator has double-sided doors, and the ones behind me open. We're on the ground floor, and people waiting in the lobby glare at us like we're the reason the elevator took an eternity to arrive—which we are.

"We're going down," I say.

A chick dressed in head-to-toe white complains. As the doors reclose, I see her flip us the finger. I want to tell her to reconsider her destination, that she might feel more at home where we're headed.

When the elevator comes to a stop, I can't help stealing a glance at Charlie. She's cowering near the back but standing on her tiptoes to see over Annabelle's shoulder. I can almost smell her excitement. It's mixed with fear and matches my own. Part of me wants to comfort her, to tell her it's just a club and nothing more. But another part, a twisted, deep-rooted part that makes my heart pump harder and my blood rush faster, relishes her anxiety. I want her to be in awe. I want her to feel the emotional rush of terror.

I hunger for her to know this is who I am.

And to accept me anyway.

The doors slide open, and I reach between Blue and Annabelle and grab Charlie's hand.

"Welcome to hell, sweetheart."

30

FIRE DANCING

I pull Charlie after me, and Blue and Annabelle quickly follow. The music is so loud, I feel it in my bones, in my teeth. It's hard-driving with a heavy bass and makes you forget who you are. In other words, it's ecstasy to my ears.

The floor is covered with black tile, and the walls are painted a dark shade of red. Throughout the room, six cylindrical tubes stretch from floor to ceiling. Slits are cut into the steel, and inside, flames lick and thrash. Though the air conditioning is cranked up to compensate, sweat still pricks my skin. The bartenders are dressed like demons, and there are people chained near the floor, dancing in chaotic, hypnotic patterns. I breathe in the rich scent of smoke, and when a waitress walks by, I buy a scarlet drink that steams in my hand.

Charlie leans in close behind me, and I imagine the way she sees this place—as a dark, sinister dungeon she'll never encounter again. If she only knew how bad hell really is. This place, this small room in a trendy club, is a tiny sampling. But it's nothing in comparison. The things I've seen people do in this room, they're not so different from the things I did in life. And in a strange way, though this room puts me on a delicious edge, I want Charlie to witness this. Maybe I'm hoping she'll somehow see through my façade and save herself.

Because I won't do it for her.

I turn and face the crew. Blue seems wary of our surroundings, but Annabelle has already acclimated. She holds a red drink similar to mine, and her smile glows in the flames.

"It's hot as hell down here," she says when she catches my eye, attempting a joke—and failing.

"Lame," I say.

She laughs and grabs Charlie's hand. "Dude, let's freaking get crazy."

Fog drifts near the floor, pulsing from strobe lights, and Annabelle and Charlie quickly disappear inside of it. Blue shoots me a look I can't quite read and follows after them. Before I know it, the three are completely out of sight—blended with the dancing mass that seems more like one single self.

Tables near the back offer solitude from the sex-crazed bodies, and though I'm usually the life of the party, I move toward them. Right now, I need time to strategize.

A waitress comes over and hands me another glass of red goodness. I pay her and toss it back. In a few minutes, I'm going to suggest Charlie and I do something crazy. Maybe yank someone's wallet or get into a fight. Something she'd never do sober or outside this room but will earn her a sin seal all the same.

Charlie has done well by requesting beauty, but this assignment is weighing me down, and the quicker I can bring her soul in, the faster I can return to my normal life.

I let my head fall back, thinking about her soul. How bright it is—how I've never seen one so untainted. She's a good girl. She deserves a long and happy life.

And afterlife.

I shake my head and comb my fingers through my hair. There's nothing I can do. I can't take on the entire Underworld to save her. I'm not even sure why I'm thinking about this. It's pointless.

Across the room, I spot Charlie dancing. Her arms are thrown over her head, and Blue is lifting her by the waist into the air. Seeing him hold her like that, my jaw tightens. He's being reckless. She could fall and get hurt. Or his hand could accidentally brush the soft skin of her stomach. My own stomach clenches. I start to head over to say something but stop when I notice she's laughing. That laugh. I remember it from the first day I met her as we walked to school. I couldn't imagine laughing like that then, and I can't now. A knot twists in my chest. I realize immediately what it is.

Envy.

I take another drink of my red liquor, drowning the thought the best way I know how. When I look again, I don't see Charlie. It drives me crazy to have her out of my sight. Whether it's because she's my assignment or something else, I'm not sure. It's a struggle I've dealt with since that night after Taylor's party.

I pound my fist on the table and push my drink away. I don't need this alcohol tonight. It's messing with my head. There's nothing I can do. Nothing. *Nothing.*

Boss Man's set his sights on her, and if she's the one destroying our seals, then it's for good reason.

Off to my left, something catches my eye. Or rather, *someone* catches my eye. I turn and see who's coming, then freeze.

Her thick red hair falls in loose waves to her shoulders, and her skin is smooth as cream. She smiles when she sees she has my attention, her red-painted lips curling into a tease. And her body. It's enough to turn any guy's head. She looks like a *Playboy* model from the 1950s, with enough curves to give an old man heart failure. And maybe a young man, too.

She sashays toward my table, her hips snapping to the right and left. All I can think is, *Boom-bada-boom-bada-boom!*

"This seat taken?" Her voice is soft as butter. Before I can answer, she lowers herself and crosses her long legs at the knee. Her skintight green blouse dips down, and I have to stop myself from checking out what it exposes. Then I wonder why I'm stopping myself. "I'm Valery."

She reaches into her gold Gucci bag and pulls out cigarettes and—oh, no, she didn't—a quellazaire—one of those long cigarette holders. She inserts her cigarette into the holder and lights up. As she blows a puff of smoke above her head, I ask, "And you're sitting at my table because?"

She smiles in my direction, completely unfazed. "Darling, I'm someone you want at your table. Trust me."

I roll my eyes. I'm not big into people with jumbo self-esteem. I've got enough of that on my own. "Listen, I'm here with someone."

"And now you're here with me." Another puff of smoke wafts above her.

My eyes travel from her sky-high heels up her lose-my-freaking-mind body and land on her soft blue eyes. She's got probably five years on me, and I wonder at the experience she's gained in that time. But I've got to concentrate on my job. I traveled too far to blow this evening. "Any other night, sweetheart, I'd eat you alive. But I've really got—"

Someone bumps into her chair and spills his drink down her back. She arches like a startled cat, and her mouth opens in a perfect red O. The drunkard stumbles off without pausing to check the damage, but another dude rushes in to help. He first tries to clean up the mess with napkins, and when that doesn't work, he pulls the shirt over his head and mops up the liquid soaking through her dress.

Valery grabs the shirt from him and checks the label. "Expensive."

"Not a big deal," the guy says. "Happy to help. You want me to beat that guy's ass?"

"No, thank you," she says with impressive poise. "You've been quite nice. Now run along."

The guy stares at her for a second, mesmerized, then mumbles something about a dance later and starts to walk away, completely unfazed by the fact he's now shirtless in a bar.

Valery pulls up her hellfire-red nails and flicks her hand in his direction. The guy's soul light flips on—and as my mouth drops open—she releases a glittery pink seal.

I jump up from the table and point an accusatory finger at her. "You!"

Valery inspects her nails with obvious disinterest. "Dante Preston Walker, please do sit down."

31

GLITTERY PINK SEALS

"You've been destroying my work," I yell.

"Correct."

"How? I mean, why? No, the first one…how?"

"How indeed."

"Are you going to talk to me or stare at your fake-ass nails all night?"

Her eyes snap on my face. "My nails are not fake. Now can you please sit down before you make a scene?"

I sit slowly, keeping my eyes locked on her as if she might slurp a chameleon tongue out and swallow me down. "Who are you?"

"I already told you, my name's Valery."

"Yeah, I got that much." I lean forward. "How did you do that?"

"Do what?"

"Stop avoiding my questions." I release a frustrated sigh. "How do you have seals?"

Valery lifts her high-heeled feet and *clacks* them on the

table. She delicately pulls up her black pants and exposes a gold cuff, same as mine. As soon as I see it, it's like I can sense her as another collector. I guess I didn't before because I wasn't expecting it. I reach over to touch her cuff.

She slaps my hand away. "Don't ever touch a lady's cuff without permission."

"You're a collector," I breathe.

"Well, of course." Valery brings her heels off the table and recrosses her legs, leaning back in her chair and inspecting the room. She waves her empty hand—the one without the cigarette—toward the people dancing. "Interesting club choice, not that I'm surprised."

"You're new." I state this versus asking. For some reason, I don't want her to know just how clueless I am.

She nods without looking at me. Then her face brightens like an idea just occurred to her. "Hey," she says. "Wanna dance?"

"No, I don't want to freakin' dance. I want you to tell me when you became a collector, and who you replaced, and who the hell trained you, since that's supposed to be my job."

Her face falls, and she lifts a hand to her impossibly red hair. "You bore me."

"Lady—"

"No!" Valery points a slender finger at my chest. "I'm not a *lady*. I'm a woman."

I suppress a laugh, wondering when *lady* became a derogatory term. "Fine. Woman…" Valery smiles and nods. "Just answer my questions. I know you're going to, or you wouldn't have popped up in the middle of my assignment."

"You mean Charlie?"

The hair on the back of my neck rises. Something is beginning to occur to me. No one would've been hired without Max running and telling me. And no Underworld collector would use pink seals. "Valery."

She looks at me.

"Who do you work for?"

Valery takes a long drag on her cigarette and blows the smoke over her shoulder. Then she raises a red fingernail and points straight up.

I shake my head and fall back in my chair. "A damn heaven-sent collector. I thought Big Guy wasn't into using collectors. I thought he was into freedom of choice and all that crap."

A roided-up guy walks by, taking his time to check out Valery's chest. She smiles at him, then turns back to me. "He does. Nothing's changed. And we're called liberators, not collectors. Same job, better boss."

"Fine. Why the hell did he send a collector—er—*liberator*?" I ask through my teeth. "Because if you think you and your damn pink seals are going to botch this assignment for me, you're dead wrong."

"I'm not here to interfere," she says. "I'm just doing my job. Same as you."

"So, what? You just give out seals when people do good things?"

"That's the gist of it."

I bring my hands together in my lap and twist. "And you're not going to mess with Charlie?"

"No." Valery licks her lips. "But if I could, I'd take you down like the rat you are. I don't know why you guys can't play fair; let her go to Judgment Day like everyone else. That girl has a near-perfect soul. She'd live a lovely, honest life if you'd just back the fuck off."

I laugh out loud. "You just cussed. And you obviously smoke.

Aren't you supposed to be saintlike?"

Valery snorts. "Hardly."

I glance to my right to see if I can spot Charlie, but she's nowhere in sight. That won't last forever, though. I've got to get rid of this liberator. "Look, if you're not here to screw things up for me, then why even show yourself?"

"Because you don't know everything about Charlie. I thought I'd try to talk some sense into you."

"Not going to happen." I cross my arms over my chest. So Charlie doesn't have seals that destroy our own. That means there's another reason Boss Man wants her. And I've realized something, I don't want to know. In fact, the less I know, the better. It'll help me keep a clear head during this assignment, and a clear-ish conscience. "Now can you kindly get out of my face and go back to playing liberator?"

Valery presses her lips together. "Fine, I'll go. But remember, I'll be close by. Watching everything you do."

She starts to stand, but I reach out and grab her wrist. "It was you. You've been following me around without showing yourself."

She waves a hand as if to say, *Yeah? So?*

"Must get boring," I taunt. "Standing outside her house, and in the middle of streets, and outside convenience stores."

Confusion passes behind Valery's eyes. Then she smiles so big, it overwhelms her face. "Sounds like I'm not the only one keeping tabs on your performance."

I realize at once it hasn't been her I've sensed. At the same moment, relief and fear wash over me. I'm glad Big Guy isn't watching me as closely as I thought. But then again, that means one of ours still is.

Valery walks to my side of the table and leans close to my ear, her enormous chest grazing my shoulder. "You're so territorial over *your* assignment, and you don't even know where she is... right...now."

I glance up at Valery, then whip my head away to search for Charlie. I don't see her anywhere. This didn't bother me before, but something about the way Valery just spoke says she knows something's up. I get up from the table so quickly that the chair beneath me grinds across the floor.

My legs can't move fast enough to the dance area. I push bodies around, trying to make my way deeper into the crowd in the hopes of finding her. "Charlie," I yell, even though it's pointless. The music is so loud directly over the dancing, there's not a chance of her hearing me.

I spot Annabelle dancing with Blue and shove my way toward them.

"Where's Charlie?" I demand.

Annabelle glances around, then points over her shoulder. "She went that way."

I glance in the direction she's indicating, but I don't spot Charlie. "How long ago?"

Blue glances at his plastic wristwatch—something the stylist really should have addressed. "Ten minutes ago." As he says this, concern sweeps over his face, like he didn't realize how long it'd been. He moves toward where he must have last seen her, but I stop him.

"Just stay here."

I bolt in the direction Annabelle indicated and turn to see Blue on my heels. I roll my eyes and keep moving. A flash of blond near the bar makes me stop. It's the Hair Toss. My question is: who the hell is she doing it for?

I push past people and get within ten feet of her. That's when I see the tall, wiry guy hovering over her with a nasty smile on his face. He's wearing a shiny douchebag shirt, and he's got his douchebag hand on Charlie's hip. She smiles and sways wildly as he hands her a shot glass filled to the brim with black liquid. The guy all but lifts her hand to her mouth.

"Charlie!" I yell.

Too late.

Down the black liquid goes.

32

I SEE YOU

I cross the distance between us and knock the laughing guy's hand off her hip. Then I grab the empty shot glass out of Charlie's grasp. "What do you think you're doing?" I ask her.

"I'm not doin' nuffin," she slurs.

I turn and face the guy next to her. "Why are you feeding her shots? She's obviously wasted."

The guy takes a small backward step, but his buddies push him toward me. He glances at them, remembers they're watching, and glares at me with renewed confidence. "What's it to you? You her boyfriend or something?"

Behind me, Blue shouts at Charlie. "How much have you had to drink?"

Charlie mumbles something about Arnold Schwarzenegger.

"You were only gone ten minutes," Blue adds.

The guy in front of me shoves my shoulder. "Did you hear me? I said, what's it—"

"I heard what you said. All you need to worry about is getting the hell away from this girl." I jab a thumb over my shoulder.

"Yeah," Blue chimes in, standing slightly behind me. "Get the hell out of here."

The guy raises his hands. "You guys are getting loud about nothing. And you obviously have some kind of threesome going on here, so I'll just let you get on with that." He starts to walk away, but he can't help adding. "Girl's ugly, anyway."

I reach out to grab the guy, but before I can, he hits the ground. Blue stands over him, face flickering in shadows from the nearby fire. My mouth opens in a gasp. Blue weighs, like, twenty-seven pounds, but he apparently knows how to toss every bit of it around when he's pissed.

I grab Charlie's arm and pull her back as Blue leans over and grabs the guy's shirt. He rips it upward so that their faces are inches apart. Then Blue says something quietly. The guy's eyes widen, and he backs away on the floor until he can stand up. Blue flicks a hand like he's releasing him, and the guy scrambles off with his friends.

Blue. Is. A badass.

Even though I itched to down the D-bag myself, watching Blue, I feel like a proud parent on graduation day.

I put a hand on his shoulder and try to shake him out of his maniacal stare. He brushes it off, stops to inspect Charlie, ensuring she's okay, then storms onto the dance floor. I'm not sure what's gotten into him, but I know I like it.

My attention falls on Charlie. She's hardly able to stand and is giving me a lazy grin. I should be happy that she's wasted. I know it'll impair her judgment and make her do things she wouldn't otherwise. But all I can think about is getting her back to the hotel where she'll be safe. This was a terrible idea. Coming to Vegas got her to request more beauty, but we should have just stayed at the hotel and hung out there. I need to stick with fulfilling the contract versus trying to get her to sin the traditional way. This—things like tonight—they're too risky.

Why are they risky? Your goal is to get her in trouble. Not save her from it.

I shake the thought away and drag Charlie to the other side of the room. I don't know why; I just feel like I need to have her alone right now. To see if she's okay even though I'm not supposed to care.

And I don't care.

Or do I?

I push Charlie into a dark corner and glance over my shoulder to see if anyone's watching. Then I bring my face close to hers and just breathe. Her breath mingles with mine, and I smell a hint of cinnamon. Those shots must have burned going down.

I raise my hands and wrap them around her cheeks. Her face is warm in my palms. She closes her blue eyes and smiles.

"Charlie," I say, my head dropping. I press my mouth to the top of her head. Not in a kiss, just to rest it there, though once my mouth and nose are near her blond hair, I can't help but inhale the scent of her shampoo. I squeeze my eyes shut and whisper, "Why are you doing this?"

"Mmm?"

I roll my head to the side and lay my cheek on the crown of her head. "Why, Charlie? Why can't you stay the same?"

She doesn't answer, and I suddenly know what I'm really asking: why couldn't *I* stay the same? I was born an innocent child. When did everything change? What made me into the person I was when I died? Was it just one mistake after another? One wrong decision chased by something worse?

Maybe I was destined to be a self-absorbed screwup.

Maybe I was born a monster.

Below me, my polar opposite stirs. She glances up, and I notice her black mascara has smudged beneath her eyes. I run my thumbs under her drooping lids, but it only makes matters worse.

"Charlie." I speak to myself, hoping at this point she's too far gone to comprehend what I'm saying—what I'm feeling. "Stay."

She only smiles and curls into my chest. She becomes heavier in my arms, as if she's falling asleep upright. Holding her, I don't feel like her destroyer. I feel like a protector. But that's not true, is it? I'm not the person she thinks I am. I'm not like her. I'm not good.

But Charlie—she is. Why else would she make her life's goal to help others when she's had such crap luck? And why else would Big Guy break his own rules and send Valery to keep watch?

"Dante," Charlie says below me. There's a sound of surprise in her voice, like she forgot where we are.

"I'm here."

I pull her closer to my chest, and she raises her head.

"Don't leave me, okay?" she says.

I hold her eyes with mine, but I don't speak. I can't.

"I'm going to tell you something, Dante." Charlie's words are still slurred, but there's an urgency to them now. Like whatever she has to say must be said now or forever lost. She raises her hands and places them on either side of my face. My skin burns beneath her touch. "I think you're beautiful."

I smile, thinking she's done. But she releases my face and places her palms on my chest, directly over my heart.

"You're beautiful right here," she says.

I close my eyes, and the breath rushes from my lungs.

"I see the good in you, Dante," Charlie continues, her words rolling together off her tongue. "Even if you don't, I do. You have a good heart. You know how I know?"

I open my eyes. She's looking at me like nothing else in the world exists. Like the entire planet and all of mankind just vanished. She slowly wraps my hands inside her own as best she can and places them on her chest. "Because I feel it here." She taps our hands against her chest. "I know you're good, Dante. Because I feel it inside of me."

I throw my arms around her and push her head against my chest. My lungs won't function. My mouth can't respond.

But the tears.

They come.

My eyes sting for the first time since my father died, and a tear trails down my cheek and drops into her hair. Her words rush up and down my body. It's the thing I've wanted to hear for the last two years, since I became a walking nightmare. It's also the thing I've never allowed myself to believe. I want to be good. But how can I be when everything I do, everything I now stand for, says otherwise? Second chances—they were never for me. But Charlie, she just gave me one. She just saw something in me.

And maybe I can be the thing she sees.

33

LIPS

"Let's get you back to the hotel." I do a quick rub of my eyes the way guys do. She can't see me like this, can't know she has an effect on me. It's something I wish I could un-know myself.

Charlie nods against my chest, so I take her hand and lead the way. We head toward the dance floor, and I realize I'm holding her against my back tighter than I need to. I glance over my shoulder a few times to make sure she's doing okay, and she smiles.

My heart pounds.

After a couple of minutes, we stumble across Annabelle dancing with someone twice her age. I drag her away, and she's none too happy about it. Nor is the guy, but I don't have the energy to deal with his ass.

"Where's Blue?" I ask Annabelle.

She shrugs and sticks out her bottom lip like I'm her freaking dad and I just grounded her. I look closely at her eyes. They're red and rolling around without connecting on any one thing.

I groan and take her hand in my empty one. "I swear, I take you girls to have a little fun—" Read: get into trouble. "—and all you do is drink your body weight in liquor and hang out with jerks."

Annabelle covers her mouth and giggles like a lunatic.

"Yeah, it's hilarious," I say.

We push through the bodies until I see Blue. There are even more people where he's dancing, enough to make it difficult for the three of us to get to him. I turn to face the girls. "Don't. Move."

Annabelle wraps her arms around a swaying Charlie. She nods with a serious face, then bursts out laughing.

I roll my eyes and head after Blue. When I get closer, I have to bite my knuckles to keep from screaming. Blue is grinding against a girl so hard, I half-expect to see clothing lying at their feet. This, however, is not what pisses me off.

People complain as I shove them out of the way and pull Valery off Blue. "Go mess with someone else, Red."

"Dude," Blue drawls.

I turn and face him and his drunken stumbling. "Seriously, Blue? You were sober, like, fifteen minutes ago."

"It kinda hit me," he says, laughing. Then he tries to move past me to get to Valery, who's busy readjusting her top.

"Red, get lost," I say. "Blue, come with me."

Blue's half-closed eyes open wide. "I thought that's what you said." He points at Valery. "You're Red…and I'm Blue. We're both on the color wheel." He roars with laughter.

"Okay, that's great." I grab his shoulders and manage to push him toward Annabelle and Charlie despite him dragging his feet and screaming for his beloved Red.

Outside the club, I hail a cab and manage to get the three drunks inside. They sit shoulder to shoulder in the backseat, and I take shotgun. As we're riding back to V Hotel, they talk over one another and fall silent in cycles.

"Charlie, Charlie," Blue slurs. "I'm sorry I pushed that guy. You know it's only because I care. It's because—"

Annabelle leans forward in her seat. "What about me? Would you do that for me? You don't care about me. You don't even care."

"I care about you," Charlie says, her eyes completely closed.

"I care about you, Annabelle," Blue shouts. "I do. You don't even know. It would blow your mind." He mimics something exploding out of his head, and Annabelle falls over his lap laughing.

"Dante," Blue says, like he has a brilliant idea, "let's get some French fries. Do they have French fries here?"

"French fries!" Charlie punches her arm in the air and hits the roof of the cab.

The cabbie glances at me with utter defeat, like he's seen this a million times and has finally accepted his fate.

"Everyone. Quiet," I say.

Annabelle covers her mouth to keep from laughing, then lays her head on Blue's shoulder. He in turn lays his head against the window, and Charlie lays her head on Annabelle's shoulder. They look like fallen dominoes. Or fallen soldiers. Or maybe just drunk asses. In tandem, they close their eyes and pass out.

We ride in silence for six merciful minutes before Charlie wakes up. "Where are we?"

I turn around in my seat and put a finger to my lips, but it's too late. Annabelle lifts her head. "Oh, my God. The lights are so pretty."

"I think they're ugly," Blue says without even opening his eyes.

Annabelle's face scrunches up like she's going to cry, and Charlie pulls her into a hug.

I take a deep breath and glance at the cabbie. "I'll pay you double if you can get us there in two minutes."

He nods and steps on the gas. I'm sure he wants us out of his cab every bit as much as I do. Two minutes later on the dot, we pull up to V Hotel. Blue and Annabelle sing at the tops of their lungs during the entire elevator ride and all the way down the hall to their rooms. Other hotel guests stick their heads into the hallway and wave their fists, though I have no idea why. This is Las Vegas, for crying out loud. So I do the gracious thing—I give them two stiff middle fingers. My humble gift on this glorious night.

After I've told Annabelle and Blue for the hundredth time that we are not, in fact, going to after-party in the casino and get them safely inside their rooms, I turn my attention to Charlie. She leans against the wall and tilts her head against a black-framed mirror.

"I'm tired," she says. "I don't want to after-party."

I bite my bottom lip to keep from laughing and walk toward her. "I know you don't, hon. Let's get you to bed."

She nods so that her neck seems to be made of jelly instead of skin and bones. I wrap an arm around her waist and hold her up as I unlock her door. As soon as it slides open, she races inside and jumps face-first onto the bed. Her head hits a pile of pillows with a *fwump.*

"Feels. So. Good," she says into the pillows, her voice muffled.

I cross the room and pull off her high heels. Then I walk to the side of the bed and remove her earrings, careful not to hurt her. This is the first time I've undressed a girl without expecting Nasty Time in return.

"Charlie," I say, "you need to roll over."

"Why?" Her face is still smashed into the pillows, and I can hardly understand her.

"Because you're going to pass out and suffocate." I push my hands beneath her and cradle her with my arms. For just a moment, I hold her there against me, her head resting against my chest. Charlie moans, and I lay her down on her back. She curls into a ball on her side. I grab the fluffy white blanket from the foot of the bed and pull it over her. Then I grab a glass of water from the bathroom and place it on the nightstand where she can reach it.

And then I stare at her.

Like a total creeper, I just stand there and stare at her.

Her breathing has already slowed, and every few seconds her mouth works like she's talking in her dreams. Knowing Charlie, she probably is. And there's no way the person she's talking to is getting a word in edgewise.

A lock of Charlie's hair falls over her face, and I move to push it back. When my hand brushes her newly smooth cheek, her eyes snap open. She wraps her fingers around my wrist, and her big blues stay locked on my face.

"Dante?" She says my name so quietly, I almost don't recognize it.

I sit on the edge of the bed and wait for her to finish.

Her mouth parts, but her eyes squeeze shut. "You can kiss me if you want."

Every muscle in my body tightens. I'm stunned into silence. I can't believe what she just said, but maybe I should. It's not like she's pushed me away these last few days, and she told me in the club that she thinks I have a *good heart*. But somehow it still feels surreal. I should have seen the signs. I should have known this was coming. Charlie's eyes stay shut, and I'm not sure whether she's fallen asleep or waiting for me to answer.

Or waiting for me to kiss her.

I study her mouth, her best feature. It's full and pink, and

I wonder for the briefest of moments what it would feel like to press my lips to hers. But I can't do it. I *won't* do it. She's drunk, and she's my assignment…and she'll forget all about this in the morning. Still, I wonder. What if I didn't work for the Underworld? What if I was just a guy, and she was just a girl I met in Peachville, Alabama?

I push a breath out through my nose and press my lips to her forehead. Below me, Charlie makes a small sound, but I can't tell if it stems from sleep or something else.

"Good night, sweet girl."

I rise from the bed and move toward the door. Near the entryway, I stop and stare at her. She looks peaceful wrapped in that white blanket, her breath coming smooth and slow. I push my tongue into my cheek, then switch off the light and move through the door.

And right away, across the hall, I see her waiting outside my room.

Valery.

34

TRELVATOR

"What do you want, Red?" I ask impatiently.

"What were you doing in there?" Valery's face is tight, like she's imagining the worst.

"If you were so worried about it, why didn't you knock?" I shoot back.

She puts a hand on her round hip. "Are we going to ask each other questions all night?"

"I don't know, are we?" I slide my plastic key into the slot, and my door clicks open. "By all means, please come in and make the remainder of my night unbearable. It's not like I need sleep or anything."

Valery sashays by me and into the room. "Such a smartass." Once inside, she lights a cigarette and blows the smoke out in small rings above her head.

I slide the balcony door open, and Valery sits down on the red leather loveseat.

"Those cigarettes look magically delicious. Care to share?"

She digs around in her purse for the pack and tosses them in my direction. I pull one out and motion for the lighter. She tosses that, too.

"So let's get this rollin'. What's your dealio, Fire Crotch?" I light my cigarette and drop down on the bed, crossing my red sneakers at the ankle. "You've obviously got something on your chest besides cheap silicone."

Valery subconsciously covers her boobs. "My girls are not fake."

"Yeah, you'd never do that. Then guys would fawn all over you."

She straightens. "I don't *need* male attention."

"Please. The worst thing that happened when you died was leaving your three boyfriends behind."

Fire burns so bright behind her eyes, my blood suddenly runs cold. Every muscle in her body is rigid, and her jaw is clenched so tight, I'm afraid she might bite off her own tongue.

"Dante Walker, there is one thing we will never talk about again, and it's this—my relationship when I was alive. But I will tell you this now: I loved my fiancé with a ferocity I dare you to challenge."

"Whatever you say." I try to play it off, but make a mental note not to discuss the fiancé again, lest she strangle me while I sleep. I take a drag of my cigarette and stare down the length of my body at her. She's glaring at me, so I shoot her my best eat-shit grin.

"You're a pig." Valery scrunches up her nose and makes grunting pig noises. Everything about her is perfect and polished, and I can't help laughing at how I've already gotten under her skin. Good. After causing my collection numbers to slip, she deserves it. Still, it's late, and I'm ready to hit the sack. And I'll admit I'm beyond curious as to why she's here, on earth, watching Charlie.

"Enough," I say. "This grows tiresome. Start talking."

Valery hunts for a place to flick her cigarette ash, then opts for the floor. Nice.

"I've come to watch Charlie," she says. "You know that. What you don't know is why."

"No. You can stop right there." I sit up on the bed. "I don't want to know. I have a job to do, Red, and I intend on finishing it. It has nothing to do with whether I want to or not. It's her ass or mine. And guess what? I choose mine. So telling me what I'm destroying in the process won't slow things down, *comprende*?"

Valery smiles. "Sounds like you're getting a bit of a conscience."

I throw my hands up in the air. "Yeah, that's the exact opposite of what I just said. I. Don't. Care."

"Which is why you treat her like she's made of glass and attack anyone who tries to break her."

I think about what she just said and realize she must have seen me beat that guy's ass and threaten Taylor at Centennial High. My tongue runs over my teeth. *Careful what you say. Remember which side you're on—the side no one walks away from.*

Valery crosses and uncrosses her legs, waiting for me to answer. "I've got all night."

I swallow, then smile like I'm about to let her in on a wonderful secret. "You know why I'm the best collector? Because I know how to play the game. I play to win. Understand? I do whatever it takes." I lean forward. "And I do mean *whatever*." Then I laugh like it's the most hilarious thing I've ever said, because I know it'll help drive home what I'm going for—which is a big, fat lie.

Valery stares at me, trying to decide if I'm telling the truth. "You're not that good, Dante."

"Aren't I?"

She takes a long drag and flicks the cigarette out onto the

balcony. From where she's sitting, it's actually pretty impressive. "You think you know that girl?" Her eyes narrow into slits. "You know nothing. You have no idea what she's capable of, do you?"

"I just got done telling you I don't—"

"But you do, Dante. You care. I see it in the way you look at her. You're no actor. You're just some washed-up collector who's terrified of pissing off his boss. So you're doing what you know how to do, looking out for number one. Because it all comes down to your promotion, doesn't it? Getting a ticket out of hell?"

My jaw snaps together, the clicking sound giving me away.

Valery shakes her head. "Even Lucifer's best man doesn't want anything to do with him. And why would you? Who would want anything to do with that place?" She frowns. "I just hope it's bad enough to warrant what you're sacrificing."

"You. Know. Nothing." My words march out like tin soldiers. "You have no idea what it's like down there."

"No, I don't," she agrees. "And you don't know what you're destroying by completing this assignment."

I want to prove to Valery that I don't care. It doesn't matter what Charlie is or isn't, because I will always choose life outside of hell. But there's also a part of me that wants to know who Charlie is and what she's capable of. Because, truth be told, I want to know her. I don't want the guilt of what this knowledge might bring, but I want to know her to the core. So I meet Valery's eye and wait for her to tell me. I won't ask for this information, but I know she'll volunteer it if I remain silent. And so I do.

Valery lifts herself from the loveseat and crosses the room, gazing out the open balcony door. "Charlie is special."

"I gathered that much."

She shoots me a look that says she's within an inch of physically attacking me. As funny as it'd be to watch her try, I shut up and let her finish.

"Her birth wasn't an accident. It was planned. Not in the way two people get married, buy a house, and plan to have a baby. Her birth was ordained by..." She stops and points upward. Apparently Big Guy has become the new Voldemort, He-Who-Must-Not-Be-Named.

Valery turns back to the cool Las Vegas night. "Charlie will change people's lives, Dante. She'll change the way they think about themselves, how they think about their neighbors. She will be...a tool in his plan."

"A tool?" I stand up from the bed. "As in, if we don't get her, then he will? And then he'll use her like a pawn to do his bidding? No. That's not going to happen. At least my way, I'll have freedom, and she'll have the rest of her life to herself."

Valery whips around and crosses the room in a breath. Her words snap from her mouth. "You idiot! You ignorant, selfish prick. Don't you understand? It's already done. Seventeen years ago, her birth fulfilled His commandment." She puts a hand on the center of my chest, and a warm sensation floods from the spot. "Three years ago, Charlie started an organization. That organization will continue to grow and flourish, and in time, it will change the face of humankind. It will remind people how to love another. It will show them how to care again."

"Her volunteer thing?" I say with disbelief. "That's what this is all about? If so, then you're wrong. I've seen it. It's a few bored people trading favors. It's nothing."

"It is *everything*. It is the beginning of the end."

"The end of what?"

"Of hate. Of jealousy. Of selfishness. Her work, her life—it will end an era of hate, and usher in Trelvator."

I push her hand off my chest. "You're making up words now."

"*Trelvator* means an era of peace, lasting a hundred years."

"You're freaking nuts, chick. Like, true psych ward material," I say. "There's no way mankind could be peaceful for two weeks, let alone a hundred years."

Valery ignores me. "Her work will touch enough people to create a phenomenon. It will feel like…Christmas, a day when people are nicer and more generous. Except that day will be a year, and that year a century."

"Something will happen. A war will start, a political fight will erupt. Something."

"Things will happen, but they won't be damaging enough to end Trelvator. Not for a hun—"

"A hundred years. Right." I sit back down on the bed and rub my hand along my jaw. If it's possible that Charlie will usher in an era of peace, isn't that all the more reason for me to stay on earth? Why would I choose hell over rainbows and cotton candy? I glance at Valery. "Why does this have to do with her soul? If I collect her soul, she'll go on living. She can still change the world and all that."

Valery turns away, but I can still see her chewing her lip.

"Oh, snap! You don't know," I say. "O Wise One doesn't have a clue what her soul has to do with any of this."

She moves to the loveseat, picks up her bag, and pulls it onto the crook of her arm. Then she faces me. "You're right. We don't know what Big Guy wants with her soul. But here's what I do know. Something big is going down. Something larger than you and me and all the other collectors and liberators. Charlie was born to help bring peace to this world, and your boss is trying to destroy that. So remember that when you're choosing sides, Dante. Remember that this isn't just about you and her. It's about the fate of mankind for the next hundred years."

Valery heads toward the door, and my stomach twists until I can hardly move.

"I don't have a choice, Red." My voice sounds serious, even to me. "Who I report to…it doesn't work that way."

She stops but doesn't turn. "Something's coming, Dante. And you better be sure you choose the right side."

Then she moves away, and even though I'm expecting it, I jump when the door slams shut.

CHOICES

"Hell is empty and all the devils are here."

—William Shakespeare

35

RETURN

I lie in bed and do everything but sleep. What Valery said replays in my mind like a spinning movie reel. Charlie will change the world. Charlie. The girl sleeping only a few doors down, wrapped in a white comforter, probably snoring, probably drooling on her pillow. And she's going to change the world.

My penny clenched in my fist, I get up from bed and pace the floor. Then I turn on the TV and flip channels, searching for normalcy. Nothing's on, and nothing helps.

Charlie shouldn't be the one in this position. She shouldn't be the girl in the middle of a heaven versus hell tug-of-war. But she is. And like Valery said, I need to make a decision.

And I have to be sure I make the right one.

In order to do that, there are things I have to take care of. I cross the room and pick up the cream-colored phone near my bed. It rings twice before someone picks up on the other end.

"Concierge. How may I assist you, Mr. Walker?"

"I need to make changes to my airline tickets," I say into the phone.

"Certainly. I'll have someone come up for the tickets and take your change requests. Would that be all right?"

I lean my head on a fist. "Yeah. That'll work. How long?"

"We should have someone up there in ten minutes."

"Perfect. Thanks."

I hang up the phone and continue my über-helpful pacing. Then I make my bed. Two minutes later, I unmake it. When the hotel staffer knocks on the door, I'm waiting less than six inches away. My muscles jerk at the sound. Then I reach over to let the staffer in. A guy four hundred and eighty years old stands on the other side.

Great. They sent an endangered species to make my airline changes.

"You know, I think I've changed my mind. I'm going to stick around," I say. There's no way I trust a guy who probably forgot his own name on the elevator ride up. If he handles this, we'll end up flying coach to Saudi Arabia. "So, uh, you can go back now."

The guy stares at me with purple-rimmed eyes. His liver spots blend together on his forehead, and I imagine hidden messages spelled out in the patterns. "Is it because I'm old?" he says in a surprisingly high voice.

"What?" I ask, feigning shock. "I don't even know what you're talking about. What time is it? I need to go to bed. Good night."

I move to close the door, but he stops it with his old man foot. "Everyone sends me away. No one wants their bags carried. No one needs their bathroom light checked. And you…" He points at me with a finger I'm sure will break off. "Now you don't want your airline changes."

Geezer starts to shuffle away down the hallway.

I let out a sigh and roll my eyes. "Hey, wait," I say. "I've decided to go home. So I guess I will need your help."

The man turns around, but now he's working the sad eyes. "It's because of what I said. You feel sorry for me."

"No, it's because you freak me out, and I want to be as many miles away from you as I can." His lips tug upward, and he proudly displays the few teeth he has left. I have a sudden urge to give him an apple. "So you going to help me?"

"Yeah," he says. "I'm going to help you."

The guy takes my airline tickets and writes down my changes with impressive accuracy. Then he leaves. A half hour later, he calls up to confirm the changes have been made. I have no idea why a place like V Hotel gave this guy a chance, but I guess they knew what they were doing.

"Can you call me a cab?" I ask. I haven't had a problem finding one yet, but considering it's three in the morning, things may be different.

"Right away, Mr. Walker."

"Dante," I say. "It's Dante."

I hang up and walk across the hall. Inside, Charlie and her friends are in Never Never Land, but it's time to wake them up and pray they're sober. I knock on each of their doors, since they're only a few feet apart.

Blue pops his head out first. "Was that you?" he asks.

"Yeah."

"What the hell are you doing out here?"

"Waking you guys up."

He rubs his face for several seconds, then makes a movement like he's going to close the door. "Just give me a few more minutes," he mumbles. He's disoriented from sleep and liquor, and it'd be funny under different circumstances.

"No. Blue, you gotta wake up. We have a plane to catch."

He pushes the door all the way back open. "You messing with

me?"

On the other side of the hall, I hear another door click open. It's Annabelle.

"What the bejesus is going on out here?" she asks.

"Dante says we're going home," Blue answers.

Annabelle finger-combs her dark, tangled hair. "Right now?"

"Yeah, right now." I head toward Charlie's door. "You two get dressed, okay? I'm going to wake up Sleeping Beauty. Oh, and you can keep the clothes and stuff from last night."

Annabelle squeals, and Blue's door slams shut.

I knock again on Charlie's door and wait. When she opens up, I get an incredible urge to pull her toward me. Her hair falls in bed-tossed waves, and her skin still glows. When she sees it's me, she smiles. And I think to myself that she's the only person who I can wake at three in the morning and still have smiled at me. But as soon as the smile appears, it's gone—and I wonder why it died so young.

It's not strange seeing her now, even knowing the things I know. I thought maybe it would be, but it's not. To me, she's still just Charlie—lover of Skittles and bed bouncing and scandalous raccoons.

"Hey," I say quietly. "It's time to catch our flight home."

She puts a hand on my chest like she can't help touching me. Then she yanks it away and retreats into the black blanket of her room.

Does she remember what she asked from me? Does she know?

I follow her into the room and turn on the nightstand lamp. Charlie looks around like she's not sure what to do.

"You didn't bring anything other than your backpack, right?" I ask.

She nods, and I'm wondering why she's not speaking aloud. It makes my neck feel stiff, and I have to rub it to loosen the muscles.

"Then…are you ready?"

Charlie makes eye contact with me but only holds it for a moment. Then she moves away and heads into the bathroom. "Just give me a minute, and I'll come out in the hallway."

She just straight up dismissed my ass, which means…

She remembers.

I let myself out into the hallway and find Annabelle waiting outside her closed door. She looks like she got run over by a semi and probably feels close to the same.

"You got your bag?" I ask.

She turns to show it mounted on her back. Then she says, "What's Charlie doing?"

Hating my guts for something I did even though it was, like, the first good thing I've ever done.

"She's getting her stuff together," I say. "She'll be out in a sec." My mind snaps back to Charlie, wondering what she's thinking and how long she's going to hide in her room. But the sound of Blue scooting into the hallway steals my attention.

"Where's Charlie?" he asks.

Annabelle and I point to her closed door.

Blue's curls are poofing out in an afro. He rubs his hands over them, trying to wrangle them into place. "Why are we leaving in the middle of the night? I thought you gave us notes for classes so we could ditch and, you know, sleep."

"Change of plans. If we leave now, you can make it back by second period," I answer as Charlie's door creaks open.

She glances at me, but her eyes pull away and land on her friends. On the people she understands. "Sorry. Didn't know I was holding everyone up. I was just getting my stuff together."

"No, it's fine," I say quickly, wondering why I needed to say anything at all. I move toward her and try to take her lime-green backpack off her shoulders. She tugs it back.

"I've got it," she says.

I bite my upper lip and head toward the elevator without another word. We ride down in silence, and it feels like every other time I've left Las Vegas—with the weight of shame and guilt hitched on my back.

Old Man greets me in the lobby. "Mr. Walker—er, Dante—your cab is waiting for you and your party." He waves an arm toward the sliding glass doors.

"Thanks for your help," I say. "Never again will I doubt the power of senior citizens."

He gives me a gummy smile, and I stuff a wad of bills into his hand. He opens his palm and stares at it for an uncomfortably long time, then glances up at me, his eyes watering.

"Get yourself a classy bag of prunes." I slap him on the shoulder and head out the doors.

For the next twenty minutes, Blue and Annabelle talk about last night as if it happened three years ago versus three hours. From the things they're saying, I'm pretty sure they're still drunk. The twosome try to involve Charlie in their conversation, but she doesn't add much. When they realize she's upset, her friends grow quiet.

Then they stare at me with suspicion.

When we pull up outside the airport, I pay the cabbie, and the four of us walk up to the check-in counter. The attendant plasters on a fake smile when it's my turn.

"Where you headed today?" she asks.

"Birmingham, Alabama." I jab my thumb over my shoulder. "I'm checking these guys in."

I motion for Blue, Annabelle, and Charlie to give me their

IDs. I hand them to the attendant, who *click-clacks* on the keyboard, managing to display every last tooth in her mouth.

Charlie brushes my arm, and I glance at her. I push her stray hair behind her ear, then snatch my hand back. This compulsion to touch her is getting out of control. I'm like a three-year-old who can't keep his hands to himself.

"What about you?" she says in a near whisper. "Aren't you coming?" Her eyes flood with worry as she wraps an arm across her stomach and holds onto her elbow.

"Charlie," I start.

"It's fine," she says, cutting me off. It's like she's already imagined the worst. "You don't have to go back with us."

Behind her, Blue grabs her belt and tugs her backward. It's terrible timing, and though I like the kid okay, right now I'd like to bust his lip and break his leg. I glare at him, but he keeps his hand rested on her.

When I speak again, my words come out in a growl. My eyes stay on Blue, though I'm clearly speaking to Charlie. "I've got some stuff to take care of. But trust me, I'll be back."

"Whatever," Charlie says. "It doesn't matter."

My gaze snaps from Blue to Charlie, and—slap me freakin' stupid—my heart aches. Actually *aches* at what she just said.

I swallow my pride and try to think rationally. There's no doubt about it, she's definitely upset with something I did. Whether it's from pushing her into a contract, convincing her she needs more beauty, or turning down her offer last night—I'm not sure. But the fact that there's a list to choose from is concerning. As terrible as this is, I'm somewhat thrilled she's upset. It shows she cares, right? But it also means she's pulling away, which is better for her than she'll ever realize. For me, though, it hurts something awful.

Annabelle takes Charlie's bag from her as a sign of affection, and in turn, Charlie wraps her arm around her friend's waist. Blue never lets go of her, either, and together the three of them stare me down. Her friends don't know what I did wrong. They just know Charlie's pissed, so they're pissed by association.

For the second time this morning, my heart throbs.

I'd kill to have friends like that.

"Look," I say, handing them their boarding passes. "You guys are at gate twelve." I pretend to speak to the group, but now I'm looking right at Charlie. "I'll be right behind you. I'll be back before you know it." I glance at Annabelle and Blue, then back at her. My stomach clenches, and I say, "I promise."

Charlie breaths out a heavy sigh and shrugs. Like I don't even matter. Like between me and a dead horse, she'd grab a glue gun.

Blue leads her toward the security gate, and Charlie doesn't glance back, even though I stand and watch her so long that people behind me talk smack. But Annabelle—*mad love for ya, girl*—she does turn around. She throws me a small wave and an *I feel kinda bad for you* look. I smile so hard, I think my face may break. Beside me, I hear the airline attendant beating the table with her palm.

I turn toward her.

She breathes out for a full ten seconds and rolls her eyes so many times I assume she's having a seizure. I contemplate calling for help, then decide to let it play out.

"Sir, puh-leeze. For the third time, there are people waiting behind you." She pauses and glares at me, waiting for my reaction.

I give her nothing.

She leans toward me. "Did you need to check yourself in?"

I nod and hand her my ID.

She snatches it away, narrows her eyes, and types my

information into the computer. Then she glances up. "Chicago?"

The second she says it aloud, a chill races down my spine. What am I doing? What the *hell* am I doing?

Again, I nod.

I'm deaf. I'm mute. I'm losing my mind.

The attendant finishes checking me in and hands me my ID and boarding pass. "Gate seven," she says.

I push the pass into my back pocket, bite down, and head toward gate seven, where I'll board my plane.

Fly across the nation.

Land in Chicago.

Take a cab to 344 Rosemarie Street.

And for the first time in two years, finally face my mother.

36

CHICAGO

During the plane ride to Chicago, I can't stop thinking about the way Charlie looked at me in the airport. She must think I'm avoiding her after the snubbed kiss incident. But nothing could be further from the truth. Already, I hate being away from her. Somehow, somewhere along the way, I changed.

The world had always been mine for the taking. Nothing mattered but me and my wants. My father never had enough time for me, and my mom never bothered. I thought this granted me the perfect excuse to do whatever I wanted. And then when I died, I had a choice: be stuck in hell 24/7, or become a collector and drag others down with me. I chose the latter, because that's what I do. I choose me. I choose the ease of sin over hardship.

But now there's Charlie. After her parents died and she was tossed into foster care, she had every reason to become spiteful and sinful…just like me. But instead, she turned disaster into benevolence.

Charlie gives me something to aspire to, and she sees something in me I never have. And for the first time in my life, I wonder if I can be that person—the one who cares about people outside of themselves, the one who picks the right and honorable path.

Valery is right.

I have a choice to make.

Flying over Lake Michigan, I glance down. Chicago buildings rise from the earth like gray, jagged teeth. Between those teeth, tucked into a brownstone, is my mother. She is the reason for this trip, the only way I can choose and be certain of the decision I'll make. If I'm even *thinking* about going against Boss Man's orders—I have to know the stakes.

I need to see exactly what I'll be giving up. As the plane touches down at O'Hare Airport, my hands find my knees and squeeze. The woman next to me glances over.

"You okay, kid?" she asks.

The *kid* part startles me. I haven't been anyone's kid in two years. But as I look outside and spot the runway fast approaching, I realize I've never stopped being my mother's son, no matter how much I try to pretend otherwise. I release my knees and stare ahead. "No, I'm not all right."

The lady reaches a tentative hand out like she's thinking about patting my shoulder, but the seatbelt sign *dings* off, and I shoot up.

"I'll be fine," I tell her, though I'm not sure why I bother. I'll never see her again.

The sun is rising as I make my way outside and hail a cab. I lower my arm as a maroon van pulls toward me and stops. Sliding inside, I pull on the Cubs baseball hat I bought in the airport gift shop. I haven't been home in a while, but I still remember where my loyalties lie.

A guy with a beard that reaches his belly button watches me

in the rearview mirror. "Where you headed?" he asks in a deep, scratchy voice.

I swallow so hard I think I might lose my tongue. "344 Rosemarie."

The cabbie punches the address into his GPS, which I think is cheating the system. As a cab driver, his job is to know the city's every nook and cranny. Isn't that supposed to be some kind of cabbie pride thing? I decide it should be.

As we get closer to my mother's house, my chest tightens. I have to keep reminding myself to relax so I can breathe. A pain throbs in my hand, and I glance down. Without even realizing, I'd pulled out my penny and had been squeezing the life out of it.

I flip the coin between my fingers and watch Mr. Lincoln change into Mr. Lincoln Memorial. My eyes close, and I wonder what it would take to get my own memorial. I think ole Abe had something to do with freeing slaves after generations of imprisonment and single-handedly holding the country together during the Civil War—which I could totally top.

I hear a crazy banging sound, and my eyes snap open. Bearded Man stares at me, his nostrils flaring with annoyance. He's obviously just knocked on the plastic slidey thing between us. Pretty sure a *hey, man* would have sufficed.

I point to his nappy beard. "You keep things in there?"

He doesn't respond.

"Like candies or baby birds?"

His jaw tightens.

"You should think about it." I dig my wallet out and pay the dude. Then I turn and look at what I've been avoiding—home. My heart skips a beat. I draw in a quick breath to kick-start it, then open the cab door and step out onto the sidewalk. Behind me, the cabbie speeds away to find his next customer—where he'll use his navigator to rob them of an authentic cab experience.

I watch the maroon van turn down a side street, then stare up at the brownstone in front of me. It's three stories tall, with a small balcony on the top floor and brick stairs climbing toward the first floor. A ceramic pumpkin is seated near the last step. The entire house is covered in creamy white stone and is sandwiched between two others. Although this row of brownstones was built in the early 1900s, they've had enough plastic surgery to match the big baller owners inside.

I realize I'm standing in plain sight, where my mother could easily spot me. Turning tail, I haul ass across the street and find a bench several yards down, hidden behind parked cars. Then I glance around, and when I'm sure no one's watching, I let my shadow swallow me.

Hours go by, and I struggle not to fall asleep. I've been watching her door all morning, half wondering what the hell I'm doing here. It feels like I've flown halfway across the country to stalk my own mother. I guess I'm hoping when I see her, it'll somehow help me comprehend my decision. I won't be able to let her see me; there are strict rules about such things. But I can see her, and right now, that's all I need.

Valery's words replay in my mind: *Something's coming, Dante. And you better be sure you choose the right side.*

I haven't seen my mother in two years. The last time I did, she was cleaning up after dinner. Actually, cleaning is probably the wrong word. *Instructing* our maid is probably more accurate.

She'd done that thing where she kisses the top of my head without seeing me. Not really, anyway. Then she went off to bed while my dad and I stayed up late into the night—long enough for him to get a brownie hankering.

Memories of that night wash over me. The sound of rap music

pounding through the speakers of his Beamer. The way he sang out of tune to Jay-Z in an attempt to show me he was *with it*. Later, the screech of tires as the deer stepped out into the road. My head rattling as the car flipped twice and slid to a stop.

And finally, the words he whispered as he slipped away: *I love you, D.*

I pound my fist against my leg. Then I do it again. And again. The physical pain feels good. Better than the one I'm feeling in my chest, the one that threatens to overtake me. This is the reason I didn't want to come back here. Too many memories I can't forget. But I guess in the end, they followed me, anyway. Not a day goes by that I don't think of the father I died beside and the woman we both left behind.

My mother. She may not be the world's best, but she's mine, damn it. And I love her something fierce.

How many times did I contemplate coming back here to watch her, to see her one more time? But why do that when the next day I could be dragged back to hell for who knows how long? That promotion, the one I've chased for two years—it means many things. Escaping from the mouth of hell, yes. But even more, seeing my mother every day. Never being afraid that I'll suddenly be ripped away. I could buy a condo near here, see her whenever I wanted. I'd have my collectors check in at my place. It'd be a headquarters of sorts. And nothing would ever take my family from me again.

I'm staring at the pavement, lost in my thoughts, when a clicking sound grabs my attention. My head pops up. The sudden movement pulls a muscle in my neck. I start to rub it but freeze.

It's her.

My mother walks out the door and onto the landing step, still pulling on her fur coat. *It's too warm for fur*, I want to tell her. But of course, I can't.

Her dark hair is pulled into a low ponytail, and her bangs are swept across the forehead she always complained was too large—which my father retorted was perfect for kissing. I catch a glimpse of her yellow blouse and white pants before they're buried beneath the mink. Her lips are painted a bright red, but she's not wearing much makeup otherwise. She seems…she appears…sort of happy, like she might not be having the worst day of her life. It splits my heart in two. I want her to be miserable that I'm gone—but I don't.

My brain sends a signal to my body, telling it to cower and hide. *Don't let her see you,* it says. My heart, on the other hand, tells my brain to fuck off. It screams for me to run across the street, waving my arms and yelling, *Mom, look! I'm here! I didn't leave you!*

My mother pulls her trusty green Prada bag over her shoulder, descends the stairs, and walks down the sidewalk like she's stepping out for an early lunch. I sit stunned for a moment, wondering what she's doing. She should be calling for a cab. My mother's never walked anywhere in her life. In fact, I'm quite certain she's selectively crippled.

I stand up and follow her. She has long legs and moves quickly, but I easily keep up. After ten minutes, she turns onto a street near our home that's littered with mom-and-pop restaurants, the kind she doesn't visit, the kind with fewer than five stars.

She crosses the street, and I notice her steps become lighter and hurried, like she can't wait to get where she's going. In front of her, a red tarp hanging over a walkway has the word *Cappello's* written in white italics. She moves beneath it…and that's when I see him.

A man much taller than my mother pulls her into an embrace. He kisses her on the cheek. It's not a quick kiss. Quick would imply informality, possibly old friends. But his lips don't flit—they linger.

And I have a sudden, detailed vision of drop-kicking his imposing ass.

37

AWAKENING

My mom and the douchebag walk to the host stand located just outside the entrance. Words are exchanged, and my mother points to an outside table. Douchebag nods. He must not know her well enough, or he would have already predicted that. It could be minus fifty degrees and raining intestines, and my mother would still insist they sit outside.

So we can people watch.

No, Mom, so people can watch *you*.

The twosome sit at a round table with a red checkered tablecloth and a shameful centerpiece of baby's breath—the scum of the flower world. Douchebag reaches across the table and takes my mom's hand. He strokes his thumb over her knuckles, and she leans her head to the side and smiles. It's a nice smile, and I almost buy it as blissful. But something's off. It doesn't consume her face like the smiles she reserved for my father. It hits me: she likes this guy…but not the way she did Dad.

The realization makes the muscles in my chest relax for the first time since I got to Chicago.

Mom has a boyfriend, which I detest.

But she doesn't love him.

I stay near the street and watch Mother and Douchebag share bruschetta and spaghetti. I can't help wondering when Mom started eating carbs, because last I remember, she put them right up there with pleather and rapists.

When the bill comes, Douchebag pays, and Mom acts all thankful—like she wouldn't have dumped his ass if he hadn't. The guy stands and helps her from her seat, and I'm able to get a good look at him. He's every bit as tall as me but quite a bit thinner. His eyes are set a touch too far apart, and his dark hair is buzzed to the scalp. Everything about him screams military—from the rigid way he moves to the crispness of his suit. I'm guessing he was a commander or sergeant or one of those other words that means you're the screamer versus the screamee.

Together, they walk across the street and move toward me. I back away and let them pass, then follow close behind. It looks like they're headed back to my mom's apartment. For what, I have no cl—

Oh, no. No.

He's going back to her apartment in the middle of the day.

He's going to try and…and…

My stomach heaves. Hello, darkness, my old friend.

Like waiting to see a car crash, I continue tailing them, matching their pace step for step. Douchebag and Mom stop outside her brownstone, and I say a silent prayer to a God long forgotten.

Don't let him come in, Mom. Don't you do it.

By some miracle, the guy kisses her and turns to go. Judging by his quick pace and stiff, something-up-his-ass suit, he's probably headed back to work. I laugh with relief and watch my mom walk back upstairs. At the door, she stops and turns. She watches him walking away with a dazed smile hanging on her mouth. But then something changes. Her eyes fall to her feet like she's thinking. And the smile vanishes. It's doesn't just disappear, it crumbles—like she's not sure how it got there in the first place.

In that instant, I know she misses us.

I can see it in the lines on her face, the ones even Botox can't erase. I can see it in the way her shoulders slump and her back hunches. She pulls her arms around her waist in a squeeze—then she unwraps herself, unlocks the door, and goes inside.

Everything I wanted to see, I saw. My mother is here, right where I need her to be. She misses us, but she's trying to move on. And even though the dude she was with looks like a real hard-ass, he might be what she needs to move forward—someone who's persistent and responsible.

Not sure what I'm doing anymore, I move away from my mother's house. My house. The one I grew up in. I know I can't stay long, but somehow I can't bring myself to leave Chicago just yet. My decision still isn't made. And my blood temperature rises several degrees when I think about what I'm choosing between: seeing my mother every day and protecting Charlie. I can't do both.

If I'm considering going against orders—and I'm not saying I am—then I'll spend eternity running from collectors. And if I get caught…

A shiver swims down my spine as I think of hell and its many torture devices. There's one thing all collectors fear most, and that's the ninth circle of hell. It's reserved for treachery, and it's the ring closest to Boss Man—a vast area of pain and suffering utilizing the terrors of ice.

I once decided being buried or encapsulated in ice for eons

wouldn't be bad in comparison to some of the other crap down there. Then Max jokingly challenged me to fill two bowls full of ice, stick one hand in each, and hold onto the cubes for as long as I could.

I tried so hard to prove I could take it, but my hands yanked themselves out after sixty seconds like they had a mind of their own. Max laughed his ass off and called me a pussy.

That pain has haunted me ever since.

Remembering it now, I can't comprehend how this is even a choice. On one hand, I have collecting Charlie's soul, being promoted to Soul Director, and spending my days on earth seeing my mother—and even Charlie—every day of their lives. On the other, I go against orders, get tracked by collectors, eventually succumb, and while the rest of the world enjoys peace and tranquility, I become a human icicle.

I've never met anyone like Charlie before. As hard as it is to admit, I care for her. But I don't think I can risk losing my mom and suffering eternal pain for Charlie's soul. Still, the fact that I'm even considering it blows me away. That Charlie girl, she did a number on me.

Running my hands through my hair, I decide to take a walk. I'll round the block and hit up the Magnificent Mile for some *real* shopping—forget Peachville Mall. Though I know I'm stalling the inevitable—making a decision—it's all I can do to stay sane. So I walk a few street lengths, and when I'm sure no one's looking, I shake off my shadow.

Soon I'm greeted by glass windows and stick-thin mannequins and crème-de-la-crème labels. Ah, Michigan Avenue, where anyone who's anybody comes to shop. I strut down the sidewalk, hands stuffed in my pockets. Even though it's Thursday afternoon, there are people everywhere shuffling in and out of the stores, hailing cabs…elbowing one another for breathing room. I inhale and catch a scent of expensive perfume. Its owner could be any one of these high-class broads passing by with their Dolce handbags and Jimmy Choo heels.

Up ahead, I spot an Armani store and decide it's time for some personal indulgences. Nothing like spending cash to get your mind off life-or-death situations. Gliding inside, I'm bombarded by the crisp, clean odor of optimism. A tall girl with white-blond hair and big brown eyes *clicks* over, smiling like a stoner.

"Business or pleasure?" she teases.

"Pleasure. Always."

She nods, her smile hitching higher. "What can I help you find?"

I glance around. "You know, I'm just going to browse. I'll call you when I see something I like."

She opens her arms wide, as if to imply the store is mine, and walks away.

A few minutes later, I'm in the dressing room, pulling on a gray sports coat. It looks damn good over this Smurf-blue tee. I turn from side to side, trying to forget what's in my head and concentrate on what's in the mirror. I'm doing a pretty good job when I think I hear a girl crying.

Cocking my head, I listen. Yep, definitely crying. I put my own clothes back on and leave the dressing room. Four Armani associates are standing near the back, hovering near a curtained entrance. I move quickly to where they stand, curiosity getting the better of me. As I get closer, I notice the curtain is a makeshift doorway into what I'm guessing is their break room. The associates are huddled around, peeking inside, watching Crying Girl pace with a phone pressed to her ear.

"What's going on?" I ask a guy in his early twenties.

His face pulls away from the girl and relaxes with false confidence. "Oh, nothing. I'm so sorry. How were your clothes? Did you find something you liked?"

I peer over the guy's shoulder at the girl, who's now hyperventilating. Another female associate rushes to her side and pulls her into a hug. "It's okay," she tells the girl. "I'm sure he's fine."

Crying Girl rips away and stares up at something in the corner.

A blast shatters the room, and the girl sobs louder. The associates push inside the room, and I follow them, wondering what the hell is going on.

All eyes in the room come to rest on the TV suspended in the corner. It's a news broadcast. Something's happened in London. I read the scrolling bar across the bottom. A terrorist attack. The channel plays the bombing in a loop, and we watch as the same people run across the screen, fear contorting their faces. It's the last few seconds that kill me, the ones where I spot a child standing alone, reaching for a mother that isn't there.

Crying Girl pushes buttons on her phone and paces the room, trying to get through to someone. She glances up, seeing me for the first time. I freeze.

The guy who spoke to me moments ago remembers I'm there and grabs my elbow. "Sir, I apologize, but I'll have to ask you to step outside. I can help you with anything you need."

I pull away, desperate to help the girl. To take her pain and make it my own, though I've never met her. "It's okay," I tell him. "I was just leaving."

He walks me to the front without speaking, but when I touch the glass door, he says, "I'm sorry about that." He swallows. "Her brother is in London."

"It's fine," I say. "Not the first time I've seen one of those on TV."

"Yeah, it happens." He shakes his head. "But it's weird knowing someone who knows someone, you know?"

I don't, but I nod anyway. Then I turn and walk out the door.

I watch cars racing down the street in a daze. It's crazy how everyone is going on with their lives when across the world, people have died. But maybe it's not that crazy, because before now, I was always able to ignore tragedies.

Glancing up at the sky, I think about what just happened. Seeing that girl terrified rocked something inside of me. I wonder how it would be if fewer people had to cry like that anymore. If Charlie saved them all. Back there, I couldn't take away that girl's pain, but I could prevent it from happening to someone else.

I could be the trigger to start the change.

In my life, I've done awful, selfish things. Things I can never take back. But I could change who I am now, couldn't I? Charlie said she saw the good in me. I wonder if she's right. If it's really there.

The sun is already past high noon, on its downward arc—and it hits me. It's Thursday, which means I only have three more days after today to either collect Charlie's soul or prepare to run. Looking back at the street, I spot a white SUV and admire the chrome rims. I'm eyeing them closer when suddenly, I get a tingling sensation.

He's here.

The collector.

I start to turn around when I feel a pair of hands slam into my back. Before I can think, I'm flying into the street, the white SUV barreling toward me.

For one terrible moment, I know it's going to hit me.

I'm going to be pancaked, and the pain is going to knock

my ass out for weeks. My brain screams at me to move, to do something, but my muscles lock in protest.

Then I think of Charlie. The way she smiles and laughs without reservation. The life in her eyes when she looks at me. The beautiful, pure light of her soul. And her mouth.

Her mouth.

The person driving the SUV lays on the horn, and the car screeches, brakes kicking in—but not quick enough. I jump up from the asphalt and, without thinking, race into the middle of the road. The SUV zooms past, but now a bus sails toward me from the opposite direction. I bite down and run. I run so hard, I'm sure my heart will explode.

As the bus *whooshes* behind me, I leap onto the sidewalk. People are yelling and asking if I'm okay. I brush them off and immediately search for the collector who shoved me into the street. There's no one there but concerned faces.

I know I can't die unless my cuff is removed, but it still takes my body time to recover from trauma. And pain—that still very much exists in my world.

This damn collector followed me to Chicago, and he's either trying to put me out of commission for a while or sending a strongly worded message.

I can still sense him—can feel his cuff. I face what I know is his direction. "You want a piece of me?" I yell, beating my chest. "Come on, I'm right here. Show yourself."

People near me move back, assuming I'm crazy.

I jab my finger across the street. "Didn't think so. The only way you can take me on is through cheap shots. That right?"

He doesn't remove his shadow, and I'm not surprised. I wait a few more minutes, and people start to move away and on with their lives. They almost saw me flattened before their eyes, but turns out I'm okay, so the luster's gone.

After a few seconds, the sense that he's near fades. The chump must have moved away. Nearby, I spot a Starbucks and race inside. I push past a line of people waiting to get their caffeine fixes and head toward the bathroom. I'm not sure what I'm doing, but I need a place to think. Inside the single-person bathroom, I lock the door and pace within the two-foot area.

At first, I thought the collector following me was assuring the assignment got completed. Now I think there's more to it. He's not tracking me, he's trying to damage me. But why?

I stop pacing. Does he know what I'm contemplating?

Crap. I never should have come here.

Another thought strikes me. If this collector is doing this to *me*, what does he plan to do to Charlie?

My assignment.

My girl.

Collectors aren't allowed to hurt humans, but they're not allowed to hurt each other, either, and that's not stopping him. This guy is a loose cannon, and he needs to be stopped. I consider heading downstairs now, reporting him to Boss Man and exterminating this pest. But I can't, because once I'm there, Boss Man may ask me to stay and send someone else in my place. It's not likely, but it could happen. And I'm not sure I want to do that, not sure I'm ready to stand by for a hundred years and let people hurt one another.

Because the next time I witness someone hurt, I'll know I could have stopped it.

What if Charlie was the next person hurt by this hate? I imagine that. Imagine knowing it's my fault she's afraid, the way her face would twist in terror.

And suddenly, my decision breaks over my head and shatters

into a million pieces. It tears into my chest and rips out my beating heart. Charlie has to help protect people from this pain. And I have to protect her.

My mind races when I realize what I'm thinking.

Boss Man has counted me as his right hand, has always trusted me.

And now I will betray him.

38

PHOTOS

Though the decision is fresh in my mind, it feels final. I've never been one to half-ass, and I'm not going to start now.

With my chest tightening, I try and determine my next steps.

Charlie could bring peace for a hundred years. I know damn well Boss Man doesn't want that to happen. He's greedy for souls, and her life would definitely put a damper on new inventory. Still, he wouldn't send a collector to hurt her physically. There's no way he could hurt a human without pissing off Big Guy and chancing war. But with these amplified stakes, I feel a twinge of doubt at what Boss Man will permit.

For now, I have to start with the soul contract. Charlie's already signed it, and though there's no way to take that back, I have to stop her before she asks for anything else. Maybe if she stalls, it'll buy us some time. Maybe we could push pause on the whole beauty requests thing indefinitely.

Though somehow, I doubt it.

I've got to return to Peachville. I have to figure out why Boss Man wants Charlie's soul. We may both know what she's capable of, but it doesn't explain why he wants her collected *now*. What could that accomplish if she'll just go on living? I also have to figure out how I'm going to protect her without sealing my own fate.

But before I do any of that, I have to say good-bye to my mother.

Brushing off my jeans, I walk the few blocks back to her house. It's been awhile since I left, and I wonder if she's still inside. A few doors from her place, I glance around and pull on my shadow. Then I cross the street and find the same bench I sat on earlier. An hour goes by, and I fidget like a crack fiend. Too much crap is flying through my head right now, but I have to see my mother one more time before I leave Chicago. Just…one more time.

After another twenty minutes, I decide I'm going to take a chance. After all, who's to say she'll even come out again today? I get up from the bench and walk toward the brownstone. I know she can't see me, but something about being this close to home makes my brain buzz.

I creep up the stairs and glance through the window, but I don't see her anywhere. She's definitely not downstairs. Glancing back down, I wonder if there's any way…

Jogging down the steps, I eye the corner brick on the last step. Back in the day, I spent my nights partying wicked late. Eventually, Dad took away my key so I couldn't sneak in after curfew. After that, I literally had to knock every time I got home and be let in by my parents. Naturally, this was unacceptable to my lifestyle. So I made a copy of my mother's key and hid it under the loose brick. I'm pretty sure Mom knew I'd swiped another key, but since Dad was mostly gone, and Mom was never a fan of waking up to let my ass in, she turned a blind eye.

I jiggle the brick. At first, I think she's had it repaired. But then it eases out, and beneath it, I see a silver key winking in the sunlight. *Score!*

Grabbing the key, I race up the stairs, take one last look through the window, and slide the key into the slot. The lock *clicks*, and I open the door and step inside, holding my breath as if that matters. I reach behind me and gently close the door.

A pang of longing forms in my chest like a fist. Looking around, it's like nothing has changed. I walk through the foyer and into our sitting room. The floor is covered in white French tile, and the walls are painted robin's-egg blue. A silver chandelier hangs from the ceiling, and the white couch and slip chairs make the room feel serene. Along the walls, English paintings are hung in ornate silver frames, and over the fireplace, I know I'll see—

My eyes freeze on the mantle.

I see my face everywhere, just as I did growing up. Me playing soccer when I was eleven, my arm around another kid. My mother and me having breakfast at a hotel in Aspen. Me as a baby, wrapped in a red blanket. There are at least a dozen pictures of me doing different things with different people. But something is missing, or rather, *someone*.

My father's pictures used to be up there, too. I particularly remember their wedding photo front and center. I run my hand over the cool wood where my father's blue-gray eyes used to stare back at me. Glancing around, afraid my mother will suddenly appear, I move toward the kitchen. It's a steel-and-granite paradise, but over the kitchen sink, I notice more photos of my father are missing. He's gone. It's like my mother erased him.

I know in an instant why she's done it. She's hanging on to my memory. My death is something she'll never forget, and she doesn't want to. But my father…his face stands in the way of her moving on with her life. How can she be a wife again if he's everywhere? I imagine she has a box hidden somewhere in her room filled with his photos. Maybe she takes it out every weekend, sifts through them, and just cries. I hang on to this thought, because I couldn't bear it if this wasn't the truth.

A flight of wooden stairs rise between the kitchen and sitting room. I move toward them. There's something upstairs I have to see. It's not my bedroom or even my childhood playroom. It's my mother's room. I need to see her jewelry and perfumes and clothing. Maybe there's a photo of her stashed somewhere I can take with me. It'll have to do in the years ahead.

I approach the foot of the stairs, grab the railing—and look up.

My mother stares back at me.

Every muscle in my body, every bone, tightens. She stares at me like she can actually see me, but I know that's impossible. I take a small, silent step back, and she follows the movement with her eyes.

I have to get out of here. Now. I continue to back away, trying to make my way to the door. With every step I take, my mother takes a step down the stairs. It's like…she senses me.

I hear a sudden thumping sound and realize she's running down the stairs. My hands flail out, looking for something, though I have no idea what. At the bottom of the stairs, she stops and glances around, searching.

Searching for me.

Her chest rises and falls rapidly, and pain crosses her face. Her eyes sweep across the room, stopping on nothing in particular. Then they fall to the floor. She pulls in a long breath and runs her fingers through her hair, which is now down around her shoulders. When she lifts her head again, there are tears in her eyes.

Slowly, she moves across the room and reaches toward the mantle. Her hand closes around the photo of me and her at the hotel. She grips it so hard her knuckles whiten, and I fight the urge to sob. I want to throw my arms around her—hug my mom and be hugged back. I want to go upstairs to my room and spend the rest of my life caring for her and being a son again.

I won't show myself, even if I were allowed to.

I can't.

She's already been through so much. I have to love her enough to say good-bye.

My mother stands for a moment, clutching the photo to her chest. Then she turns and shuffles up the stairs like someone twice her age. I relax, and a breath rushes from my lungs. I take one last look around the house and move toward the door.

With my hand on the knob, I stop. I don't want to leave. Not without doing something first. I dig into my pocket and retrieve my lucky coin. Pulling my hand out, I open my palm and stare at the blurry printing. I've kept this coin for two years. Having it with me, it felt like my father hadn't left. Not completely, anyway. But I know with the risks I'm facing that I could lose everything. I always want to know where my father is. Even if I'm trapped in eternal pain, I want to know where a small piece of him lies. And with the disappearance of his photos from my mother's mantle, I want even more for it to be here, with her.

I walk quickly to the mantle, keeping an eye on the staircase. Then I slide the penny behind one of my photos, so that it lies against the backing, hidden.

There. Now I'm sure my father will always be here with my mother, right where he should be. I'm suddenly blindsided by a wash of emotions as I remember my dad. I like to imagine he'd sacrifice himself to make the world better for my mother and me, so I know he'd understand. Maybe he'd even be proud of the choice I'm making.

I cross the room, open the door, and leave unnoticed. Walking down the stairs, I notice how ugly Chicago looks. Leaves breaking off from the trees, dead. Grass robbed of its rich green color. Even the sky seems unremarkable. I squeeze my eyes shut, then put my hands over my ears and…just…push.

I don't want to see anything. I don't want to hear anything. But mostly, I don't want to *think.* Dropping my hands and opening my eyes, I walk down the sidewalk but keep myself hidden from the world. If people don't see me, then maybe I'm not here… maybe I don't exist.

I'm somewhere else, some*one* else. But that can't really happen, can it? I can't escape myself or the things I've done. When most people die, they get to forget who they were. But for me, I'll always remember what I *was.*

I was the center of the universe.

I was king of the world.

I was the son who watched his father die.

I was the one who killed him.

I was the driver of that damn car.

39

FLYING BACK TO CHARLIE

I board the plane back to Alabama and breathe a sigh of frustration when the stewardess plops a ten-year-old down next to me. I mean, this is first class. Why a ten-year-old? She's wearing a blue-jean skirt, a white tank, and enough thin silver bracelets to give me a headache every time she moves. Pulled back in her short brunette hair is a white sweatband.

As soon as the girl sits down, she reaches over me to see out the window. Her eyes are as big as Alaska, and she couldn't appear more terrified if someone bit the end off a grenade and tossed it in her lap.

When the plane rolls, then races, down the runway, she goes full-on possessed, swinging her head around and speaking in tongues. After a few minutes, she calms down. But when mild turbulence hits halfway through the flight, the tears start a-comin'.

I don't even notice she's crying until I lean forward to take my drink from the stewardess. But once I realize the girl's cheeks are wet and her chest is convulsing, I can't get it out of my head. Now typically, I'd play dumb. Act like I didn't know that the kid next to me is having a nervous breakdown. But I can't. And I know damn well why not. It's Charlie. That girl got in my brain and dug around. She found the one morsel of good in there, held it up to the light, and said, "See here? See this? Look how sparkly! Let's make it *grow*."

Setting my drink down and facing the kid, I ask, "Freaked out?"

At first, she seems surprised I'm speaking to her. But then she swallows and nods.

"Tell you something? I was totally freaked out the first time I flew."

"Really?" she asks.

No. Not really. I can't remember being afraid of anything when I was alive.

"Totally," I answer. "But you know what? These people who fly these planes? They're, like, flipping geniuses. You're in safe hands."

The girl glances toward the cockpit and gives a small smile, but she's not convinced.

I try to think of something to get her mind off the flight. Her sweatband catches my eye. "Why you wearing a sweatband? Is that what all the kids are doing these days?"

She laughs and touches the headband. "LeBron James wears one. He's playing tonight so I got to be…you know…"

"Supportive," I finish for her.

She nods.

"Want to see something cool?" I pull my foot up and turn back the tongue on my red sneaker.

Her eyes bug out. "Is that what I think it is?"

"If you think it's Dwyane Wade's autograph, you'd be right."

"Dude," she says.

"Dude," I say back.

"I would, like, never take those off." The girl sits back in her seat, visibly relaxing.

I put my foot back down. "I don't."

She pulls her mouth up to one side like she's thinking. "What if you'd gotten LeBron's autograph, too?"

"Pfft. Please," I say. "I got the only one I wanted."

Her face gets all excited like she's got a million arguments on the subject of Miami's best player. Turns out, I'm right. And as we approach Birmingham, she's still defending her stance. I hold up a hand to stop her and point out the window. She sees the city and gets a confused look, like she's not sure what I'm referencing.

"We're here," I say.

She glances from the window to me. An enormous smile covers her face, and she throws her little kid arms around my neck. The sensation strikes something inside of me. Something I haven't felt in a very long time.

Like a warm fuzzy or some shit.

• • •

When I get to Peachville, it's late, but I need to see Charlie right away. Even though I'm not sure it can be done, I've got to try and stop her from fulfilling any more of the contract. But I'm afraid of where this conversation could go. My biggest fear is that she'll uncover my secret. That I don't work for Big Guy. I think about the way she'd look at me if she knew—with fear and betrayal and disgust. My shoulders tighten, and I have to roll them several times to relax.

I wonder whether she'll be disappointed in not receiving all the beauty wishes she'd expected. But I feel sure I can make her see reason. I'll just tell her the truth—that seventy-five percent of attraction comes from exuding confidence. I'll teach her how to enter a room, how the tilt of her chin can make people believe she's too good for them. I'll also hold her in front of a mirror and show her the things I see. The elegant slope of her collarbone, the soft, flat plane of her stomach, the way the corner of her eyes crinkle when she laughs. There are a million little reasons why someone could fall for Charlie; I just have to remind her of those things. I just have to say, *You're beautiful. If you believe it, they'll believe it.*

I pull up to Charlie's house and walk up to the bright red door. Raising my hand to knock, I hesitate. She was upset when I last saw her. Will she still be tonight?

I drop my hand. That kiss. I couldn't have taken it. It felt wrong. I've never cared about deceiving someone before, but with her—I don't know. I just couldn't do it. Maybe one day, if I can find a way to save her soul, then we can…

But even as I consider this, I realize it'll never happen. Charlie is meant to do big things. And me, on the other hand, I'm just trying to escape my past.

I bite the inside of my cheek, and this time, I manage to knock without stopping myself. Grams opens the door. She seems surprised someone's here so late, but when she realizes it's me, her expression changes. Anger flashes behind her eyes.

"Man Child," she says, cocking a hand on her hip.

"Can I talk to Charlie?"

She smiles, but it's a non-teeth smile, which isn't promising. "No, you may not. She came home from school today pretty upset."

I lean against the frame outside the door, wondering if Grams knows about Vegas. "She stayed at Annabelle's last night," I say. "Maybe you shouldn't let her stay over there anymore."

"I don't think that's the problem."

She eyes me, so I eye her right back.

"Look, I really need to talk to her," I announce in my best gentleman voice. "It's important."

Grams shakes her head. "That is unfortunate."

I've had enough of Grams right about now. I push past her as she hollers for me to stop, that she's going to squash me like a bug. But something besides Grams's empty threats stops me.

Charlie.

She's standing at the top of the stars, gazing down. She seems worn, like she's been fighting a battle all night.

"Charlie," I say, "I have to talk to you."

"It's late, Dante. I'll see you tomorrow."

"Charlie…" My voice has a pleading tone, but I don't care. Seeing her now, I can't believe I ever imagined not saving her. I can't believe I never really *saw* her before this. That I didn't see how beautiful her soul is, how the life she lives is one I've always wanted but never had the guts to claim. My heart throbs, and I know it's over for me. I'm done. Putty in her hands.

She turns and walks back toward her room. Over her shoulder, she says in a shaky voice, "Please. Go home."

I'm too shocked to move. I knew she was upset, but I didn't think she'd kick me out. Grams grabs my arm and gives a gentle tug. The anger has drained from her face. Instead, she looks at me with pity. I yank my arm away and glare at her because I don't need anyone pitying me. Ever.

"I'm fine," I bark.

"I know you are," she says.

I march past her and out the door. Behind me, I hear the *click* of the lock sliding into place, and moments later, the front porch light flips off. I stand alone in the dark, looking up at Charlie's bedroom window. A warm light glows behind her sheer curtains, and my nerves fire. Maybe I should climb up and talk to her. But seconds later, the light snuffs out.

Hanging my head, I walk back to Elizabeth Taylor. Charlie is really upset, and I know now this isn't just about the kiss. There's something bigger going on. I think back through all the times she requested beautiful features. I remember how she immediately sought my opinion on her blonder, shinier hair, and how she asked if I knew what color her eyes were before changing those, too. And finally, in Vegas, when she asked if I thought she should ask for more beauty.

In every single instance, I practically begged her to fulfill the contract. And why wouldn't I? At the time, all I cared about was finishing the job and getting my promotion. But now, all I feel remembering these last few days is shame.

Briefly, I try that putting-yourself-in-their-shoes thing I've heard about. I wonder how I'd feel if someone suggested I change my appearance. My face pulls together, and I wince. I'd tell that someone where to shove it. But like a sudden slap, I realize I'd also be hurt.

Starting the engine, I pull away from Charlie's house and drive toward Wink Hotel. I never checked out, and even thinking about the bed makes me drowsy. Right now, I should turn around, charge up the lattice outside her window, and demand she speak to me. But maybe she's right. It's late. And technically, I still have three days to finish this assignment. Knowing how quickly Sunday will be here, my stomach clenches.

Fatigue overtakes anxiety as I park outside Wink Hotel and then let myself into my room. I have no idea what I'm going to do to protect her. I don't know how I'm going to keep her from finding out who I really am. And I really don't know how I'm going to do both without being cast into the ninth ring of hell.

These, and other equally lovely thoughts, are the last I remember as I succumb to sleep.

• • •

I bolt upright in bed and listen. I heard something. In fact, I think I've been hearing it for a while and am just now realizing it.

Cocking my head, I listen for whatever woke me. I'm about to accept that I'm imagining things when four quick raps sound outside my door. I glance around the room, attempting to pull myself awake and trying not to panic. It could be anybody. Just because someone's outside my door doesn't mean crap's about to the hit the fan.

I slide off the bed and move toward the door, holding my breath.

"Dante, dude, it's me. Open up. I know you're in there." Max's words sound muffled through the steel door, but sure as hell I know it's him.

I swing the door open, and he strolls past me into the room.

"Where have you been?" he says. "I couldn't sense you anywhere for the last twenty-four hours. I thought you'd gone rogue and busted your cuff off or something. Committed demon suicide."

I flip on the light, and Max pushes himself up on the dresser to sit.

"I had to take care of some stuff."

"I bet you did." Max acts like he's slapping, then squeezing, someone's rear.

Running a hand through my hair, I say, "Max, I need to sleep."

"I bet you do."

"Cut it out. I'm seriously exhausted."

Max frowns. "It's that Charlie girl. She's got you whipped or something. You're really pulling out all the stops to bring this one in. Taking her to parties. Flying her around the world."

I freeze, then shoot a cold look at Max. The memory of the collector watching me pours over me like lava. Heat pricks my skin as I realize this collector…could be anyone. Very slowly, I ask. "How do you know we left Peachville?"

He points at me. "Busted! I knew it."

Inspecting him closely, I wait to see what else he'll say.

"Simmer, man." He raises his hands. "Like I said, I knew you were gone because I couldn't sense you anymore. You know that unless we're downstairs, we have to be pretty close to pick up on the cuff. I knew you were in Peachville because that's where everyone said your assignment was, and when I couldn't sense you anymore, I knew you'd left. Figured you'd taken a trip with your old lady."

What he says makes sense, but suddenly, I can't shake the paranoia. What if it's him? What if he's watching me? Most collectors would do anything to get the promotion I'm up for. Can I really trust Max right now?

I nod toward the door. "I think you should go."

"Dante…" he says, and it sounds exactly the way I said Charlie's name earlier.

"Max, get out before I make you get out. I've got three days to bring Charlie in. And like you said, I don't want any of those pesky consequences for failing to deliver. I'm sure you understand."

Hurt twists his face, but I've known Max for two years, and I'm certain if he wanted to, he could be an Oscar-winning actor.

Max's eyes open with disbelief, and his head drops. Then he remembers himself and glances up. "Yeah. Fine. Whatever."

I cross my arms as Max turns to go and fight the temptation

to stop him. He's been a good friend. No, a great one. And I can't believe this assignment has made me into someone who can't trust his best guy.

The door closes behind Max, and I sit down on the bed. For several seconds, I just stare at the brown-and-black damask carpeting, feeling like I just lost the only person who really knows me.

A sharp, high sound startles me, and I jump up, half-hoping that somehow it's Max. If it's him, I'm certain I won't be able to send him away. But as I listen, I can tell it's coming from farther away, and it doesn't sound anything like him.

Opening the door, I hear the noise coming from the stairwell. It sounds like a woman screaming. I walk, then run, toward the shriek. Swinging the stairwell door open, I hear that she's calling for help about two flights down. I jog down the stairs, wondering what I'm doing, why I'm running after a screaming lady.

When I see her just standing there, I reach out and grab her arm.

"Hey, what's wrong—"

I stop.

Max is slumped over on the ground, holding his head. Blood, dark and thick, is running down the front of his face from beneath his hands. Beside him is a fire extinguisher, blood splattered over one end.

40

SECRETS

My heart lunges as I move past the woman and pull Max up.

"It's fine. He fell," I tell her. "Go back to your room."

"But—" she starts.

"Go back to your room," I say, louder.

I sling Max's arm around my shoulders and help him walk back to my room. When he moans about a killer headache, I know he's going to be fine. We're immortal, but it'll still take time to heal.

Inside my bathroom, I sit him on the toilet lid, wet a towel, and push it into his hand. He presses it to his head.

"You okay?" I ask.

He nods, then smiles. "Look how scared you are. You totally love me."

I shake my head, but he's right. Seeing him busted up scares the crap out of me. "What happened?"

He pulls the towel away, inspects it, then pushes it back to his head. "I don't know. I just got knocked the hell out."

"With a fire extinguisher?" I soak another towel and hand it to him, but he pushes it away.

"Guess so. Maybe I hooked up with some dude's girlfriend or something."

My jaw clenches. "Who tracked you down at the Wink?" I pause, watching him. "Do you…do you sense another collector besides me right now?"

He gives me a surprised look, then narrows his eyes in concentration. "No," he says finally. "You think one of our own did this?"

I hesitate, then nod.

Max pulls the towel away, and I glance at his head. Already the wound has stopped bleeding.

I lean against the doorway, take a deep breath, and fill Max in on everything. Big Guy's liberator. Trelvator. The collector following me. I leave out the part about me falling for Charlie and that I'm planning to go against orders.

Max whistles when I'm done talking. "Damn."

"Right."

"So you think this a-hole collector hit me tonight because I'm bros with you?"

I shrug. "Maybe. I don't really understand his deal. All I know is, it's getting worse."

Max cocks his head, thinking. "I guess I did sense a collector when I was in the stairwell, but figured it was you since I was still so near your room. You know we can't really pinpoint how *many* collectors are nearby."

"So you can't think who would be tailing me out of our team?"

He shakes his blood-caked head. "Not at all. I mean, everyone worships you downstairs. You're Boss Man's *numero uno*. But then who else could it be?" Max crosses his ankle over his knee, and his eyes fall to his cuff. "Sometimes I really hate this thing."

I consider telling Max what I know and realize I have nothing to lose at this point. "Max," I say, "I know how we got these cuffs."

His eyes bulge. "What are you talking about? No one knows where these things came from."

"Boss Man explained it while training me for my new position as Soul Director."

I motion for Max to follow me out of the bathroom. We move into the room, and he sits across from me on the other bed. I fold my hands together and try to retell the story as I heard it. "Did you know that, back in the day, Boss Man was a high angel for Big Guy?"

Max laughs a quick, dry laugh.

"I'm taking it you weren't a churchgoer before you died, either."

"Uh, no. That's kinda how I got this gig."

"Right," I say. "Okay, well, Boss Man used to work for Big Guy. But one day he decides he doesn't appreciate the attention Big Guy gives to humankind. Boss Man feels like that attention should be on *him*. So in a jealous fit, he decides to overtake Big Guy, figures he'd look pretty awesome sitting on Big Guy's throne. So he gets together with these other angels on earth, where they can conspire unheard, and plots to overthrow Big Guy."

"No shit?" Max interrupts.

I nod. "So as Boss Man is plotting, he asks one of his comrades to fashion him a crown. That way he can wear it as soon as he's ruler. But he doesn't just want any crown, he wants one to rival Big Guy's. So his comrade spends days seeking these particular sheets of gold, known to angels as *dargon*. It's said that there are only two sheets of dargon in existence, and that Big Guy fashioned them when he created the world. They were meant to be used for a crown and throne for the future son he knew he'd have. Well, eventually Boss Man's comrade gets his hands on one of the sheets of gold, but before he can fashion it into a crown, Big Guy finds out about Boss Man's plan and tosses him and the other angels into hell."

"So Boss Man never got his crown," Max repeats.

"No, he didn't get his crown. But he did make it out with a stolen piece of dargon."

"So…what does that mean?"

"Well, after Big Guy learns about his angels plotting against him, he pulls every last one of them off earth and back into heaven. He decides that the only being who can step foot on earth again is his son—the person wearing the crown."

"I think I know where this is going," Max says, his face twisting with awe.

"Yeah. Right. Because Boss Man had stolen a sheet of dargon, he was able to walk the earth, too. But Boss Man was all vengeful, and he wanted payback. So he took his dargon, and he created six cuffs and chose six collectors to steal souls from Big Guy—figured he could do more damage that way.

"Now Boss Man just ensures he always has the cuffs on his best six people, those who had particular skills on earth." I shake my head. "Not sure what's better, working as a collector or retiring in hell."

Max glances down between his shoes. "Why don't they want us to know about this?"

"I think…" I say. "I think because Boss Man doesn't want to appear weak to his collectors. Like, he doesn't want us knowing that Big Guy tossed him out on his ass like that."

"So you think Big Guy knows about us?" Max asks.

I think for a second. "Yeah, he knows. I think he's known all along. But now he's creating his own collectors—the liberators.

And I think Boss Man knows he's on Big Guy's radar. That's why we're not allowed to hurt humans, because Big Guy would bring war, and Boss Man isn't strong enough to take him."

Max touches his head and checks his hand to see if there's blood. "The cuffs. They're why other collectors and Boss Man can sense where we are when we're close by, right?"

I nod.

"And they're also why we can shadow?"

I run my tongue over my teeth. "Yeah, I think so. I often wondered if…you know…we can do other things that we don't know about."

"Dude," Max says. "Me, too. I always feel like I have big stuff bottled up, you know?"

"Yeah."

Max lets out a long sigh, and his face pulls together, like he just thought of something. "Why do you think Boss Man wants Charlie so bad? I mean, other than avoiding the whole peace-on-earth thing."

I shrug. "I have no idea."

He turns and faces me. "Have you heard of the soul scales?"

"The gauge thing?" I tick my finger back and forth.

"Yeah. The whole thing where if either side gets too many more souls than the other, heaven or hell will break open, and all the angels or demons will spill out onto Earth?"

I stand up. "Holy crap. Charlie. She's going to sway the scales. Max, you're a genius."

"Yeah," he says. "Yeah, that's totally where I was going with that."

It makes sense. If Charlie can really bring a hundred years of peace, it could turn the tides for heaven. But she could still do that through her charity without a soul, couldn't she? Which means

Boss Man may be trying to claim her soul before taking more extreme measures. Maybe collecting her is just the first step.

"But why would Big Guy even want that?" Max asks. "He doesn't want angels on earth anymore."

"No," I say. "That was then. Things are different now. His new liberator is proof of that."

"So if Charlie lives, she'll be the reason angels can walk earth without dargon."

My breath catches, and a bolt of fear shoots through me. "And if she dies…"

Max's face whitens. "Oh, man. If she dies, does that mean hell may eventually gain the advantage? Like, without her, we're headed toward a world where demons walk freely?" His eyes gloss over. "Boss Man is going to try and kill her, isn't he?"

"I'm not sure. All I know is right now he's focused on collecting her." I turn to Max. It's time he knows. It's now or never. "I'm not going to let him have her soul, and I'm definitely not going to let him hurt her."

He physically pulls back like someone gut-punched him. "Dante," he says. "You're talking about treason."

I hold his eyes and nod once, a quick acknowledgement.

Max stands and moves toward the door in a daze. He spins around and faces me, his skin pale. "I can't hear this. I can't…I can't know this." He reaches up and absently touches his head. "He'll send us after you. You're my best friend, and I'll be forced to hunt you. And when the collectors find you—and you know they will—they'll drag you back downstairs, and Boss Man… He'll torture you, Dante. You've seen what happens down there. He'll put you through every part of hell and deposit you in the ninth circle. I mean, what are you even thinking? Are you out of your freaking mind?"

I square my shoulders and raise my head higher. This is the first of many challenges I'll have to face over the next thousand or more years. If I can't have conviction before my best friend, I don't stand a chance. "I won't get caught."

His face falls to the side, and his eyebrows pull together. "You will," he says gently.

I turn away, because I know he could be right. Behind me, I can feel his eyes burning into my back. "She's worth it, Max."

His words boom when he speaks again. "You're wrong. She's not worth my best friend. I don't care what kind of peace she'll bring if it means seeing you imprisoned."

I turn and take two long strides toward him. "You don't see what I see. You don't know how freaking pure she is in here." I jab myself in the chest. "I know we're trained to only care about ourselves. But if you felt what I do right now, you'd have to try and protect her." My voice drops. "I can't lose any part of her, Max. I don't expect you to understand that."

My friend's jaw tightens, and his eyes lock on mine. "Don't act like I don't know about loss. You may find this hard to believe, but I had love once." He nods. "Yeah, I had a girl. She was my everything. Her hair, her skin." He touches his neck and, catching himself, quickly drops his hand. "We were going to get married, man. Married." Max loosens his jaw and works it back and forth. "But she died."

"Max," I say, because I don't know what else *to* say.

He shrugs. "So yeah, I know about losing people. And if it meant fighting the king of hell himself to bring her back, I would. But she's gone. And Charlie, she'll be gone one day, too. And you'll be locked down there. With him. So don't do this. Finish the assignment, and get your placement on earth. Then you can spend every day with her until—"

"Until she dies, or he kills her off, and she takes my place in hell?" I interrupt. "Max, I'm so sorry about what happened to you. No one should have to lose the person they care about, which is why I have to fight for her." I move closer to Max and slap him on the shoulder. "I can run. Faster than you can imagine. I can protect her soul, and I can keep one step ahead of the collectors." I smile. "Even you."

Max backs away. "I've already lost my girl."

I know what he means. He's lost her. He can't lose me, too. But he's not going to say that. Saying it makes it real. Part of me wants to scream for Max to stay, for him to help me protect Charlie. But I can't ask that of him. I can't ask him to risk eternal pain and suffering for someone he doesn't know. So instead, I rush across the room, pull him into a hug, and slap his back hard. "I love you, Max. Now get the hell out of here. I can take care of myself." I give him the best smile I got, the one that says I'm confident and self-assured and can tackle Lucifer with my bare hands.

Max's eyes water, and he rubs them roughly, like he's pissed off at his body's reaction. "Screw you, man."

I smile and raise my middle finger. "Right back at ya."

He shakes his head and laughs. Then he opens the door, glances over his shoulder, and nods good-bye.

41

CHARLIE OUT

I wake up feeling like I spent the last three days in a massage parlor. My muscles are relaxed, and I feel refreshed, like I could climb Mount Everest or build an ark or cure the world of minivans.

Then I glance at the clock on the nightstand.

Noon.

I've had a standing wake-up call set for every day, but I'm guessing I slept through it. Not surprising, since Max didn't leave until almost 4:00 A.M. Thinking about my best friend, my heart clenches. I wonder if I'll ever see him again. And if I do, if he'll be chasing me down with a pitchfork.

I climb out of bed and pull on a T-shirt, jeans, and my red sneakers. Then I half-jog to Elizabeth Taylor and speed toward Centennial High.

One goal has my attention this morning, and that's finding Charlie. I've got to get her alone so I can explain everything in a way that doesn't make her hate me. Maybe I can tell her Big Guy has changed his mind on the contract, and that he'll be pissed if she asks for any more beauty. Maybe that way I can avoid telling her what I really am.

I pull up outside the school and make my way inside right as Charlie's lunch hour starts. Perfect. I won't even have to drag her out of class. Nearing her table, I realize Annabelle is the only one there. I glance around, searching for Charlie or Blue, and see neither.

Annabelle's stops eating her chips when she sees me. "Hey."

"Where is everyone?" I ask. "Why are you sitting alone?"

She takes a swig of her drink. "Charlie bailed."

"Bailed? What do you mean 'bailed'? Like she skipped school?"

Annabelle bobs her head from side to side. "Kind of. She came for the first half, then just a few minutes ago, she said she wasn't feeling it and that there were too many people."

"Too many people? What does that even mean?" My brain isn't able to process this information. Charlie never ditches. Someone always has to talk her into it, that someone usually being me. "Did she leave with someone?"

"Yeah, she left with Natalie. The girl that asked Charlie about her hair that time. Remember?"

I think back, trying to place the girl's face. I remember she was hot and reeked of money and popularity, which is why I don't understand why she'd ask Charlie to skip with her.

Annabelle seems to read my mind, because she says, "Something about Charlie is off today. I mean, even this morning. It's like she came to school this whole different person, like she's trying to prove something."

The way she's talking makes me nervous. I don't know what's gotten into Charlie, but I need to find her. Stat. "Do you know where she went?"

She shakes her head. "No, but Blue went with her."

I let out a frustrated sigh. I'm not sure whether to feel better or worse that Blue's with her. I decide on worse. I run a hand through my hair and think. Peachville isn't big, but it's big enough to hide in.

"Don't you see?" Annabelle says, interrupting my thoughts. She tilts her head and stares up at me. "That girl's lost her head to you."

I look at her for a long time, like she just grew a third eye—one that sees right through my crap. My chest constricts, and inside, buried deep beneath skin and bone and muscle, I pray what she says is true. That Charlie has fallen for me. It's a selfish wish, because it'll be easier to keep her safe with a level head. But I can't help the jig my heart performs at hearing Annabelle's words. If they are, in fact, true.

"Thanks, Annabelle. Seriously." I start to move away, ready to jump in my car and drive all over Peachville if that's what it takes to find Charlie. But Annabelle surprises me by reaching over and grabbing my wrist.

"She's going to a party tonight. At Natalie's house. Near Preston and Parker, I think." She lets go of me. "I don't know what you've done to her, Dante, but you better make it right. Understand?" With that, she gets up and walks away, and I can't help thinking she had that speech and dramatic exit planned in case I showed today.

Still, she's right. I need to make this right. I'm just not sure how. An orange-and-black-clad table catches my eye. I glance over to see people crowded around, buying tickets to the Halloween dance tomorrow night. Inwardly, I sigh. But I know it's not going to get better dragging my feet.

I make my way over and wait my turn to shell out sixty bucks for a pair of tickets to the last thing I'd ever like to do. Then I shoot the student council chick beaming at me a mocking grin and stuff the tickets into my pocket. Maybe this will help win Charlie over—a gesture of the things I'm willing to do to make her happy.

With any luck, she'll agree we can't actually go, that we've got to get as far away from Peachville as quickly as possible.

Two days. That's all I have left after today before Boss Man calls my assignment a bust. Will he send the other collectors in? That is, the ones not already stalking me?

I hop inside Elizabeth Taylor and spend the next three hours searching for Charlie. I swing by her house, I walk around inside the mall…I even go by the town square and glance though all the restaurant windows. For the first time in my life, I curse myself for not having a cell phone, and I curse Grams for not getting Charlie one. If I wasn't about to go on the run, I'd get one of those smartphones that people hunch over all day like shitting dogs.

When I've looked everywhere I can think of, I decide to circle back by her house. If she's not there, I'll have to wait it out until the party. Pulling up beside the curb, I kill the engine and walk to the door. I knock several times, then ring the doorbell an ungodly number of times. If there's anyone in there, they've got the temperament of a coma patient.

I back up a few steps and glance up at her window. It's obvious no one's home, but I decide to check if her window's open. Maybe I can leave her a note to call the hotel. I scale up the lattice and nearly scream a victory cry when the glass of her window slides up beneath my palm. Though I'm thrilled it's open, it also makes me nervous. I don't like thinking of Charlie being so exposed.

Inside her room, I search for anything that might clue me on where she is, but I can't tell if anything's different. It's strange being in here without her. A sense of longing twists through me when I look at her bed. I remember holding hands, jumping on the mattress like a couple of idiots. Thinking back, I should have known it then, known she was working her way under my skin. It's no wonder she was born to change the world, seeing how easily she changed me.

I feel desperate to see her. Even though I saw her briefly last night, it wasn't enough. There are things I need to tell her, but that's not the only reason. I just want to be close to her again. Opening her nightstand drawer, I find a pen and paper and write out a quick message:

Charlie, I need to talk to you. It's urgent. It's regarding the thing we signed. Call me at Wink Hotel. I'll be waiting.

I stare at the note and try to decide how to sign my name. *Dante? Love, Dante? Obsessed with you, Dante?* I feel like a freakin' twelve-year-old, like I'm seconds away from zits and wet dreams.

Shaking my head, I decide on: *—D*

Folding up the note, I lay it on her pillow. Then I decide that's too creepy and move it to the dresser. Then back to the pillow. I let out a frustrated groan, because I'm getting on my own nerves.

It's time to leave, I realize. Because being caught in her room really would make me a creeper. I'm moving toward the window when something catches my eye. There are two tin cans near the wall next to her bed. Narrowing my eyes, I walk toward them, then bend down.

Sherwin-Williams. One can of primer, one can of red paint. My hands ball into fists. I should be happy she's doing this. She told me herself she wanted to repaint her room. I wonder if Blue knows she's repainting her room. I wonder if he's asking if she wants a ride to the party tonight. I wonder if he knows what being strangled feels like.

Sliding her window open, I steal one last look around her room. Then I crawl out and climb down. There's nothing else I can do now. I've got to get back to Wink Hotel and wait for a call that may never come—while Charlie's out there…changing.

42

PARTY CHARLIE

Charlie doesn't call. This tiny fact crushes me like a bug.

Earlier today, I had a clear goal: keep Charlie safe. But now I'm just trying to hold onto my freaking sanity.

I feel like a maniac, pacing the floors of my hotel, replaying everything she's ever said to me. Her words, they're like pieces of a puzzle, and I'm sticking them together to see what they create. What does the picture say? Does she feel the same way I do? Am I sure?

At 10:00 P.M., I decide I can't wait another minute. I change into a button-down shirt and pull on a belt. All in all, my wardrobe takes thirty seconds to update. About as much time as I ever spend getting ready, but tonight it feels like an eternity.

Grabbing my car keys, I go outside and slide inside Elizabeth Taylor. Even this small act brings on a pang of nerves. After all, she's the one who named my ride. I've known Charlie for nine days, yet she's touched so much of my life that I can't escape the thought of her.

I blast the radio and drive to where I know I've seen Preston

Road. Then I head down it until I see Parker. Turning right, I see short, squat houses kept in pristine condition. It's a neighborhood built to emulate the rich.

After a few minutes, the houses become farther apart, and I decide I'm headed in the right direction. I may not have the exact address for my GPS, but I shouldn't have a problem finding Natalie's pad. Party locales are almost always in the middle of nowhere so the po-pos don't bust them. I lean over my steering wheel and catch a glimpse of cars parked alongside the road. As I get closer, I realize just how many there are, and I know I've found the place.

Parking Elizabeth Taylor, I kill the engine and click off my seat belt. I'm about to head inside when I stop. It's been forever since I've come to a party alone. Not like I care—it just feels strange. This must be what dorks feel like. I decide I'll pour a little out for the nerds of the world next chance I get.

I walk up the long driveway and open the door. I'm three steps inside when a girl dressed as a slutified sailor runs toward me. I recognize her immediately as Natalie, the chick who talked Charlie into skipping this afternoon.

"No. Stop," she says, stabbing a manicured nail in my direction.

I wonder what I'll do if she tries to kick me out. Maybe I'll join an alien conspiracy group, decide anything's possible.

"Take off your shoes. Do you see this?" She points toward the cream-colored carpet. "My parents will kill me if anyone jacks it up."

"Then prepare thyself because you're having a party, sweetheart. That carpet's hours are numbered."

"Off," she repeats. "Now."

"I'm not taking them off," I tell her. And I mean it. If I have to wrestle her to the ground, my babies aren't coming off. "Where's Charlie?" I quickly add.

"She's in the barn."

"You have a barn? Seriously?"

"Take your shoes off."

I try to move past her, but she steps in front of me.

"I will mace you," she says. "In the face…I will mace you."

As I strategize how to come at Natalie—like a linebacker, or a raving lunatic, or perhaps both—I spot Annabelle near the back of the house. I think I must be imagining things, but no, it's her. Charlie must have made a quick climb up the social ladder to get herself and her friend an invite to this party.

"Annabelle," I call out. She doesn't hear me, or if she does, she doesn't acknowledge my presence.

Sensing I might make a break for it, Natalie pushes a palm to my chest. "Down, boy."

"Woman, you're getting on my last nerve." I consider going around the house to avoid taking off my beloved reds, but I need to talk to Annabelle. Shaking my head, I kick off my Chucks and throw them in a heap with the others near the door. "Happy?"

"Elated."

"I care."

"This is my house, you know?"

"Whatev."

I move past her and toward where I last saw Annabelle. It seems she's disappeared into the crowd. I'd love to pick her mind, get the lowdown on Charlie before I face her. Is she still pissed? Still being weird?

But it appears I'm on my own.

Grabbing a beer from the kitchen counter, I make my way out back and immediately search for her. There are people everywhere, even more than at Taylor's party a week ago. Some are dressed in costumes, and all are completely plastered.

A chick in a cowgirl getup grabs my hands and starts to sway to the music. She's dancing like it's a slow song, though it's anything but.

"Dance with me," she slurs. "Like Romeo and Juliet."

What?

"Gotta go, babe." I push her onto the closest guy I see. When she lands in his arms, he smiles like I just handed him a bib and a warm teat—which I kinda did. "Where's the barn?" I ask the guy.

He nods toward the woods, and I spot a dirt path winding through tall, barren trees.

Why does everyone's backyard here look like a set for a horror movie?

I kill my beer and shove it in the guy's hand. His tongue is so far down the girl's mouth, he doesn't even notice where it came from. He just wraps his hand around it and moans as if the empty can just added to his overall enjoyment.

I make my way toward the path but stop before setting foot on it. Glancing around, I notice a pile of white socks. Guess I'm going barefoot. I pull off my own socks and toss them in with the rest. It'll be the last time I ever see them, because I'm sure as hell not chancing picking up someone else's on my way out. The thought alone makes me cringe.

Dirt from the path rubs between my toes as I follow a barefoot couple holding hands farther ahead. It takes a solid five minutes of walking before I see the barn. I have no idea why anyone would build this thing so far from the house, but my guess is someone in Natalie's family is enjoying less-than-honest recreational activities out here.

The barn is red, which brings a smile to my lips. I do enjoy red barns. I mean, if there's one thing in this world that's meant to be red, it's a barn. And that's a damn fact.

Inside, I can see people dancing and sitting on squares of hay. Above their drunken heads, multicolored lights are strung across wooden rafters. In the center of the strands, a small disco ball dangles on a cord, spinning and casting dots of white light across smiling cheeks and laughing mouths. This barn was built for partying.

My eyes take in everything before landing on her—on Charlie. She's standing on a bale of hay and is dancing back-to-back with another girl. Draped over her slender body is confidence I've never seen before. Confidence I was all prepared to teach her about. I notice it in the way she moves, the way she laughs. My mouth falls open when I see what she's wearing.

Thin, bare legs stretch out from tiny, barely there white shorts. She raises her arms over her head and does the drunk-girl anthem scream. As she does, her low-cut red silk blouse tugs upward, exposing her midriff. I want to walk right over there and flip her over my shoulder. I want to rip that shirt back down so the guy sitting near her, ogling her, will mind his fucking manners.

But I wait. I want her to see me, and I want to see the look on her face when it happens.

She turns in my direction, and my heart pounds something furious. And then it stops, right there in my chest, just forgets its purpose and refuses to function. Her eyes don't fall on me, but no matter, mine are on her. Her lips are pulled into a wide smile, and she's laughing at something Ogle Boy is yelling up at her.

Charlie's mouth has always been beautiful. Full, plump lips. A small pink tongue. A delicate line running from the bottom of her nose to the top of those adorable lips. But her teeth, they were always wrong—a stop sign on a busy highway. The only thing that kept her from being every dentist's fantasy.

But as I step closer, I see I'm not imagining things. That her teeth are white and straight and that everyone she smiles at seems drawn to smile right back. Her mouth, it's become contagious. Addictive.

A secret weapon that just reached its fullest potential.

She's asked for more beauty. And I wasn't there to stop her. I shove my way toward her, and she finally spots me. Her face pulls into a smile, the biggest I've seen tonight.

Then it's gone.

She jumps down from the bale of hay and storms away from me to the other side of the barn, pushing past people as she moves.

"Charlie," I yell.

She keeps going without turning back.

I run to catch up to her, and people start to stare. I don't care. I don't give a rat's ass about anything but her.

Charlie reaches the back of the barn. There's no door. Nowhere for her to go. She turns and faces me, her eyes blazing. "Get away from me," she growls.

The sound of her voice shocks me. It makes my muscles feel like glue, sticky and thick. I reach out to touch her but stop myself. I'm afraid she'll pull away.

Terrified she'll insist I leave.

43

PLAYING GAMES

"Charlie." I say her name so softly it hurts my throat. Like her very name is too much for me to manage. "Please. I have to talk to you."

"It doesn't matter," she spits. "I don't want to talk to you."

Some dude walks up between us, stands near Charlie. "There a problem?"

He glares at me, and I fight every impulse to rip his head from his shoulders.

"Move. Away," I snarl.

The guy stares at me for a moment, his eyes running up and down my frame, sizing me up to see if he can take me. Realizing he can't, he raises his hands and moves away, the look on his face saying he never cared in the first place.

I glance back at Charlie. She's eyeing me like I did something unspeakable to her, like she's found me out. Still, I can't walk away.

"Can we go outside for a minute?" I ask. "I promise I'll leave once you hear me out."

Charlie steps close to me. She leans her head toward mine, her lips brushing my ear. Her voice is so calm, it raises goose bumps on my arms. "I want you to leave, Dante. I want you to stay away from me. You came for one thing, and I'm giving it to you." She pulls back, and I notice her eyes have filled with tears. I reach up to rub them away, but she jerks away like I slapped her. Her head tilts, and her face swims with pain. "Go. I'm begging you."

I came here tonight to protect Charlie, to keep her safe from collectors, from people trying to take her light. But I've already done it. It was me who asked her to sign that contract. Me who pushed her to fulfill it. Me who brought the tears slipping down her cheeks. She may have cared about me once, but that's gone now. I can see it in the way she's looking at me. She sees me for what I am. Arrogant. Egotistical.

Selfish.

I back away from Charlie, because as much as I want to protect her from what's coming, I can't stand seeing her cry while knowing it's my fault. Charlie is generous and happy, a loyal friend and an honest person.

And she is beautiful.

Inside, Charlie glows—her soul's the most precious thing I've ever seen. And on the outside, she's even more beautiful. Not just the way she is now, though she is killing it tonight, enough to take my breath away, but the way she *was*. The bounce of her hair when she jumped on the bed, the glow of her skin when she told me about the charity, the curve of her mouth when she said she liked the sound the world made. And her eyes—I've never seen as much life in anyone's eyes as I do hers.

Charlie is beautiful.

And I convinced her she wasn't.

She knows what I did was wrong, making her feel bad about who she is. She went along with it for a while, maybe because she secretly desired traditional beauty and popularity. Or maybe because she sought my approval. And I bet...when I didn't kiss her...she decided I wasn't interested—that I'd been playing her all along. This last thought stings going down.

I take one last look at Charlie, her drowned eyes and parted mouth, and turn to go.

Not sure where I'm headed, I leave the barn and head for the woods. I don't make it twenty feet outside before stopping. Charlie may hate me, and I have to live with the fact that I caused that. But there's something much bigger to think about. In two days, I'm certain Boss Man will send another collector, or all his collectors, and force Charlie to fulfill the contract faster.

A jolt of nerves rushes through my bloodstream like a shot of adrenaline. I have to take my feelings out of this. If Charlie hates me, is disgusted with me, so be it. I won't leave here without her. If I have to drag her out kicking and screaming, I'm not going to let someone hurt her the way I have—or worse.

My heart pumps hard as I march toward the barn. Nothing will stop me from rescuing this girl. Not even if she despises me.

I spot Charlie sitting in a circle of people, leaning against Annabelle's shoulder. I walk toward the circle, but no one notices me over the music, which sounds much louder than before. Overhead, I notice someone has killed the multicolored lights so that the only glow comes from the disco ball. I swallow hard, then open my mouth to call for Charlie. I'll make a scene. Yell her name over and over until everyone pushes for her to go just to shut me up.

But I stop before her name reaches my lips.

In the center of the circle, I see a bottle. More importantly, I see Charlie reaching for it, her fingers closing over the green glass. It spins beneath her hand, and every breath I'd been holding rushes out. My head spins. This isn't the girl I know. The girl I met eight days ago would be inside, searching for a soda amongst the liquor, making awkward conversation with people who don't care. But now she's here. Playing a make-out game. Wearing way too little clothing.

She watches the bottle spin to a stop, and so do I, because my body won't operate anymore. It's frozen in horror, anticipating what I don't want to watch. In my head, I make bargains with no one in particular.

Don't let her kiss anyone, and I'll start being a better person. I'll eat vegetables. Save baby seals.

The bottle lands on a guy I can't identify. From where I'm standing, I can only see the back of his head. Charlie leans forward, and so does the guy. I gasp like a chick, and my blood solidifies.

Please. Don't do it. Decide I'm too important. Decide you care too much. That you never realized it until now.

Charlie's head tilts to the side, and her lips connect with the guy's lips. With their heads turned like that, I can see that the guy she's kissing, the guy who's shaking with nerves, is Blue.

Something explodes in my chest. It turns my entire body inside out until all my organs, all my muscle and tissue, is exposed.

Red flashes in front of my eyes, and before I know what I'm doing, I'm storming toward her.

Moving like a hurricane.

44

FIRE

I grab Charlie's arm and yank her up. "What the hell do you think you're doing?"

Her blue eyes widen, like she's surprised I'm still here. "Dante," she says.

It's all she can get out, because before she can add anything else, I'm scooping her into my arms and carrying her ass out of the barn. She screams and kicks and yells just like I thought she would. Behind me, I wait for a blow from Blue. But it never comes—whether it's because Annabelle's telling him to stay put or he doesn't know how to react, I'm not sure. And I don't care.

I carry Charlie into the forest, far away from the barn and the path and the people who might interrupt. Ensuring we're alone, I set her down. Once her feet hit the ground, she stops yelling and limps a few steps away from me.

"You have no right," she says, and I can tell she means it.

"The hell I don't," I retort.

She spins around and steps toward me. "What did you just say?"

I think about it, because even though I said it two seconds ago, I can't remember.

"Who do you think you are?" Charlie's lips push out, and her head falls to the side like she's inspecting me, like I'm an exhibit at some dusty museum. "You wanted me to sign that contract. I did. You wanted to convince me I wasn't beautiful. It worked. Then…then you pretended you cared. And I bought it." She covers her mouth like she wants to stop what's coming. Her words slide out quiet and muffled, but they slice through me like blades. "Everything I did, I did because of you."

I concentrate on breathing. In. Out. In. Out. It seems like the only thing I can do, because my body is trying to absorb what she just said. This is my fault, and she knows it. I was sure she did, but to hear her say it, to hear it out there—it kills.

I turn my back to her and take a few steps away. There are things I need to say, and I can't watch her face as I'm saying it. "Charlie, I know you're angry with me."

I pause, waiting for her to tell me just how angry. She doesn't.

"But you need to know the truth. I didn't mean for this to happen." I stop, considering what I just said. "Actually, I guess I did mean for this to happen. At first. But then I got to know you, Charlie. I got to see how you are, the things you do for other people. The way you smile when there's nothing left to smile about, and the way you laugh…it hurts to even hear it. Because it reminds me what it's like to live. To be happy." I take a deep breath. "You are beautiful, Charlie. You're so beautiful, and I can't believe I let you think you weren't."

I turn around but focus on the ground. I can't see her face. It'll end me. But my eyes are deceitful, and before I can gouge them from my face, they slide up and land on her. On Charlie. And she's crying. Tears rolling down her cheeks, sliding into a wide, happy smile.

"You're smiling," I say.

She nods, her grin stretching further.

The way she's looking at me, like she never really stopped believing in me, it shatters my heart, reveals something I buried long ago. And it's suddenly too much. I can't take it anymore, can't deny what I'm feeling. My breath catches, and before I can stop myself, the words tumble out.

"I love you, Charlie," I say. "I fucking love you so much."

A gasp escapes her throat as I race toward her. I tug her against me and smash my mouth over hers. I feel everything—her hair between my fingers, her skin pressing against mine. And her lips. I feel those soft pink lips freeze for a moment beneath my kiss. And then I feel her relax, opening her mouth and mirroring my movements. She leans into me, twining her arms around my neck, pulling me so that there's nothing between us.

I grab her thighs and hoist her up, and she wraps her legs around me. Fumbling toward a tree, I press her back against it and push toward her, my hips locking against hers. An animalistic groan escapes my throat as I kiss her harder, deeper. I trail my lips down her neck and along her collarbone, and Charlie softly moans. Then I bury my head against her chest and take her in—her smell, her chest rising and falling. The wild thumping of her heart.

Slowly, I let her down, easing her legs from around my waist and back to the ground. I pull her head against me and hold it there, never wanting to let her go. Not for anyone or anything. My arms pull her closer and closer until I'm afraid I may crush her. But I can't let up. I'm afraid if I do, she'll realize I'm not worthy of her. Afraid to hear her say she doesn't feel the same way. That she thinks I'm great, but she's completely toasted, and we shouldn't mention this tomorrow.

Even though I've got her in a death grip, she manages to pull her head back and gaze up at me. Her pink lips are bright and swollen, and I can't help rubbing my thumb over them.

She kisses the tip of my finger, and I squeeze my eyes shut as tightly as I can. So I don't see when she opens her lips. I don't see when she pulls in a breath and swallows and whispers to me, "I love you, Dante. I've loved you from the start."

But I *hear* her say it, and that's all I need to crumble. Almost choking on my words, I manage to ask, "Why?"

I open my eyes and find Charlie smiling. She runs her hand over my cheek, then leans back against my chest. "Because I see you. Even though you try so hard to hide, I see you, anyway."

What she says feels so good that when my breath rushes out, it's mixed with laughter. Two days ago, I couldn't imagine chancing my life for hers. And now I wouldn't have it any other way.

I will protect this girl with everything I have, because if something happens to her, I will lose myself. I will cease to exist. And I will take everyone with me.

With unfathomable effort, I pull away from her and take her face in my hands. "Charlie, I need to tell you something."

Her eyes lock on mine, and she smiles wider, assuming I have more good things to tell her. Things that will bring us closer together. I imagine the way her face will change when I tell her everything, and the weight of it drags me down. I need to protect her. I need to tell her the truth about me and the contract. But I can't lose her. Not after what just happened between us.

"I want you to stop asking for beauty. I love the way you look, okay?" I gently squeeze her face between my hands. "Can you promise me you won't ask for anything else? It's important to me."

Charlie's eyes fall to my chest. I sense it instantly, that there's something she's not admitting.

"What is it?" I ask. "What's wrong?"

"I'll try not to," she says. "I really will."

"What do you mean, you'll 'try not to'? Can't you just promise me?"

She pulls her face from my hands and steps away. "It's getting harder…to not ask for things. It's like the longer I go without asking for something, the more anxious I get. It started after the first time, but I figured I was just excited to add new things." She pauses, wrapping her arms around herself. "But flying back from Vegas after I, you know, changed my skin…I felt physically sick. Like my body was screaming for me to do something else, something new. It scared me, so I waited as long as I could. Decided I should take a break to get some perspective."

Charlie turns and faces me, and I find I can't move. I don't want to hear what she's saying, but she opens her mouth and continues anyway.

"But the more I resisted, the sicker I felt. When you came by last night, I was feeling the worst of it. I was shaking and sweating. I knew what it was, and in the middle of the night, I couldn't take it anymore. So I asked for something. Something small. Just a little wish to better my smile. The second I made the request, it's like the sickness was vacuumed from my body. It was just…gone." Fear flashes behind her eyes.

"Why is this happening, Dante? I thought I could go at my own pace."

I fight to control my anger—anger with Boss Man for putting a target on her, and anger with myself for following orders. I take Charlie's hands. "Because they know how perfect your soul is, and they want it. But listen to me, you have to fight it. You have to fight it for as long as you possibly can, understand? Do you feel okay right now?"

She nods, but she still looks terrified.

"Good. If it hits again, the sickness, call me and I'll be there. We'll work through it."

Charlie presses her lips together like she's thinking about something. "It's okay, though, right? I mean, my soul will go to heaven." She shakes her head like she's being silly. "I'm being stupid over nothing."

"You're not being stupid. The truth is…" I grab Charlie by the shoulders and swallow hard. "The truth is, your soul may be in danger."

"Danger?" Her eyes widen, and even that tears me apart. I don't want her to be afraid, but she has to know.

"Charlie. There are collectors for heaven, like I told you." So far, I'm not lying. I just have to get through this. Get it over with. "But there are other collectors, too. Different ones."

"Different how?" she asks, her voice barely a whisper.

"They…they don't work for…" I point upward.

"Oh, my gosh," Charlie says, pulling away from me. "There are collectors from hell, too?"

I nod, because I can't get any words out.

She covers her mouth, and tears spring to her eyes. When she speaks again, I can barely hear her. She starts crying, because she already knows. She knows something feels off, and here's the explanation. "Do they want my soul, too?"

Again, I nod.

"But I signed the contract," she blurts, dropping the hand from her mouth. "Everything's okay. I'll just fulfill the contract, and then they can't get it. Right? Right, Dante?"

Charlie steps toward me, lays her hands on my chest, begs me to tell her she's right. That they can't take her soul.

I realize then that I'm not strong enough to tell her. I've spent nineteen years being selfish, taking whatever I wanted without question. And there's nothing—*nothing*—I want more than Charlie. I can't tell her. I can't have the fear on her face be because of me.

"The paper you signed," I say softly. "It's a general contract. I didn't know it was going to work out like this."

It's the truth. I imagine if Big Guy had a contract, it'd include the same verbiage. The only thing that matters is who it's presented by. Which side they work for. And it's true that I didn't know it'd work out like this. I never could have predicted that I'd fall in love with my assignment.

I'm about to try and explain why we can't be certain her soul will go to heaven—without exposing myself—when I sense him.

The collector.

He's here.

45

TRUST

I step in front of Charlie, ready to protect her with my life if needed.

"What is it?" Charlie asks, noticing the way my face changes.

I step toward where I feel the pull, keeping Charlie close behind me. Then I see it. A flash of red. When I realize it's Valery and not the collector sent to tail me, I relax. Still, I can't talk to her with Charlie here.

I face Charlie and wrap my hands around her jaw. "Can you do something for me? Can you wait for me up at the house?"

"Dante, you're scaring me."

"No. Don't be scared, baby." I kiss her lightly on the tip of her nose, then again on her forehead. "I'll be right behind you. Go now, okay?"

She glances into the forest where she knows I was just looking and nods. Over her shoulder, she watches me as she makes her way toward the path. When I can no longer see her, I head toward Valery.

"Come out, Red," I say. "I know you're here."

Valery steps out from behind a tree like a mass murderer and struts forward. Her face scrunches in disgust as her heels dig into soil and dried leaves.

"What are you doing out here?" she asks.

"Talking."

"Liar."

"You know what we're doing out here; you've been hanging around like a stage-five clinger," I say. "So what's going on? What do you have to say?"

Valery smooths her hair back, then perches her claws on her hips. "I've come to warn you. We believe you're being tracked by one of your own. And that he may try to harm you, or maybe even Charlie."

"No shit, Sherlock." I lean against a tree and kick my foot up on the bark. "What else you got?"

"You know?"

"Of course I know."

"Then you're going to tell her."

My eyes pull to the right. "I'm trying."

Valery laughs. It's quick and sharp and says this is anything but funny. "Well allow me to give you some motivation. You have until tomorrow to tell her who you really are, or I will."

I push away from the tree and step toward her. "Thought you weren't going to interfere?"

"Plans have changed," Valery says, pulling out a cigarette and lighting it. "Tell her. Soon. Let her choose for herself who she wants to side with."

My mind races. I have to tell Charlie, and chances are that after I do, she'll want to get as far away from me as possible. Maybe she'll run right into Valery's waiting arms. It wouldn't be the worst thing in the world. Valery would try and protect her. But she couldn't do what I would, wouldn't go to the same extremes to keep her safe.

She doesn't love her like I do.

But if Charlie won't come near me after I tell her the truth, Valery may be my only option to ensure Charlie stays safe. Though in order for Valery to do that, I have to tell her everything.

"Charlie signed a soul contract," I confess.

Valery's cigarette drops to the ground. Her eyes dart around like a crazy person's. "I knew it. I freaking knew it. It's why she looks so different. Isn't it?"

I nod.

She paces past me and back again, muttering to herself. When she walks by me for the third time, I grab her arm.

"Valery." I can't believe what I'm about to say, what I'm about to do. "Work with me. Together we can keep her safe."

She rips her arm from my grasp. "Work with you?" she snarls. "You're crazy. I mean, freaking *loco*." She rolls a finger near her temple to mimic just how crazy I am. "We would never work with one of you. We have standards. Morals. Things you demons don't give a second thought to. You think I buy that you care about her? That you wouldn't say or do anything to ensure you get a promotion? You said it yourself, didn't you?" Valery huffs. "*I* can protect Charlie, and I certainly don't need your help to do it."

I storm away from her, flipping her off over my shoulder.

"Dante," she yells from behind me, "don't you walk away from me."

I spin around and walk backwards. "Forget I said anything. I won't let anything happen to her. I'd die first. I'd die *again*."

Valery's face changes. It softens, like she sees something she missed before. "Tell her, or I will."

It's the last thing I hear her say before landing on the path and finding my way back to Charlie. I spot her waiting near the front door and quickly pull her into my arms.

Kissing the top of her head, I mumble, "Ready to go?"

Charlie glances around like she wants to tell Blue and Annabelle good night. When she doesn't spot them, she looks back at me and gives a halfhearted nod.

I pull one arm around her and open the door. I'm about to step out onto the patio when I remember I'm barefoot. Stepping back inside, I flip through the pile of shoes, searching for my sneakers. I've spent all of ten seconds on the task when the realization hits me.

They're gone.

I dash around the house, looking for anyone who may have them. No one does, and it doesn't surprise me. Those puppies were autographed by Dwyane Wade. And now they're gone. Stolen. Jacked. I want to scream and throw things and possibly find that mace Natalie was talking about and hose every third person I see. Instead, I walk back to Charlie and sling my arm over her shoulder.

As we walk toward Elizabeth Taylor, Charlie asks, "Where are your shoes?"

I bite the inside of my lip and take a deep breath. "It doesn't matter," I say. Then I kiss the top of her head and open the car door.

It's quiet in the car as I drive toward Charlie's house. I feel like she's waiting for me to say something, but I'm just not sure how to tell her what I am. That this was all my fault.

Eventually, she breaks the silence. "What was out there? In the woods?"

I glance at her, then back at the road. "You know."

"One of them?" she gasps. "One of the bad ones?"

I nod, and my heart tugs at hearing her call my fellow collectors…me…*bad ones*.

"How many are there?" she breathes.

"Six."

"That doesn't seem like too many," she says, sounding relieved. "How many good ones are there? The ones like you?"

"I…I'm not sure, Charlie." It's the truth, but it's getting harder to answer her questions without lying. And I really don't want to lie to her. Not anymore. I anxiously await her next question, wondering how I'll dodge it. How much longer I can do this.

"I was excited about the dance," she whispers, staring out the window. "Now it feels so trivial. You know?"

"You found the tickets." I reach over and grab her hand.

Her eyes stay locked on the passenger window, watching the world speed by way too quickly. "Yeah."

I can't stand the defeat in her voice. Eight days ago, Charlie's only worry was whether to wear purple or pink jeans to school. Now she's fighting a soul contract I pushed her to sign, terrified the wrong people will claim her soul.

Before I can rationalize how terrible an idea this is, I say, "We're going."

She glances over. "Yeah, right."

"We are." I squeeze her hand. "We're going to go. And when it's over, we'll face what needs to happen to keep your soul safe."

"How?" she asks. "How will we be sure my soul isn't in danger?"

I clench my jaw, because I'm terrified of how she'll react when I tell her. I pull in a deep breath. "We'll have to run." When she doesn't respond, I keep going. "We'll have to run for a long time, Charlie. A really long time. And you'll have to fight fulfilling the contract. It's going to be really hard. The hardest thing you've ever done." I rub up and down her arm and deliver the final blow. "You won't be able to call home. You'll have to tell your grandma and your friends—you'll have to tell them good-bye."

For a long time, Charlie stays quiet. She nods several times and squeezes my hand. I pull up to her house and face her.

"Are you okay?" I ask.

"Yeah." She looks at me and smiles. Then her voice breaks, and tears roll down her cheeks. "I did this to myself."

I pull her into an embrace, and she sobs into my chest. I know she's angry with me, that somewhere down deep she blames me instead of herself. And she should. But right now, she needs me to hold her. So I do. I keep my arms wrapped around her for as long as she wants. I let her cry until her blue eyes are red and swollen. Then I lift her chin in my hand and rub the tears from her cheeks and from beneath her eyes.

"I'm sorry, Charlie."

She nods and chokes on more tears. "I don't understand," she says. "If I fulfill the contract, if I can't resist the sickness, what will happen?"

"I'm not sure," I say, which is true. I think because I signed the contract, her soul will slide inside of me. Then the collectors will try and steal it from me, or drag me back to hell and kill two birds with one stone. And then there's Charlie herself. Once her soul leaves her body, I feel sure Boss Man will give the green light for her death, and he may send someone to take her out. I know killing a human could cause war, but it's clear Boss Man doesn't want to take any chances with Charlie, with what her life's work could bring about.

I'm going to tell her this, all of this, but not tonight. I want Charlie to have one more day of happiness. Just one more.

I have two days to bring her in, so I'll give her tomorrow night. It'll allow me the time I need to book our flights and pack some things we'll need along the way. I know I'm pushing my luck, but I need her to have this. One last day with her grandmother and one last night with her friends.

Then we'll go.

"Listen," I say, pulling her head against my chest. "I want you to spend time with your grandmother tomorrow. I want you to forget all about this and trust that I'm going to handle everything." I lift her face and kiss her lips, tasting salt from her tears. "Tomorrow, I'm going to pick you up at seven o'clock and take you to that dance. It's going to be perfect. I promise. Then after that..."

"We'll run," she finishes for me.

"Go upstairs and go to sleep. Imagine me lying next to you. Tomorrow this crap doesn't exist. None of it, okay? It's only you and me and the people you care about. Let me take care of everything."

I wait for her to argue, to ask me questions I can't—or don't want to—answer. But she wraps her arms around my neck and pushes her forehead against mine. Then she closes her eyes and whispers, "I trust you."

Her words trigger a warm current down my spine. I could never trust anyone the way she does me. I'd want every question answered, every rock overturned. But not her. She believes in people.

She believes in me.

I kiss her softly, taking my time, trying to memorize the taste and touch of her tongue. Then I lift my head and nod toward her house. She gets out of the car and limps her way up the sidewalk. As I watch her go, I wonder how I'll ever protect her. I roll my ankle and silently curse my cuff. Other demons envy our cuffs—wish *they* were chosen to walk the earth. But I've always hated it, and now... Now it feels like a prison sentence. As long as I'm wearing it, they'll always know where I am—and where *she* is, too. But there's nothing I can do about it. Because without it, I can't stay with her. Can't ensure she's safe.

At the door, Charlie turns and faces me. A tentative smile tugs at the side of her mouth. I give a small wave, and she blows a kiss. It's such a funny, innocent thing to do. I can't help but laugh.

The sound startles me, like I never expected to hear myself do that again.

46

THE DANCE

The next evening, I drive to Charlie's house. I'm early, but I want her to know I'm looking forward to seeing her. It was all I could do to stop myself from parking outside her house last night just to ensure she was safe. But I didn't want to have to try and explain what I was doing if she spotted me, and I certainly didn't want the collector following me to question my actions.

Pulling up outside Charlie's house, I try and relax. This night is for her. Besides, I've done everything I can to prepare us.

I've packed two bags full of food and clothing and booked two tickets to Tokyo, where an enormous population will shield us. Then I pulled out the maximum on my Amex Black, and cut the card—and a piece of my soul—in half. I won't be able to use it once we're on the run.

Inside one of the bags, I've stashed maps and names of places we can flee to at a moment's notice. And wrapped in those maps... is the Glock .45 I bought this morning. It's not usually my style to rely on a weapon to fight my battles, but we're talking about demons here, not school-yard bullies. We'll play everything else by ear, because the more planned we are, the more predictable we become.

Brushing off my charcoal blazer and red button-down, I take a deep breath. Charlie deserves this night, and I intend on giving it to her. I slide out of Elizabeth Taylor, head toward the porch, and ring the doorbell.

I wait for Grams to open the door, to give me the stank eye. Inside my head, I'm coming up with solid one-liners to throw her way. I've pretty much decided on something to do with a drunken shar-pei, when the door swings open.

I lift my eyes and gasp.

My heart clenches in my chest, and my muscles lock in place. I feel like I can't breathe, like I never could in the first place. In fact, I'm quite certain I will never fill my lungs again. Even though I'm looking right at her, my eyes refuse to believe what they're seeing.

Charlie stands inches away, her *entire* body transformed. She's wearing the red dress I bought her, and on her back are two silk angel wings she must have picked up at a Halloween store. Her blond hair, smooth skin, and glasses-free eyes all look the same. I imagine if she were smiling, I'd still see perfectly straight teeth. But she's not smiling. Not even close. That probably has something to do with the rest of her.

The way her cheekbones jut out, and the way her chest appears larger. The way her hips seem a bit fuller and her nose slightly thinner. I reach out and run my hand down her arm, the skin beneath my hand kissed with a fresh bronze glow. She is stunning, enough to stop a guy's heart with a glance, but already, I yearn for my old Charlie.

"When?" I whisper.

"Last night. I was going to call, but it happened so fast. I couldn't stop it, Dante." Her eyes glisten with tears. "But I do look beautiful, don't I?" She manages a small smile that shatters my dead soul.

"You've always been beautiful, sweetheart." My forehead pricks with sweat, and my hands curl into fists. I'm afraid to turn on her soul light, afraid of what I'll find. Is it over? Have I collected her soul without realizing it?

She steps toward me, and I notice something that makes my brain sing.

Her limp.

I point to her hip and grin so hard I'm afraid my face will break. "You still have—"

"Yeah," she says. "No way is anyone taking that from me. I got it the night my parents died. It's mine. No one else's."

I yank Charlie into a hug. I'm overwhelmed by her. Not her beauty, but her soul. It terrifies me that more of the contract was fulfilled. That the only piece left of her to give is that blessed limp. But I won't let anything destroy her night. I'm not sure what to say to make things better, or to mask the fear I'm feeling, and before I can think of something good, I blurt, "You're my girlfriend."

Charlie stares at me, her mouth quivering, threatening to transform into a smile.

"Yeah, you are. And tomorrow, I'm going to show you just what I'm willing to do to keep you safe." I lean over and kiss her gloss-coated lips. "But tonight we're going to party school-safety style—punch and cookies and cheesy decorations. It's going to be awesome."

Her quasi-smile blossoms. "I shouldn't be scared," she says, and it sounds like something between a statement and a question.

"You should be terrified," I say. "Because I'm going to show you dance moves that'll have you *begging* for my shit."

She slaps my chest, and though a nervous hesitation lingers in her eyes, she allows me to take her hand and lead her toward the car.

"Where's Grams?" I ask as she carefully crawls into her seat, ensuring her wings don't get crushed.

"Said she was really tired, but she made me take a million pictures before I left."

As we drive toward Centennial High School, I wonder how Charlie explained her new look to Grams. I decide not to mention it for fear of bringing the subject up again. Instead, I take her hand and squeeze. And a part of me—the tiniest little piece—gets excited about this stupid school dance.

Because I know it may be the last time I'll see Charlie truly happy.

• • •

Charlie and I walk into the school gym, and I let out a long sigh. It's just as I feared. It's like every loser in Peachville got together and shopped for the most horrifically cheesy decorations.

Near the floor, a fog machine blasts hazy clouds, and dangling from the rafters are a bazillion black and orange streamers. Along the walls, some douchebag has taped paper spiders and pumpkins. And the band—oh, sweet mercy—the band. They're like a cross between mini Justin Biebers and the Jonas Brothers, and the Halloween covers they're playing make my ears bleed. But when I glance at Charlie, decked out in her red dress and angel wings, everything becomes wonderful again. If she's here, I'm happy. But if she steps out to, like, pee or something, I'm lighting a match.

As Charlie and I walk toward the dance floor, all eyes take her in. Whispers are exchanged, and fingers are pointed, and I can't help getting pissed off. I mean, why couldn't they have noticed her before? She was just as amazing then. But I guess I'm just as guilty of overlooking her.

Seeing Charlie now, I almost don't recognize her myself. It causes a twinge of nerves to rush through me. Will she move on now that she's physically perfect?

But almost like she's reading my mind, she absently reaches her polished nails into her dress pocket and pops a few Skittles in her mouth. I bite my lip to keep from laughing, because that tiny action tells me she's still Charlie. She's still my girl.

Annabelle sees us and races over. "Char-char!" she squeals. "You look phenomenal." Her face changes, like she's realizing exactly how phenomenal. "In fact, you look different. Like, way different."

"I let Grams do my makeup," Charlie chirps.

Annabelle eyes her. "Yeah, I don't know."

Charlie pulls her friend into a hug, going for distraction. "Come on, squeeze me," she says. "I like your costume. It's…uh…"

"I'm Katharine Hepburn," Annabelle says, her face relaxing somewhat.

I inspect Annabelle's colorless clothing and cream-painted face.

"See?" she says. "I'm black and white. Like she was in most of her movies." Annabelle's wide-brimmed hat bounces as she considers me. "Big surprise. You didn't dress up."

"I came as Awesome Sauce," I say. "You probably wouldn't recognize it."

She leans back and puts her hands in a square like she's gazing through a camera frame. "No. No, I see…I see…" She drops her hands. "Tool-wear."

Charlie tugs on Annabelle's arm. "You know, you guys could drop the act and admit you like each other."

Annabelle glances at me to see my reaction. I form a gun with my hand and fire in her direction. "Pow."

A grin sweeps across her face, and she fires right back.

Charlie rolls her eyes. Then she gets a nervous edge to her voice. "Hey, uh, where's Blue?"

My shoulders square at the mention of his name. After seeing his lips on hers, I'd like nothing more than to tear him a new one. Even if it was a stupid game.

Annabelle points over her shoulder. Her face squishes together, like she can't believe we're asking. "Seriously?"

As soon as I spot him, I have to stifle a laugh. I'm supposed to hate him, not get off on his costume. But Blue came as... blue. He's dressed in all-blue clothing and even painted his face a dark blueberry color. Standing near the refreshments table, he's pouring himself a glass of green punch. Blue's eyes land on Charlie, then quickly glance away. He knows she's here—probably watched her from the time she came in.

I flick my eyes over Charlie's face. She seems upset, and it strikes a dark flame inside me. I can't stand thinking she cares about him. To keep her mind where it should be—on me—I take her hand. "Want to dance, beautiful?"

She beams up at me and nods. Then she turns toward Annabelle. "You okay if we dance real quick?"

Annabelle waves us away like she couldn't care less.

As I guide Charlie toward the middle of the floor, Taylor turns and stares at the girl on my arm, her jaw hanging open. She can't believe how beautiful Charlie is, and I can't believe I ever missed it. Taylor meets my eyes, then quickly glances away, acting like she doesn't notice us.

I tug Charlie's head against me and press my lips into her hair. A slow song washes over us, and I move my arms around her waist and rock back and forth. Charlie seems to be having trouble with the swaying.

"You okay?" I ask.

Her pink mouth opens, but her eyes divert away from my face. "It's harder for me."

I'm not sure why it's harder, and I don't care. Without thinking, I sweep her into my arms. She laughs long and hard. The sound splits open my heart and fills it with candy-coated goodness. I dance in a circle, occasionally dipping so that her hair falls in a yellow blanket. Being here—surrounded by bad costumes, listening to even worse music—I'm as happy as I remember ever being. The feeling is overwhelming, like at any moment I won't be able to handle it anymore. Like my body will explode from pleasure.

Charlie leans her head against me and mumbles into my chest.

"What'd you say, sweet girl?" I ask.

She looks up at me, her eyes large with joy. "I said I'm so in love with you."

"'Course you are," I say. "I'm freaking outstanding."

Charlie laughs and presses her head back against me. "Thank you, Dante."

"For what?"

"For this. For tonight." She pauses. "And for telling me everything."

A chill races through my arms, and for a second, I'm afraid I'll drop her. I set her down gently but keep my hold around her body. "For telling you everything?"

"You know. The stuff we're not supposed to talk about tonight. Which I'm not talking about. I'm just…I'm happy you told me," she says. "You could have lied. It probably would've made it easier on you if you had. But since you didn't, it makes me realize I can totally trust you."

My gut clenches like a fist, and I feel dangerously close to puking. I've tried to forget about how this night is going to end—with me telling her who I really am—but maybe it's best I get it over with. A cold sweat breaks across my brow. Charlie reaches up to brush her fingers across my skin.

"Are you hot?" she asks. "Want to get a drink?"

I nod, because if I'm going to tell her this, I need to find a quiet place. Charlie takes my hand, and I can't help wondering if she'll still hold it afterward. At the table, she grabs a glass of punch, takes a sip, and passes it to me. I taste it and inwardly sigh to find it squeaky clean. I could seriously use a hit of something strong.

Swallowing down every bit of courage I have, and remembering Valery's threat to expose me, I glance at Charlie. My vocal chords threaten to stop operating at any moment. But somehow, I manage to say, "Hey. I need to talk to you." The words feel thick leaving my mouth, like I just ate peanut butter. And now I'm sure—absolutely positive—that I'm going to hurl.

"Okay," she says, a wide smile touching her lips. "Let's hear it."

"Can we go somewhere?"

Charlie's face falls. She's the most innocent person I know, but even she recognizes the sound of doom. "Oh, no. Do I want to hear this?"

I run my hands through my hair. "Probably not."

She steps back, inspecting my face. Then she glances around. "Come on."

She heads toward an empty hallway, and I follow after her. When the double doors close behind us, she spins and faces me. "What's going on?"

I pull in a long breath and reach for her. She curls into my arms, and I lay my chin on top of her head. I don't want to tell her, don't want her to hate me. But I have to do this. Not because Valery threatened to tell Charlie herself, but because it's the right thing to do. I love her, and I don't want this lie between us.

"Sweet girl," I say into her hair. "Tell me you'll always love me."

"I always will," she says without hesitation.

I close my eyes and clench my teeth. Then I open my mouth and say, "I'm not who you think I am."

Charlie pulls her head back and looks up at me. "What do you mean? You already told me this."

"I didn't… I didn't tell you the whole truth."

I expect her to push away from me, to put distance between our bodies. But instead she tugs me tighter against her. She stays quiet for too long, then whispers, "Tell me."

I pull in a breath through my nose. "I *am* a collector, and I *was* sent to collect your soul. That much is true." I lift my hands to the top of my head, twining my fingers together. I can't stand the sound of my own voice. I let my head fall back, and before I can stop myself, before I can fabricate another lie, I say, "But I don't work for who you think I do."

Charlie holds onto me for a moment. In those sacred seconds, I think she's going to forgive me—that everything's going to be okay between us. Then I feel her arms loosen from around my waist. I feel her head pull away from my chest. And slowly, she moves away, taking small steps until her back presses against the wall. Her face says she understands everything I haven't fully explained.

"No," she says. She shakes her head. "No. No, please." Her voice cracks. I reach for her, and she bends at the waist. "Dante, please. Tell me you're lying. Say it."

I try to pull her to me, but she yanks away.

"Please." She says it so softly, I almost miss it. Then she jerks upright and jabs a finger in my chest. "You tell me you don't mean it. You tell me you're lying."

"I can't," I whisper. A stinging sensation pricks my eyes, but I can't cry. I can't. If I do, I know I'll never stop.

Her face twists with pain, and she starts to shake her head again. Tears slip down her face. "Say it," she cries. "Say what you are."

I push my fists against my eyes and fight against the burning behind them. "I'm a collector," I breathe. "I'm a demon." I pull my hands away from my face, because I have to see her face. I have to see how she's looking at me now that she knows.

When I do, I can no longer stop the tears. They crash over my cheeks and free-fall to the ground.

Because her face.

It's filled with fear. And betrayal. And disappointment.

"Charlie," I say, my voice broken from crying. "I'm a demon."

A cry escapes her throat as I repeat the word. She pushes away from the wall and starts to move down the hallway. Her tears morph into sobs.

"Charlie," I yell. "Please. I love you. I'm going to protect you."

Charlie stops walking. She swivels around and marches toward me, her eyes blazing with anger. "Protect me?" she growls. "*Protect* me?" She raises her hand and slaps me hard across my face.

I cover the stinging spot, and at the same time, I reach for her. She tears away from me and runs down the hall.

"Charlie!" I chase after her. The gym doors fly open under her hands, and I watch as she crashes into Blue. She throws her arms around him and sobs. He immediately pulls her to him and looks for what could have hurt her.

His eyes land on me, and I stop dead in my tracks. Blue pushes Charlie behind him, and his chest swells. His hands ball into fists, and his chin lifts slightly. He's preparing to fight me, and from his blazing eyes, he won't stop until I cease breathing.

Charlie breaks away from him and runs across the dance floor and out of the gym. People stop and stare at me and Blue. I move to go after Charlie, but Blue steps to the side and catches my eye. He shakes his head back and forth, and for the first time in my entire life, I'm actually afraid I'll lose the fight.

I nod once, then turn and walk back down the hallway—away from the only girlfriend I've ever had. The only girl I've ever loved.

Away from Charlie.

47

DESPERATION

Alone in the bathroom, I splash cold water on my face. I almost don't recognize the person staring back at me, broken and ashamed. Someone should have warned me about love's dark underbelly, about the rejection and despair.

Drying my face with a rough brown paper towel, I wonder where she is right now. The last I saw, she was racing out the gym. It couldn't have been more than fifteen minutes ago, but it feels like forever.

As hard as it'll be to face her again, I'm already looking forward to it. I'd rather have her hate me to my face than be without her. Besides, I made her a promise that I intend to keep. I'm going to protect her, body and soul. I'm going to right my wrongs. And maybe one day, she'll forgive what I've done.

I walk into the gym and spot Annabelle on the dance floor. Her eyes connect with mine, and she strides toward me. I brace myself for a second slap, but she just looks at me funny.

"Where's Charlie?" she asks.

I glance around, searching for her. "She hasn't come back

inside?"

"I didn't know she went outside." Annabelle narrows her eyes. "Why *did* she go outside?"

"Because she hates my guts."

Annabelle's face softens, which surprises me. Then it opens with alarm. I turn to see what she's staring at and spot Blue racing toward us.

He's breathing hard and bends over on his knees to catch his breath. "I can't find Charlie anywhere," he tells Annabelle, completely ignoring me.

"You searched everywhere?" I ask.

He glares at me, and I'm certain he's debating kidney-punching my ass. "Yes," he says through clenched teeth. "What did you do to her?"

"Enough to make her hate him," Annabelle chimes in.

I race outside the gym with Blue close on my heels. Together we call her name, circling the school.

"Maybe she went back inside," I say.

"Maybe you should get the hell out of here and leave this to her *friends*," Blue snarls.

I bite my tongue because I don't want to give Charlie another reason to hate me. Instead, I say, "I'm going to run by her house. Maybe she called her grandma to pick her up. I'll take care of this. I'll find her. Just call me at Wink Hotel if she shows, okay?"

Blue clenches his jaw.

"Blue," I say, louder.

"Fine. Fuck." He stomps back toward the gym.

Racing toward Elizabeth Taylor, I fight the fear that something terrible has happened. If it has, I will never forgive myself. This close to deadline, I shouldn't have let her out of my sight. Not even for a second.

I drive around the parking lot a few times, then head toward her house. On the way, I speed like a lunatic and manage to make it there within five minutes. Without even considering knocking, I run toward the trellis and climb toward her window. I need to see for myself if she's here, and I don't want Grams freaking out and calling the 5-0s.

The window slides open beneath my hand, and I remind myself again that this lax safety needs to be remedied. Inside her room, I look for anything suspicious, but nothing seems off. Then I head toward Grams's room. Near her door, I hear the noise of chainsaws and garbage trucks—all sounds coming from Grams's sleeping body. I ease the door open and move to her bedside. If she wakes up, I can't imagine what she'll think. But I know when she does, her granddaughter will be gone. I know the pain she'll feel, the abandonment. It hurts what's left of my heart.

Silently, I lean forward and gently kiss her forehead. She's been good to Charlie, and I'll always be thankful to her for taking care of the girl I love. I pull her blanket closer to her chin and turn to go.

• • •

At Wink Hotel, I barrel down the hallway toward my room, praying there's a message from Blue.

Pushing the door open, I breathe a sigh of relief.

There on my cream-colored retro phone is the red blinking light I've been hoping for. I dash across the room and push the message button. The sound of Annabelle's voice fills my head.

"Dante, it's Annabelle." She pauses, like she's letting that sink in. "We can't find Charlie. We've looked all over the school. We even looked in the places nearby where she might have walked to. Billy's Burgers, Movie Buzz, the Arcade…"

She continues to rattle off places they've searched. But I can't listen anymore, because the room is spinning. I hang up the phone and lean over, gasping for air. The realization burns through me like fire.

They have her.

I jump up and pace the room in a panic. I always figured I had until the end of tomorrow. *One more day*, I'd said. Somehow, Boss Man figured out what I'd been planning. And he'd acted.

My failures rush through my brain like poison. I lived my life like a selfish brute. I watched my father die. My mother found a replacement for the husband I killed, and the only piece I have left of him is now with her. I lost Max, my best and only friend. My favorite shoes were stolen at the stupid party where I lied to Charlie for the last time. And now the only girl I've ever loved has been taken by a collector.

Everything that has ever been important to me is gone. And though I want to fight for hope, to feel like I can turn this all around…right now, it's too much. I cover my face with my hands and scream into them.

I can't lose her. I can't lose Charlie, too.

My mind ticks off the possibilities of how to get her back, but each time I hit a road block. Even if I can find her, he'll know I'm coming. My cuff will give me away.

An electric shock bolts over my spine, and I stiffen. I peek between the fingers covering my face and stare down at my ankle. My cuff.

It's the reason they knew where to find her, the reason they know where I am this very moment. That piece of blasted dargon has kept me prisoner for two years, caged like a filthy animal. I pull my hands away and cross my leg over my knee. Pulling up my dark jeans, I run my fingers over the cool metal.

Boss Man gave me a choice the day I became a collector. Wear the restraint and walk among the living, work for hell and be traceable by him and the other collectors. Eat, breathe, and carry on a normal existence on earth.

Or.

Break it off and die a final death. No afterlife. No Judgment Day. No nothing. Just an eternity of silence. I'd heard of one collector who did it before. I believed it a rumor, but now I'm not so sure. I heard he lived for several hours before starting to fade. And now I wonder…

Being locked in the ninth ring of hell is one thing. It's pain beyond my imagination, but deep down, I figured there'd always be hope. Someone, maybe Max, would spring me from my torture, and I'd be back in action. But this… This is final. No backup plan, no last-minute resolution. Just death.

I imagine Charlie afraid. About who she's with at this very moment. It stirs something hysterical inside me.

And just like that, my decision is made.

48

COINKIDINKS

I push my jeans back down over my new lame sneakers and head for the door. For now, I need my cuff. But my hours as a collector are numbered. The realization is both exhilarating and terrifying.

Elizabeth Taylor has been packed since this afternoon, and when I get outside, I ensure our bags are still in the backseat. I note the size and wonder if they'll fit into Valery's tiny trunk. She no doubt has one of those sporty chick cars. Guess she'll have to figure it out, because I won't be around to ensure the bags are properly packed, or that she stays ahead of the collectors, or that Charlie fulfills her destiny.

I'm about to slide into the driver's seat, trying to keep my mind focused, when something seizes my attention. Spinning around, I spot a figure standing against a car near the back of the parking lot. In the dim lights, I can't quite make out who it is, but the gut sensation I feel tells me everything I need to know—it's a collector. Pulling my blazer back, I wrap my fingers around the Glock in my waistband. If Creepy McCreeperson doesn't announce himself soon, I'll bust a cap in his ass.

The guy takes two quick steps toward me, and I raise the .45 and aim. His hands fly up, and he screeches to a halt.

"Holy crap," he says.

I narrow my eyes and smile when I realize it's Max.

"What do you think you're doing, Captain Psycho?" he says, breathing hard. "You almost shot my ass."

I put the gun away and pull Max into a hug. "What are you doing here?" I say, laughing. "I almost killed you."

"Dude." He starts motioning toward his body. "You know you can't hold this down. Besides, you're going to need me."

When I realize what he's saying, I push him lightly. "Shut up. You're going to help me?"

He nods and grins, but a flash of fear fires behind his eyes. "Figured you'll need someone to talk to when you turn into a Popsicle."

My chest aches when I remember that I'll never make it that far. Realizing this, I know I have to stop him. I won't let him be locked away because of me. "Max," I say, "I'm not going to let you do this."

"The hell you're not," he says. "It's done."

I inspect his face, searching for any sign of wavering. But he looks as determined as a bull. And if I'm being honest, this works out even better. I'd planned to find Valery first, but this will save time. If Max says he'll help me, then I trust him to take Charlie to Valery once I rescue her. "I'm not going to talk you out of this, am I?" I ask.

"No," he says. "So what's the plan, man?"

I rub my forehead, remembering Charlie and feeling a knot of dread form in my stomach. "They've got my girl."

"Seriously?" Max asks.

"Yeah, you didn't hear?"

He shrugs. "Never got a call."

I think about what that means. If Max didn't get called, and I didn't, either, then maybe only one collector has Charlie. And I have a good idea which collector that would be. "I've got to find her," I tell Max.

He nods, runs around Elizabeth Taylor, and jumps in the passenger seat like we're headed to freakin' Disneyland. I get into the driver's side and glance at my best friend. "Thank you, Max. For helping me. For helping *her*."

"Meh," he says. "Figured the world could use some peace. I've been giving it hell for a while now." He winks, and I punch him in the shoulder. My way of saying, *I freaking love you, man.*

For the next twenty minutes, we drive around town with our heads stuck out the windows like dogs trying to sense another collector. When we near an enormous grocery store, Max grabs my shoulder. He looks over at me with big eyes, and suddenly I sense it, too—another collector. I pull into the store parking lot and park near a line of Dumpsters. We watch people coming in and out of the sliding glass doors. I'm not entirely certain what the collector will do to Charlie, but if he wants witnesses, this would be the place.

"You think he's in there?" I whisper, like the guy can hear us from here.

"I don't know. But I think I feel him, don't you?"

I nod. "Look, Max. When we find Charlie, I want you to grab her and run. Let me deal with this dick, okay?"

"No way," he protests. "I came for a fight, yo."

"Dude, if you care about our friendship, you'll do this. Please? I want her safe. It's the only thing that's important to me."

He rolls his eyes and sighs. "What am I supposed to do with her?"

"Find Big Guy's liberator. Hand Charlie off to her. Then run. I'll be right behind you." The last part is a lie, but I can't chance Max's safety.

As Max mutters about Big Guy calling his collectors *liberators*, something moves across my line of vision. When I glance forward, I don't see anything, but I know someone was just there.

"Hey," I say slowly. "Does the collector feel closer to you?"

A banging sound rings near my head. Max screams like a girl, and I jump in my seat. I turn to my left, ready to punch through the window if I have to—and stop when I see a mane of red hair.

"You scared the crap out me, Red," I snarl, rolling the window down.

"Who is it?" Max asks. He leans forward but doesn't say anything.

In front of me, Valery's eyes get so big, I'm sure they'll explode right out of her melon head.

"What's your deal?" I glance at Max, who has a similar look on his face. "Uh, Valery, this is Max. Max, this is—"

"Valery," Max chokes out.

"Max!" she screams.

"What the H, guys?" I say.

Max flies from the car and races around the front. Valery meets him right in front of Elizabeth Taylor's grill and leaps into his arms. She wraps her legs around his waist, and he presses his mouth over hers.

And then...then they just kinda start getting it on right there on the hood of my car. Like I'm not sitting right here. Like we're not trying to save my girlfriend from hellfire demons.

Through my open window, I can hear Max moaning. My face scrunches in disgust. I lay on the horn. "Can someone tell me what's going on?" I yell out the window.

Nothing.

They keep making out like I'm freaking invisible.

Then it hits me. Valery turning into a nut job and declaring her devotion to her fiancé. Max telling me his fiancée died, saying *people change when shit happens* after I questioned him about his playa ways.

I get out of the car and move to stand in front of them. Over their slobbering bodies, I say, "Seriously?" I scratch my head. "I mean, *seriously*?"

When Valery comes up for air, she giggles like a psych ward junkie. "Max," she coos, running her fingers down his cheek.

"Baby," Max says, nuzzling her neck.

"Not that this isn't terribly romantic and wildly coincidental," I say. "But I've got to find Charlie."

Valery's head twists to face me, Charlie's name snapping her out of it. "I knew something was up. You've been driving around town like a maniac, and I just *knew* you'd lost her."

I look at Max but point at Valery. "Meet the liberator."

Max stares at her, wide eyed. "No way."

She nods and gives him a devilish smile. "I've been busy since…you know…the accident. So, are you…?"

Max nods, appearing ashamed. "I work with Dante," he says, no doubt hoping that sounds better than *I work for Lucifer. Heard of him?*

She bites her lip and seems for a moment like she's going to cry. Max pulls her close and whispers in her ear. She shakes her head back and forth. Then her head snaps up.

"What are you going to do?" she asks me.

"We're going to find Charlie," Max answers.

Her body relaxes against him. "You're going to save her?" she breathes. "You're going to risk your life?"

He nods, clearly pleased with himself.

Valery steps away from him. She studies him for a long time without saying anything. Then she turns to face me. "Then I'm going to help you." She glances back at Max, and I fight the urge to mention that this was already my plan, to have Valery help us. "And once this is done," she continues, still staring at Max, "once that girl is safe…you and I are going to make up for lost time."

The twosome snuggle and laugh, and I have to practically drive a stick between them to wrench their bodies apart. "Both of you," I say, "in the car. There's time for that later."

Valery looks at Max and nods. Then she climbs into the passenger seat, and Max jumps in the back. When I slide into the driver's seat, I notice Max running his fingers over Valery's neck and whispering in her ear.

I roll my eyes, but a small smile tugs at my lips. I'm happy for them. And with Valery and Max both on my side, I allow myself to get excited that this will work—that I'll save Charlie from the collector and get her safely under Valery's protection.

Before my time is up.

49

I QUIT

Valery, Max, and I drive around Peachville. The music is off in my car, and now there are three heads hanging out the windows instead of two.

"You'd think," Max says, "that between heaven and hell, we'd be more helpful than a pack of German shepherds."

"My boss doesn't want us having too much power after what happened with your boss." She says *your boss* like it's an insult, but Max only nods.

"Does anybody sense anything yet?" I ask.

"Oh, yeah," Valery says. "I did a few miles back but decided not to mention it."

I grip the steering wheel tighter. Apparently just because we're working together doesn't mean she's going to cut me any slack. As much as I'd like to, I can't manage a comeback because I'm struggling with the feeling that we're being followed. It's not a sensation that my cuff delivers. This is different, like someone is staring at me from across the room and I just now noticed.

Pulling the car over and onto the shoulder, I ask, "Sure no one feels anything?"

"Why?" Valery asks, her mocking tone gone. "Do you?"

"I feel like we're being followed." I turn around to look behind us but don't see anything.

"How in the world do you feel that?" she asks, also turning around.

I shake my head. "I don't know."

She falls back in her seat. "Just keep driving. We're wasting time."

I press my lips together and pull back onto the road. We've already explored the heart of the town, and Valery assured us she checked the major retail locations. The only thing left to do is circle the perimeter, where the lights are limited, and the trees are thick. In other words, total axe murderer territory.

As I'm driving down a long and narrow dirt road, surrounded on both sides by a dense forest, Max asks, "Does anybody—"

"Yes," Valery says, clipped.

Hearing their suspicion, and feeling my own, I shiver from a wave of anxiety. I drive farther down the road while Max and Valery become restless. We're getting closer. Remembering I want an element of surprise, I pull Elizabeth Taylor over and throw her into park.

"What are you doing?" Valery hisses. "Keep driving."

"No. I'm going to sneak up on them," I say. Then, knowing they'll wonder what I mean, I add, "I can be quieter than the two of you." I glance back and forth between Max and Valery. "Remember the plan. When I find Charlie, I'm going to tell her to run, and I need you guys to be here when she does. I can handle the collector. Don't wait for me, just start driving."

"Yeah, I've changed my mind on this," Max says.

But Valery nods. She looks at me like a human being just sprang up where a swine once sat.

"Hey." Max waves a hand between our faces. "Why is everyone ignoring me? We're not really leaving Dante."

I turn in my seat and face him. "Max, I need you here. You have to trust me. Take care of Charlie when she gets here. And take care of your fiancée. I'll find the three of you. I promise." I know I'm lying again, but at least now my lies help protect the ones I care about, rather than serving selfish desires.

Grabbing Max's shoulder, I squeeze. "You're my best friend."

He pulls back. "Screw you, man. Don't be a freaking martyr."

I slide out of the car and glance once more at Valery. She smiles, but it's mixed with pain. She thinks the collector may overtake me, that I'll be dragged back to hell for sentencing. But I know it'll never get that far.

I'm about to close the door when Max says, "Hey."

I tilt my head so I can see him in the backseat.

He looks at me for a long time, then smiles. "Bring the thunder."

I close my fist and raise it. He bumps it with his, and we both say, "Pow!"

The door clicks shut beneath my hand, and I turn and face the forest—and the final hours of my life—alone.

After only a few seconds of walking, I turn around. Already, I can't see the road or my candy apple-red Escalade. Goose bumps rise on my arms. It's now or never. The collector I'm searching for most likely already knows there's another of his kind nearby. Because if we can sense him, he can sense us. I glance around, then drop down onto the ground. Pulling up my jeans, I inspect the cuff. The collector won't notice I've removed it. He'll just assume I've moved from where I stand now to where Valery and Max are. It's why I needed Valery with me. That, and she had to be here to get Charlie to safety.

Fingering my cuff, I know this won't be too difficult. Our cuffs are strong but can easily be broken if the will is there. I search the ground for a rock and find one. My pulse quickens, and my mind spins. This is my life. This is it. I stare at my cuff, at the rock cold in my hands. If I do this, there's no going back. I won't be able to protect her once I'm gone. I swallow hard, thinking of that word. *Gone.*

Maybe I was never meant to protect Charlie. Maybe Valery was always the best person for the job; she has Big Guy to back her up, to help her hide his precious cargo. Maybe keeping Charlie safe was never my destiny.

Maybe dying for her was.

A cracking sound splinters the night. I raise my arm and hit the cuff again. And again. And again. The noise is earsplitting as stone meets metal. I try not to hurt my ankle in the process, but at this point I don't really care.

A fracture forms in my cuff, and I laugh out loud. I hit the metal three more times, and the cuff breaks apart and falls to the earth. I jump up and toss the rock over my shoulder. Then I raise my middle fingers and point them toward the ground, hoping Boss Man sees me real good right now, and scream inside my head, *I quit asshole! Pow!*

I smile big and wide like Charlie would. My breath comes strong, and I feel like I could take on the entire world.

My hours may be numbered, but damn it, I'm going to live them *free.*

50

GUESS WHO?

I stare at my newly exposed ankle. Part of me can't believe what I just did, but it's too late to dwell. My time is limited, and if I don't rescue Charlie from the collector, I'll have died again in vain.

The guy I'm tracking should here should be here soon, drawn by the noise. I retrieve the broken dargon, move behind a tree on the other side of the small clearing, and wait. Sure enough, after only a few moments, I hear the sound of leaves rustling. I can't sense him coming, but I know he's there. Even if he is sporting his shadow.

I've never fought one of my own before, and the thought that I will makes my forehead prick with sweat. In my head, I flip through the alternatives. There are six of us. Max and I make up two of those, which leaves only four people it could be. Each has his own strengths and weaknesses, but since I've had a hand in all the collectors' continued training, it should be easy to predict their actions.

Still, this knowledge does little to calm the nerves pulsing through my body as the footsteps grow closer. I feel like a gas leak waiting to detonate—like if someone lit a cigarette on the other side of Peachville, I'd explode into a billion pieces. It's a wonderful thought as I'm stalking a demon in the middle of a dark forest.

I still as the leaves stop crunching and hold my breath. After what feels like an eternity, I see the ground rustle. Footprints. He's so close, I see his footprints in the dirt. And now they're leading away. I wait for as long as I can and then follow him. Right about now, I'd love to utilize my own shadow, but I kissed that ability good-bye when I broke off my cuff. Instead, I walk lightly and just keep moving.

Then I hear her.

Charlie sobs, and it takes everything I have not to race forward. Listening, I notice the sound of her voice is muffled, like something is stuffed in her mouth. I continue taking soft steps, ensuring I've stayed behind the collector in front of me. Every few seconds, I glance around. I'm still not sure there's only one collector out here, and I don't want to be surprised. When finally I see Charlie, I freeze.

Her back is to me, and her arms are tied behind a tree. She's still wearing her red dress, but her costume angel wings are missing. Everything in me wants to run to her, to untie her hands and scoop her into my arms. Fury that I can't burns through my veins.

I inch closer, removing the gun from my waistband. Not knowing who's done this to her is driving me crazy. I need to see his face, need to know who I'll destroy tonight. And then I do.

One of my collectors—Kincaid—shrugs off his shadow and glances around. He still thinks he heard something.

That was me, asshole. And I'm watching you. Right. Now.

Kincaid is the newest collector. Younger than me and one I trained only a few months ago. Out of all the collectors, he'd be the most naïve, the one most likely to try a stunt like this. I can just picture him thinking how easy it'd be to trump me as I taught him how to seal a soul. I bet the second he heard about my assignment, he drooled all over himself. He just knew I'd screw this up, and he'd be there waiting when it happened.

Cocky bastard.

He doesn't know who he's messing with.

I prepare myself to lunge toward him but stop when I see a glint of chrome tucked between his belt and dark jeans. No matter. I'm still taking this guy out; it's just going to take the right moment.

Kincaid finally decides there's no one watching and crouches down next to Charlie. He pulls the rag out of her mouth and quickly replaces it with his hand. "I know you want to scream, pumpkin," he coos. "And I'm going to let you. Know why?" He pauses as if giving Charlie time to think. "Because if your boyfriend is out there lurking, he'll come running when he hears that scream of yours. And that's exactly what I want."

Kincaid is kind of squatting so that I can see his profile. I just need him to turn a bit more toward Charlie and away from me. That's all I need. One moment of surprise to attack. He slowly uncurls his fingers from Charlie's mouth.

He stands up. "Go ahead," he says. "Scream."

But Charlie doesn't. Her eyes are locked on him, and her jaw is clenched.

Kincaid bends down again. "You think you're saving him? You're not. Even if he doesn't come here tonight, I'll find him. And I'll kill him. Just me." He smiles and rubs a hand along his jaw. "See, Dante? He thinks he's hot shit. But one on one, there's no way I won't come out on top."

The last statement tells me everything. He's here alone. He's that sure of his ability to wreck me and my assignment. But what else does he know? Does he know about Trelvator? And if he gets through me, will he try to collect Charlie's soul? Even worse, would he *kill* her?

Kincaid pulls his leg back and kicks Charlie hard in the ribs. "I said *scream*!"

Kincaid probably has plans to hide now that she's cried out, to wait and see if I close in. But that's not going to happen because I'm already here. I consider capping his ass now, but he's too close to Charlie. Too close. Rage floods my body—

And I run.

I run hard and fast, moving like I never have before. I'm an animal racing toward him—all legs and lungs and muscle. Hearing Charlie scream in pain messes with my head, flips a switch that removes all rational thought. As I close in on Kincaid, it feels like I'm not even inside my own body, like I'm controlling my movements with a joystick in a video game.

Kincaid turns to see me, but I leap before he can react. My body pummels into his, and we land hard on the ground. The gun flies from my hand, but it doesn't matter. I've got this. I pull my fist back and smash it into his nose. He hollers and fumbles for his own gun. I grab his shoulders and shove him back down, landing another shot to his kidney.

Somehow he gets out from underneath me and jumps to his feet. We circle each other like beasts, like demons. Kincaid fakes like he's going to charge to my right, then turns and slams into my left. We fall to the ground again, and again I pound my fists into his face. And his stomach. And his shoulder. And because I suddenly remember how he kicked Charlie like a dog, I rear back and send a blow crashing into his ribs. He groans but doesn't stop fighting.

Kincaid's hands fly up, and he wraps them around my throat. It's a good move, because I have no choice but to stop hitting him and start defending myself instead. I grab onto his wrists and yank as hard as I can, but he's determined to choke the life out of me. My lungs burn, and I feel like if I don't get air immediately, I'm going to black out. I can't fathom how this has happened. How even though I'm on top, he's somehow winning this fight. My vision blurs, and I steal a glance at Charlie. She's yelling something, but I can't make out what it is, because all I'm thinking is, *I can't breathe. I can't breathe!*

I yank myself onto my feet, trying to tear Kincaid's hands from my throat. But he mirrors my movements like a freaking anaconda. I finally stand upright just to have my knees start to buckle beneath me. *I just have to get his hands off my throat,* I think. *Get them off!*

And then, even though my thoughts are starting to slide together in a tangled mess, I realize something. I have a choice. Being choked makes me think that the only thing I can do is play defense. It's a false assumption.

I let go of his wrists, and throw everything I have—every available knee, elbow, and fist—into his groin. He curls in on himself and groans. Yanking him onto his side, I grab the gun from his pants and point it toward his chest.

Kincaid tries to speak, but his words are too soft, and I can't hear him. What I can hear is Charlie screaming my name. I realize she's been yelling this entire time, and I never heard it. Keeping Kincaid's gun aimed on him, I run toward Charlie. As I start to untie her, I hear Kincaid mumble something over and over.

The second Charlie is free, she dives into my arms. "You're okay," I tell her. "It's going to be okay. I've got you. I'm not ever going to let anything bad happen to you again." Charlie doesn't say anything back. She just presses into me, and I wrap myself around her. "You're hurt?" I ask.

She shakes her head against me, and I rub my free hand over her hair. Then I look back at Kincaid. I've got to figure out what I'm going to do with him. Break off his cuff? Put a bullet in him so we have time to flee? I know I can't leave him here to follow us, but I don't want to make a rash decision. I've got to calculate my every move with what time I have left, give Valery the best chance to get Charlie hidden.

Kincaid crawls like a beetle across the ground, watching us. He repeats himself but grows louder.

"You got something to say?" I bark, standing and pulling Charlie up with me. "Go ahead," I yell, fueled by adrenaline. "You're done now. One way or another, you're dead. So go ahead. Want to say something? Say it!"

He smiles at me, his teeth laced with blood. "I *said*." He licks his lips and fills his lungs like he's going to scream. "He's here! He's over here!"

My head snaps up, searching for who he's calling. When he calls again, I raise my gun in his direction. "Stop it. Stop yelling." I contemplate pulling the trigger, but now I'm afraid I might need the six rounds this gun holds. Searching the ground, I find my Glock and grab that, too. Twelve rounds. Now I may have one to spare for this jerk.

"Dante, look," Charlie yells.

Kincaid turns and glances behind him. When he faces me again, he's pulling himself off the ground. "Did you think it was only me?" He laughs, then coughs. My finger twitches over the trigger. "You did, right? Man, how stupid do you think I am? I was just the bait, baby."

I step in front of Charlie when I see the final three collectors—

Patrick, Zack, and Anthony—coming up behind us. Zack and Patrick are hanging back, but Anthony is pointing a gun at Max and Valery. My two comrades are walking in front of Anthony's enormous frame like two inmates. As Max comes closer, I notice a gash across his cheek, probably received from fighting to keep them from taking Valery.

My blood runs cold as I reach my hand behind me and feel for Charlie. This isn't good.

Kincaid nods toward Anthony but speaks to me. "You can take those guns off me now," he says. "Unless you want us to blow holes in your friends."

"I'll kill him," I tell Anthony, stabbing the gun in my right hand in Kincaid's direction. But I already know what he'll say.

Anthony shrugs as if he's read my mind. "Then do it."

Kincaid bows. "I'm the sacrificial lamb if need be," he says, standing upright again. "But it's cool. You won't kill me. We're immortal, dickhead. But the second you pull that trigger, Anthony will pull his." He wipes blood from beneath his nose. "Drop the guns and kick them over here, or we'll kill the girls."

I know they must be bluffing. They can't know Valery is a liberator, not with so many other cuffs in the vicinity, and they wouldn't chance killing a human. And I'm not certain they'll hurt Charlie, either. At least not without collecting her soul first. Still, I can't take the risk. So I do what he asks. *I'll get another chance to get everyone out of here*, I tell myself.

"Great, we're all here," I say as Kincaid picks up one gun and puts it in his waistband, then grabs the other and aims it in my direction. "So what's the plan?" I continue. "You've been following me for days. So what the hell do you want?"

"I wasn't following you," Kincaid spits. "Why would I ever follow you?"

I narrow my eyes at him. "But I sensed you." I glance across the four of them. "Or one of you, at least."

"I already told you, pretty boy. It wasn't me." He glances at the other three collectors. "Was it you guys?"

The three jackasses shake their heads and sneer like villains in a cowboy movie.

Kincaid turns back to me. "You know, come to think of it, I might know someone who was following you."

The collectors laugh and move back as if something big is coming. I narrow my eyes, gazing deep into the forest over their shoulders—and gasp when I see who steps out of the shadows.

A man walks toward us, head held high and shoulders squared. His dark hair is buzzed short to his scalp, and his clothes are crisp and clean. Every movement he makes, every tilt of his head, screams military.

"You!" I race toward the man, but Kincaid leaps in front of me and pistol-whips me across the face. Blinding pain shoots through my body as Charlie cries out. My vision blurs, but when I glance up from the ground, he's still there.

My mother's boyfriend.

51

HUSH

The bastard stops walking and stands a few feet away. He digs into his pocket and pulls out a coin, flips it into the air, and catches it. Then he holds it between his pointer and thumb.

"You like my coin?" he asks. His voice is deep, and each word he speaks is clipped, as if his biggest fear is slurring.

I drag myself up, gritting my teeth against the pain, and look closer at the coin he's holding. I clench my fists when I see it's *my* penny, the one my father gave me. The one I left in my mother's house.

"How about these?" He turns his foot to the side, and I spot my red Chucks on his gnarly feet. "They're a little big, but I made them work." He spins around in a slow circle, holding his arms out wide. "I was going for a grand entrance. What do you think? You think I nailed it?" He places a hand on his chest. "My name is Rector, and I am here to finish your assignment."

"You motherfucker," I growl.

"No," he says, holding up a finger. "Not yet, but I'll go back for your mama later." He smiles and lets his head fall to the side. "Just think, I could be your daddy one day."

I charge at him, but Max grabs me and holds me back. He has trouble keeping me grounded until Charlie and Valery grab onto me, too. I brush them off and stand still. As evenly as I can, I say, "Listen to me closely, Rector. I am going to kill you. I am going to end your life."

He flips my father's coin again and says coolly, "Doubt it. I have so much to do, I just do not have time to die." He stuffs my coin into his pocket. "Did you know I only died a few weeks ago?" He eyes me, searching for the answer in my face. "No, of course you did not know that. So many demons downstairs fighting to be a collector."

I feel my eyes widen, and my breath catches. "You can't be."

"Oh, but I can." Rector lifts his pant leg and exposes a gold cuff. "The seventh cuff."

"Liar," I snarl. "There are only six cuffs."

He shakes his head. "I'm afraid you have been misled. Six are reserved for collectors. But the last one, the seventh, is reserved for Boss Man himself."

My heart stops beating. A seventh cuff? It wasn't possible. I would have known. Boss Man would have told me. I was his right hand man. He never hid things from me.

"You can understand why I feel blessed to be here," Rector taunts. "Boss Man must be so very confident in my abilities to relinquish his ability to walk the earth. I will admit, it took some convincing. You actually helped me out, taking as long as you did to get the girl to sign the contract. Boss Man was feeling antsy, and I promised him—no, I *assured* him—that I could make you complete this assignment."

My head spins as he spews words. I can't comprehend that Boss Man kept the seventh cuff a secret from me. And that he had no problems telling this dickhead about it. It dawns on me that I was never Boss Man's number one, that he was always waiting for someone else to fill the spot. What's more, I can't believe I didn't sense this prick in Chicago when he was with my mother, but I guess I was too preoccupied being creeped out that Mom was dating.

Rector taps his chest. "And look here, he gave me a shot. I showed him early on that I could get close to those important to you. Like your sweet mother." He moves his hands to mimic a woman's curves, and I bite down to keep from screaming. "After that, he offered me a deal: bring in the assignment myself, and the promotion is mine."

"Yeah," Kincaid chimes in. "And Rector's promised us more time above ground."

The other three collectors nod and mumble under their breath, showing their support for their potential new Soul Director.

"You know, I watched you before this," Rector says. "You were always so cocky. Such an arrogant prick. I just could not wait to take it all away from you. And," he says, scratching his jaw, "I think I have done a fairly good job." Rector moves toward us. "I had a good time screwing with you and Max. But let's get this over with, shall we?"

Something snaps inside of me, and I lunge. But before I can get to Rector, Kincaid barrels toward Charlie and sticks that blasted gun under her chin. She chokes on a scream, and the sound breaks me. I want to believe he won't hurt her, but I freeze, anyway. Then I throw my hands up to show them I'm not moving any closer. I find Charlie's eyes as Kincaid drags her toward Rector. "Charlie, listen to me," I say. "I love you. I love you so much. I'm not going to let them hurt you. Do you hear me?"

Tears slip down Charlie's cheeks, but she keeps her jaw

clenched, like she's trying hard not to show fear.

I feel a sudden jab in my back and know it's a gun. Next to me, I spot Max on the ground. He must have charged when I did and got taken down. Valery is kneeling over him, her eyes glued to the gun under Charlie's chin.

"Please don't hurt her," Valery begs.

Kincaid points the gun at Valery. "Who the hell is this chick?"

"My fiancée," Max interjects, trying to cover what she really is.

Kincaid scrunches up his nose. "You're going to marry a mortal? That's disgusting." He puts the gun back on Charlie, and the collector behind me, who I've now realized is Anthony, slides his gun up near my head.

"Thank you, Kincaid. You've been quite helpful." Rector takes Kincaid's outstretched gun and nods for him to step away. Then Rector pulls Charlie against him and presses his lips together. He glances at me as Charlie squeezes her eyes shut. "She does look good, doesn't she?" Rector thrusts his hips at her, and the collectors laugh.

"Stay away from her," I growl, heat flooding my veins.

Rector leans over and whispers in Charlie's ear. "Open your eyes, girl. Look at Dante. Look at this boy you love."

She opens her eyes, and seeing the gun pressed against my head, her face fills with fear.

Rector motions toward Kincaid, who steps forward and hands him a roll of papers I can only imagine is the soul contract. He flips Charlie's soul light on and grins when he sees how little is left uncovered.

He presses his nose against her cheek. "Come, child, just ask for one more thing." He pauses, thinking. "How about that limp of yours? Don't you want it gone?"

Tears continue to rush down Charlie's cheeks, but there's still fortitude in her eyes.

"Don't do it, Charlie," I say. "Look at me. Charlie! Look at me!"

She meets my gaze.

Rector nods toward Anthony, the collector holding the gun to my head, and he presses it harder against my temple. A clicking sound rings near my ear as he cocks the gun.

"No," Charlie says calmly. "You will not hurt him."

Anthony puts his finger on the trigger and pretends to squeeze, and in that moment I see Charlie's confidence waver.

"Charlie, it won't hurt me," I lie. "I'm immortal. They can't kill me."

"He is right," Rector says. "We cannot kill him with a bullet. But that gun will put him out for several days, and in that time, we will drag his body downstairs and lock him in eternal torture. Do you want that for him?"

Charlie's chest rises and falls so quickly I'm afraid her heart will give out.

"I said, *do you want that*!" Rector yells into her face.

Her body shakes uncontrollably in response to his words, and I have to shut my eyes against the sight. If I grab the gun at my temple and put a bullet in my own head, would it end this? No. They'd just press her with something else until she crumbled. The only thing I can do is beg her not to give them what they're asking for and pray they don't hurt her.

Charlie opens her mouth.

"Don't, baby," I plead. "Remember where you got your injury from. Remember your parents."

Charlie's face pulls together in pain, like she's remembering the loss. And I realize suddenly it was the wrong thing to say. Her eyes snap open, and she lets her head fall back.

"I can't lose you," she whispers.

"No," I say, but I know it's too late.

Charlie closes her eyes and says gently, "I wish to be beautiful."

As soon as the words leave her mouth, a seal releases from my chest, crosses the distance between us, and attaches to her light. Then, as quietly as a sigh, a bright light breaks open around Charlie. It hovers there like a warm cocoon.

And as I cry out, Charlie's immaculate soul slowly floats toward me and slides gracefully into my body.

52

LET THERE BE LIGHT

Rector opens his mouth in a great circle of black and laughs deeply. He yanks Charlie against him, licks the tender flesh on her neck, and throws her to the ground.

"Good girl," he says, locking his eyes on me. "The contract is fulfilled. Your soul has been collected by Mr. Walker here, and now I just have to bring him in."

My hands flatten over my chest. I can't believe I have her soul, that I was still able to collect it without my cuff. It doesn't seem right.

Rector motions for Anthony to lower the gun from my head and back away, and he does. "This should be easy enough. I am fairly certain that between the five of us, we could bring you downstairs without harm. But tracking you these last few days has been highly annoying, and I feel like blowing off steam." Rector raises the gun in my direction and takes aim.

"No!" Charlie jumps up and throws herself in front of him. A loud crack thunders around me, and my mind screams. I see my girl crumble, and everything around me tilts. For a second, even

Rector seems terrified at what just happened. But then Charlie rolls to the side, holding her arm, and I see that the bullet only grazed her.

Rector crows with laughter. "Oh, shit," he says. "I thought I killed her. That certainly wasn't on my to-do list, so I'm pretty effing happy she's still breathing. Boss Man probably wouldn't have been very pleased about *that.*"

I feel sick with relief from seeing Charlie okay and learning that no matter what happens tonight, these guys don't have orders to kill her. At least not yet. But that doesn't change the fact that Rector almost *did* kill her. Blinded by a mix of fury and fear, I race toward Rector, no longer caring if the collector behind me fires. I charge toward his body, and we fall to the ground. We struggle, and I manage to get on top of him. I grab his head and slam it into the ground twice until I feel the barrel of his gun jab into my stomach, prepared to fire.

Rector smiles. "Nighty night."

A sudden voice booms through the woods. "Stop!"

Everyone stares, waiting to see where the sound originated from. Taking my chance to get away from Rector's gun, I jump back.

"Your weapons bring shame upon even *your* kind. Put them down," the voice commands. "Now."

I narrow my eyes and watch as a guy steps into view. He looks to be in his early twenties and has shoulder-length blond hair. Standing tall with his shoulders held back, his dark eyes pierce into Rector.

"Kraven," Valery yells.

The guy, Kraven, turns quickly to glance at Valery. Then his eyes return to Rector.

"Who the hell are you?" Rector asks.

Kraven glares at him. Slowly, he repeats himself. "Put. Your weapons. Down."

He has a way of speaking that seems regal, but Rector only rolls his eyes and says, "Somebody please take this guy out."

Kincaid runs toward Kraven, and suddenly, the entire area is blasted with white light. It radiates from Kraven's body, and I have to shade my eyes. When the light recedes, I pull my hand away and gasp.

Surrounding Kraven's body are two enormous white wings. They arch over his head and stretch toward the sky, and he looks like a complete badass.

I glance at Rector, whose face is momentarily frozen with panic. Then he glances around at his collectors, remembering his quest, and barks, "I said *get him*!"

The collectors, more afraid of Rector's wrath than of Kraven, rush toward the winged guy. Kincaid is closest, so he gets there first. Kraven wraps a wing around his body and swings it back out. The movement is so fast, I feel a rush of wind on my face. Kincaid flies through the air and smacks into a tree with a *thud.* I can't be sure, but it doesn't appear as if Kincaid is breathing.

Rector seems outraged at what Kraven just did to his collector. "Liberator!" Rector roars. "You want a fight?"

With Rector distracted, I race toward Charlie. But I stop when Rector leaps in front of me. His face. Something is wrong with his face. It's like his skin is stretched too tightly across his bones. I take a step back even though everything in me screams for Charlie. Rector cocks his head like a bird, and then I hear a chilling, splitting sound from behind him. He stomps his right foot into the ground over and over.

"You want to fight *me*?" he yells again, and it almost feels like the ground is shaking. Behind Rector, Charlie stumbles backward.

And then I see what's caused her to stagger.

Massive black wings stretch slowly out of Rector's back. They aren't like Kraven's. They aren't covered in feathers and glowing. Instead, his wings are like a bat's, slick like new leather and frayed in several places. My jaw drops open as he beats his wings once, causing a gust of wind to lash across my face. Rector bends at the waist like he's going to leap. I feel certain he's going to slaughter my ass, but then I notice his eyes are still locked on Kraven's.

Rector jumps, and right as he's about to sail over me, Charlie dives onto his back.

I can't believe what I'm seeing until I watch both Charlie and Rector slam into the ground. She knocked him off balance. My Charlie…just took down a demon with freaking wings.

This time I do make it to Charlie with seconds to spare. I pull her up as Rector forgets all about Charlie's soul and charges toward Kraven. Rector's remaining collectors, clearly stunned at what Rector's capable of, continue trying to fight Kraven. Max and Valery stand beside Kraven, trying to free him of the other collectors so he can focus on battling Rector.

"Run, you idiot," Valery screams. "Get her out of here!"

And so I do. I nod my head once in Valery's direction, because I'm not sure I'll ever see her or Max again, and I run. Hand in hand, Charlie and I make it almost half a mile before agony tears through me, and I crumble to the ground. Pain sears the inside of my head and twists my muscles until I scream.

Charlie's face floods with concern. "Dante," she says between heavy breaths, "what's wrong?"

For a moment, I don't understand. And so I try to get back up. But when I'm blinded by pain once again, I remember why this is happening. I remember what I removed to save Charlie. I remember that my end is near.

After a few seconds, the pain subsides. I feel impossibly exhausted, like it's hard to breathe, let alone run. But I know I have to get her to my truck. I don't know how long I'll make it, but I have to get her at least that far.

Gritting my teeth, I pull myself up, and after assuring Charlie I'm fine, we take off running again. I try and head in the direction of the dirt road, moving as quickly as my failing body will allow. It feels like we're only a few yards away from Elizabeth Taylor when I hear a whooshing sound. Spinning around, I see Rector *thud* to the ground. I can't decide whether he chased after us, or flew after us, or whether he can even fly at all. It's the only thought I have before he lands a blow to my gut.

"This is so much better," he says, his face still jacked up. "Now I know none of this will get back to anyone."

When he pulls his arm up, I figure he's going to hit me again. But then he says, "This is for getting in my way, bitch." His hand flies across Charlie's face, and she hits the ground.

I'm on him before he can even bring his arm forward again. Wings and freaky face be damned, this dick is about to get what's coming to him.

I crash into Rector like a bulldozer. He flies off his feet, and his fugly head slams against the ground. He seems rattled by the sudden attack, and that confusion gives me just enough time to climb atop him. I land a blow to his chest right over his heart. Rector pulls in a ragged breath and gasps for air. As he tries to fill his lungs, I reach over his shoulder and grab hold of his right wing. Then I tear it toward me with everything I have. The wing feels rubbery in my hand, and Rector screams in pain. With a burst of energy, he pushes himself forward using his wings as arms.

Charlie rushes toward him, but before she can do any damage, he wing-wipes her like Kraven did Kincaid. She flies for several feet and then rolls to a stop. My throat closes as I remember what Kincaid looked like after the same thing happened to him. That he looked *gone.* But then I see her struggling to stand up and realize she's okay. Afraid Rector will hit her again, I spring to my feet and race toward him.

But before I make it there, pain rips through me, and I tumble to the ground. Squeezing my head between my hands, I cry out.

"Dante!" Charlie yells.

"Shut. Up," Rector says. I hear a terrible sound and know he's hurt Charlie. "You know what I hate? That I cannot harm one measly human. I mean, this girl could have ruined things for a hundred years, and I have to wait to kill her? Wait for *what*? So God can have a chance to ruin our plan?" He spits Big Guy's name like it's poisonous.

I try to crawl toward Charlie, but I can hardly see her anymore. *I'm dying,* I think. *I'm dying for the last time, and I don't know what will happen to Charlie's soul when I do.* Blackness swirls before my eyes, and I feel like I'm floating above my body. The pain blisters my skin and wrenches my stomach into a fist. It's unimaginable pain—and it's the last thing I'll experience as my girlfriend gets beaten in front of me.

"What's wrong with you?" Rector kicks me in my ribs, and I bite down against the blow. "My guys get ahold of you back there?" He laughs. "Well, I am glad you made it. You will love watching this. Just because I can't kill her does not mean I can't hurt her, am I right?"

Rector raises his gun like he's going to use it to hit Charlie. Right as he's bringing it down, I see a flash of something colorful race toward him.

Blue crashes into Rector.

Blue!

As they fight for the gun, I realize it must have been him I felt tailing me tonight.

Charlie screams Blue's name. Then she struggles to stand and tries to take a swing at Rector. He shoves her down and hits Blue in the jaw, Blue's face paint covering his knuckles.

"Charlie," I choke out. "Run."

She races to my side and tries to pull me up.

I push her away. "Run, Charlie. Now. If you love me…run!"

She looks at Rector, like she's thinking if she runs that maybe he'll follow her and leave Blue and me alone. She glances at me, squeezes my hand, and turns to go. She runs with a limp for a moment, but when she realizes her hip is no longer damaged, she races. My hearts lifts watching her fly forward, her legs pumping with precision.

I hear Valery calling her name, and I know if she gets to Charlie before Rector does that Charlie will have a chance at being safe.

Rector knows it, too, because he growls like a rabid animal and moves to race after her. Blue jumps on his back, dragging him down. Blue's a twig, but right now he's a pit bull, using every pound he has to attack. Swinging around, Rector fights against him. They brawl for several minutes, screaming and tearing at each other.

A sudden sound shatters my dying thoughts and rings through the night.

Blue's eyes swell, and his face contracts in shock. Slowly his body slumps down. When he falls to the earth, Rector is holding a gun limply in his hand, a gun I hadn't realized he had. His eyes meet mine, and he appears…terrified.

As much as Rector wants this promotion, as much as he wants to prove himself to Boss Man, he knows what we cannot do.

We can never—*never*—harm a human.

Boss Man clearly has plans to hurt a human—Charlie. But not now. Now is not part of his *plan*. Rector has screwed that up, and he'll have to answer to the devil himself for what he's done.

The look on Rector's face says he didn't mean for the gun to fire. But it may not matter, and he knows that. Striking Charlie was one thing; her bruises will heal. But this… Rector's *accident* will ignite war between heaven and hell.

He drops the gun and leans down. Then he pulls me up by my shirt and presses his chest against mine. I feel something tug inside my ribs, but I'm so far gone, I'm not sure what's happening.

Rector smiles darkly like he got what he wanted. Then he drops me to the ground and runs.

With Rector gone, I drag myself over to Blue and try to press on his wound. He gasps for air, and I wrap my other arm around his brightly painted face.

"It's okay," I tell him. "We'll take you to the hospital." Even speaking takes the life out of me, and I know that, like Blue, I'm fading fast.

Blue sputters and squeezes his eyes shut. His entire body shakes like it's thirty below. I grip him tighter and tell him all the lies I've learned to tell so well. I tell him it's not that bad, that help is on its way. I tell him whatever I can to keep the truth from tumbling out—that there's no way he's walking away from this.

Blue whispers something I don't catch, and I have to ask him what he said.

His eyes still closed, he says with shallow, jerky words, "I…. love…her."

"I know you do," I say. "*She* knows you do."

Blue opens and closes his mouth several times like he's trying to breathe but can't.

"Blue," I say, pulling closer to him. "Blue!"

His body relaxes.

I close my eyes tight and try to block out what's just happened. Try to convince myself Blue is still here. *He's right here.*

Somewhere in the distance, I hear the sound of a car's engine. I pray it's Valery behind the wheel of Elizabeth Taylor, that Charlie's next to her and Max is in the back. I pray my friends get out, and they remember Blue, who died for them tonight. And I hope they remember me, too. Deep down, I hope I was someone worth remembering in the end.

I lie back and let the pain slam into me. Gripping the dirt with my nails, I think of Charlie. I think of her beautiful, smiling mouth. I think of the feel of her skin against mine and the sparkle of life in her bright blue eyes.

Reaching beside me, I fumble for Blue's hand and find it. I squeeze it hard and thank the boy who's gone from this world. I turn toward him, feeling a tear race down my check, and I tell him, "I loved her, too."

Blackness floods over me in a thick blanket.

It smothers everything that's left of my life.

And with Charlie's smiling face in my mind and her name on my lips, I let go.

53

REBIRTH

Bright light stings in front of my eyes, and I think to myself, *Really? This is death?*

Lame.

But then I hear something, and I'm certain that's not right because A) There's no noise after death, and B) I shouldn't actually be thinking at all.

My eyes open, and I see Charlie's big, goofy grin, and I decide if this is eternity, I'll take it.

"He's awake," she squeals.

That squeal. Do it again. Please, *do it again.*

Imaginary Charlie grabs my hands, and I pull my imaginary ass up in bed and stare. She looks exactly the way she did the last time I saw her—covered in small battle wounds but otherwise perfectly beautiful.

"Careful," she says. "Don't overdo it."

I glance around and notice this place is like Grams's house, all floral and tackiness with a mild stench of poor people. I love it so much I could scream.

"Overdo it? He can't overdo it. He's Dante Walker, am I right?" Max strides into the room, beaming like a real live person.

"Is this happening?" I'm surprised to hear my own voice and decide right then and there that I have a positively perfect Man Voice.

"Damn right it is," Valery says, stepping out from behind Max. She wraps her arms around her fiancé and smiles up at him, then back at me. "We saved your ugly ass. Though I must say, removing your cuff? Idiot move."

"It was heroic." Charlie leans over and kisses my cheek. "And yes, idiotic."

"I don't understand," I say, shaking my head. "How am I here?"

Charlie and Max glance at Valery, and I realize there's something big I'm missing.

Valery clears her throat. "Um, there's someone here to see you, if you're up for more visitors."

I nod, and they turn to leave.

"No, wait, don't go. Not yet," I say, sitting up straighter.

Valery's mouth tugs into a sympathetic smile. "You're going to want a minute. Trust me."

The three of them leave the room, and a few seconds later, someone else steps inside. When I see him, my heart thumps hard inside my chest, and my mouth drops open.

"Dad," I whisper.

My dad rushes toward my bed and pulls me into a hug. He holds me against him for several seconds, then takes my face in his hands. "My son. My D."

"You're alive," I gasp, not able to believe he's really here.

He grins, and I suddenly remember how much I've missed his face. It opens something wonderful inside of me.

"Kind of," he answers. Tossing his leg onto the bed, he pulls his pant leg up and shows off a gold cuff wrapped around his ankle.

I gasp. "You're a liberator?"

"Nah, I got this cuff on loan," he says, sitting on the side of my bed. "I put in a special request to help with your…situation."

I can't get any other words out, can't do anything but stare at my father.

"Listen, Dante, I can't stay long. But I wanted to tell you something." He takes my hand and pats it hard. His eyes stay on my hand as he speaks, like it's too difficult to meet my eyes. "That night. It wasn't your fault. And I've watched you carry it around for two years." My dad lifts his head and looks me dead in the face. "Let it go."

I swallow past a lump in my throat. Finally, I choke out, "But if I'd been paying attention to the road instead of bitching about you missing my birthday…" Hot tears burn behind my eyes, but I refuse to cry in front of him.

"It as an accident, son," he says firmly.

I bite down and stare at his hand over mine.

"Dante Walker, you tell me right now that you'll let it go."

"Fine, Mom," I say.

My dad lets out a single sharp laugh. "Good," he says, a smile sweeping across his face. "Now I want you to take this opportunity to be the man I know you can be."

I don't know what he's talking about, but I'm too stunned by everything that's happened in the last few minutes to do anything but nod. My dad—*my dad!*—pulls me into another hug.

"I love you, kid," he says.

"You too, Dad." I slap the outside of my dad's arm in a friendly gesture but find myself holding onto him. For several moments, I study him in awe: his thick, gray-streaked dark hair, his wide shoulders and warm smile. Then, slowly, a sense of dread drowns out any other thought. He said his cuff was a loaner, which means he'll have to leave soon. But he can't leave. Now that he's in front of me, I don't know how I could handle seeing him go.

Almost as if he senses what I'm thinking, he stands from the bed and moves toward the door. He turns as if it pains him to do so and gives me a soldier's salute.

"Dad…" I say.

"I know this is hard, me leaving," he answers, his smile faltering. "But it has to be this way. I need you…I need you to say good-bye and keep living any way you can. Understand?"

Because I can't speak, because I'd break down if I did, I salute him back, my chest full of fireworks.

He walks out the door, and I have to bite down to keep from begging him to come back.

Charlie pokes her head back in and walks to my side, the limp gone from her step. Valery and Max trail in after her.

"Will I see him again?" I ask Valery, hoping she knows the answer. Hoping they don't notice my voice shaking.

She shrugs. "Maybe."

"Seeing my dad is like…" I breathe, and a laugh tumbles out. "Amazing," I finish. Inside my head, I try to balance the agony of losing my dad again with the joy of seeing him. "I don't understand why he had to go," I mutter. "And I still don't understand how I'm even here."

Max opens his mouth to answer, but Valery lays a hand on his chest. "Please, allow me." Then, turning to me, she says, "The first question I can't help you with. But the other…" She walks to the end of my bed and pulls back the covers. "Have a look-see."

I bend at the waist and can't believe what I'm seeing. "No," I say.

"Yes," Valery says with obvious delight. She clinks her long red nail against the gold cuff around my ankle.

"You fixed my cuff?" I ask, the happiness draining from my body.

"Not exactly," she replies.

Charlie pulls my arm into her lap, and I glance at her. "You're one of them now," she says.

My eyes widen, and Charlie nods to assure me it's true.

"Oh, hell, no," I say, leaning down and pulling on the cuff. "I ain't no angel."

"You are now," Valery says. "Your father delivered the cuff, straight from Big Guy himself. He apparently thinks you can be useful on the home team. You best be happy. You'd be rotting in the ground if it wasn't for him."

Hearing her words *rotting in the ground*, I glance around the room, hoping by some miracle I'll see him.

"Blue?" I ask quietly.

Tears fill Charlie's eyes, and I brush my thumb beneath them.

"You've been out for a while," Max says gently. "Blue's funeral was a few days ago."

My throat burns as I think about my fallen comrade—my friend. He was the real hero. The reason Charlie's alive and here next to me. The reason she's safe. Thinking about him and my dad at once is nearly unbearable.

"And Annabelle?" I manage. "Does she know?"

Charlie nods. "I told her."

The look on Valery's face says she doesn't agree with involving anyone else, but she doesn't understand Charlie's loyalty to her friends.

"What now?" I glance at Valery. "I mean, I have her soul,

right? Do we just go upstairs and turn it in or something? If we give it to Big Guy, will that be it? Will the collectors leave her alone?" I squeeze Charlie's hand in hope. But even as I ask the questions, I know there will be more battles ahead. Even if Ex-Boss Man didn't get her soul, he still won't want to risk leaving her alive on earth to bring Trelvator.

Valery shifts like she's uncomfortable. "Um, we'll have to wait for word on what to do." Almost like she's changing the subject, she says, "How'd you like Kraven?"

"Dude!" Max interjects. "For the hundredth time, why can't I have ninja wings? Black or white, I'll take either."

Valery laughs and kisses his chin. Then she turns to me.

"Yeah, what was up with that shiznit?" I say, feeling a strange stab of jealousy that Rector knew how to sprout wings and I didn't. "Did you know collectors and liberators could do that?"

Valery bites her lip. "No, I didn't, actually. Not anymore, anyway."

Max steps forward. "Valery says Big Guy and Boss Man took away our abilities back in the day so we didn't get too powerful, but now that shit's hittin' the fan, we might be able to awaken them."

"Okay, yeah," I say, excitement granting me a small reprieve from pain. "Let's get on that." In my head, I imagine sprouting superhero wings and being unstoppable. If Rector and that Kraven guy can do it, then I can, too. I wonder what other mad skills I can awaken. I vow to figure it as soon as possible.

Valery and Max suddenly get pushed aside, and Grams strolls in, wearing enough perfume to freshen a landfill.

"Out," she says, shooing Valery and Max from the room. "Come on. Man Child has to sleep."

"Later, dude," Max yells as Valery waves over his shoulder.

Watching them leave, I wonder how long Max can hide from Boss Man. He's committed treason, and it's only a matter of time before the collectors are ordered to bring him in.

With my friends gone, Grams turns to face me and Charlie. "Now," she says, a serious tone to her voice, "I'm going to close this door, and I don't want any funny business. Understand? No making it or snogging or whatever it is you kids call it."

"Grandma," Charlie pleads.

Grams winks and grins like a fox, closing the door behind her. She obviously doesn't know we're the living dead, because I'm pretty sure that'd categorize us as Friends to Not Associate With. I wonder briefly if she's admitted to Charlie yet that she's sick. I know Charlie realizes what's going on, so they both need to just face the facts. But maybe now's not the time, not when the pain of Blue's death is so raw.

Charlie's face is stretched into a wide smile, but I can see the anguish behind her eyes for the friend who's not here.

"Come closer," I say.

Charlie crawls into the bed with me and lays her head against my chest. I wrap my arm around her and pull her as close as I can. If I could, I'd pull her inside of me, where I could keep her safe forever. Charlie's presence makes everything easier. It makes me feel certain I'll see my dad again, and that Blue is at peace.

"My sweet girl," I whisper. "You'll change the world."

She digs her head deeper against my chest. "No pressure or anything."

I laugh lightly. Then I stop and press my mouth into her hair, closing my eyes. "I love you, Charlie," I say. "And I'm so sorry I ever lied to you."

Charlie raises her head. I want her to tell me she's forgiven me, that she won't ever leave. That we're going to be okay. But she doesn't say anything. Instead, she leans forward and kisses me.

My lips move against hers, and the kiss says everything I'd hoped to hear. It tells me she loves me, and that she's in this forever.

Her faith reminds me that I can have a second chance.

That I can leave behind who I was.

And be what I am now.

Bad to the bone.

ACKNOWLEDGMENTS

There are so many bomb people who have helped me during this journey. First, a fist bump for my girl, Trisha Wolfe. You loved Dante from the start, and yes, he's totally yours. To Mary Lindsey, Wendy Higgins, Veronica Rossi, C.C. Hunter, Rachel Harris, Jenny Martin, Lindsay Cummings, and Mindee Arnett, thanks for reading an early version and giving me valuable feedback. I heart your faces.

A big thank you to Kevin Maus who has a big house and completely nailed the trailer for my book. To my publisher and editor, Don Liz Pelletier, thank you for believing in Dante's story enough to buy it. *Look.* Heather Riccio and Jessica Estep, you two are my publicists, and you are big pimpin'. To my agent, Laurie McLean, who gave me a chance and has sold my books like the hustler she is. Onward!

Hugs to my friends who have supported me through every step, especially Gianina Bailey, Eiffat Karp, and Angee Webb. Also, to my peeps at the Lincoln Park B&N Starbucks, thanks for all the (decaf) coffee.

Tyse Kimball, my big sis, you talked me down more times than I can count during this process. You also beat the crap out of me that one time on the way to Grandma's. Let's call it a wash. Jeremiah Kimball, thanks for making my sis happy. I bet if I tried, I could totally sing better than you. Taylor Stanley, thanks for getting into YA books because your sister writes them. Also, you totally rocked the Christmas play this year. To my grandma, who loves me so deeply I almost don't know how to handle it; I love you back times a million. Thank you also to my grandparents who have moved on to be with Big Guy; you'd make excellent liberators.

To the entire Scott family, especially Linda and Royce, thank you for being so welcoming and for always asking about my books. Love you guys!

To my mom, Vicky Stanley, who introduced me to books at an early age, and who celebrates every publishing milestone with me. I love you, Mama. And to my dad, Mark Stanley, who I love beyond reason, and who is never surprised when I accomplish something big. Hey Dad, short version, huh? Look who's laughing now.

My deepest gratitude for the V Mafia and ALL my readers, thank you for embracing Dante. He and I know how lucky we are to have you.

To my husband, Ryan, you are my reason for breathing. Marrying you was the best decision I ever made. You and me, babe. Forever.

Finally, to God, who has mad swagger just like D-Dub. Thank you for blessing me with everyone I just mentioned. Sorry Dante is so bad. He's getting better.

Get tangled up in our Entangled Teen titles...

***Inbetween* by Tara Fuller**

It's not easy being dead, especially for a reaper in love with Emma, a girl fate has put on his list not once, but twice. Finn will protect the girl he loves from the evil he accidentally unleashed, even if it means sacrificing the only thing he has left...his soul.

***Onyx* by Jennifer L. Armentrout**

Thanks to his alien mojo, Daemon's determined to prove what he feels for me is more than a product of our bizarro connection. Against all common sense, I'm falling for Daemon. Hard. No one is who they seem. And not everyone will survive the lies...

***Gravity* by Melissa West**

In the future, only one rule will matter: Don't. Ever. Peek. Ari Alexander just broke that rule and saw the last person she expected hovering above her bed—arrogant Jackson Locke. Jackson issues a challenge: help him, or everyone on Earth will die. Giving Jackson the information he needs will betray her father and her country, but keeping silent will start a war.

***Toxic* by Jus Accardo**

When a Six saved Kale's life the night of Sumrun, Dez was warned there would be consequences. But she never imagined she'd lose the one thing she'd give anything to keep. Dez will have to lay it all on the line if there's any hope of proving Jade's guilt before they all end up Residents of Denazen. Or worse, dead...

1.15